"Can you cut the leash?" he said at last,
his voice grating.

"I'll try."

She touched the fresh scar near his temple, felt the steady pulse under his warm skin, and then the sizzle of data flowing through the link. Her eyes closed and she sensed him breathing, slow and deep beside her.

As soon as she jacked in, she knew something was different: instead of the cold, flat flow of dry-teck in the datastream, she heard the unmistakable chime of bio-cyph. A strand of biocyph burrowed into his cerebral cortex like a tiny, immature version of her wet-teck interface. It anchored and controlled the explosive device that would detonate if she went out of range, and it was wired to painfully paralyze him if she triggered the jolt. It was immune to reprogramming and impossible to remove. They must have known she'd try this.

Finn knew there was a problem at the same moment she did.

"Back off," he hissed.

With a gasp, she pulled back her hand, opened her eyes to stare into his, into the dark gold flecks radiating across the irises. "They've injected biocyph into your cerebral cortex. It's a real disaster in there."

Finn nodded. "So if you die, my brain fries."

Song of
Scarabaeus

SARA CREASY

WITHDRAWN

An Imprint of HarperCollinsPublishers

This is a work of fiction. Names, characters, places, and incidents are products of the author's imagination or are used fictitiously and are not to be construed as real. Any resemblance to actual events, locales, organizations, or persons, living or dead, is entirely coincidental.

EOS
An Imprint of HarperCollins*Publishers*
10 East 53rd Street
New York, New York 10022-5299

Copyright © 2010 by Sara Creasy
Cover art by Christian McGrath
ISBN 978-0-06-193473-5
www.eosbooks.com

First Eos paperback printing: May 2010

HarperCollins® and Eos® are registered trademarks of HarperCollins Publishers.

Printed in the U.S.A.

10 9 8 7 6 5 4 3 2 1

For my dad,
who always takes the time to answer every question

ACKNOWLEDGMENTS

Thanks to my agent, Kristin Nelson, for working with me on improving the manuscript; to Diana Gill and everyone else at Eos Books involved in the book's production; to Olga Lorenzo at RMIT, Melbourne, for her enthusiastic encouragement; to David Bardos, Liz Burrage, Jenny Creasy, Laurie McLean, and Keith Stevenson, for commenting on early drafts; to my wonderful critique group partners Alison Hentges, Suzanne Moore, and Cindy Somerville, for their invaluable input; and to MCP, with love, for making it all worthwhile.

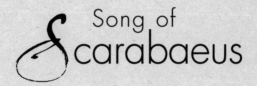
Song of Scarabaeus

CHAPTER 1

Turquoise and black. She watches the beetle stalking over stones and dirt. Its long, feathery legs sink into a patch of woven moss and it flounders. But the harder it struggles, the more tangled it becomes. With one finger she could rescue it.

Rolling onto her back, she closes her eyes. It's been years since she felt the gentle heat of the sun on her face, and then it was a different star. It's been years since she cried. The sun dries each tear on her cheek.

She turns her head, opens her eyes to focus beyond the beetle to a seed falling in the distance, clean metal lines gleaming. Six meters long, bullet-shaped and deadly. Another falls, even farther away. And another. One thousand silent intruders drop from the sky to burrow into the planet's skin.

The beetle chirps incessantly. A distress call. But she hasn't come here to save it.

She has come to destroy.

"Gotcha!"

Edie's boot slammed into the bulkhead with a satisfying squish.

She scraped the remains of the hapless roach off her heel,

wrinkling her nose and making a mental note to inform pest control—yet again. She was so used to doing their job for them, her interface didn't skip a beat.

Below the maintenance platform, the sharp, repeating *clang* of something hitting hollow metal was more distracting.

"Torres!"

He didn't answer. Edie withdrew her mind completely from the clutches of the biocyph connection, feeling the remaining trickle of the datastream disperse within her mind. She leaned over the handrail and squinted into the dimly lit freight car. Torres was propped against the bottom of the ladder, directly below, throwing a kid's ball against the opposite wall.

"Can you cut that out? You're driving me and the roaches crazy."

Torres scowled, caught the ball, and stuffed it into his jacket pocket. Poor guy—the latest milit sent by CCU to stand guard while Edie went about her work on Talas Prime Station. A post so dull, he must view it as punishment.

Settling in front of the access panel, Edie pondered her next move. The call to check out a malfunctioning freight car had come through twenty minutes ago, dragging them both away from lunch, and she still hadn't figured out what was wrong. According to the log, the car's automated rails had jammed. The departures of three ships, including a schooner at the VIP dock, were delayed as they waited for cargo.

She jacked into the car's loading systems again. The stream of data flowed through her wet-teck interface. She had de-merged the program layers twice already and analyzed each tier in turn, searching for the glitch. It had to be simple. The freight loading system, though it looked like an impressively choreographed mechanical ballet from the cargo docks, was controlled by a straightforward set of routines. But this particular car ignored its instructions and refused to join the dance.

Edie switched the loading routine back into diagnostic

mode. It blinked a random command and promptly stalled.

"Damn." She sat back on her heels and called out again. "Torres, you sure you checked those servos like I told you?"

No answer. He wasn't the most talkative guy, but a little cooperation would've been nice.

"Torres?"

From down below came a muted thud. The sound of blows, and then the murmur of low voices.

"*. . . no, I'll do it.*"

The ladder rattled as someone climbed up in a hurry, and instinctively Edie backed against the paneling. Over the lip of the platform a woman appeared, wearing a remarkable gold flight suit. Striking dark skin, tightly braided hair, a navpilot badge on her sleeve. Her weapon lay extended along her forearm. She was entirely out of place. Beauty and elegance armed with a spur.

"How did you like my brainteaser?" She nodded toward the open panel. Her clipped accent was Crib—this, at least, was nothing unusual on a station where hundreds of outworlders passed through every day. "Don't be upset you couldn't figure it out. It's a sensor glitch feeding back from the railings. The car is fine."

Edie hissed a soft breath between gritted teeth. The first thing she'd done after responding to the call was send Torres under the car to check the railings. Not that he could be expected to do the job properly. He wasn't supposed to help fix things. He was supposed to protect her.

Speaking of which, he wasn't doing a bang-up job of that, either.

The navpilot beckoned with her spur and stepped one rung down the ladder. "I have a job for you. Come on."

"You need to—" Edie choked on a false start as her heartbeat thumped in her throat. "You need to file a request with Station Maintenance."

"Maintenance doesn't provide the kind of service I'm after. Come, Edie." Her tone was pleasant, but there was no mistaking the underlying menace.

Edie eyed the spur on the woman's arm and hesitated, fighting the rush of adrenaline that screamed at her to run. Trapped on a platform wedged into the top corner of the freight car, she had nowhere to go.

"I don't want to start making threats," the woman added.

Edie grabbed the console with both hands and pulled herself to her feet, locking her knees to stop them shaking. The navpilot allowed her to squeeze past and climb down the ladder, following close behind. Torres was nowhere in sight.

A man moved out from the shadows of the crates. A serf. The gray uniform, the close-cropped hair, the powerful muscles gave it away. Lithe muscles, the result of hard physical work rather than grav weights or sterospikes. He was a roughly handsome brute, years of labor etched into his face, and he stared at her with unwavering intensity. Edie forced herself to stare back, felt the heat of defiance rise. She'd heard it was never wise to back down to a serf.

Behind him, the freight car's main hatch slid open a fraction and a second serf slipped inside the car. He shrugged his shoulders into Torres's jacket. The simmering panic in Edie's gut started to boil.

"Where's Torres? Is he dead?"

The woman ignored her. "What's it look like out there, Ademo?"

"All clear for now," the second serf grunted. He snapped the hatch closed and ambled over.

The woman turned to Edie. "Listen carefully. My friends here have boundary chips in their heads—you know what that means?" Edie nodded mutely. "I need you to deactivate the chips so we can leave."

"Deactivate them? I don't even know if that's possible."

"Make it possible."

A surge of anger overrode Edie's fear. "And what the hell makes you think I'll do anything to help—"

Ademo moved quickly—a blur at the corner of her vision—and his hand closed around the back of her neck. She yelped as he shoved her forcefully to her knees. The sheer brutality of the act sent a wave of terror through her. Catching her breath, she kept perfectly still.

"You changed your mind yet, teckie?" He squeezed her neck so hard the blood vessels compressed and stars danced across her vision. She concentrated on staying conscious. Focused on a pair of boots—the other serf's boots—on the scuffs and scratches that crisscrossed the leather. The metal deck was ice cold against the palms of her hands.

"Steady on. Let's play nice," the navpilot said lightly, but it was an order.

"You're the boss, Lancer." Ademo released his grip, leaving Edie to grab the deck to stop from keeling sideways. A dizzying wave of blood rushed to her head.

The navpilot—Lancer—addressed the other serf. "Finn, you're up first. Ademo, get back out there and reboot those railing sensors. I'm going to prep the car."

Ademo muttered a reply and left, his boots clunking dully. Lancer headed to the ladder leading to the maintenance platform, where Edie had been working only moments before. Halfway up the ladder and still climbing, she looked down.

"You've got about ten minutes before these two are reported missing. I intend for us to be on the far end of this track by then." She moved to the back of the platform, where the consoles were, out of sight.

Edie forced her breathing to slow as the nausea passed and her mind clicked back into order, overwhelmed with relief that Ademo had gone. But he'd be back within minutes and furious if she wasn't ready. The serf Finn had not yet spoken a word. What would he do if she simply ran? The hatch was open a crack, three meters to her right, and she might get past Ademo if he was occupied under the railings. Neither serf was armed, although that hadn't stopped them taking out Torres.

All she had to do was raise the alarm. She weighed the options. The navpilot wanted her to help a couple of Crib serfs escape. That was all. She knew nothing about these men except that they were convicts. Perhaps they deserved freedom, perhaps not, but when she thought about it—which wasn't often—she'd always found it distasteful that they could be bought and sold as property for the duration of their sentences.

She resolved to go along with it and make sure she got out alive. Talas Prime had half a dozen serf gangs onsite, maintaining the gate around Talas's jump node. What did she care if two laborers jumped ship?

She hauled herself to her feet. Finn took a step forward and caught her arm to steady her, but she shook him off sharply. He was a head taller than she, with a solidly imposing build. She'd feel more in control of the situation with him sitting down, so she indicated a nearby crate. He took the hint.

Edie reeled out a line from her tool belt and pressed one end to his left temple, over an old scar. The other end she pressed to the matching position on her temple. A direct connection through the embedded lines in her fingertips seemed too intimate, considering the situation.

She let her eyes glaze as her wet-teck interface sought out the connection. A crude flash of data caught her by surprise. She gasped and pulled back.

"That's some piece of work," she spluttered.

Finn's lips twitched in what was perhaps a bemused apology. He regarded her steadily, uncommunicative, very still. Perhaps he recognized her—her job took her all over Talas Prime in the course of a normal day, following fault logs from TrafCon to the warehouses to the docks. With his head tilted up, Edie could see the narrow metal strip across his throat—a voice snag. That explained his silence. Someone must have taken offense at what he had to say.

Swallowing hard, she sent out feelers again. This time his chip spat out a few curt phrases of pidgin but let her in.

She probed deeper. This was definitely not a Crib chip, and that made her wonder what the serf's background was.

Most likely he'd had a black market chip implanted in the past, and the Crib had hijacked the device for its purposes. She'd never explored a boundary chip before, but knew in theory how it worked. It wasn't supposed to fight her like this. The chips were primed to receive regular signals from a marker, placed within the area to which the serf was confined—in this case, somewhere on Talas Prime Station. If the serf moved beyond the marker's perimeter, the signal was lost and the chip reacted by detonating. It was an effective incentive to stay put.

Several layers of encryption protected the chip's receiver, but ultimately it was meant to be accessible. The boundaries would have to be changed every time the serf was moved to another job, and most serfs were freed eventually. There must be a way to deactivate it. Edie closed her eyes to concentrate on mapping the layers. The obvious course of action was to start at the first layer and work through each in turn. As soon as she tried that, a security blip courteously threatened to detonate if she didn't back off.

Well, killing the serf would be one way to facilitate her own escape, but she wasn't ready to do that yet. Ademo had better behave himself when it was his turn.

She withdrew and set about de-merging the layers instead. This wasn't something a regular op-teck might try, because it could go horribly wrong if the tiers started recombining at random. But she had tools at her disposal that a regular teck didn't—the wet-teck in her cerebral cortex created a smooth interface and she could keep the tiers separated but aligned, like melodies playing in counterpoint. She teased them apart one by one and imprinted a decoder glyph at each encryption point so the layers would be easy to find later.

At the fringes of awareness she heard Lancer call out for Ademo, then the sound of the outer hatch sliding open and closing again. Heavy footfalls jogged past. She allowed their voices to filter through to her consciousness.

"Just checked the bulletins," Lancer told Ademo. "Your

escape's been reported. They're on the alert. First thing they'll do is lock down the docks."

Edie's heart skipped a beat. Station security would be here soon.

Ademo swore as he climbed up to the maintenance platform. She heard the two of them arguing. Lancer tried to mollify him, assuring him they would make it out in time. As if to confirm this, the car suddenly powered up, servos whining, hatch clicking shut.

"What the hell are you doing?" Ademo screamed. "We can't leave yet!"

"Calm down," Lancer said. "I didn't do anything. It's queuing up on auto."

It sounded like the woman's patience with the anxious serf was wearing thin. They exchanged more angry words. Edie tried to block out the sound but it was no use. She opened her eyes, keeping the link on standby.

The striplights had powered on. A milky glow illuminated Finn's face, a handspan from hers. Strongly masculine features, olive-brown skin weathered around the eyes. He might have been five years her senior, or fifteen—impossible to tell.

He was staring at her throat, at the pearlescent inlay between her collarbones. She wrenched together the lapels of her coveralls to hide it. Now he looked straight into her eyes. His penetrating gaze both frightened and compelled her, his eyes reflecting two pinpoints of light that hid a depth of experience beyond her understanding and destroyed her determination to not back down.

She looked away quickly, steadying her breathing, and focused on the link, gathering the strands of data together and double-checking they were fully separated before going back to find the first glyph. The encryptions were standard Crib fare, and it was now only a matter of time before she could break through them.

She hesitated. She could delay, hope Security showed up, hope TrafCon realized what was happening . . .

The car shuddered and grated against its railing. It started moving.

"Edie!"

Startled by Lancer's voice, Edie turned toward the maintenance platform just as the first code of Finn's chip locked into place and the second glyph sang out, demanding her attention.

Lancer leaned over the handrail. "How do I stop this thing? Where's the manual override?" She sounded annoyed but not particularly concerned.

They would clear the dock and be out on the main track within seconds. Unless the docks were locked down soon, there was nothing to stop the car traveling all the way out to its destination—presumably Lancer's waiting ship. And at some point along that track, the boundary chips would fire.

"It's under TrafCon control," Edie replied. "You can't stop it." There was a way, but it would take several minutes to climb up into the platform, patch in, and trigger the necessary overrides. And both serfs would be dead by then.

Lancer was yanked backward and Ademo appeared at the handrail. "You, teckie! Get over here and help me!" He moved out of view again, and the sounds of a struggle came from the platform.

Edie remembered Ademo's earlier brutal rage and went cold with fear. Pulling back, she reached up to disconnect the line from Finn.

"No."

Finn forced the word through locked vocal cords, little more than a hoarse breath. His hand closed firmly around her wrist, but not painfully so. It was his eyes that held her there. Behind her and above, the navpilot cried out. The spur fired once, the round sizzling harmlessly into the bulkhead.

Edie twisted her wrist and Finn released it abruptly, catching her by surprise. In his eyes she saw a calm, accepting trust—the knowledge she would save him.

She would try anyway.

Pressing her eyes closed, she filed rapidly through the glyphs, setting each one to its task. Her mind flooded with the datastream, the familiar melody she both welcomed and despised. Her subjective sense of time slowed as the biocyph thrummed its rhythm and each tier sang its tune.

It was a juggling act, keeping the glyphs balanced, but one by one they clicked into place. She was aware of the sporadic jolting of the car, of Ademo coming down the ladder, screaming in a wild panic. He must have jumped the last couple of meters—she heard him land heavily and crash into the crates, thrashing about.

Then silence.

The datastream slipped away, the last eddies chasing down the link like whispered echoes. The car swayed and purred. Edie was shaking again. Then the warmth of human flesh as a hand cupped her cheek and Finn disconnected the line at her end, then at his.

She opened her eyes as he stood up. His gaze flicked over her shoulder and refocused, and Edie swung around to see what had caught his attention.

"Ah, jezus." Lancer staggered down the ladder, nursing a gash across her knuckles. "And I so hoped for a happy ending."

Ademo lay crumpled against a pile of crates, eyes open, filled with blood, seeing nothing. More blood oozed from his left ear and trickled down his jaw. He must have given up wrestling for Lancer's spur before plunging down the ladder to get to Edie. Lancer still wore the weapon but it was retracted. She hadn't used it to kill Ademo. The boundary chip had killed him.

Lancer addressed Finn. "Glad to see you made it through. Told you she was good." Then her brow knitted as she looked to Edie. "Why's the car moving?"

Edie dragged her eyes away from Ademo's blank, bloodied face. "It's automatic. Once he fixed the railing, the car took its assigned place in the loading schedule." She was mentally exhausted and her voice was unsteady—the kickback from making her wet-teck interface jump through hoops—but the words flowed easily enough now it was over.

"How long until they lock us down?" Lancer asked.

"I don't know. I don't know why they haven't yet. They're probably wetting themselves in all this excitement." Edie had spent three months dealing with Talas Prime Security, and knew the routine. "Give them time to triple-check their emergency protocols," she added bitterly. The serf would still be alive if they'd acted faster.

The navpilot grinned. "Hooray for red tape."

The whine of the car's servos changed pitch abruptly and the docking hatch mated with a soft clunk.

"We're here." Lancer stepped around Ademo's body and raised her arm to allow the spur to slide forward. It clicked ominously into place.

Edie felt Finn's presence close behind her. She was trapped.

"Hey—I tried to do what you wanted. I couldn't save them both."

"Don't worry," Lancer said, "you did the galaxy a favor letting that one pop. Never would have recruited him if I'd known what a shit he was. Finn, get the hatch."

The serf moved past Edie, a momentary brush of warmth. She shivered.

Lancer lowered her voice. "You did well. Honestly, I didn't think you could do it. Never heard of anyone hijacking a boundary chip before."

Edie frowned. If the navpilot thought she couldn't save the serfs, what was she doing here? As realization dawned, her unease returned.

"It's me you want."

"Of course."

"If you think I'm going anywhere with you—"

Lancer took a step closer, casually menacing. "You're about to get the offer of a lifetime, Edie Sha'nim, so think long and hard about your options before you reject it out of sheer stubbornness."

"I can't leave. I can't just walk away from my Crib contract."

"But I bet you'd love to, huh?" Lancer waved her spur toward the hatch as Finn snapped the doors open. "Go through there."

The mated hatch slid aside. Beyond it was the murky hold of a ship. Two men waited, shadowy shapes in the dark.

A siren blared through the freight car. One of the men in the hold gave a cry of alarm as the hatch doors started to close by themselves. He jumped up to help Finn shoulder them open.

Lancer clutched Edie's arm and pushed her toward the exit, the barrel of the spur bruising her ribs. "They've recalled the freight cars. Dammit, hold those doors!"

Edie grabbed the nearest crate and dug in her heels. If the hatch closed, there was nothing they could do to stop the car returning to the station. She'd be safe.

Lancer yelled and cracked the spur against the side of Edie's head. Disoriented, she tried to wriggle out of the navpilot's grasp. The hatch servos screamed in protest as the men forced them apart.

Something slammed into the back of Edie's knees, and her legs buckled beneath her. The scruff of her coveralls was wrenched aside by a huge black hulk of a man, a manic grin splitting his face. He hauled her up with ease and dragged her out. Struggling against such strength was useless, but she gave it her best shot.

She tripped over the lip of the hatch, and he released her. She tumbled into the hold of the ship, rolled down a ramp, and hit the musty deck. Hard. Her first bodyguard, Lukas, had taught her how to roll safely—years ago, eons ago—and she'd never once needed to know. Until now. She failed him dismally, slamming unceremoniously into the bulkhead, hitting her skull.

A face hovered nearby. A man—an angel with pale bright eyes, but she couldn't make out his words. The siren faded a notch as the hatch screeched shut, and half a dozen voices tumbled around her in confusion.

The cold of the deck seeped through her clothes. Her head throbbed.

Then a sharp pain against her neck brought instant relief, and she drifted away.

CHAPTER 2

She had the sense of having been unconscious or semi-conscious for a long time. Her head felt like it had been split open. Fractured events drifted through her mind. The navpilot. The unknown fate of Torres. The bloodied face of the dead serf. The other one, who could have been violent like Ademo, but instead had compelled her with a look to save him.

And a more recent memory, an image recalled from the days while she drifted in and out of consciousness—two people having sex, hushed and hurried, in this very room. The navpilot in her gold flight suit, and the angel-man from the ship's hold. Whispered words between them that made no sense, then or now.

She opened her eyes to smooth white contours. White walls, white sheets, white monitors. The unmistakable smell of antiseptic singed her nostrils. A medfac. Compact enough to be on board a ship or station, rather than dirtside. Blinking to clear her vision, she saw the whiteness was marred by scrapes and chips. Not dirty, but very worn.

Out of habit, she pressed her fingers into the crook of her elbow, feeling for her implant. It was still there, just below the skin. An umbilical cord to her homeworld.

Voices soaked through the bulkhead. Real and present voices this time.

". . . Never seen anything like it. It's lethal stuff. Interesting. Very interesting."

"And you can't synthesize it?"

"No, just like her med records say. It has to be concentrated from natural sources. She'll last a few months on that implant."

And then what? Would they let her go home? Leave her to die?

The voices faded. Edie pushed back the sheets and swung her legs, heavy and stiff, over the edge of the bed. Someone had put her in bland hospital PJs. The sharp pounding in her head made standing up difficult. It wasn't just the fuzzy disorientation of tranqs. A dull but centered ache throbbed at her left temple.

Her splinter. They'd done something to her wet-teck interface. She gritted her teeth and rubbed her forehead. She did *not* like people poking around in her head.

Walking took even more effort. She grabbed the bed rail and monitors and a solitary chair to keep her balance as she hobbled across the room to the wall opposite the door. A palm-sized med tom that had been monitoring her scuttled around the bulkhead to follow her, its sensors flashing. Filling the wall was a shutter screen, covering a window that might give her a clue where she was.

"Would you like to see the view?"

She spun away from the screen, the sudden movement stabbing her head with pain. Two men had entered the room. The speaker was pushing forty, clean-cut, with pale puffy skin that reminded her of any number of outworld daytrippers who spent too much time in the artificial environment of a ship. His clothes marked him as a spacefarer, too—jacket and flight suit modeled pretentiously after the milit cut, popular among higher-ranking commercial vessel crew. He had a palmet clipped to his belt but no weapon.

Looking at the second man, Edie recoiled. It was the huge

man with the shiny black face who had hauled her out of the freight car during her kidnapping.

She recovered with some effort and put on a bold face for her visitors. The first one flipped a switch near the door and she glanced over her shoulder as the screen faded. The view was obscured by a lattice of girders, cables, and access tubes. Between them, in the geometric shapes formed by the haphazard crisscrossing, was space, splattered with stars.

"Where am I?"

Her voice was a scratchy croak. The man in the fake uniform fetched a beaker from the nightstand and brought it over, watching her carefully. As she drank, he spoke as if he hadn't heard her.

"I'm John Haller, executive officer of the *Hoi Polloi*. This is Zeke." He thumbed the big man at the door. "I believe you've met."

Zeke looked a little older than Haller, though his bulky build and obvious strength gave him vitality. "Sorry about grabbing you like that." He had the decency to offer a rueful grin. "Had to move fast."

"Zeke is our op-teck." Haller backed away, for which Edie was grateful. "We'll be in spacedock a few more hours and then transfer to the *Hoi*. How are you feeling?"

"I'm feeling like I'd rather go home, thank you." She'd never heard of the *Hoi Polloi*, but she had heard about cyphertecks being blackmailed or bribed into doing illegal work. Even kidnapped. Hence, the Crib had seen fit to assign her a guard on the station, and before that a series of body-guards, or so-called bullet-stoppers, for her offworld missions.

"We're rather hoping you'd like to work for us." Haller gave a thin smile, a halfhearted attempt to put her at ease.

"I can't say I'm impressed with your manner of recruitment. You attacked my guard, kidnapped me, made me feel responsible for a man getting his head blown up—"

"He was just a lag," Haller said dismissively. "Part of a

Crib labor gang on the station. They knew the risk involved with deactivating the boundary chips, and they chose to take that risk for the chance of freedom. As for your guard—I've no information about what happened to him."

"Ask that woman. Where is she? How is she connected with this?"

"She's our navpilot. Cat Lancer."

"She's really a very sweet girl," Zeke added.

"I'll remember that, next time she jams a spur in my ribs and starts ordering me around."

"I think you'll find we're all on the same side here." Haller gestured toward the chair. "Why don't you take a seat and I'll explain."

Something Lancer had said during their encounter flashed through Edie's mind. *You're about to get the offer of a lifetime.* Being forced to leave her homeworld and work for pirates—rovers, they had to be—wasn't her idea of an offer. Then again, her Crib contract wasn't exactly voluntary, either.

Edie wrapped her arms around her rib cage and stayed where she was. Unperturbed, Haller took the chair for himself. Zeke folded his arms and leaned back against the door. His presence was perhaps intended to intimidate her, yet the executive officer's polished poise was far more threatening than the big man's sheer size. If it weren't for the way Zeke had manhandled her earlier, she would've conceded that his expression was friendly.

"I'm sure it'll come as no surprise to hear we're interested in your special talents." Haller took the palmet from his belt clip, tapped it, and was silent for several seconds as he studied the holoviz, rubbing his forefinger slowly along his lip in a show of concentration. "Before Cat picked you up on Talas Prime Station we'd been keeping an eye on you, poking around in your CCU records—some of which are highly classified, by the way." He looked up. "Took us a while to dig that deep."

Edie shifted uneasily. "I don't have any secrets."

"Perhaps not, but the Crib Colonial Unit has secrets about you." He cocked an eyebrow as if waiting for an explanation, but she said nothing. "For example, your involvement in Project Ardra."

That project was highly classified. Their infojack must be good.

"I'm not involved in Ardra."

"*Yet.* CCU approved Project Ardra's implementation phase a few months ago. It's only a matter of time. Your contract compels you to participate—and from your performance reviews, I know how you feel about that."

Edie didn't respond, but the simmering trepidation she always felt when she thought about Ardra made her stomach clench. She'd taken a three-month assignment on Talas Prime, working as a mere op-teck in maintenance, in order to delay her reassignment to Project Ardra. Liv Natesa, sector head of the CCU's BRAT seeding program, had allowed her to work on the station—under milit supervision—because she hadn't had a break in years. But Haller was right. Within days she was due to return to Natesa's new and improved seeding program.

"Your Crib training makes you particularly valuable," Haller said when she remained silent. "These assessments from your training days are nothing short of commendable—at least from a technical perspective. Have you ever read them?"

He held out the palmet. She felt safer on this side of the room, with the bed between them, so she didn't move. But she couldn't take her eyes off that palmet. Her records. She'd never been allowed to see them, but she was certain they held other information—details Haller would have no use for, but that she wanted very badly.

Edie forced herself to look at him. "Crib-trained tecks are two a penny. Why me?"

"It's a cypherteck we need. A good one. A cooperative one."

Her heart lurched as she wondered what might happen if she refused to cooperate.

"Just how long do you need my cooperation for? As a native of Talas, I have a biological dependence on the planet. You must have read that in my records."

"We're certainly aware of your condition."

"Then you know I'll die in a few months when my implant runs dry." She'd been using neuroxin implants since the Crib took her, at the age of ten, from the Talasi resettlement camps. Other Talasi got what they needed in their diet, but the Crib kept her secluded at the institute or offplanet on missions. Every few months, her doctor had to distill the drug from crops of native vegetation.

"We'll get your drug for you—if you prove your worth." Haller didn't expand on what would happen if she didn't prove her worth. "Despite your exemplary training reports from Crai Institute, it's clear you were never exactly enthusiastic about working for CCU. Your superiors note your questionable level of commitment to both the Crib and Talas, your lack of interest in the career they so carefully mapped out for you—"

"So you rescue me from a job I don't like by kidnapping me?" It was hard work maintaining a defiant attitude while her head pounded and her knees kept threatening to buckle under. "Don't paint yourself as my savior. What do you want from me?"

Haller flicked off the palmet with a deliberate gesture. "I want your help. Billions of people *need* your help." He opened his hands in supplication, as if those statements alone should be enough to make her swear loyalty to him. "The colonies that won so-called independence with the Outward Reach treaties over the last twenty years are being held hostage. The technology that created their worlds, decades or centuries ago, is still controlled by the Crib." He was referring to biocyph retroviral automated terraformer seeds, known as BRATs, the complex machinery that first terraformed and then fine-tuned the environment of every inhabited planet. "Every year, the BRAT seeds sustaining their ecosystems automatically fail unless the colonies pay the Crib for a renewal key. If they don't pay up, the seeds shut down and the ecosystem quickly collapses. Those fees have crippled hundreds of Fringe worlds, turned generations of people into little more than serfs who have to export most of their resources just to buy renewal keys. And all because the Crib wants to keep the colony worlds under its thumb—"

"Nice speech." He was making her head hurt again, and she rubbed at the sharp pain in her skull. Still, she had to struggle to keep the curiosity from her voice. "So you steal BRAT seeds and trade them to the Fringe worlds, right? You need a cypherteck to hack them, calibrate them to new environments."

"That's right. But we have a cheaper and more efficient method than replacing all those failing seeds. We dig out seeds from recently seeded worlds—the biocyph needs to be in the embryonic stage to be pliable. Then we reprogram the biocyph to create what we call keystone seeds. Only works ten percent of the time, but with your help our success rate will soar."

Edie ignored the sweet-talk. "Are you talking about some sort of override?"

"Yes. It counteracts the inbuilt failure mechanism of BRATs. We program a keystone for our customer's specific ecosystem—just one per planet. It transmits the override to all the other BRATs on the planet, making a renewal key unnecessary."

"That's . . . impossible." Even as she said the words, her mind was figuring out how it might be done. "The override wouldn't hold for long before the existing biocyph on the planet rejected it."

"It's not a perfect solution, by any means. The keystones do fail after a couple of years, but still it costs the colonies a fraction of what the Crib charges. Their resources are freed up to pay for more important things, like infrastructure and med-teck."

"It's irresponsible. You can't throw biocyph around like that. The Crib has to control it—it's dangerous."

"I never said otherwise. But do they have to charge so much for it? Must populations be forced into serfdom, generation after generation, to pay the ransom to keep their worlds alive?"

"I think you're exaggerating." Her protest sounded lame. What would she know? The decades-long Reach Conflicts had fizzled out four years ago, but everyone knew the Crib still censored information flowing in and out of the Central zone for "security" reasons.

Of course, the Crib must already know about these keystones. If CCU wasn't getting its payments, and yet those worlds weren't falling apart, it would investigate. But the Outward Reach treaties protected the independence of the colonies. There was nothing the Crib could do if people on the Fringe found a way to misuse their BRATs. These rovers, on the other hand—their actions were outrageously illegal. Haller and his crew would end up lifers on a serf labor gang if they were ever caught.

Edie's rebuttal hung in the air as Haller tapped a finger against his chin, contemplating her. "Your world was almost destroyed, your ancient race of people decimated over the last few decades by the new wave of colonists on Talas."

She bit her lip at the mention of *her* people, but kept silent. She had never thought of them that way.

"Your people are hanging on by a thread. Have some compassion for the Fringers, Edie. Millions have already died or been dispossessed after they failed to pay up and their worlds were left to rot. And now Project Ardra will expand the Crib's territory at an ever-increasing rate as it terraforms and mines advanced worlds that were previously off limits. You have to admit, helping the Fringers become truly independent is more palatable than feeding the Crib's endless greed."

Edie frowned. "You can't blame the Crib. Humans have always taken the worlds they want, and always will. Sometimes I think the eco-rads have a point."

Zeke spoke up, his voice low but scathing. "Rads killed your trainer, isn't that right? Don't go defending them."

If Haller had chided her like that, she'd have bitten back. But she could only stare at Zeke and feel her face warming with shame. She lowered her gaze quickly and then glared at Haller, hating herself for being tempted. Not because she cared about the Fringers—Haller was no doubt misrepresenting their plight—but because stealing BRATs was an appealing way to thumb her nose at the Crib. Her status as an abductee would protect her if they got caught.

"Why not hire a cypherteck from the Fringe? I heard there are illegal training programs out there. And Crib Central is swarming with legal cyphertecks, ripe for kidnapping."

Haller seemed very pleased with the question. "Do you know what CCU's overall success rate is for seeding planets?"

"Those figures aren't released to the public."

"But you're not the public. You know the figures."

"Well, they're not great."

"One in five is a success. Eighty percent of terraforming missions fail, often within a few months of dropping the BRATs, and usually due to cypherteck error."

"It's not an exact science."

He waved that aside. "And what's your success rate, Edie?"

"I don't have any successes yet. It takes years to assess whether—"

"Eighteen missions, eighteen new worlds molded by your hands, your mind, over the last seven years. And not one has failed. Two of them have already been announced publicly as colony worlds, with recruitment calls going out for settlement within the next five years. The others are well on the way to success. You're the best there is."

There had been *nineteen* missions. Nineteen. And yes, she

was good at what she did. She also recognized clumsy attempts at flattery when she heard them.

"Forgive my cynicism, but I don't believe you're doing this purely out of compassion."

"It's a business operation, of course. And we don't expect you to work for free."

"What are you offering?" She had no idea how much she was worth. She'd never been a commodity on the open market before.

"Twenty thousand for your first run and another twenty in bonuses, depending on how the mission shapes up."

Edie couldn't help herself—her eyes popped wide. Haller and Zeke exchanged a look.

"How many missions?" she asked.

"As many as we can manage over the next few months."

"Until my implant runs dry?"

Haller *tsked* but didn't address that concern. "Here's how it works. Our client sets up the runs, finds us the customers at the other end. There's even a little downtime to spend your earnings. 'Course, we may have to monitor your downtime—wouldn't want you skipping out on us early. But I think you'll come to see things our way. I think you'll want to stick around." His equanimity and confidence were irritating, as though he was certain of her eventual capitulation.

"What happens if I refuse?"

"That would be a pity," Haller said, still affable. "I don't want an uncooperative teck aboard, one with wires in her fingertips and wet-teck in her head so she can talk to any teckware just by touching it. Makes the crew nervous. This is a big dock—I'm sure we can find a rover ship that's not so fussy. We'll get a good price for you."

Edie clenched her fist, feeling the wires crackle under her skin. The offhand manner of his threat was infuriating, but that didn't change the fact that his proposal was more appealing than anything the Crib had to offer. And it was more creds for one mission than she'd see in a year with CCU. Assuming she could trust anything he said.

"We're doing you a favor, Edie, and you know it. The Crib trained you for eight years and you owe them twice that in service—eleven years to go, and no way out. You were a kid when they signed you up. Doesn't sound like a fair deal to me."

It was better than the camps. Better than spending another day with *her people*.

"So, what do you say? Are you with us, or shall I start looking for another crew that might be interested in you? Of course, I can't promise they'll be as concerned as I am about your medical requirements."

With her life on the table, it wasn't as if she had a choice. Her only decision was whether to go willingly, how far to play along. A likely outcome, after all, was that the Crib would track these rovers down and take her back. Perhaps she could at least bargain with Haller for the one thing she really wanted that the Crib had always refused to give her.

"I want my Crib records." She pointed at his palmet. "All of them. Everything you have."

That took him by surprise, and Edie was perversely satisfied that something could disturb his smug demeanor.

"You can have them. But not until we board the *Hoi* and get under way."

That would have to do.

Edie drew an unsteady breath and glanced at Zeke. That one she felt safer with, if only because she identified with the no-nonsense approach of a fellow teck.

"Given my options, I guess I'm in."

Haller's eyebrow twitched. Perhaps, after all, he hadn't thought it would be that easy.

"By the way," he said, standing up to leave, "what's with that pretty little thing at your throat? The medic tells me it's organic, but the DNA doesn't match up with anything on record."

Edie touched the smooth warmth of the beetle shell. "What about it? You want one?"

He must have taken her sarcasm as some kind of breakthrough in their relationship, because he grinned. "Latest fashion on Talas, huh?"

Zeke chuckled.

She cut off further conversation by turning back to the window, looking past the girders to the polygon patterns of space beyond. And the stars, those blazing pinpoints crowding the view—she'd visited a handful in her years on the seeding team and she'd left her mark on their planets, but it had all been dictated by the Crib. Here was her chance for a new start.

The possibilities were out there.

CHAPTER 3

She can make the lights sing.

In waves of silver and crimson she spins them in the night air and they sing their pure, clear drops of music. Carving ever-decreasing spirals, trailing fire, and then bursting outward again in an explosion of color and sound, raining down like glowing embers.

Her audience gasps, awestruck. She shuts out their voices and concentrates on the lights. They leap over each other, chanting arpeggios as they gambol in a wide circle, racing and turning. They jump out of line, three by three, pulsing with simple chords and then falling back to resonate with the dance of melodies. And then she makes them fade away, their song becoming a hum, a whisper, until they vanish into the night with the faint curlicue of a sigh.

The camp guards whoop and cheer and applaud the performance, and it isn't the effusive artificial praise one gives a child. It's real. She unhooks the sensor from behind her ear and hands it back to Ursov, along with the small flat holoviz projector. He grins and pats her on the head.

They're inside the double-ribbed perimeter fence, near the hog pens where the talphi that nest in the feed troughs are settling down for the night, chattering among themselves.

Gossiping women, Ursov calls them. She doesn't know what gossiping women sound like. The women in the camp gather in groups to weave or carve or cook, their hands flying in stilted conversation, often one-handed while the other hand attends to their work. But it's almost entirely silent conversation.

The guards start to disperse. They'll get into trouble if they're found shirking their duties or interacting with a Talasi child. Some of them break those rules, like Ursov. She was wary at first. It was hard to shake the fear that the other children instilled in her, those who deigned to communicate with her at all—but she's always been treated well by the guards. She trusts their kind actions more than she trusts the warnings handed down by the Talasi elders.

Sometimes Ursov shares food. She likes it best when he shares his stories. Now he squats down beside her.

"They're very impressed with you," he says.

"Why? It's so easy to do." Her hands sign the words as she vocalizes them—a habit she's not yet broken when speaking aloud.

"It's not easy, you know. Controlling the lights like that. You've got a special talent."

"Can we play the swan-dive game?" This is another trick from that little flat box, a game for two using the lights to battle for territory.

Ursov laughs. "No. You're too good for me now. I'll have to go back to playing it with my son." She must look crestfallen, because he smiles and holds out the box toward her. When she reaches for it, he draws it back. "Tell you what, I'll make you a deal. I'll let you have the holo if you promise to do something for me."

"Okay."

"There's a lady in the city, in Halen Crai. She's very interested in your special talent. I've told her all about how good you are with these games. She wants to meet you. Will you talk to her and show her what you can do?"

She thinks about that. The very mention of the city churns up strange emotions. The people who live there are the ones responsible for killing off the forests and ultimately forcing the Talasi into camps. She's supposed to fear and hate those people. But the city is also where the camp guards come from, where their families live, where they board ships to the space station and to the mysteries beyond.

She would perhaps be very pleased to meet a lady from Halen Crai who is interested in this silly game of musical lights.

"Okay, if she really wants to meet me."

"She really wants to meet you."

"Can I have the box now?"

"One more thing. She's going to ask you questions. About your life here, how they think there's something wrong with you because your mother wasn't Talasi, and how they make you live out here minding the animals, and won't let you eat with them or play with the other children . . ."

She shuffles her feet uncomfortably. She doesn't want to talk about that. It will certainly cause trouble. But Ursov's voice is very gentle and kind.

"You can tell her everything, Edie. The truth. If you promise to do that, I'll let you have the holo and you can keep it. Because Ms Natesa is a very important lady, and she's going to want you to be properly looked after. If you tell her how unhappy you are, she might be able to get you away from here. Let you live in Halen Crai."

Her eyes pop wide open. "Just because of this game?"

"That's right. So will you show her what you can do and tell her everything? Do we have a deal?"

She reaches again for the little flat box. They have a deal.

Edie woke with a clearer mind—and a clearer understanding of the deal she'd struck with Haller. The last time she'd made a deal that dramatically changed her life, at least she'd trusted the man on the other end of the handshake. This time she might be in over her head.

But she'd play along with these rovers, at least until Haller handed over her records. Maybe even go on a mission or two, if they lasted that long before the Crib found them. And if they could evade the Crib and she could escape the *Hoi*, the creds they'd promised her would pay for someone to steal neuroxin for her. With a sufficient supply of the drug, she'd finally be free of Talas, and free of Natesa's stifling grasp.

The rhythmic low-frequency engine thrum told her she was shipside and they'd left dock. Being shuffled from place to place while unconscious only reinforced the feeling of being viewed as a commodity. An adolescence spent at Crai Institute on Talas meant she was used to that sort of treatment, but she'd never learned to accept it.

The room was small and dark, the bulkhead lined with locker doors, with a washbasin in one corner. The gray and blue décor was as worn as the medfac's, in contrast to the well-maintained CCU vessels she was accustomed to. A jumble of clean clothes on the end of the bed signified her welcome to the *Hoi Polloi*.

Checking the lockers, she found more changes of clothes, a personal palmet, and other essentials. Among the clothes that someone had preselected for her was a long-sleeved zip-up navy-blue tee, which she discarded and replaced with a gray one from the locker. This minor act of defiance felt ridiculously good.

She grabbed the clothes and looked for a shower. The only door in the room led to a tiny annex with a console and, curiously, a narrow bunk. She'd never had a roommate before. Opening the main hatch from the annex, she looked up and down a long corridor. No one in sight. She found the shower room directly opposite her quarters and went in. Behind a frosted panel that divided the room in half was a row of showerheads. Edie flung the clothes over the door of a toilet stall and gratefully shed her hospital garments. Hot water and steam lifted the last of the drugged stupor from her mind and muscles.

Done with her shower, she pulled on the tee, dark gray pants, and a paneled sleeveless jacket shaped by vertical spines around the rib cage. Typical space-flight gear for a teck. Back in her spartan quarters was a pair of ankle boots, new and stiff and a size too big. She tossed them across the room in a flash of frustration and doubt. The unknown future felt more like freedom than anything she'd known, but did she have any more control over her life now? She didn't even have her own boots.

She wandered into the annex and touched the dataport. The information she could immediately access was limited. She scanned the ship's manifest, the crew roster, the flight plan. From these she learned that the captain of the ship was named Francis Rackham, a decorated war hero from the Reach Conflicts. Apparently, piracy suited him more than basking in that glory.

The "client" Haller had mentioned was a prospecting and mining company called Stichting Corp. It legitimately employed the crew of the freelance *Hoi Polloi* and then covertly organized and funded their illegal seeding activities to make the real profit under the table. It was a shell company and there was no way to trace its ownership, at least not with the information at Edie's fingertips. The ship carried all the necessary survey equipment in its holds and had all the correct flight plans in its logs to support its cover story, in case it was ever inspected.

Ignoring the internal memos blinking for her attention, she considered how she might breach security. She was at the mercy of these rovers, and if things turned sour she needed all the information she could get. She was no infojack—her expertise was biocyph, not dry-teck—so the higher levels of security were out of reach. But she didn't doubt that she could hack the lower levels. It would take time—that was a task for later.

She ran a scan of her quarters to make sure she wasn't being spied on. The process took a couple of minutes. When that was done, she resisted the urge to poke further and withdrew to explore the physical environment instead.

Barefoot, Edie stepped into the corridor, searching the wall paneling for directions. From the length of the corridor and number of hatches leading to crew quarters, the ship seemed to be a mid-sized cruiser—as befitted its cover.

A tom darted into her path and inspected her with a glittering eye, decided she didn't require cleaning or reporting, and trundled away. The little dome-shaped mecks, a ubiquitous feature of ship and station life, were programmed for cleaning, maintenance, medical monitoring and first aid, or as gophers to fetch and carry. Edie called after the tom with the intention of jacking in and getting to know it, but not surprisingly it ignored her. The toms would need to be primed before they responded to her voice. She could probably do that via one of the ship's consoles, but she didn't want Haller to know exactly what she could and couldn't do. Not yet.

At the end of the corridor, a ladder cut through the deck in both directions. She climbed down the well to the lower deck and found herself in a shorter corridor with a faded striplight. She pressed it firmly and it flickered to full strength. In front of her, a hatch swung ajar on old-fashioned hinges. Someone approached from the other side. Not wanting to be found snooping around, Edie returned to the ladder.

"Hey, there." It was Zeke, the op-teck. There was no reproach in his voice. "Glad you decided to join our merry little crew."

Hardly an accurate statement, but she let it slide. "What's down here?"

"Main engine, aft." He waved a hand in the direction of a large double hatch behind her. "We have a couple of engineers, but I doubt you'll see much of them."

"I was . . . looking for the seeding equipment," she bluffed.

"Ah, the rigs, my babies." His white teeth flashed in the dim light. "Most of them are here belowdeck. I'll show you later. The extractor rigs are stored in the landing skiffs. Saves having to move them around."

"What about back there?"

Zeke glanced over his shoulder at the room he'd exited. "Come on, you may as well get reacquainted."

"What . . . ?"

But Zeke was already heading back in. Edie followed him, and noticed a heavy bolt running the full width of the outside of the hatch.

"Primitive but effective," Zeke commented.

Through the hatch, she found herself in a narrow room lit by the sickly green glow of a bank of monitors near the door. At first all she could see were pale striplights marking a regular pattern down each side of the room. As her eyes grew accustomed to the darkness, she realized the strips were attached to grilles, and the grilles formed two rows of cubical cells.

"Serfs," she breathed.

"Sure. We use them to work the rigs. Cells are empty now, but we'll be loading them up at the first stop."

Zeke disappeared into the gloom, striding past the empty cells. Edie hung back, a sinking feeling rolling over her. The Crib claimed that renting out serfs—convicts and POWs— for labor gave them a more useful and interesting life than rigid incarceration, but that didn't mean she wanted to travel and work with them. The seeding team from Talas had never used them.

At the last cell, Zeke stopped. The cell was slashed in red light, indicating it was locked.

"Come on." His matter-of-fact tone contrasted with the cold despair of the place.

Edie approached the grille with caution. A bunk clung to one wall of the cell and a water drain ran the length of the floor at the back. The occupant was a silent shadow in the corner.

"Edie Sha'nim, meet your new bodyguard."

She drew in her breath. A serf for a bodyguard? How could that possibly work?

Zeke noted her reaction and gave his characteristic grin.

"You didn't think we'd set you loose in the Reach without protection, did you?" He cooed into the cell. "Don't be shy."

Edie moved closer, feeling the soft heat of the striplight on her face. The man inside the cell shifted almost imperceptibly, as though he was reacting to the sight of her and deciding what to do next. Then he moved forward in three smooth strides, coming to stand against the grille directly in front of her. Despite the instinct to back away, she forced herself to hold her ground.

"Say hello to an old friend," Zeke said.

She stared at Finn. He still wore his Crib coveralls, sleeves rolled up to reveal strong forearms, voice snag fitted at his throat. His eyes bore a hard expression that had been missing the first time she'd met him. What had they done to him?

"I—I don't understand," she stammered, gripping the grille. Finn had been cooperative when she was deactivating his boundary chip, when his life was at stake, but she sensed a tension in this caged man, like a coiled spring—restrained, calculating, and frighteningly unpredictable. She shook her head and dragged her eyes away from him. "I don't want a bodyguard—not a serf, not him."

"Don't think you got the choice, kid." Zeke shrugged, renouncing all responsibility. "The client thinks you need one. Captain Rackham agrees. When they found out he was a Saeth . . . it was a done deal."

"A what?"

"The Saeth were hotshot fighters in the Reach Conflicts." At her bewildered expression, he added, "You'll have to ask Cat about it. Or maybe not—she fought on the other side."

"How am I supposed to . . ." *Control him*, she almost said. She wished she was having this conversation somewhere else, out of Finn's presence. She wished someone had warned her.

Zeke took her elbow and drew her away from the grille, but though he lowered his voice she suspected Finn could still hear. "They rigged his chip. He's got a boundary chip, like all of them, understand?"

"So he has to stay within a perimeter, I know. How does that motivate him to protect me?"

"The *chip* keeps him motivated," Zeke hissed, tapping her skull with his forefinger.

Edie flinched and put her hand where he'd touched her as realization dawned. "They did something to my splinter, at the medfac."

"Your what? Is that what you call it?"

She nodded. That was how she'd always thought of it. A splinter driven into her brain.

"They linked his chip to the wet-teck in your head," Zeke continued. "You're his perimeter now, see? His chip picks up brainwave signals from your chip. A leash, they called it. So he stays alive as long as he keeps within a couple of klicks of you."

She guessed the next part. "Or as long as I stay alive."

She couldn't believe what they'd done to her. To *him*. Finn was forced to keep her alive, forced to stay by her side, or he'd end up with his brains scrambled and bloody like Ademo.

A surge of anger flooded out her shock and confusion. "Why didn't Haller tell me he planned to do this? He must have known I'd never agree to it."

"Well, that would be why he didn't tell you." Zeke was unmoved. "Believe me, I'd sooner pay for trained security but we're on a budget."

"Did he agree to it?"

"We hauled his criminal ass off that labor gang on Talas Prime and put him on babysitting duty. I'm sure he's very grateful."

"*Grateful?* Why don't you take off the snag and ask him? No sane person would sign up for this."

Then again, she had no proof Finn was sane.

"Well, he should be grateful. He's a lag who got a lucky break. He doesn't get to choose his work conditions. I'll take off the snag after I finish processing him. I've still got to run a—"

"No, stop it. This has to stop," Edie said raggedly. "You can't do this to him. I want out. The mission, the creds, the whole deal."

Zeke opened his hands in a helpless gesture. "It's done, Edie. Too late. The leash can't be cut."

"Never?"

"That's what they told me. It's not like he ever had a long life expectancy anyway."

Edie pressed her temples between her palms, digesting the implications, but nothing made sense.

She walked away. She had to get out of this dismal place so she could think straight.

Zeke caught up, grabbed her arm. "You made a big mistake letting him see you react like that," he said under his breath, before raising his voice as if addressing the cells. "You have to show them who's in charge, understand? They're lags. They do what they're told or what the zap of a drub tells them."

Edie yanked her arm free and left the hold. Thankful that Zeke hung back, she climbed the ladder, grabbing at the rungs. They dug painfully into the arches of her bare feet. She ran down the corridor, snapped the hatch to her quarters and locked it behind her. Pacing the tiny room, she tried to think.

These rovers had tempted her with the creds and a way out of the Ardra project, and she'd fallen for it. She'd even get to see what her files said about Lukas, assuming Haller came through on that promise. Participating in their dubiously honorable work, at least until she had the chance to escape, had seemed like a fair enough trade for freedom from the Crib bureaucracy, which had manipulated her since she was ten.

But now someone else's life was involved. Finn's alternative was a labor gang—maybe he'd rather be here, leash or not. And what options did she have? For now she'd play their game, learn what she could, let them think she was cooperating. But she had to find a way out, for her own sake and Finn's.

* * *

Hunger finally forced Edie out of her quarters again in search of the mess hall. The ship was in nodespace now, judging from the engine sounds. She had no idea which spacedock they'd just left, and that meant she couldn't trace the hired infojack who had created the leash. He or she would be able to cut it, regardless of what Zeke had been told. Infojacks always left themselves a back door.

Ascending this time, she went up the ladder two decks to the top. She'd seen no one on decks three and two, and deck one was deserted as well. At the end of a short corridor was a common room with a large oval viewport, its window shuttered. Most spacefarers did not enjoy the sight of nodespace—it tended to induce nausea or even neurosis—so external ports were usually set to darken during node travel. Couches and tables littered the floor, and a huge holoviz blinked silently to itself. Sensing Edie's approach, it flared to life and ran through a default display of alien vistas—places humankind had visited or scanned but left untouched. Terraforming was legal only on planets with primitive ecosystems, not these lush worlds.

A row of consoles lined one wall and she ran a finger across them as she passed by. Her wired fingers brushed over dataports, sending frissons up her arm.

At the far end of the common room were two hatches to the left and right, with a ramp to the bridge between them. The bridge hatch was resolutely shut. Edie chose the hatch on the right, which was open, and almost ran into a woman hurrying in the other direction. They both pulled back and appraised one another. The woman was small and wiry, with the worn-out look that comes from decades of hard work.

"Excuse me, ma'am. Can I help you?"

Edie wasn't used to such deference. Perhaps the woman was a serf. In any case, the blue apron and simple tunic identified her as the cook.

"I'm looking for food."

"Supper's not served for an hour, ma'am. You can raid the

galley, if you like." The cook pointed vaguely toward one side of the mess, and Edie nodded her thanks.

"I'll do that."

The woman scurried off. Edie had never been addressed as "ma'am" in her life and it didn't sit well. Somehow she didn't think Finn would call her that.

In the galley, a small room in the corner, the remains of lunch had been left warming. Edie poured a flask of water and picked at pieces of soft, meat-filled dumplings. The dough was spongy and slightly sweet—a good deal better than her usual fare on Talas Prime.

Near the warming pan was a serving window covered with shutters. She cracked open the shutters and peered into what must be the captain's dining room. A wooden table surrounded by eight upholstered chairs stood in the center of a lavishly appointed room. Paneled walls displayed a range of original paintings, not a holo among them. An impractical rug covered most of the deck. Twisting up the bulkhead in one corner was a grotesque sculpture that must pass for art on some benighted world, and a coffin-sized decorated crystal box—possibly a musical instrument—occupied another corner. A large glass-fronted wine cabinet displayed dozens of bottles in its softly lit interior. As her first glimpse of Captain Rackham's tastes, this was certainly intriguing.

Voices approached from behind, and she quickly closed the shutters. She'd rather not be discovered yet, especially when she recognized one of the voices as Haller's. But the cook must have told him where to find her, because within seconds he was in the galley looking at her with amusement.

"We may be pirates, but we do use plates and spoons around here."

She glanced at her fistful of dumplings and felt her face coloring. Haller handed her a plate from an overhead locker. He gave her bare feet a pointed look.

"We wear boots, too."

"They were too big."

Haller sighed dramatically, as if she was going to be more

trouble than she was worth. With the crook of his finger, he beckoned her out of the galley. She set her jaw and suffered the patronizing gesture. Zeke waited in the mess with Finn. They made for an ominous pair—of equal height, the younger with toned muscles where the older was turning to bulky middle-aged fat. To her dismay, Finn still wore the voice snag.

Edie slid onto the nearest bench with her food, hunger pangs mingling with the faint nausea of panic.

"This is Finn," Haller said.

"We met." Edie couldn't bring herself to look at the serf, even though she sensed he was looking at her.

"We've finished up his psych and med tests. I'm putting him in your charge."

His turn of phrase annoyed her, and she couldn't resist a sweet smile at the executive officer. "Why, thank you."

Haller folded his arms and exchanged an amused look with Zeke. "He's in the curious position of being both serf and crew. Stichting Corp wants him clinging to you like a bad smell, so he'll be sleeping in your quarters. I understand Zeke has explained about the boundary chip. There's a couple more things we need to discuss."

While Edie digested the startling information that she was to share her quarters with a stranger who looked like he could crush her windpipe with his little finger if he wanted to, Haller signaled to Zeke. The op-teck threw a belt onto the table with enough momentum to send it slithering across the top. It came to rest against the back of Edie's hand.

"Standard tool belt, courtesy of the *Hoi Polloi*. You got your basic swissarmy tools, a commclip, datacaps, diagnostic rod, and a couple of spare hardlinks for your fancy biocyph tricks." Zeke seemed inordinately pleased with himself for having put together such a gift for her. "Oh, and a big fat drub there in the recharge bracket"—he patted the drub in his own belt where it rested against his thigh—"just in case."

He gave Finn a brief but meaningful glare. The serf hadn't

stopped looking at Edie, with the same stony expression she'd seen earlier in the cellblock.

Turning the belt over with one hand, Edie flicked the bracket open to extract the drub. It gave a beep to signal its readiness for action. She'd seen the handlers use them on Talas Prime Station—mostly as a simple cudgel, but it could also deliver a shock. The idea of her using it on Finn was comical. In a mirror image of Zeke's action, she tossed the drub back across the table and he slapped down his hand to catch it.

"Don't need that," she said, and a frown creased the big man's brow.

Haller was unmoved. "Why don't you head belowdeck, Zeke? I'm sure you have work to do."

Zeke started to protest but Haller held him silent with one raised finger. Zeke belted the drub, looking more confused than annoyed, and left.

Haller sat down beside Edie, facing outward, and leaned back against the table on his elbows, stretching out his legs. He gave Finn a slow once-over, and Edie found herself doing the same. Finn was powerfully built and instantly intimidating, with no hint of Zeke's good humor to soften the effect. The sense of lurking danger lingered in his eyes, but Edie felt no malice directed at her. If he knew anything at all about her situation, he'd presumably figured out they were on the same side here. He'd been given basic crew garb to wear—charcoal cargo pants and sleeveless jacket with utility pockets, a tee, and boots. So he wasn't to be treated like a labor-gang serf, at least—other than the voice snag at his throat.

"Despite appearances, his psych profile checks out," Haller said. "Cooperative, smart. Not impulsively violent, but good in a fight."

How exactly did they know that?

"His instructions are to keep you alive, pure and simple," Haller continued. "No idea what else he might be good for." He chuckled, then pulled himself upright and his nonchalant air dissolved. "Now, I'm not saying you're in any great danger. I want to reassure you of that. On a ship like this, everyone looks out for everyone. We're all armed whenever we leave the *Hoi* outside Crib space—even him. We're not milits but we know how to handle ourselves. You're the heart of the mission and you'll be protected. This guard dog is extra insurance that Stichting Corp, bless 'em, seems to think we need."

With a twinge of satisfaction, Edie realized Finn's presence damaged Haller's pride. He was annoyed his people weren't considered capable of protecting her themselves. And yet the more he talked about the danger she wasn't in, the more she felt he was worried about her safety.

And what of Finn? Was she safe from him? The leash gave him a good incentive not to kill her, but there were ways he could hurt or bully her. If he somehow forced her away from the others, how could she protect herself?

Haller noticed her wary appraisal of the serf and guessed her thoughts. "You can jolt him. You know what that means?"

Edie shook her head, transfixed by Finn's dark eyes as they slid toward the XO and narrowed. He knew what Haller was talking about, even if she didn't.

"At the medfac, when they hijacked your wet-teck interface, they installed a trigger. Take a look."

She mentally filed through her interface's setups and found the implanted subroutine.

"You flip the switch and his chip overloads momentarily," Haller explained. "Minces up his neurons. He's incapacitated for a few seconds. Do it a few times and you can knock him out. Oh, and it hurts like hell, too. Give it a try."

"I'll take your word for it, sir."

"Test it. Just once."

Her throat dry, Edie ignored Haller's forbidding expression and swung back to her food with a quick shake of her head.

"Finn looks hungry," she muttered.

Haller glared at her for a long moment. Finally, he stood up, indicating with an elaborate wave of his hand that Finn should sit. The serf moved around the table to the bench directly opposite Edie. She waited for Haller to leave. Instead, he leaned over her, resting one hand on the table near her plate, and spoke with chilling precision.

"Something else you should know. Around here, when someone gives an order, you obey—like the good boy over there. I just gave you an order. Maybe you didn't realize because I asked so nicely, but that's what it was." His free hand traced slowly down the length of her spine, and she suppressed a shudder. "Now, this time you get a free pass because you're new here and because I like you. Next time, you ask me how high to jump. I don't care if you *yes sir, no sir*, or not, but you do what you're told. Understood?"

Edie slid her hands into her lap so he wouldn't see them tremble. After what he'd done to Finn, he'd already gone too far with their deal. She wasn't about to put up with his sleaze as well. "I *understand* the 'heart of your mission' might inexplicably forget all her expensive CCU training if the XO doesn't keep his hands to himself. *Sir.*"

Haller's fingers froze. The briefest flicker of a muscle at the corner of Finn's mouth told Edie he appreciated her response.

Edie slipped sideways along the bench, out of reach, and said to Finn, "I'll fetch you a plate."

Finn's eyes flicked from her to Haller, and she followed his gaze. Haller straightened, a smile fixed to his face, but the twitch in his jaw signaled his suppressed anger.

"Please, sit and enjoy your meal," he said with forced congeniality. "I'll feed the dog."

He sauntered into the galley and Edie was left staring at her plate, wishing she'd voiced an objection to the insult on Finn's behalf, but not wanting to further aggravate Haller. Haller returned with a large dish heaped with dumplings and a loaf of sour nut-bread. He placed the food on the far end of the table, forcing Finn to lean across to drag it closer—which he did without hesitation.

"One more thing," Edie said, knowing she was pushing her luck. "The voice snag—Zeke said he'd take it off."

"Let's see how he behaves first, shall we?"

"What use is he as a bodyguard if he can't even speak a warning? Don't you think this will work out better if I have his cooperation rather than his resentment?"

Haller raised his brows in a shrug of disinterest. "I don't even have *your* cooperation, apparently."

She had no intention of obeying the order to jolt Finn, not even as a trade for the voice snag. But this was nothing to do with the snag. Haller was simply savoring the power game and didn't want to let her win any more points.

She'd have to tackle it another way. Much as it irked her, she proceeded with a deferential tone. "I'm sorry about my earlier insubordination . . . *sir*. If he misbehaves, I'll jolt him." A lie, but to her ears she sounded fairly convincing.

Haller considered her a moment before unclipping a magkey from his belt. Edie held out her hand, expecting him to reconsider at any moment. But he pressed the small tool to her palm.

"Since you asked so nicely."

"Thank you."

"There. Isn't that much better?" He seemed genuinely relieved. "Now get some rest. Read your memos. CPT at six sharp, tomorrow morning." He walked off, calling over his shoulder, "And keep that snag handy. I can't vouch for his manners."

CHAPTER 4

With Haller gone, Edie could breathe again. She was used to dealing with people who needed her cooperation, and while Haller's attitude was less refined than that of the Crib 'crats, his method was the same. He was willing to make small compromises to keep her on-side because she had a talent that would make him rich.

Seated opposite her was a man who probably didn't know, and certainly didn't care, that she could create valuable new worlds with little more than a well-aimed thought. Depending on what they'd told him, he might not even consider her an ally, but she intended to gain his trust. The jolt that excited Haller so much was the worst possible way to achieve that. She couldn't imagine using it any more than she could use the drub. She wouldn't discipline him like an animal.

Nor would she keep him silent.

Finn tucked into the food, ignoring Edie's frank gaze as she picked thoughtfully at the bread, savoring the spices that stung the roof of her mouth. His age was difficult to estimate. His position as a serf may have added a few years to his appearance, but she guessed he was under thirty. Old scars marred his jaw and cheekbone, and fresher ones slashed across one arm, snaking under the sleeve of his tee.

His midtoned skin made the pale lines stand out. Patchy yellowing bruises ringed his wrists, and his long fingers were calloused, the nails worn down though fairly clean.

Edie forced herself to stop staring and concentrated instead on fastening the tool belt around her waist—a delaying tactic. The familiar, encouraging weight of the belt boosted her courage.

Finn lifted off his seat to reach across the table with a quick, controlled movement that made her sit back in alarm. He flicked her a calm look that held neither query nor reassurance, took her cup and drained it. His presence set her on edge. She couldn't tell if it was an overreaction on her part or something more. The carefully directed defiance told her this man had learned to survive his servitude but had never succumbed to it.

She'd been rolling the magkey between her fingers as she watched him. Not once had he looked at it, yet she knew that was by conscious effort. She'd heard that the voice snag was the single most despised tool that serf handlers used on their charges. Cleanly and silently it removed identity. The uniform garb rendered them unseen, while the snag ensured they remained unheard. It was easy to assume a man lacked normal human thought processes when he was unable to speak them.

As Finn wiped sticky crumbs off his fingers, Edie mentally braced herself before walking around the table to stand beside him. As obediently as if she'd given him an order, he swung a leg over the bench to straddle it, and tilted his head. The snag, a flat metal strap the length and width of a finger, was locked with a magnetic seal into his throat. It prevented the vocal cords from moving and made even whispering too painful to attempt.

But she'd heard him whisper, once, when he asked her to save his life.

His skin was warm under her fingers. She fitted the magkey against the indentation in the center of the snag and it fell away. It didn't detach completely. Three thick wires were embedded into the corded flesh of Finn's throat, and the snag dangled from them. He reached up and tugged at it firmly. The hard line of his mouth was the only clue to his pain, while Edie winced at the sight of the slick red wires emerging. The snag finally came free. Three parallel trails of blood dribbled down his neck.

Finn drew a ragged breath and started to choke. The snag clattered to the floor as he coughed up blood onto the table top. Edie backed away involuntarily. Was this normal? As she retrieved the snag, she noticed the cook hovering nearby.

"Go on, I'll clean up." The cook swept in without taking a second look, as though crewmembers depositing blood on her tables was a daily event.

"Will he be okay?" It seemed both logical and absurd to be asking the cook, of all people, such a question.

"He's been snagged a long time, this one, eh?" The woman stopped wiping long enough to give a sympathetic shake of her head. "Infirmary's on deck two."

Edie touched Finn's shoulder. "Come on."

Finn followed her out of the mess, doggedly wiping his mouth and throat with the back of his hand as though this, too, were nothing out of the ordinary.

In the infirmary Edie handed him medigel and swabs and watched him clean up his wounds. From there he trailed her down another ladder to her quarters. The tiny annex seemed ridiculously small to serve as his berth. With the portable bunk and the console, there were barely three square meters of floor space.

She indicated the bunk. "I guess this is where you sleep."

Finn walked past her and entered her room without a word. He hadn't yet spoken and she was worried perhaps his vocal cords had been permanently damaged. For the first time, he seemed to take an interest in his surroundings. He investigated her quarters with methodical precision—which took about thirty seconds. There wasn't much to see. He checked the hatch between the two rooms, flipped open the lockers, ran his hands briefly along the interior bulkheads as though feeling for something.

"We're not bugged, if that's what you're looking for. I already checked."

He spared her a thoughtful glance, apparently decided to believe her, and stopped his search to face her squarely.

"The leash," he rasped. "Can you—"

A coughing fit interrupted his question. He leaned against the bulkhead and choked up more blood.

"Hey." Edie tried to sound annoyed, but it was hardly his fault. She went to the washbasin in the corner and filled a beaker. He slid down the wall to sit on his haunches and drank the water. Crouching beside him, she took back the beaker and placed it aside, waiting.

"Can you cut the leash?" he said at last, his voice grating.

"I'll try."

He jerked his head up, as if surprised by that.

"Of course I'll try." She lifted her hand and almost changed her mind when he shied away. He recovered quickly, although he still looked wary. "Keep still. I'll use a softlink this time."

She touched the fresh scar at his temple, felt the steady pulse under his skin, and then the sizzle of data flowing through the link. Her eyes closed and she sensed him breathing, slow and deep beside her.

As soon as she jacked in, she knew something was different: instead of the cold, flat flow of dry-teck in the datastream, she heard the unmistakable chime of biocyph. Considering the simple task his chip performed—monitoring her splinter to check she was in range and alive—it seemed like overkill. Then again, they must have known she'd try this. She'd deactivated his boundary chip before, and they'd made sure she couldn't do it again.

There's always a way in. That's what Bethany had taught her. Climb over, dig under, smash straight through . . . But she could see it was hopeless. A strand of biocyph burrowed into his cerebral cortex like a tiny, immature version of her wet-teck interface. It anchored and controlled the explosive device that would detonate if she went out of range, and it was wired to painfully paralyze him if she triggered the jolt.

The graft was artless, not the work of a cypherteck. But now that it was integrated into his brain and locked with unbreakable biocyph coding, it was immune to reprogramming and impossible to remove. It was already part of him. Attached to it was her ident code—in fact, her wet-teck sought out the ident like a voice calling her name across a crowded room. But nothing else was familiar. She circled around the thread, prodding at the edges, creating dissonant notes in the datastream. Was there anything here she could piece together to create a meaningful melody?

A single, pure chord disengaged itself from the rest. Edie grabbed it and traced its source, certain she was doing the wrong thing, but it was all she had. Her interface kept the chord separated, but the cacophony surrounding it obliterated its path. A hard vacuum of silence cut through the link for an instant, and then a warning glyph screamed.

Finn knew there was a problem at the same moment she did.

"Back off," he hissed.

With a gasp, she dumped the chord and let his splinter kick her out. She pulled her hand away, opened her eyes to stare into his, into the dark gold flecks radiating across the irises. For a long moment she couldn't speak. She had to make herself breathe again. Staggering to her feet, she felt like she should apologize but didn't know how he'd take it.

Instead, she stuck to the technicalities. "They've injected biocyph into your cerebral cortex."

His eyes widened. "Biocyph? In my head?"

"Just a single strand. But it can't be removed or interfered with, or the little bomb in your skull will go off. I don't know what to do."

"How does it work?"

"It tracks my splinter—my wet-teck interface. Specifically, it monitors my brain waves via the splinter so it knows I'm still alive and within range. And it's a hatchet job. A real disaster in there. It'd be dangerous to mess with any of it."

Finn nodded. He believed her, then. He believed she wanted this to be over as much as he did.

"And if you die, my brain fries," he said.

"That's it."

"You're not suicidal, are you?"

She examined his face for any trace of humor. His tone was deadpan, but his eyes glittered.

"That warning we got," she said, sticking to the subject, "that's supposed to let you know you're going out of range. Or, in this case, that the splinter doesn't like being interfered with." Her wet-teck interface quickly analyzed the stored reflection. "You get zero leeway, instant detonation, once we're separated by two thousand meters." The interface fed her new data. "Make that one thousand, nine hundred and eighty-nine meters."

"Hatchet job," he echoed. "They couldn't even get that right."

Edie leaned against the opposite bulkhead. "How did this happen? You didn't agree to it, did you?"

He stared at the patch of blood drying on the deck. "That outworlder woman on the station, Lancer, she bribes our handler to let us escape—if we help her grab this A-grade teckie so her people won't have to risk their own asses in case it goes wrong. She told us we'd be freed."

He paused, swallowed, rubbed his throat, having trouble speaking through disused vocal cords. He continued more slowly.

"I didn't believe a word of it, except the part about you." His eyes met hers again, and Edie remembered his trust in her abilities, back in the freight car. "I'd seen you around. Heard things. I knew you could break the boundary link, just like she said. Figured it was worth it, even if they were lying about the rest. It was worth trying, for a shot at freedom."

"But this leash—they didn't tell you about that." It wasn't a question.

Finn set his jaw. "No, I never agreed to *this*." He flicked his hand at his skull. "Now it's a life sentence, right?"

More like a death sentence. Edie hugged her arms around herself. "So what do we do?"

Finn considered in silence. She could see the cogs turning in his mind behind those unwavering eyes. Then, "When do we jump?"

"We already jumped once. I don't know where from, or where to."

"What's the mission?"

She shrugged, feeling out of her depth. "These guys are BRAT seed rovers. Trading illegal biocyph." She remembered Haller's unread memos. There must be information in there about the mission, or at least about a briefing.

Finn stood, eyeing her carefully. "So what are you thinking?"

"I'm thinking we have to get back to that medfac. Find the infojack who made the leash. Or someone else who knows what they're doing. I mean, if it's even possible without . . ." *Without killing you.* She couldn't say it.

"How much will that someone cost us?"

"A lot. It's not a service you pick out of the catalog."

"Well, I don't know about you, but I'm broke."

She smiled grimly, appreciating his levity. "They told me I'd get twenty thousand for this run, plus the same in bonuses."

"Is forty enough?"

"Might be. So you're saying we should go ahead with the mission?"

"What do you think?"

"Don't keep asking me that. It's your life we're playing with."

"I need to know where you stand."

Where did she stand? She'd been trying to figure out her own future, but now his was inextricably intertwined. "I didn't ask to be here, either. I might've stuck with them for a while. But not now. Not with you forced along for the ride." She swallowed a bitter lump in her throat, remembering the dead serf on Talas Prime Station. She wanted no more deaths on her conscience. "We have to cut the leash—and to do that, we need the creds from this mission."

He didn't look convinced. "And you'd spend it all to free me?"

In her mind, there was no question. In his mind, clearly, there were plenty of questions. He had no reason to trust her, or anyone.

"It would be freeing us both."

Disbelief flickered again in his eyes, but he didn't voice his doubts. "So, one mission. Then we split, find an infojack."

Edie nodded, wondering if he had a plan for himself after they cut the leash. "What did Zeke mean—who are the Saeth?"

"Never heard of them."

His quick response and cold glare told her he was lying and that he didn't care if she knew it. She let it drop and pinched the bridge of her nose—the burden of the cached data had left her wet-teck groaning in protest. She should copy it to file at the console in the annex, but she didn't particularly want to leave evidence around for someone else to find, so she wiped it and forced herself to relax. As she turned from the wall, something jabbed her thigh. The voice snag in her pocket.

"Here." She handed it to him. "A souvenir."

Finn crumpled it in his fist and headed for his little annex.

"Aren't you going to say thank you?" She regretted the words as soon as they were out. She had no right to do that, to treat him as a subordinate, no matter how the rest of the crew thought of him.

Finn hesitated in the hatchway, looking down at the twisted metal strip in his hand, and his lips curled into a sneer.

"Thank you."

The hatch snapped shut behind him.

Edie went to bed, exhausted, not caring what he did or where he went. Caring even less about the XO's precious memos. She slept solidly. No dreams. The best kind of sleep.

CHAPTER 5

"First morning on board and in trouble already."

Stifling a yawn, Edie stared at the woman in her doorway. Armed only with a breakfast tray, Cat Lancer still managed to look as formidable as the first time Edie had seen her. She wore a white tank top that showed off the well-defined muscles of her arms and shoulders, and colored pins sparkled against her hair braids that shone black as the Reach. Her cobalt-blue pants were unlike anything that had been provided in Edie's wardrobe.

"Um, trouble?" Edie said.

Cat grinned and pushed the paper tray at Edie, who took it reflexively. The doughy bread looked unappetizing and she set the tray aside.

"You missed CPT. You do know what the *C* stands for, don't you?"

Haller had mentioned CPT the day before, and Edie hadn't bothered wondering what it meant.

"*Compulsory* physical training," Cat said helpfully. "Can I come in?"

Edie didn't feel like having a visitor this early in the morning, but didn't object when she saw what was sticking out of the duffle bag near Cat's feet. Her old boots.

"Where did those come from?" Edie grabbed the boots and jammed her feet into them.

"You're welcome." Cat picked up the bag as she entered, and dropped it on the deck between them. "Haller dug them out of the recyc bins, or so he claims. Where's Finn?"

"In the shower." Hands on hips, Edie faced Cat and tackled more important questions. "What happened to my guard back on Talas Prime Station? Did you kill him?"

Cat settled into the console seat and pointed at the bag. "Brought you some stuff. How are you feeling?"

"Please, I need to know."

Cat sighed, her gaze wandering over the holoviz where Edie had been exploring the ship's accessible logs while meticulously avoiding Haller's memos. "The guard's fine, Edie. We just tranq'ed him."

Edie had no choice but to believe her. External comms were locked down for the duration of the mission—not just because the ship had a captive cypherteck on board. It was necessary because the rovers would soon deviate from their flight path and didn't want to be tracked. Edie couldn't get news from Talas Prime or contact anyone there to confirm Cat's story.

Cat leaned down to unzip the duffle bag all the way. "Bought you a new palmet at the last dock. You don't want to use the piece of crap they gave you. And a few other things. Some book caps and girl things. There's stuff for Finn, too—"

"That's great, thanks," Edie said without feeling. She didn't want to deliberately antagonize Cat, but she didn't need a best buddy, either.

Cat caught on fast. She gave Edie an earnest look and switched tactics. "Look, I'm sorry about how this went down. Haller will never tell you this, but I had this great plan where I'd meet you on the station, make you an offer you couldn't refuse, convince you to join us freely. Get you on-side from the start."

Cat sounded genuine, but she had every reason to get Edie on-side *now*.

"I might've said no." She wondered if, in fact, she would have. Edie had dreamed a thousand times of leaving Talas, but it had always seemed so impossible she'd never seriously thought about how to achieve it. The Crib had her bound by a contract and the planet had her bound by her dependence on neuroxin.

Cat looked dubious. "We knew you were unhappy with your Crib contract and with Project Ardra. As for our XO—well, there's two things you need to know about John Haller."

"Uh, let me guess. He's slick and he's creepy."

"Yeah, a real slimemold." Cat chuckled. "Though I have to admit, he smells better. So that's one thing. The other thing—sometimes he gets his priorities screwed up. When the client sent us to Talas to pick up a Crib-trained cypherteck with credentials to die for, Haller wasn't listening to anyone's ideas but his own. He always barges into a situation like the engine room's on fire and relies on his charm to extricate himself later."

"He doesn't have any charm."

"Well, he thinks he does."

That was a fair description, considering Edie's experience so far with Haller. She sat on Finn's bunk, tugged the duffle bag toward her, and rummaged through the contents. There were bottles of toiletries that were a cut above the stuff in the shower room, a clip of entertainment datacaps, a crew key, and several colored tees—surprisingly subdued, considering Cat's tastes, but perfect for Edie.

As Edie folded the tees in her lap, she asked the other question that had been bugging her. "Who was the blue-eyed man in the *Hoi*'s cargo hold when I was kidnapped? I recall the two of you getting rather friendly at the medfac."

Cat didn't answer at once, and Edie looked up to catch her guarded expression.

"That was the infojack."

"The one who hijacked my interface to make the leash?"

"Yes." Cat anticipated the next question. "I don't know exactly who he was, Edie, so don't ask. I don't know his name or anything about—"

"You don't know his name? You two were having sex right next to my bed."

"We were killing time. Look, he helped us kidnap a cypherteck—that puts him top of the Crib's shit list. He's long gone."

That infojack was her best chance—perhaps her only chance—of cutting the leash, and she didn't believe that Cat really knew nothing about him. But if she was going to get Cat to talk, she needed to befriend her. She pulled a piece of fabric from the duffle bag, shook it out, and realized it was a pillow slip. Plain white, gloriously soft. There was no denying Cat's gifts were thoughtful.

She opened her mouth to say thank you, but closed it at the sound of footsteps from the corridor. Finn strode through the hatch, eyeing the navpilot with a look that said he would prefer she leave at once.

Cat gave him an arch smile. "We meet again."

He didn't respond. His resentment of Cat was understandable—she'd promised him freedom and he'd been tricked back into slavery. The navpilot wasn't oblivious to his feelings, either. She seemed to lose her nerve, a far cry from the situation back on Talas Prime where she'd taken for granted his yielding to her authority.

Edie watched with bemusement as Cat forced a smile. "So, Finn. How d'you like your new quarters? Cozier than the Catacombs, I'll bet."

Finn took the tray of food from the console and sat next to Edie to eat it, stabbing at the pieces of bread with a fork. He ignored both women until Cat, with an impatient glance in Edie's direction, backed down with a shrug.

"See you at the briefing, okay?"

She left, snapping the hatch shut behind her.

Edie's spine prickled self-consciously as she felt Finn's

eyes on her, watching her fold the clothes and make a neat pile of them, along with the pillow slip and the bottles of shampoo on top.

"Hey, I didn't ask for this stuff," she said, feeling guilty for accepting gifts from the woman who was at least partially responsible for his current situation.

"Don't get too cozy with the enemy. You're not part of this crew."

"But it makes sense to play nice, right? She brought things for you, too." Edie tapped the duffle bag with the toe of her boot. "And she gave me back my own boots."

His looked down at them and his lips curved in a half formed but real smile. Edie ran her hands over the familiar zips and buckles of her boots. They felt great. Despite everything that was wrong, something was right when she had her own boots.

"I should find out when that briefing is." Edie slid into the console and pulled up Haller's memos. When she saw the first one, she forgot about the briefing. It was the files she'd asked for—her records.

She glanced over her shoulder to see Finn digging into the pockets of the duffle bag. He pulled out some new clothes, a basic tool belt for shipside duties, an empty spur bracket, and a datastick of caps that must be the books Cat had mentioned. While he packed away the clothes, Edie downloaded her records onto her new palmet, deleted the memo, and went to her room. She didn't want Finn reading her personal stuff over her shoulder.

Sitting cross-legged on the bunk, Edie opened the files. The palmet extruded a glowing holo-cylinder that displayed her records in a revolving field, each one labeled haphazardly and filed apparently randomly. *Education reports. Training program: biocyph interface. Psych evaluation, age 14 . . .*

She searched the files for Lukas, her first bodyguard and her only friend after Bethany's death. He'd been an ex-milit, a loyal Crib citizen who'd guarded Bethany for years and then her. He'd just disappeared one day—"retired," or so they told her. It had been a while since she trusted anything the Crib said, including that.

The search turned up zero hits. She tried again with different parameters, not believing her eyes. Nothing. They'd wiped Lukas from existence. Having controlled Edie's life since she was ten years old, they could certainly control what got written into her records.

Edie scanned through the data again, swallowing the anger that made her throat ache. She could've jacked in and absorbed the facts five times faster via a softlink, but there was something about seeing the stark words before her eyes that made cold reality seem more real. And even colder.

One of the oldest documents was her guardianship-transfer paper. After the Crib discovered her extraordinary affinity for biocyph, her rescue from the camps had come in the form of Liv Natesa, a newly promoted 'crat from the Crib Colonial Unit whose personal ambition drove her to argue for establishing a seeding program on Talas. The idea had the full support of the local gov, which would do anything to boost its standing with the Crib. With Natesa's help, they'd petitioned Crib Central for a year to get the CCU program up and running, and to get permission to train Edie. From Central came a string of excuses: she was too young, she wasn't a Crib citizen, she was native born and should never have been taken from her people in the first place. What stopped the flow of excuses was a change of minister, quickly followed by a change of policy.

The Talasi Elders had had no say in the matter. Natesa had accused them of mistreatment—only slightly embellishing the extent of it—and brought Edie as a ward of state to the institute in Halen Crai.

Edie lingered over a three-line consent form, signed by Natesa, for the splinter and softlink implant. She remembered the surgery, the pain, the itchiness in her fingertips where the wires were embedded. She'd accepted everything they did to her.

There were education and training schedules, psych as-

sessments and recommendations, ongoing evaluations of
her rapidly developing skills. She skimmed the copies of her
seeding missions with CCU, and of Liv Natesa's investigation into her first mission. They'd buried a thousand BRATs
on that world, but the world described by Natesa bore little
resemblance to the one Edie recalled. The investigation was
a sham, its purpose designed to salvage Natesa's career after
the mission failed.

Bethany's death was dealt with in a few brief lines.

"What's wrong?"

Edie jumped at the sound of Finn's voice. He stood with
one foot inside her room and made no move to come nearer,
respecting her space. She blinked, hoping he hadn't seen her
crying. But her eyes were dry. She'd cried out her tears for
Bethany a long time ago. Why would he think there was
something wrong?

When she said nothing, he nodded at the holoviz. "What
is that?"

"My records from Talas." She switched to on-screen display so he couldn't read them from where he was standing.

"You've got a memo saying the briefing's in ten minutes,
top deck." His voice was hoarse, as though speaking was
still a huge effort.

"Give me fifteen and we'll head up there." She didn't want
to arrive early and appear over-eager.

"I'm going to skip it. Still sleeping off those tranqs they
gave me." He looked unsure of himself, as though he hated
to admit to any vulnerability.

"But they won't dose you up any more, right?"

"That's what they told me."

"Well, I'll fill you in later, if you're interested."

"I'm interested in keeping you alive. That's it."

He didn't sound as bitter as he probably should have.
Maybe because he was tired. As he turned to leave, Edie
called after him.

"Why did you think there was something wrong?"

He faced her again. "You were quiet."

"I was reading."

"I don't know. I just . . ." He shrugged but didn't leave. "You're a native of Talas, aren't you?"

"Yes."

"On the station I heard rumors that the natives would die if they left the planet."

"Don't worry. I have a neuroxin implant." She touched her inner elbow. "These rovers have assured me they'll replenish it before it runs dry."

If she was a good girl.

He surprised her by coming over to cup his hand around her arm. He examined the faint scar, his fingers firm on her skin as he prodded the tiny disk below the surface.

"Subcutaneous." He frowned. "They should've injected it deeper."

Edie slid out of his grasp. "It works just fine."

"How did that happen—the dependence on neuroxin?" He seemed genuinely curious.

"The ideology of the original settlers on Talas forbade them to meddle with the ecosystem to remove the toxins. This was hundreds of years ago, before terraforming advanced worlds became illegal. Anyway, the Talasi wouldn't do it. Instead, they used biocyph to change themselves—to break down the neuroxin they encountered in the environment."

"And this stuff is toxic?"

"It's lethal to non-Talasi."

"Then your body must break it down fast. I mean, I touched you and I'm still alive."

"My blood, sweat, and tears aren't toxic, if that's what you mean." She'd explained this a hundred times to nervous schoolmates and lovers. "There's biocyph in every cell of a Talasi's body. It instantly metabolizes neuroxin that's eaten or touched or breathed in, into harmless by-products. But the Talasi screwed up. Or perhaps it was deliberate—a way to ensure their descendants couldn't be uprooted again. If the level of those by-products in the body drops because of a lack of neuroxin, the biocyph metabolizes other compounds instead, like common neurotransmitters. That causes neuroshock. Death, eventually. So they're . . . we're dependent on neuroxin. I'm only half-Talasi—my mother was an outworlder—but still . . ."

Her voice dwindled away. Talking about herself, especially to a virtual stranger, caused the usual discomfort to resurface. She took a moment to collect her thoughts.

"Anyway, when the Crib Colonial Unit took me in for training, they developed these implants so I could leave the planet for short periods. It's my lifeline."

"Then it's my lifeline, too. Don't lose it."

They shared a grim smile and he returned to the annex without probing further.

Returning to her files, Edie found an appended report on Talasi history, written by a Crib 'crat but drawing on published articles by researchers who'd studied the natives. Naturally, the report reeked of Crib spin. Edie's unique experience from both sides of the controversy had given her what she believed was a more accurate picture. Five decades ago the new colonists had arrived, bringing clumsy blackmarket biocyph to tame the toxic ecosystem. The resulting ecological disaster had devastated the native population, while the colonists were forced to build their city, Halen Crai, inside a mountain where their air and water and food could be controlled.

Their forests dying, the desperate Talasi tribal elders finally allowed a small team of researchers to document their plight. The resulting anthropological articles caught the Crib's attention, but the end result was not what the elders had hoped for. The Crib's ever-changing tactics in its efforts to control the escalating Reach Conflicts placed Talas's jump node in a prime position. The new colonists were allowed to stay, and the Crib sponsored the building of a gate around the node to make transit easier. While the Talasi barely clung to life in their poisoned forests, the colony of Halen Crai quadrupled in size.

The only voice speaking for the Talasi was that of the researchers. But when one of them gave birth to a half-Talasi child, the elders felt betrayed and threw them out. The baby was left behind. Born with a dependence on neuroxin, like all Talasi, she couldn't survive offworld. The Talasi raised her but they were slaves to their superstitions—Edie was a half-breed, born out of season, and they never let her forget that stigma.

Shortly after Edie's birth, the Crib moved the Talasi into camps for their own protection. In those camps Edie had grown up—among a race desperately trying to maintain its tribal culture and traditions while its youngsters learned to speak Linguish from the Crib guards and heard unimaginable tales of adventure from the stars.

As for Edie's parents—the elders had exiled her father to a neighboring tribe and he'd never revealed himself to her, even after the tribal structure had broken down in the camps. Nor had she ever heard from her mother. She didn't even know her name. And some time during the last twenty years—she couldn't pinpoint exactly when—she'd given up waiting for her mother to come back to her.

Edie had had enough of reliving her childhood through the Crib's piecemeal reports. There was nothing here that would help her find Lukas. Shutting off the palmet, she walked through to the annex. Finn lay on his back, apparently asleep, one arm thrown over his eyes. His powerful frame dwarfed the too-narrow bunk. She couldn't help wondering about his background and whether she'd ever learn more about him. Considering her reluctance to talk about herself, it was unfair to expect him ever to open up. Every scar on his body told a story she'd probably never hear.

It was time for the briefing. If she left now, she'd be three minutes late—not quite late enough for a charge of insubordination.

CHAPTER 6

Haller's office doubled as the briefing room, a triangular bay below and to the port side of the bridge. Edie showed up just as Zeke delivered the punch line of a joke, causing a ripple of bored laughter from the crew. They fell silent as she entered. Cat gave her a friendly wave, while a young man with unruly hair and a ruddy face—it must be Kristos, Zeke's young op-teck according to the crew roster—jumped up to offer his chair, one of two on the near side of Haller's desk. But Edie planted herself on a cabinet along the back wall instead. Kristos sat again, beside Cat, while Zeke lounged against the bulkhead. Haller worked the holoviz controls on his desk. There was no sign of the elusive captain.

Haller launched into the briefing without commenting on Edie's tardiness. He was all business, boosting Edie's faith that he might actually be competent, at least when things were running smoothly.

"Our full brief's come through from Stichting Corp. After our next stop, we make nine more jumps to system fourteen in the Valen Sector. Navconn's still working out the best route." The holoviz displayed a graphical representation of several possible routes, which probably made little sense to anyone in the room except Cat. "The third planet in this system was seeded seven years ago, and that's our destination. We grab—"

"Uh, seven years?" Zeke interrupted, frowning at the display. It now showed the third planet in a long-range scan, a CCU file dated several years ago. "You can't extract BRATs after they've put down taproots." He looked over his shoulder at Edie for confirmation. Rovers were known for diving in and grabbing BRATs a year or two after terraforming had begun, while the taproots were shallow, but beyond that the task was more trouble than it was worth.

Edie watched the holo planet turning slowly on its axis, a pale blue sphere with the outlines of continents burned into it. The globe was scattered with tiny bright spots to indicate where the BRATs had been buried. Edie's vision narrowed on the image as a deep memory stirred. It couldn't be . . .

With a frustrated shrug at Edie's silence, Zeke turned back to Haller. "Even if we could get the BRAT seeds out of the ground, they'd be useless for making keystones. The biocyph is primed for that ecosystem and it's been brewing away for seven years."

"Thank you, Zeke. I can always count on you to announce the impossibility of every plan." But Haller was looking at Edie as he spoke.

"You're telling me it's not impossible?" Zeke persisted, incredulous. "We're supposed to uproot them after—"

"These seeds never germinated," Haller said. "No taproots. It's embryonic biocyph."

He had Edie's full attention now, and waited for her reaction. The memory, now fully formed, pushed to the front of her mind.

"Scarabaeus." As she breathed the word, four pairs of eyes turned to look at her. She drew an unsteady breath. "We're going to Scarabaeus?"

"If you mean Candidate World VAL-One-Four Tee-Three," Haller said, a smile tugging at his lips, "absolutely."

Edie sat in stunned silence while he continued to explain for the benefit of the others. She gripped the edge of the cabinet as the sound of blood rushing in her ears swamped the conversation. VAL–14 T3 had been her first mission, and the first major assignment for Liv Natesa's newly established seeding program on Talas. Natesa's big chance to impress CCU and to make herself indispensable when it came time to implement her grander vision. In hindsight, it was also a test run—albeit a failed one—for what would become Project Ardra. An unremarkable world, the commander in charge had called it during that briefing session so long ago, yet Edie remembered its serenity and her heartache at the thought of destroying ancient beauty, working it over, recreating it to please humankind.

"Edie?"

Startled, she looked at Haller through the glow of the holoviz, realizing he'd asked her a question. "What?"

"I'd like to hear your perspective on this."

She swallowed hard, staring at the glowing planet. It showed a detailed image of the locations of each BRAT drop, generated shortly after they finished the job.

"Our information on the initial seeding mission is sketchy." Haller's tone was patient but he couldn't have failed to notice how this was affecting her—in fact, he seemed to be enjoying it. "We do know that an unmanned scout returned a year later and reported the BRATs hadn't germinated. Our current intelligence indicates that CCU never returned to claim the BRATs. So unlike our usual hit-and-run, we can take our time with this one."

Kristos spoke up. "Why would they abandon all those BRATs?"

"Cheaper to make new ones than dig up the old," Zeke said, "if you have the biocyph templates. And no one but the Crib's got them."

He didn't bother to hide his resentment of this fact. With access to templates, the Fringers could make their own seeding technology. During the Reach Conflicts, plenty of desperate people had tried everything in their power to get their hands on the templates—blackmail, terrorism, humanitarian appeals. The Crib had ruthlessly crushed them all.

"Edie?" Haller insisted.

"What you said is correct." Edie heard the tremor in her voice. "The BRAT seeds didn't germinate, and I don't know much more, sir." She regretted that admission as soon as it was out. What would they do with her if she couldn't help them, if she was of no use?

"But why didn't they germinate?"

Because of me.

She had no idea how these people would react if she admitted what she'd done, all those years ago. She needed to fit in, to play along. She needed them to trust her so she could get through this, take the creds and run.

But she couldn't stomach the idea of these rovers profiting from Scarabaeus. She didn't want to go back.

"We . . . we never figured it out. That planet wasn't suitable for terraforming in the first place. We weren't supposed to be there. The ecosystem was too advanced."

"The Crib breaks its own rules when it suits them." Zeke shook his head like he had intimate understandings of the workings of that bureaucracy. "And then it just makes up new ones. That's what Project Ardra is, right? A loophole that's going to let them legally terraform advanced ecosystems like—what was it you called the place? Scara—?"

"Scarabaeus." Edie was embarrassed to explain why. "That's just my name for it. I found a beetle there."

"A beetle?" Kristos scoffed. "You mean, like, an insect?"

"An insect analog, yes. A sort of scarab." She wished she hadn't brought it up. Kristos's astonishment didn't surprise her. For a candidate world to be eligible for terraforming, its life was supposed to be no more evolved than basic multicellular organisms. "Like I said, the world was too advanced. Marine vertebrates, insects, vascular plant analogs. Seeders showed up three hundred million years too late. We should've left it alone."

And in the end, she'd made sure of that.

"Crib antics aside," Haller said, "you just let me know when you remember something useful, okay? That's why you're here."

The hint of a threat was unmistakable. Edie was going to have to justify her position on the team. It was now clear that their destination was no coincidence. They may have wanted her because she was the best cypherteck in the Crib, but once Stichting Corp had found out from her files that there was a world out there packed with dead BRATs, abandoned forever, they realized they'd hit the jackpot. Who better to help in a recovery and hack operation than the cypherteck who'd been present on the initial mission?

"Give her a break," Zeke said after a moment of tense silence. Edie threw him a quick look of gratitude. Haller scowled, and the big man responded by jutting his chin defiantly.

Edie stared at her boots and let the XO's voice wash over her.

"We've scheduled six days on the surface. If we can avoid tripping the security beacons and CCU isn't alerted, we can come back later for more. With the help of our brilliant cypherteck here, we'll have dozens of keystones ready for our customers by the time we reach the Fringe in a few weeks. There's a fortune out there and nobody else knows about it. Fat bonus checks for all of us. One thousand gold mines . . ."

One thousand deadly bullets.

She'd saved Scarabaeus, but she wanted no part of this reward.

Haller ordered Edie to produce a detailed report on Scarabaeus. That afternoon, while Finn worked with Zeke in the equipment holds, which she'd yet to see, she sat at her console and attempted to comply. Scarabaeus had been her first mission and the many runs since then had clouded whatever recollection she had of the technical specifics. But worse than that, she didn't want to remember. She'd tried for seven years to forget.

The actions of Liv Natesa and her team on Scarabaeus had been officially illegal. The mission had failed, but the 'crats in the Crib Colonial Unit that ran the seeding programs hadn't given up. As Edie became CCU's most successful cypherteck, Natesa's career quickly recovered and she set her sights on Project Ardra, a controversial and secret program to seed ecosystems that were up to half a billion years more advanced than had previously been permitted. But Ardra was more than just a career move for Natesa. Her personal ambition had morphed into a single-minded obsession to stamp humanity's footprint on every world in the galaxy.

Natesa called it her duty as a Crib citizen. Edie likened it to religious zealotry.

And now . . . Ardra would go ahead without Edie—there was nothing she could do about that. But for as long as she was in hiding with the rovers, she wouldn't have to be involved or go to prison for refusing to be involved. Her abduction was turning out to be unpleasantly convenient.

As Edie stared at the scant sentences she'd written, her pleasure at the thought of leaving Natesa high and dry evaporated. Had she known Scarabaeus was the rovers' destination, she'd have refused Haller's offer. Not that it would have made a difference. They controlled her life now, as surely as the Crib had until a few days ago. Haller had convinced her to help the Fringers instead of remodeling planets on the Crib's whim, but considering the man whose life now depended on hers, it was hard to calculate whether or not she'd traded up.

Finn returned in the evening, looking like he'd spent the day down a mine. His face was smudged, his clothes filthy.

"I thought you were hauling rigs?"

"No. Greasing drills."

"What? They don't even use those drills. They're just for show." The *Hoi* carried mining equipment because it was supposed to be a prospecting vessel.

"They have to *look* like they're being used."

"Did they feed you?"

He nodded. Edie had skipped supper and not even noticed until now. She tossed him a palmet.

"I put the mission briefing on there for you, and a few details about CCU's seeding program." Project Ardra. She wanted him to know why working for rovers was a better option than the alternative—at least for her. "Maybe you could take a shower first."

"One shower a day is my limit."

She wrinkled her nose, wondering if he was kidding. Leaning against the hatch, Finn scanned the briefing.

"It doesn't sound so bad," she said helpfully. "Secret location, no Crib monitoring. Pretty safe."

"I imagine working with rovers is never safe."

"You know about that stuff—security, I mean?" Presumably the rovers had singled him out because they considered him bodyguard material.

He didn't answer, but perched on the edge of the console and considered her. Edie was starting to realize she'd never get more out of him than he wanted to give. On the other hand, she'd already told him far more about herself than she'd intended to.

She began to feel warm under his appraising stare, but when he spoke, it wasn't what she expected.

"You any good in a fight?"

"I had basic training."

"Had?"

"It's been a few years."

He quirked a brow, unimpressed.

"That's your job anyway." Edie risked a question of her own. "What are the Catacombs that Cat mentioned?"

"That's where I was before Talas Prime."

"But what are they?"

"Asteroid mining."

He didn't elaborate. She'd heard a few horror stories and didn't push it. He handed back the palmet and she wiped a smudge off the screen, throwing him a mildly accusatory look.

"I guess I'll take that shower now," he said, as though it was his idea all along.

"Good idea."

Alone again, Edie turned back to her report, but it was hard to concentrate with the echo of Finn's brooding presence lingering in the room. She leaned back in her seat and ran her hands over her face, trying to relax. Including their outgoing trip and then the long journey to the Fringe, she had four weeks cooped up in here with Finn. Four weeks with Haller breathing down her neck and Cat cozying up to her.

She stepped through to her room, undressed quickly down to her underwear and curled up on the bed. She must have dozed off, because the sound of the hatch snapping woke her up. Finn returned in clean casual pants and put away his things, shifted a few items on the console, threw a blanket onto the bunk. He moved with an economical grace that captivated her attention, his chest glistening with moisture in the half-light of the annex. Everything about him projected strength and assurance.

Things could be worse. Had Ademo not died back on Talas Prime, *he* might have been assigned to protect her, and tonight she'd be sharing her quarters with him instead— living in fear of his cruel temper. Finn didn't exactly set her at ease, but she felt safe enough.

She found herself seeking out the marks on his skin, the bruises, the wound at his throat, and old scars crisscrossing his back that could only have come from a flogging. He glanced over and caught her watching through the open hatch, and she was thankful that her room was in near darkness so he couldn't see the heat rising in her face. A vertical crease formed between his brows as he held her gaze in an unspoken query while he stuffed his dirty clothes into a laundry bag. Then he slid into the console and turned it on.

Edie rolled over and tried to sleep.

CHAPTER 7

She counts the bruises while she waits. Four little ones on
Ursov's neck where someone grabbed him. Two along his
jawline. One very black eye. Eight grazes in a neat row
along his knuckles, each one now ringed in white because
he's clenching his fists as he sits opposite her, still smarting
from the indignity of it all.

In her arms she clutches a white teddy bear that he gave
her. Her legs are swinging because her feet don't reach the
floor. A clean floor made of stone, unlike anything she's
seen before. She's never seen so many straight lines, either.
Perfectly flat and vertical walls aligned with perfectly level
floors and ceilings. Who would have thought the rugged
mountain peaks of Halen Crai were hiding such perfect
form and structure within?

Ursov gives her an encouraging smile, and she returns it.
But she's devastated by those marks on his skin. It's all her
fault. One of the elders sent a group of young men to attack
him as they were leaving the camp. She's ten years old and
they've always ignored her, and now they suddenly decide
she's worth fighting for? She hates them for hurting Ursov
as he was trying to help her. His milit uniform is torn at one

sleeve, and from the way he fussed with it all the way here, she knows he's ashamed of that.

"Don't be nervous," he says, but she is very nervous.

She knows that her life starts today.

A perfectly square door slides open. Ursov stands and leads her inside. She grips his huge hand, feeling dizzy, and the teddy bear dangles from her free hand. The room is enormous, bigger even than the elders' council meeting hall, and the ceiling is a lot higher. Looking up, she sees a balcony running all the way around the wall, supported by intricately carved stone arches.

Ursov's boots tap and echo on the hard floor. She trots to keep up, her new boots scuffling softly. They don't fit properly and she has a blister on her heel.

At the far end of the room is a tall woman in quiet conversation with two smartly dressed people. It takes a long time to reach them, and then the woman turns from the group. She has silver icicles hanging from her ears and her hair is pulled back so tightly that it stretches the skin around the edges of her face. Her scarlet lips curve into a smile but her eyes are frowning.

"Does she understand me?" she asks Ursov.

"Sure," Ursov says. "She speaks Linguish real good."

"Goodness, she's very . . . small."

Ursov gets defensive. "You said you'd help her."

"Well, we have many tests to run before we'll know if she's suitable."

"But you can't send her back there. They don't treat her right."

The woman's smile turns brittle. She doesn't want to deal with difficult questions. She doesn't want to deal with Ursov at all.

"Thank you for bringing her to Crai Institute. Leave her with us now."

Ursov falters, realizes he's been dismissed, lets go of her hand. He squeezes her shoulder once and then he's gone, *he's nothing but fading footsteps while she stares up at the woman who has saved her, who will give her a future.*

"Edie, it's lovely to meet you. I'm Liv Natesa." She reaches for the teddy bear, her dark painted lips a cruel smudge. "You don't need this anymore."

"I do need it," she whispers, keeping a firm grip on its paw as Natesa tugs.

"You're a big girl now. You need big-girl things. I'll give you everything you need."

Natesa smiles at her, but the smile is brittle. Edie wants the real smile back. She needs to please this woman, or Ursov will get into trouble and she'll go back to the camp. She lets the bear out of her grasp. The soft thing disappears, dropped on a table and discarded. Insignificant.

"You're very special to me," Natesa says, holding out her hand.

She doesn't want to take it. It looks cold and bony, not safe like Ursov's. But Ursov is gone, her old life is gone. There's no one else. And she's no longer insignificant. Not to this woman.

She takes Natesa's hand.

"Hey. *Hey!*"

The dark shape of Finn's body filled the hatchway. His voice had woken her up, and apparently that had been his only intention—once he saw her eyes were open, he returned to his bunk.

In a cold sweat, Edie drifted on the surface of consciousness, floundering in old memories and dream images as her heart raced. Had she cried out in her sleep? Did Finn care enough to wake her from a nightmare?

Ursov's face came back to her, his heavy weathered features and toothy smile. She couldn't remember how she met him—one of dozens of milits who guarded the Talasi camps—or how they'd become friends. She only knew he'd meant more to her than anything else on that lonely, frightening day. But the moment she stepped through that square stone door, everything changed. Natesa's obsessive schemes and detached concern were no substitute for his stories and warm smile.

The annex glowed faintly from a single striplight. Part of Finn's bunk was visible and he turned restlessly under the covers.

Finn threw off his blanket with a grunt and again moved to the hatchway. As he leaned against the arch, he rubbed the back of his neck slowly with his hand.

"You need to calm down."

Edie stared at him. "What?"

"Your mind. Whatever is going on in there—I can feel it." His voice was gravel-edged. "You need to stop."

She sat up, confused. "I don't know what you mean."

"I can feel it. In here." He touched his temple. "Your mind, your body, your . . . *awareness*. It's not pleasant."

"That isn't possible."

"Well, it's there. Ever since they initialized the link when I boarded. Thought at first it was a side effect of the surgery, but it's not. It's you. All day, all the time. Right down to that nightmare you just had."

She set her jaw, refusing to be drawn: "My splinter sends out a signal to let yours know I'm alive. A basic brainwave pattern and a locator, that's all. It shouldn't even reach your consciousness."

"Well, something's getting through." He glared at her. "Just stop it."

As he turned away, Edie slipped out of bed and grabbed a diagnostic rod from her tool belt. Padding into the annex, she found Finn sitting on his bunk, elbows on knees, massaging his temples. He flinched when she touched his skull, and she opened her hand and let him see the tool, then tipped his head and pressed the sensor against the scar at his temple. It calibrated to his splinter and blinked a brief display.

"It's reading fine," Edie said. Was he just trying to unnerve her? But she remembered when he'd come into her room that morning, wondering if she was okay. He'd picked up on her state of mind then, too—even if he hadn't been fully aware of it.

Finn's brow furrowed. "It's not *fine*. It's . . . a whisper. An itch. With these flashes of light when your emotions run hot." He brushed her hand and the tool away and looked at her pointedly. "Irritating."

The mention of her deeper emotions left her feeling vulnerable. Standing in her underwear before Finn, who was himself half-naked, wasn't helping. Too much skin and tension in a confined space, and her heartbeat was still unsteady from the dream. In a self-conscious gesture she wrapped her arms around her body.

"You're telling me you can feel what I'm feeling?"

He shook his head. "More like an untuned comm. White noise. Nothing specific. And then it fires out of control. You need to learn some mental discipline."

"This has nothing to do with me. I'm not doing anything."

Finn shook his head and stretched out on the bunk with his hands behind his head, leaving her helpless in the face of his resentment.

"You would not believe what I've seen dished up on some cruisers and called food." Cat tore apart her fried roti and shoved a piece into her mouth.

Edie pushed around bite-sized patties with a fork and tried to work up an appetite. Cat had cornered her in the gym that morning, by jumping into the exercise bay next to hers, and made her agree to sitting together for lunch. Edie decided to return the friendly attitude. She and Cat would have little contact with each other during the course of their shifts, and as the only other woman on board—except for Gia, the cook, who apparently had no contact with anyone outside of meals—Edie decided to make the effort with Cat.

Finn found himself a seat at a long table that Edie suspected was reserved for the serfs. For now, the table was otherwise empty.

"You worked on other ships?" she asked Cat.

"Sure. I had a life before the *Hoi*."

"Where are you from?"

"Originally? Cameo. Left when I was fifteen. What a place."

Edie gathered from her disparaging tone that she meant it was a bad place. "Is that an original Terran colony world?"

Cat nodded, mopping her plate with the last of the roti. "A forgotten, abused hellhole. Only reason we didn't completely wipe ourselves out was because the Crib came to the rescue after our government—if you could call it that—offered up a few hundred recruits to fight in the Reach Conflicts. I jumped at the chance to leave. They taught me to fly. I did it for the thrills. Earned a few medals, then decided I'd had enough of their war." It seemed Cat thrived on stress and adventure. She'd obviously enjoyed her wartime action.

"So, illegal seeding is more your thing."

"It's illegal only because the Crib decides the rules, Edie." Cat waved her fork for emphasis. "We're all taught to think of the Crib as this wonderful and benevolent force because it's the birthplace of humanity. But it just wants control. It controls worlds. It controlled your life, and mine."

"Why did you leave the milits?"

"I did my tour. It's not like my heart was devoted to Fleet. I just wanted to fly." She noticed Edie's thoughtful expression, but must have mistaken it for disapproval because there was a hint of defensiveness when she added, "You think I'm a rat for switching allegiances."

"No—actually, your story is kind of familiar."

Cat gave her a dark look. "It can be a dangerous thing."

"What?"

"Not trusting, not belonging. Losing faith. You can end up with no indicator for what's right, and they use that. They grab pieces of you, pushing you every which way. They can make you do things and you don't even know or care if it's wrong."

"Is that a warning?"

"Eh. Call it a life lesson."

Edie considered the advice but said nothing. If Cat was referring to her own situation on the *Hoi Polloi*, she was perhaps hinting that her loyalties were flexible. That could be useful down the track.

Cat looked over Edie's shoulder. "Huh. Rackham just came in, and he *never* comes in here. I guess you must warrant special consideration."

Edie turned to see the captain heading straight for them, ignoring the murmured greetings from his crew. Zeke sat with an older man, presumably one of the engineers. Kristos sat alone eating a sickly-looking fluorescent dessert. Haller must be manning the bridge.

"Remember, say yes sir, very good sir," Cat said with a wink. She pushed back her chair and stood up as Rackham stopped at their table to fix Edie with a steely glare. "Good afternoon, Captain."

"Lancer." He flicked her a look, then returned his attention to Edie.

"Sir, may I introduce our new teck, Edie Sha'nim. Edie, this is Captain Francis Rackham."

Rackham was less imposing than Edie had imagined. Her impressions had been of a mysterious, elusive leader with exotic tastes in art. He was compactly built, middle-aged, with cropped salt-and-pepper hair and a trimmed beard. His clothes were neat and traditional, and looked expensive. She bobbed out of her seat to exchange a nod with him, unsure of the protocol, and sat when Cat did so.

"Welcome aboard, Sha'nim. I trust my executive officer has seen to your needs."

"Yes, sir."

Rackham tipped back on his heels and glanced casually around the mess, as if searching for a conversation topic. His attention was drawn to, of all things, a gray splotch on the floor near their table.

"What the devil is the matter with our cleaner toms today? I don't expect to walk in here and see this morning's breakfast on the deck."

He wasn't talking to either of them in particular, so they stayed silent.

"How's it going with your bodyguard?" he asked Edie.

She looked over at Finn, who was finishing his meal and watching her with his usual impassivity. If he was curious about the captain, he didn't show it.

"No complaints."

Rackham's absently fingered a badge on his lapel as he studied her. Edie realized it was a medal, and remembered what she'd read about him being a war hero.

"Word on the bridge is that you have an aversion to using the drub."

Cat shifted uneasily in her seat and reached for her drink. Edie would get no help from her.

"Finn isn't violent, sir," Edie said, "or disobedient."

"Generally, we don't let lags wander about on the loose. The rest of the crew would feel better if they saw you carrying it." Rackham bestowed a benign smile upon her, nodded to Cat, sneered at the stain on the floor, and moved off to the galley to speak with Gia.

Cat looked like she was about to say something when Zeke, who had hopped up from a nearby table, dragged over his chair and straddled it backward.

"Ladies."

Cat regarded him with good-humored annoyance. "You're interrupting."

Zeke chuckled and placed his drub on the table before addressing Edie. "Since you're now under captain's orders." He gave an apologetic shrug. "Haller told me to send you belowdeck this afternoon. I'll be portside for a couple of hours, but Kristos will introduce you to the rigs. Any questions, ask him. Just don't expect the right answer. He's keen, but green as snot."

Kristos looked up at the sound of his name, showing no particular reaction to Zeke's words. As the most junior member of the crew, he probably endured such insults on an hourly basis.

"Hey, take me portside, Zeke," Cat said, throwing her arm around the big man's shoulders. The way their brown eyes flashed at each other made Edie wonder if they were lovers. Cat looked at Edie. "I've got some creds to burn at Neuchasley. You want anything?"

"A couple of one-way tickets to Port Paradiso," Edie said. Zeke guffawed. Cat just looked uncomfortable.

Edie thumbed her tray aside, pushed back her chair, and grabbed the drub before Zeke had time to remind her. As she headed out, aware that Finn had risen to follow her, the drub was an awkward weight in her hand. Maybe she could find a use for it if the machines got temperamental.

CHAPTER 8

Kristos fired up a tracker so Edie could calibrate her wet-teck interface and practice some commands. The young op-teck had spent a couple of hours showing her the rigs and the only thing she'd learned was that Zeke was the most disorganized teck she'd ever met. Finn was attempting to bring some order to the chaos by sorting a chest of tools into trays over in the corner of the equipment hold, a job Zeke had assigned him before leaving for the dock to pick up a gang of serfs. Finn's hands moved quickly to accomplish the mind-numbing task. Every so often he paused to adjust a tool, to dismantle or reset it. He handled them with a practiced flair that convinced Edie he must have meck experience.

For the better part of the afternoon, Kristos kept up a monologue—although much of what came out of his mouth was information-free. Edie discovered he was a year younger than she, far too fresh-faced to be shunning legal teck work for this gig. When she asked what he was doing with rovers, he evaded the question with a shrug. Maybe he had a juvenile record that prevented him from joining the civil service, at least until he turned twenty-five and could wipe his slate. Not that he'd ever get a foot in the door at a Crib recruitment center if they found out the specifics of his current job.

"So cool, being able to control teckware just by thinking about it." Kristos watched Edie with awe. Edie had never considered it *cool*, nor shown any particular enthusiasm for her work. She was just good at it and had never been given other options.

"That's not quite the way it works. I don't control the biocyph. More like, coerce it. The whole point of biocyph in an operation as complex as terraforming is that it works best when it's left alone to interact with the environment, learn from its mistakes, and evolve its own solutions."

Looking over Zeke's rigs, she wondered how the crew had coped over the last few years, considering the state of the equipment. It represented a broad mix of technology: some rather dubious-looking security tracking units, a bank of outdated—and certainly stolen—CCU biocyph interface units for hijacking and reprogramming the BRATs, and an assortment of spare parts for repairs. There were even a few BRAT seed husks, many of them wrenched apart, lined up against the bulkhead like open coffins built for six-meter-tall giants.

"What happened to those BRATs?" she asked Kristos.

"I don't really know. Most of the time the biocyph just sort of falls apart when you force the BRATs open. It was one of Jasna's projects."

"Jasna?"

"Our last cypherteck. Take a look at those stasis modules over there. We use them to stabilize the BRATs while we hijack them."

Edie used a hardlink to jack into one of the modules, a flat unit not much bigger than a tom. The datastream buzzed along her arm, up her spine, into her wet-teck.

"So, what happened to Jasna?"

The good humor left Kristos's face. "They didn't tell you?"

Before he had time to explain, the external hatch snapped open. Zeke exited the airlock followed by three men who were instantly recognizable as serfs—the cropped hair and sullen looks, the identical garb. A few days ago, Finn would not have looked out of place among them. A chorus of toms skittered out of their way as the men shuffled in, carrying crates and cases.

Zeke instructed them where to put the supplies by pointing to apparently random places in the hold as they went back and forth, unloading the airlock. The only case he seemed concerned about was a shiny rig that one of the men wheeled in on a trolley. Zeke stopped him and sent him back through the airlock to the far hatch, which led to the landing skiff.

Zeke had on a bright orange tee that he hadn't been wearing earlier. In the multicolored light sources of the surrounding striplights and consoles, it seemed to glow. It was a good guess that Cat had picked it out for him portside. He caught Edie's eye and thumped his chest as he called out to her, "Nice, huh?"

He joined them, nodding with approval to see Edie checking out his rigs.

"What d'ya think, then, teckie?"

"Uh, I have questions."

"Fire away."

"I don't mean to question your competence, but how do you intend to disable the planet's security beacons with those trackers over there?"

"Aw, beacons are the least of our worries on a planet that's not even being monitored."

"These stasis modules aren't much better. It's a miracle you can make usable keystones at all."

"What's wrong with them?"

She tried to explain it diplomatically. "Your cypherteck cut corners. She forced simplistic start-up routines onto the biocyph."

"Yeah . . ." Zeke scratched his head. "Uh, why would she do that?"

"Makes the modules easier to handle once they start doing their job, but it also stifles the natural inclinations of the biocyph, makes it less adaptable in new situations or if something goes wrong."

"Can you fix it?" he asked. "Cuz something always goes wrong."

"The biocyph's responded predictably, writing itself some clever leapfrogs." Edie paused and tried more commands through her interface. "And it's produced defensive coding to try and counteract her overlaid routines. They were fighting each other all the way."

Zeke grimaced. "I always thought she looked kinda stressed out."

"Biocyph needs to be prodded and coaxed, not forced into submission by aggressive commands. Otherwise it's wasted—you may as well be using regular dry-teck."

"I know, I know." He glanced around the hold. "Is Haller about?"

"He's off duty," Kristos replied.

That seemed to be the answer Zeke wanted. "Edie, come with me. I'll show you something that'll impress you."

She followed him into the landing skiff, which had a hold that was marginally better organized thanks to rows of brackets to hold the equipment in place for atmospheric flight and landings. In the center of the hold stood the main drill, a permanent fixture surrounded by a scaffolding of platforms and conduits. It was exactly the equipment that a prospecting vessel would carry, but these rovers probably never used it. Beyond it was a short ramp leading to the cockpit.

Zeke drew Edie's attention away from the drill and flicked open the case that she'd seen the serf carry in.

"Just picked up this baby from a Neuchasley merchant." He handed her a hardlink. "Take a look."

"What is it?"

"Some sort of booster. The guy said it can turn around a failing ecosystem in ten months."

She shook her head. "Zeke, you know that's not possible."

"Sure it is. I've seen it. Or something like it. Listen, the insides are probably a bit screwy. Maybe you can work your magic on it. I don't want to sell it to some poor buggers and have it turn their planet into mash."

Mash. An ugly word for ugly failure. CCU had its share of them. Most terraformed planets never made it past the first half-decade—the ecosystem tended to crash within months, and a few years after that the lingering cyphviruses reduced all living matter to decaying organic sludge. A fallen world, the Crib elegantly called such a disaster when it felt the need to announce the failure. Tecks in the seeding program called it mash and wrote long reports about why it wasn't their fault. Meanwhile, the planet rotted.

The ecosystems of colonies that couldn't pay their renewal fees suffered the same fate.

"It's very pretty," Edie conceded, because in truth she was curious to take a look at the device. It sounded something like a reverse bio-bomb. "But our priority is to prep the rigs for Scarabaeus, right?"

"I just wanted to show you. And don't tell Haller, okay? He doesn't need to know where every penny of the supplies allowance goes."

So that was Zeke's game—overreporting the cost of new equipment and using the leftover creds to make his own trades. This wasn't an industry that used invoices and re-ceipts. By confiding in her, he'd made her an accomplice. That was fine by Edie. Because they shared a profession, Zeke was the one person on the ship she was closest to im-plicitly trusting, although she recognized the irrationality of her reasoning. If he wanted to bond with her by confessing his subversive acts against Haller and Stichting Corp, she'd accept that.

He caressed the control panel with affection and Edie re-lented, squatting for a closer inspection.

"Thanks. And I forgive you for insulting my rigs back there." He gave her a friendly smile that she couldn't help returning. "You were pretty unhelpful in the briefing yester-day." His tone was conversational, but she sensed tension, as though he was wary of saying the wrong thing and threaten-ing their newfound comradeship.

"I was a trainee during that mission. They didn't tell me

much." Thinking about Scarabaeus set her pulse hammering. She still couldn't believe she was going back.

"Want some friendly advice? Learn to fake it. Bluff your way through the details. Haller won't know the difference. He's very much the big picture guy. You need to be useful to him."

"I know that." The conversation made her uneasy, even though the same thought had already crossed her mind. She sat back on her heels and changed the topic. "Kristos told me you trained with CCU."

"Sure did. Not with biocyph, mind you, just as an operations teck. Did some seeding work. Gave them ten years before I came to my senses, realized the real action was with rovers. Maybe you'll see that too, eventually."

She made a noncommittal sound. She and Finn had a plan and it didn't include running with rovers in the long-term.

She tapped the rig. "This biocyph is decades out of date. Looks flashy, but its guts are obsolete. I hope you weren't ripped off."

"But you can train it, can't you? Catch it up with the latest specs?"

"I can try. If I have time."

"Terrific." He lowered his voice, although there was no one else around. "If you feel like making a little extra, just let me know. I got contacts all over the place, but half the time I don't know what to do with the shit they sell me. All kinds of stuff I can pick up cheap. Boosters, med units, those regulator things they use for hothouse ag-teck. You fix the biocyph up for me, maybe track down some customers on the Fringe, I'll cut you a share of the profit."

"How do I track down customers when there's a comms blackout?"

"You can override that."

Edie sighed, shaking her head dramatically. "Zeke, leave me out of your games."

"Suit yourself. Just saying, us tecks should stick together."

"Doesn't mean we have to go down together. You want to answer a question for me?"

"Fire away."

"What happened to Jasna?"

Zeke's expression turned hard. "Eco-rads happened to Jasna." He let that sink in, then continued. "Couple of months ago we were docked at some port on the Fringe and they . . . it's like they jumped out of the walls. Went straight for her, cut her throat, and vanished." That was how they worked. They didn't need to kill the entire team. Taking out the cypherteck had the same effect. A seeding team couldn't do anything without its cypherteck. "She was a good kid—even knew how to charm Haller. Everyone liked her. Not exactly a wiz with biocyph, but as good as any cypherteck who hasn't had the benefit of Crib training."

Edie didn't know what to say. These people worked outside the law and she didn't understand their motives, but they had their own code, formed bonds like normal people. It was clear Zeke had cared for Jasna.

She could relate to that. She'd lost someone she loved to eco-rads, too.

"This is a good gig, the *Hoi Polloi*," he went on, but it sounded like he was trying to convince himself more than her. "Rads are still a problem, and sometimes we have to deal with rivals. But we've got client backing, a nice cover story in case CIP noses around. And now we've got a Crib teckie complete with a bullet-stopper." Edie winced at his choice of words. "I'll leave you to this. I've got three more serfs and a bunch of supplies to bring over."

"You're returning portside?" She peered through the hatch into the *Hoi*'s hold beyond. "What about the—the guys in there?"

"Kristos can handle them. They're tranq'ed and stable. But keep the hatches closed until I get back."

He went to have a word with Kristos and then left. At the sound of the hatches snapping shut, Edie realized she was only meters from freedom. She hadn't allowed the idea of escape to take form in her mind, not now she and Finn had agreed to complete the mission and use the creds to deal with the leash. But it was tempting to fantasize about making a run for it . . .

A blinking light on the hatch panel caught her eye. Zeke had left the hatches unlocked. He was only a few dozen meters away and wouldn't be leaving the vicinity of the dock, so he hadn't bothered about security. She went over, snapped the skiff's hatch, and looked into the airlock. Every one of its six walls had a hatch—she'd heard that such a connection was called a six-way. Only three hatches were in use—one leading to the skiff, one to the *Hoi*, and one to the gangway that connected to the dock.

Edie's hand shot out and she pressed her fingers to the gangway hatch's lock before her brain caught up to what her subconscious mind had made her do. Dry-teck wasn't her forte, but her splinter allowed her to deal with complex code better than many op-tecks. With the lock disengaged, she was able to copy its code to her splinter and rip apart the tiers with impunity. The lock was primed for a crew key in combination with an authorized thumbprint—a print from any of the *Hoi*'s senior crew. The latter was something she couldn't replicate, but she could fool the lock into accepting her thumbprint as well. Her heart racing in anticipation of Zeke's imminent return, she altered the code to accept a new input and fed it back into the lock. It beeped for input, and she pressed her left thumb against the optical panel.

It felt good to plan ahead, and unfamiliar. Everything she did now to infiltrate security might come in handy when the moment was right for her and Finn to escape.

She turned her attention back to Zeke's new rig. She recognized the booster from CCU documentation—it was not an approved model, but a highly illegal supercharger. No doubt there were desperate people on the Fringe willing to pay for it, but they'd be foolish to use it.

A loud clatter rang through the bulkhead from the other

side of the airlock, followed by Kristos shouting what sounded like a reprimand.

Edie hit Kristos's callsign on her comm. "Kristos? Is there a problem?"

"No problem. One of these guys is a bit skittish." The nervous undertones to his voice were unmistakable.

Edie moved gingerly into the airlock and peered through the window of the *Hoi*'s hatch. Someone moved past the window only a couple of meters away—Finn. He backed up a step and looked at her through the plaz, then spoke via his comm.

"Stay where you are." He sounded calm, but firm. He moved out of sight.

If there was trouble going on, it made sense that Finn wanted her out of it. That didn't mean she wanted him *in* it. She called Haller on her comm.

"Sir, can you come belowdeck? Zeke's dockside, and Kristos might need help with the serfs."

After a moment's pause, Haller's irritated voice came through. "Christ, he can't babysit for five minutes?"

Another crash from inside the *Hoi*'s hold, as though something had been thrown, and this time it was a serf's voice yelling in frustration. Edie backed away from the hatch, uncertain of what the danger was. She hit her comm again.

"Kristos? What's going on in there?"

"Everything's under control!"

"Haller's on his way."

"Damn, I don't need him." From the pitch of his voice, either panic or anger was taking hold. Edie regretted calling Haller. It made Kristos look incompetent, and the kid wouldn't thank her for that.

Over Kristos's still-open line, she heard further scuffling and voices calling out, then Haller's authoritative voice in the background as he arrived on the scene. The line clicked off and Edie breathed a sigh of relief. This crew was used to dealing with serfs, and Haller would sort out the problem, whatever it was.

Just as she stepped back, another wave of noise erupted inside the *Hoi*. Straining her ears, she tried to make sense of the muted sounds—scuffles and cries, boots clattering on the deck. Haller barked orders and there came the sound of steady thumping, as though someone was being hit or punched, along with the unmistakable crackle of a live drub.

She heard Finn yell, quickly followed by an almighty crash as a pile of crates tumbled down. One of the serfs screamed something unintelligible while another started whooping with excitement. So much for being tranq'ed.

The airlock beeped, startling her. The panel showed that the hatch on the far side of the gangway was open, which meant Zeke was returning. She punched his callsign.

"A fight's broken out." Her voice sounded weak, breathless. "Zeke, hurry. I don't know what's going on in there."

"On my way, kid. Get into the skiff."

"Haller's in the hold. I think the serfs started something. I don't know . . ."

She looked through the hatch window again, but other than the occasional flash of motion, there was nothing to see. It was clear from the sounds, though, that a serious ruckus was going on.

Zeke arrived at last, along with three serfs and another load of crates.

"Get in there." He pushed her into the skiff and snapped the hatch shut before she could protest. She watched through the window as he ordered the serfs off the gangway and trapped them in the airlock where they would be confined while he investigated the trouble. Then he disappeared into the *Hoi*'s hold.

One of the serfs turned slowly and gave Edie a blank look through the window. She pulled back, her pulse racing.

Her comm crackled.

"Edie, jolt your damn lag." It took her a moment to figure out the voice was Haller's. "Jolt him! He's out of control."

Whatever was going on in there, she wasn't about to jolt

Finn without seeing for herself. She snapped the hatch with her crew key, much to the surprise of the three men on the other side, and stepped into the airlock. One of them made for the open doorway without any particular enthusiasm, so she snapped it shut. She pushed past the men, but to her dismay found the far hatch locked on the other side.

Kristos's face appeared at the window. "Do it!" he yelled through the bulkhead. "He's going to kill him!"

Edie's instinct was to doubt Kristos's assessment—surely Finn wouldn't kill anyone. Would he? She hammered on the hatch.

"Kristos, let me in!" She could see him moving about on the other side. Thumbing her comm, she tried again. "Unlock the hatch, Kristos. Let me in."

Behind her, the serfs milled about in dazed uncertainty. One of them started whimpering, disturbed by what he could hear going on inside the ship. Another touched her hair and she spun around, wishing for the first time in her life that she had a drub. But the one Zeke had given her was sitting in the *Hoi*, somewhere among the rigs where she'd dropped it after starting work.

"Get back," she hissed.

The serf jumped away, startled. She looked into his glazed eyes and fought back her fear. She'd never had to deal with serfs before, and now here she was crammed into a tiny airlock with three of them. She should have stayed in the skiff.

Kristos's distraught face appeared at the window again. "Edie, do something!"

"Open the hatch!"

A second later, the hatch snapped and Edie stumbled through. Kristos had the presence of mind to wave his drub at the three serfs, clutching the tool white-knuckled, his expression controlled to hide his nervousness. But he succeeded in keeping them inside the airlock.

Edie ran toward the fight, almost tripping over a man curled up on the deck, cowering in a fetal position. His tunic was scorched across the back where he'd been hit with a drub.

Ahead, in the shadowy corner of the hold, one serf sat cross-legged, hugging his knees, motionless, as though he'd been ordered to assume the position. Zeke manhandled another to the ground with his drub, though it wasn't turned on, yelling at him to sit.

Beyond them, Edie saw Haller strutting back and forth in front of a jumble of equipment. As her eyes grew used to the darkness, she saw movement near Haller's feet. Finn sat in the shadows, in the same submissive posture as the other serfs. With calculated intent, Haller whacked him on the side of the head with a drub. Edie cried out in disbelief at the unprovoked attack, and Haller spun on her.

"I told you to jolt him," he growled.

Edie's first instinct was to run to Finn, who had slumped forward, hand over his ear where he'd been hit. His arms and scalp glistened with sweat and blood—there must have been a vicious fight. But Haller's murderous expression kept her rooted to the spot, several meters away.

He turned on Finn again and kicked him hard in the chest, flinging him backward. Finn groaned and rolled onto his side.

"What are you doing? He wasn't moving!" she yelled.

Having subdued the third serf, Zeke ran over and hauled Finn up by the scruff. Finn staggered on his feet, but remained upright.

"He can cool off in lockdown," Zeke said, nudging Finn to move with the tip of his drub.

"No. Wait." Haller pointed at Edie. "Jolt him."

The hold seemed unnaturally quiet after all the chaos. Silence pressed down on Edie as she stared at Finn.

"Jolt him *now*, or I'll throw him off this ship."

She willed Finn to raise his head, to tell her what to do. Would Haller really leave him at the port, to die when the ship went out of range?

"He wasn't doing anything," she retorted, surprised by the ferocity in her voice. "He wasn't fighting." More than anything, she was confused. She hadn't seen what started the fight, but it was clear Finn had surrendered by the time she arrived.

"Either you punish him," Haller snarled, "or I'll get rid of him and then flog you for disobeying orders. Now *do it*!"

Edie wasn't sure if she believed him about the flogging, but what she saw in Haller's eyes convinced her that he'd carry out the threat against Finn. It was a look of pure terror—terror that his world was spinning out of control. In front of half his crew and a quartet of worthless lags, his authority had been undermined and he was about to shatter. And when he broke, there was no telling what he'd do.

But she couldn't bring herself to jolt Finn just to satisfy Haller's power-lust. She shook her head. *No.*

"Throw him out," Haller told Zeke, and she knew he meant it.

Zeke hesitated. "C'mon, boss, let's just slam—"

"Throw him out. *Now.*"

Finn raised his head at last to look at Haller, and saw, perhaps, the same thing Edie had seen. A man on the precipice. As Zeke started to drag him away, Finn shot out an arm to catch the op-teck neatly on the jaw, sending him spinning into the equipment racks. Zeke landed messily.

As Finn turned to face Haller, the XO raised his arm and extended his spur. The weapon clicked into place, Haller's thumb flexing in preparation to fire, and Edie had no time to think.

Her mind latched onto the trigger and she jolted Finn.

The force of the jolt snapped Finn's neck back and he cried out, a bloodcurdling sound ripped from his throat. He dropped to his knees, his body stiff, his expression frozen in pain. Then he toppled to the side and hit the deck.

Edie stumbled across the hold, numb with shock, her knees threatening to buckle. Allowing his spur to retract,

Haller gave her a triumphant look that made her feel sick to her stomach. His hand closed around her arm, preventing her from getting nearer to Finn.

"He's not breathing," she gasped.

"He'll be fine. Get back to work." He didn't immediately release her. With a glint in his eyes he said, "That was impressive." She scowled and he gave her a sharp push in the direction of the rigs. "Zeke, get these men under control. I'll deal with the lag."

He prodded Finn with his boot until Finn drew a ragged breath and started to move. He got slowly to his feet. He didn't look at Edie, and she was grateful for that. But she caught a glimpse of his bewildered expression. She didn't want to see more.

CHAPTER 9

What happened? Edie's mind churned over that question. Crouched in the corner of the hold, she ignored the blinking and whirring of the nearby rigs that she was supposed to be prepping. She couldn't stop trembling—possibly a kickback effect of triggering the jolt, but she knew it was more than that. Devastated by what Haller had made her do, she kept playing the scene over and over, wondering why it had got out of hand, agonizing over whether she could have done anything differently. She and Finn had made a plan—and no part of that plan involved getting violent with the crew to the point where his life was endangered.

Had he been violent? She hadn't witnessed that. She'd seen only Haller's relentless provocation while Finn was already on the ground. What had she missed? She needed to talk to Kristos. He was in the cellblock with Zeke, just beyond the equipment holds, helping assign the serfs to cells and doling out the evening meal.

She went through her options for the hundredth time. Whichever way she turned it, the outcome was the same: her bodyguard would die. Haller had shown he was prepared to discard Finn at the slightest provocation. Even if he didn't have the balls to execute him—and she'd never know if he would have pulled that trigger—he could achieve the same result by sending Finn out of range.

Cutting the leash was the only way to remove that threat. They could hope to complete the mission and get paid before Haller found some excuse to get rid of Finn, or they could escape at the first opportunity and find another way to scrape together the creds. The second option was starting to look a lot more appealing.

With Haller back in his quarters, or wherever he went while off duty, Edie felt it was safe to enter the cellblock. She found Kristos fiddling at a console while Zeke worked at the other end of the room, attending to the injured serf—the man with drub burns.

Kristos wouldn't meet her eyes. "That was not my fault. I didn't tell you to do it. Haller kept screaming the order."

"You told me Finn was going to kill him. Was that true?"

Now he looked up. "No, I said *Haller* was going to kill *Finn.*"

"What? Just tell me what happened."

"One of the serfs started freaking out because the toms were bugging him." Kristos pointed to a couple of toms in the corner of the hold. "There's something wrong with them. They kept buzzing around, and the serf started yelling and kicking at them. I think his tranq mix must've been screwed up. No big deal until Haller shows up. He starts beating on the guy." Kristos thumbed the serf being treated by Zeke. "Keeps drubbing him until your guy steps up and says, *That's enough!* Just steps right up and says it like he expects Haller to obey. Haller turns on him and goes crazy."

"Did Finn retaliate?"

"He just tried to ward him off. Generally these guys don't put up a fight. They know that in the end it only makes things worse for them. And if they're tranq'ed properly"—he indicated the drug regimen listed on his console—"they *can't* fight. Doesn't affect their ability to work, of course."

So, Finn wasn't the instigator and had done nothing more than defend himself and another man. That hadn't stopped

Haller from pulling a spur on him, and Edie was certain he'd find another excuse to kill him.

They had to get out of here, and fast.

She watched Kristos plugging seven spikes into a med unit attached to his console.

"Is that the evening cocktail?"

"Yup. Double dose for everyone after today's excitement."

Edie glanced at the regimen as he fiddled with the seals. Finn was due to be tranq'ed just like the others. As the half-baked plan that had been forming in her mind over the past two hours solidified, she knew she was going to have to stop Finn being dosed.

With Kristos's attention on the spikes, Edie surreptitiously slipped her fingers onto the console and jacked in.

"Where's Finn?" she asked to distract him. "I'd like to check on him."

"You'll have to ask Zeke if you're allowed. He's in lock-down, far end of the cellblock." He pointed in that direction.

"How's the guy who was drubbed?"

"A drub scorches like a sunburn—no big deal."

By the time he'd finished the sentence and turned back to the console, Edie had pulled her hand free and Kristos was none the wiser to what she'd done. She'd dialed Finn's dose to zero, so his spike was now filling with pure saline.

Zeke put the injured serf in his cell and came over. As he looked at Edie with troubled brown eyes, she noticed the bruise on his jaw.

"Hey, I'm sorry it went down like that," he said.

She bit back a smart reply. She needed his help.

"Let me go patch him up, Zeke."

"I already hosed him down. Nothing serious."

"I'd like to take a look myself." She reached for the medkit.

Zeke shrugged and pushed the medkit into her arms. "Ten minutes, then meet me out there—we've still got work to do before supper. Kristos has the key."

He told Kristos to administer the spikes, then returned to

his rigs. Delaying near Kristos's console, Edie waited impatiently for him to finish up. Each serf fitted his arm into a tray attached to the front grille of the cell to hold it still for the injection. They seemed used to the routine, obeying without a fuss.

She followed Kristos to the lockdown hatch and he used his crew key to open it. One faint striplight glowed on as they stepped inside the large cell that doubled as a storage area. Finn sat on a narrow bench, facing away, leaning against a holding frame. His wrists were cuffed and hooked to the railings. To her surprise, he was naked. That didn't faze Kristos, who boldly approached him, spike in hand.

Finn pulled away from the spike as far as the restraints would allow, rattling the railings. Kristos flinched, losing his nerve, and looked over at Edie.

"It's okay." Her words were meant for Finn, not Kristos, although from her position near the hatch she couldn't see Finn's expression. He tensed at the sound of her voice but didn't move again as Kristos jabbed the spike into his arm.

Kristos seemed eager to get out of the cell as fast as possible. "Just snap the hatch when you're done, and don't forget to bolt the other door."

As his footsteps retreated down the cellblock, Edie edged around the cell to face Finn. The green-tinged light hit the hard angles of his body, emphasizing every muscle in his back and shoulders. The area around his left rib cage was colored with bruising. When he turned his head, she saw that his lip was split and his cheekbone sported a livid bruise. She couldn't hold his hostile glare.

His clothes lay in a heap on the far side of the cell. She picked up his tee and discovered it was sodden. All his clothes were wet, as was the deck around his feet. Zeke had mentioned hosing him off—the traditional daily bathing routine for serfs. Having done that, he must have decided that Finn's injuries weren't worth his time because the scrapes weren't dressed. Edie approached him with some trepidation, set down the medkit and unfolded it.

"That spike was just saline. I made sure of it."

"Get me out of here." His voice was scorched with anger.

"Not yet. Soon. And then we're leaving."

He hadn't expected that. "Thought we had a plan. We need the creds."

"No. Haller's going to kill you. He'll find an excuse to shoot you or leave you behind or—"

"I can deal with Haller."

"Can you?" Edie's voice rose, forcing back the tears of anger burning her eyes. "He put a spur to your head. He was going to kill you."

"If I thought that, I'd have stopped him."

She marveled at his conceited belief in his own indestructibility. "You're not bulletproof."

"I've taken care of myself to this point. Last thing I need is you cracking open my head every time the order is given."

Too annoyed to respond, she selected a swab and moved closer to wipe a graze along his jaw, concentrating on keeping her eyes averted from his body. Then she set to work on a small puncture wound on his shoulder where he'd smacked into something jagged during the fight. His breath hissed out at the sting of the swab.

"My job is to take care of you," he said. "It doesn't work both ways. I don't need anyone looking out for me."

She wouldn't let him get away with blaming her. "You're not being fair. I thought I was saving you."

He considered that, and in the silence that followed she met his gaze. The bitterness left his eyes.

"Forcing me to bend me to your will won't save me. Don't do it again."

"I won't. I swear. I'll never do that again."

Finn held her gaze for a moment, then turned his head aside without acknowledging her words. They must mean nothing to him. He was a serf, used to threats and punishment. Maybe he didn't know how to deal with a promise.

She turned her attention to the bruising on his ribs. If he had more than minor injuries, it would hamper her escape plans. Running her hand over his skin, she checked for wounds. His muscles tensed briefly, then he relaxed and sat back, casually unselfconscious, hiding nothing. Perhaps that, too, was a habit learned through incarceration, a lack of modesty about a body that someone else owned. Edie chewed on her lip, avoiding letting her gaze wander too low, acutely aware of the forced intimacy of their situation.

"There's a lot of bruising here," she said, because she had to say something.

"I think I cracked a rib." He rattled the restraints. "Let me check."

She hesitated. Would he retaliate if she let him loose? He hadn't actually agreed to her escape idea yet.

"Are you in on this?" she asked. "I meant what I said. I have a plan but you have to stay here a while longer. I need an hour to organize things first, to give us time to get to the docks and find a ride before they know we're missing."

He gave her a wary look. Did he not think she was capable of pulling this off?

"We have to try, Finn."

At last, he nodded. "Okay. Let's do it."

She inspected the wrist cuffs. They didn't need a key, just two-handed brute force to unhook the catches. As quietly as she could, she opened them. Finn methodically worked his fingers over his rib cage to check for breaks, his masked expression giving no clue about whether he was in pain.

"Well?"

"Just bruises. Give me bandages and painkillers."

She wasn't sure he wasn't hiding a more serious injury, but found what he needed in the medkit and watched him do the job that she had come to do. Clearly he knew more about it than she did. More about everything, no doubt. Outside of a datastream, did she really know anything? Her entire life, she'd been protected from whatever was out there—by the camps of her childhood, the institute walls, the milits who guarded her on missions. When she and Finn finally went their separate ways, could she survive on her own?

Finn pushed a spike into his biceps, discarded the empty, and handed her back the medkit.

"I'll fetch dry clothes," she told him. "The serfs are doped up for the night, so they won't raise a fuss when you leave. I don't think anyone will come back here this evening. I'll leave this hatch unlocked, but stay here. One hour, okay? I'll come for you."

CHAPTER 10

Edie rammed the bolt home. There was something horribly barbaric about keeping humans confined with metal locks and cuffs and chains. In this instance, however, such quaint old-school measures would work to her advantage. Nothing but the attentiveness of the crew stood in the way of their freedom.

She found Zeke in the equipment holds.

"How is he?"

"He's fine. You'll let him out in the morning, won't you?" Zeke shrugged. "That's up to the boss."

For the next fifty minutes they worked in companionable near silence. If not for her anxiety about the escape, she'd have enjoyed the work. The security buoys were familiar but different enough to be interesting, and had she been concentrating better she might have learned something new.

She was constantly aware of the minutes ticking by. "Didn't you say something about supper?"

Zeke checked the time. "Sure, let's go. Cat's meeting us in the mess."

He dropped his tools and left them where they fell. Edie followed him as far as deck three, then excused herself, saying she wanted a quick shower before eating.

She ran to her quarters and stuffed clothes for herself and Finn into her duffle bag. She grabbed the fake idents Cat had given her and slipped them into her jacket pocket. Her hands shook and she fumbled with the zipper. Only a few hours ago she'd made the mental switch from kidnapping victim to outlaw—not much of a step up, but free of the Crib, at least. Now she was going on the run from both the Crib and the rovers, with no idea of where she'd end up. She only knew she wasn't going to let the one person who depended on her die.

She hit Zeke's callsign.

"Zeke, I changed my mind. Not really hungry. I'm going to turn in."

"What, you don't like my company?"

"I'm just tired. Another time, okay?"

She could almost see him shrug. "Okay. But you're missing out on Gia's famous curry."

In the background, Cat muttered, "More like *infamous*."

Edie removed her commclip and set her console to cycle through spec sheets. If anyone jacked into her account it would give the appearance that she was working and, she hoped, fool the crew for a while that she was in her quarters.

Her heart thudding, she returned belowdeck and heaved open the bolt on the cellblock hatch. Finn waited just inside, holding his boots. She thought she detected a flicker of relief in his eyes.

In silence she watched him pull on clean clothes. Then he slung the duffle bag over his shoulder and followed her out. She locked the bolt and headed for the external airlock.

"What's the plan? You got any arrangements portside?"

"No arrangements. We hop on the first ship that'll take us."

He gave her an incredulous look as if to say, *that's it?* But, thankfully, said nothing. She was locked out of comms on the *Hoi*, so she'd been unable to contact the port, even to check the job boards.

Her crew key snapped the airlock, and her thumbprint

opened the gangway hatch. They ran down the narrow tube—four, three, two seconds from freedom . . .

One step to freedom. They entered the airlock and Finn hit the panel to cycle it. As they stepped into the slightly heavier but more stable gravity of Port Neuchasley, Edie's stomach flip-flopped.

Freedom.

She felt light-headed. With Finn a pace behind, she moved through the busy dock area toward sec-check. The checkpoint was not their last hurdle, but it might be the toughest. Time to find out if their fake idents were worth what Stichting Corp had paid for them.

Edie moved toward a gate with a short line. The officer was a young woman her own age, wearing a starched uniform with the Neuchasley logo stamped on her sleeve. The officer began to argue imperiously with a tourist in line.

Edie felt Finn's hand on her elbow.

"This way."

He led her to a gate at the other end of the checkpoint, manned by an older security officer with a crumpled jacket and a bored expression. Edie handed over her ident and he swiped it, offering only a cursory glance in her direction.

"You got papers for him?" He nodded toward Finn.

Edie froze. The officer had mistaken Finn for a serf—or, rather, accurately identified him as one. The stubbled scalp was one clue, but there was something in Finn's demeanor that marked him, too. Edie had seen it all too often—the disinterested but wary look in his eyes, the hard expression.

Finn slapped his ident onto the desk, glaring at the officer with a harsh confidence Edie had never seen before. She watched his transformation in amazement. It was the perfect act of a respectable man insulted by the accusation that he was a criminal.

The officer picked up the ident with a small shrug of apology. Edie held her breath as he checked and double-checked the readout that told him Finn was a registered miner from

Pelingrat, a large colony just within Crib borders. He waved them on without further question. Behind them, the young officer whose line Edie had almost joined was still giving the tourist a hard time.

The main concourse of the station was a riot of color and noise. Edie was used to the busy crowds of Talas Prime, but that station was much smaller than Neuchasley and somewhat more remote. She pressed against Finn, drawing courage from his strength and confidence. Despite the open construction of the common area, its hyperactivity and stark patches of light rendered the atmosphere claustrophobic. Mezzanines jutted out from the walls, linked by steps and small elevator cars. Holos flashed information and advertisements from every wall.

They found a console and pulled up the departures board. This was where outgoing ships placed work-for-passage ads. With no money, it would be their only way to get off the station quickly.

"There's a couple of commercial haulers looking for engineer tecks," Edie said, scanning the holoviz. To her ears, her voice sounded breathy, nervous, hyped up on adrenaline. For the first time in her life she was doing something truly independent, and it terrified her.

"Engie tecks? You know what that means, right?" He appraised her blank look. "Scrubbing the fusion rings, degaussing the injectors. You get paid in radiation, carcinogens—take your pick."

"What about a freetrader?" She pulled out the ads, magnifying them on the holoviz. "Mostly small family-owned vessels. Ah, no good. They're offering passage for cash and goods. We're a little short on assets."

"Check the Fringe-world vessels. We have one asset they need—you." He indicated an ad that had caught his eye. "This one's leaving in an hour."

He sent a brief text message. Edie couldn't see clearly what he was writing, but caught the phrase *wet-teck*—halfway to an admission that she was a cypherteck. Perfect bait for any desperate Fringer.

"You really want to go to the Fringe?" Despite her desire to escape the Crib, she hadn't fully accepted the idea of stepping quite that far into the unknown.

"Don't care where we go. We can jump ship along the way."

A face appeared on the holoviz—a young woman with worn features framed by tight sandy curls. She peered at Finn with open curiosity.

"Tilda Skardi, captain of the *Drakkar*. You an op-teck?" Her accent was thick and stilted.

"No. I have one. D'you want her?"

"Already have an op-teck on my crew. She does wet-teck?"

"The very wettest."

"A cypherteck? She can fix biogenerators? Med stuff?"

"She can fix anything you want. Nanoteck, sequencers, seeding biocyph—"

Seeding biocyph: the magic phrase. Tilda Skardi's eyes sparked greedily, and then narrowed.

"We have no seeding equipment on board."

"Of course you don't." Finn gave her a wry smile. There wasn't a Fringe-world ship in the Central zone that didn't trade in biocyph. It was the most valuable commodity on the Fringe, where people had no means of making the technology for themselves and very few skills in fixing it when it broke. They needed cyphertecks, and the Crib wasn't about to share them.

"And what about you, Garrison Wyle?" Skardi said, reading Finn's fake name off her holoviz. "Any special talents?"

"Where she goes, I go."

She wrinkled her nose as she considered him. "Not such an impressive talent, Mr. Wyle." She cut audio and spoke urgently to someone out of view before turning back to Finn. "Okay, we'll meet—the *Drakkar*, dock B43. We'll give her a little test, check her out."

"We'll not come on board until we've checked *you* out,"

Finn said. "Find a booth on the docks." The booths were in
safe neutral territory, on the far side of sec-check so they
could leave in a hurry if they had to. And it was a weapons-
free zone.

Tilda scowled again. Her gaze slid to the side as she
scrolled through data.

"Okay. I put a hold on booth B4–11. See you there in fifteen minutes."

Finn nodded and cut the link. Edie had to admit that she
had a newfound respect for the man. She'd worried about
how they might survive alone, with her almost complete
lack of knowledge about the worlds beyond Talas and his
years of crushing imprisonment. Seeing the way he negoti-
ated gave her hope they'd make it.

Hovering holos signposted the way to Dock B, and Edie was
relieved that it took them farther away from the *Hoi Polloi*'s location in Dock C. Port Neuchasley's offensive décor
became progressively shabbier as they moved away from the
main concourse.

They took an open elevator down to the fourth level of
Dock B and found the area almost deserted. There were only
two sec-check gates, and only one was manned.

"Leaving so soon?" The security officer's computer told
him Edie and Finn had boarded the station only twenty minutes earlier. Edie opened her mouth to invent an excuse, but
Finn took back their idents with a nod of thanks to the officer and nudged her through the gate. Apparently he didn't
want to risk getting caught up in chit-chat with a stranger.

A multilevel honeycomb of booths lined one side of the
dock. The tiny rooms were designed for waiting, trading,
liaisons, even spending the night for those who wanted a
cheap alternative to a portside hotel.

Edie walked to the opposite bulkhead, which was lined
with angled windows. Each one overlooked a docking bay,
some containing a berthed ship, others darkened and empty.

Unlike the *Hoi*'s berth via an extendable gangway, smaller ships that could handle grav landed inside the docking bays at Neuchasley.

Edie stopped at B43, the *Drakkar*. It was much smaller than the *Hoi*, although the *Hoi* was excessively large considering the size of its crew. Under the *Drakkar*'s bulky belly sprawled a three-pronged landing foot.

"Zed-class Raven." Finn's voice, so near, startled her. He leaned on the railing beside her.

"Is that good or bad?"

"It's small. Just enough mass to get through a jump node. Crew of three, maybe four. They won't want me tagging along."

"They'll have no choice."

They exchanged a look, and written on his face Edie saw an edginess that unnerved her. Did he think she'd leave him to die if it was her only way out? She wanted to reassure him that she wouldn't do that, but what was the point if he didn't believe her? She'd helped him this far. If that wasn't enough to convince him, mere words wouldn't help.

They would make this work. Disappear, find a way to put together enough creds to cut the leash.

She focused on the *Drakkar* again. "It looks reptilian. Kind of ugly."

"I think she's charming." He stared at the ship for a long moment. "Come on."

He pushed back from the railing, slinging the duffle bag over his shoulder. She followed him to the booths.

"Don't give away too much to these people," he said as they started up the metal steps. "They already want you. Don't make them desperate to have you."

As if lack of trust in Edie wasn't enough, now he seemed worried they might grab her and leave him behind. The crew of the *Drakkar* probably had no reason to take him. Another mouth to feed, another pair of lungs sucking air.

They climbed several flights to reach B4–11. The room's screened plaz wall was turned off, so they could see inside.

Tilda Skardi waited at the table. Behind her stood an older woman with the same curly hair. A relative, probably. From her limited interactions with outworlders on Talas Prime, Edie knew these traders frequently worked out of family-owned ships. Despite the ramshackle state of their vessel, it was an expensive piece of hardware that required generations of family money to fund.

Finn hit the door panel and it slid aside. The older woman tensed and Tilda stood, and both of them stared at Finn. They shifted awkwardly on their feet, looking like they wished they were carrying weapons. There was an automated checkpoint between here and the bays that prevented weapons coming through.

They turned their attention to Edie and their expressions took on a hint of hope. Hope that Finn had told them the truth, that she was a cypherteck, that she could help them.

As Edie followed Finn into the booth, she noticed a child on the floor, a girl of about six, her unruly blond hair puffing out like a cloud around her face. She sat cross-legged, oblivious to the people in the room, and amused herself with colored disks—some sort of toy.

"This is Amma, my sister." Tilda indicated the other woman.

Amma nodded a greeting, stepped forward, and put a small med unit on the table.

"That's a biogenerator," Tilda said. "It's not working so well. You fix that, you're welcome on board." She deliberately avoided looking at Finn, excluding him from the offer, at least for now.

Edie stepped out from behind Finn, hoping it would show she trusted them. They both took half a step back. Perhaps they were worried they'd walked into a trap. A cypherteck had just landed in their laps and they must be wondering if someone was setting them up.

"I'm not a medic," Edie said. That sounded too negative. "But I'll see what I can do."

She drew the unit to the edge of the table and used a

hardlink to jack in. It was a jury-rigged piece of equipment, patched together from half a dozen models, some Crib, some not. The biocyph matrix growled with discontent as she explored it. Its function was to create nanofinds—custom-built DNA machines to be injected into the body to seek out and destroy damaged tissue and tumors, clean up burns, and stimulate healthy growth.

The problem was incompatibility between the components. Nothing a few subroutines couldn't fix. Edie fired up the sequencer and coded a patcher that would do the job for her, tracking down the broken links and distorted layers created by the haphazard melding of circuitry from various sources.

"Leave it running a couple of hours," she said, disconnecting the line. "Then we'll flush it out and run a live test." She spoke as though she was going to be doing the job herself—as though they'd already agreed to take her on.

Tilda didn't look convinced. She glared at Finn, as though Edie had tricked her and it was Finn's fault, and then she took a diagnostic rod out of her jacket pocket and jacked into the biogenerator. The readout seemed to satisfy her. She gave her sister a nod, closed up the unit, and handed it to Amma. Amma cradled the unit like a baby. Her hands and nails were filthy.

"What's your name?" Tilda said.

Edie flashed her ident, which read Beata Szwaja. The client's infojack must have a sense of humor because she had no idea how to pronounce it.

"Call me Bee," Edie said.

Tilda's lips thinned into a tight smile. So she knew, and didn't care, that the ident was fake.

"We got a bay full of broken biocyph doohickies on the *Drakkar*," Tilda said, "Keep you busy. After that we got an ecosystem that's six months from turning to mash."

"Mash!" the little girl piped up.

To Edie's surprise, the child had come right up to her without her noticing. She offered Edie one of the colored disks. It had become a flower. Edie took it, turned it over in her palm. The flower melted back into a flat disk. The girl took it back, gave it a twist, and it blossomed again. Some sort of memory-plaz.

"Inga!" Tilda snapped.

The girl heeded the warning note in Tilda's voice and moved away to sit on the floor.

"I'll do whatever I can for you," Edie said, and she meant it. Finn's plan was to make their own way as soon as they were free of the Crib and the rovers, but looking at Inga playing with her pathetic toy, at the child's unwashed hair and torn-up boots, Edie wondered if she'd be able to bring herself to leave these people to their desperate plight. Maybe she could make herself useful to them, to others like them whose equipment was failing, whose worlds would only survive with the help of a cypherteck. Maybe she could make a life out there.

"Okay, passage to the Fringe if you help us. You." Tilda looked at Finn. "You're a lag."

"I'm Garrison Wyle," Finn said.

"Yes, Garrison Wyle." Tilda repeated the name with a mocking lilt. "We're not looking for labor, Mr. Wyle."

They were so close to freedom. There wasn't time for this—they wanted Edie, needed her, and she wanted to be on board with Finn and safely away from Port Neuchasley. She wasn't going to let Tilda call the shots.

"He protects me. The deal is both of us, or neither." She debated whether to tell the whole truth—that he'd die if she left without him. But she couldn't risk them knowing that and using it against her.

"C'mon, Tilda, we got room," Amma hissed, eager to get back to her ship, to stow her precious biogenerator, to bring home a cypherteck.

Tilda gave Finn another hard look. It was understandable that she didn't want a runaway serf on her ship, but she couldn't pass up a cypherteck. Edie watched her expression change as she relented, first mentally, then verbally.

"Okay, okay, we'll take your man."

Amma sighed with relief. She reached out her free hand for the child, and Inga gathered up her toys and went to her. As Amma turned to the door leading to the docking bays, a figure suddenly loomed into view in the corridor beyond. A man with shaggy hair and bloodshot eyes. For a brief moment Edie wondered if it was another crew member from the *Drakkar*, someone who wanted to check out this alleged cypherteck for himself, but as soon as the man's eyes swung in her direction, piercing her with pure hatred, she knew who he was. What he was.

An eco-rad.

CHAPTER 11

Tilda sensed the danger immediately. "Who the hell—?"

The man shouldered open the door and lunged into the tiny room. Amma darted to the corner with the little girl, still cradling the biogenerator.

Edie felt Finn's hand close around hers and he yanked her backward, toward the other door. She turned, instinctively pressing close, but he pulled up sharply. Another eco-rad appeared there, a huge man, bulk and muscles, heavier than Finn. And behind him, a wiry woman with cropped hair.

They were trapped.

"Get down!" Finn pushed Edie to the floor.

The room erupted into chaos. All three eco-rads lunged for Edie, without weapons but with an obvious intention to kill with their bare hands. Edie scrambled underneath the table as Finn knocked back the wild-haired man with a powerful punch and confronted the second one. The two grappled, colliding into the wall.

The woman rad dived under the table and grabbed Edie's ankle—the nearest body part she could reach. Edie kicked out sharply with her free leg, connected with air, and forced herself to think instead of react. A moment later the woman reached in farther, and now her head was within range. Edie let her advance, kicked again, felt the satisfying crunch as a connection was made. The woman retreated with a yelp, but not because of the kick. Finn had grabbed her from behind.

The first eco-rad was back on his feet and heading for Edie. From underneath the table, she saw Tilda running across the room, toward her sister. The eco-rad stood between them. He grabbed the edge of the table and upturned it, throwing it against the wall. It bounced off the little girl's body in Amma's arms.

"No!" Pure instinct pulled Edie to her feet and she tried to reach them, to help them, despite Amma's accusing glare in her direction. The eco-rad pounced, bringing her down. She rolled and slithered out of his grasp, but he was quickly on her again, grabbing her in a choke hold. In the confusion, she saw Finn fighting off the other two rads. The woman had something in the palm of her hand, and as the large man held Finn in a lock, she slapped it against Finn's neck.

A tranq dart, or perhaps poison. Edie gasped his name in anguish. If he died . . . if he was put out of action, she had no hope. She couldn't expect Tilda and Amma to help her, especially with the child injured.

As Edie struggled against her attacker, she realized he, too, was trying to connect his palm with her bare skin. She jerked her head back sharply, catching him on the bridge of his nose. He grunted, his grip loosening momentarily. Edie slipped through his arms, swinging her legs as she fell, tripping him up. He dropped heavily and blood spurted from his nose. He would be back on his feet in seconds . . .

Her throat aching from the eco-rad's grasp, Edie staggered across the room to help Finn. She was vaguely aware of Tilda lifting Inga's limp body, of Amma's sobs, and of the precious biogenerator that had been smashed to the floor in the mayhem.

"Run," Edie choked.

Much as she needed their help, it was too dangerous, and it wasn't their business or their fault. The rads weren't after them and wouldn't harm them if they stayed out of the way.

Edie leapt onto the woman who had poisoned Finn, and pulled her back. At the same moment, Finn lashed out, using the man who held him as leverage, and kicked the woman in the chest. She and Edie were flung against the window, which shattered around them, and they tumbled onto the catwalk outside the booth.

Edie took the brunt of the fall, but the woman on top of her took the shards of plaz-glass. As Edie pushed her off, she felt the woman's slick blood on her fingers.

Seconds later, two men crashed out of the window and Edie crawled out of the way just in time. Finn and the larger eco-rad were locked together in a struggle. Finn managed to disengage himself. Ignoring the shards of plaz that sliced into his jacket, he grabbed the man's lapels and threw him over the railing of the catwalk, taking part of the railing with him.

It was a four-story drop. Finn didn't wait to see the outcome. But as he turned to the second man, Edie realized there was something very wrong. Finn's movements were slow, as though his arms weighed too much. He blinked sweat and blood from his eyes, shaking his head as though he couldn't focus properly. He reeled even before the eco-rad's fist connected to his jaw. He wavered against the railing, almost losing his balance. A second punch drove him to his knees. A third, to the deck.

The eco-rad turned to Edie where she crouched on the catwalk. His face was wild with fury and marred with small cuts where he'd been hit by pieces of plaz. Behind her, she was aware of the woman hauling herself up and staggering along the catwalk in the other direction, crying out someone's name. The name of the man who'd gone over the railing.

The remaining eco-rad loomed over her. Confronted by a man intent on murdering her, Edie's basic training fled and her mind went blank, paralyzed by pure terror. He moved toward her as if in slow motion, a lumbering, shaggy beast with bloodied outstretched hands.

She was aware of footsteps pounding the metal stairs.

More eco-rads? Or someone coming to help? Security must be aware by now that something was going on, but it was just as likely that the eco-rads had backup. No, the footsteps were receding. It was the woman, running away to help her friend. If he was seriously hurt, which seemed likely, there would be questions, and Edie and Finn would never get off the station.

In the brief moments of silence, Edie heard the woman calling for backup over her comm.

That jump-started her brain into action again. She gathered her muscles into a tight knot and darted out of the man's path, through the broken window, back into the booth. Her boots crunched and slipped on the broken plaz and she almost lost her footing.

She raced for the far door, hearing him stumbling along behind her. Grabbing a chair, she turned sharply and smashed it into his head. He slipped on the broken shards and went down. Using the few seconds of time she'd gained, she pressed her fingers against the control panel of the door of the booth as she left the room. The door slid shut behind her and locked.

She hoped Finn could still defend himself if the eco-rad went back for him. Eco-rads weren't supposed to kill indiscriminately. She was the target. It was even more important to get herself to safety than to stay and help Finn, because her death would kill him anyway.

She had to get to the docking bays, where there were people to help her, or at least to deter the eco-rad. She had to shake him off long enough to find her way back to Finn, or hope he found her. If he hadn't been knocked out by whatever drug they'd used on him.

To her surprise, Amma and Tilda had made it only a few meters, the child draped against Tilda's shoulder. Unlike the scaffolding of catwalks on the far side, the docking bay side of the booths opened into wide platforms with elevators at the other end.

To Edie's relief, Inga was screaming—at least she was no longer unconscious, although she was terrified and in pain.

"Get away from us!" Amma yelled over her shoulder as they struggled toward the elevators. Edie hesitated. A nearby *boom* startled her and she turned to see the eco-rad launching himself against the door of the booth, trying to force it open with his shoulder. He left streaks of blood on the plaz.

There was one elevator car waiting, and the women entered it. Edie opened her mouth to call to them, to ask them to hold the door, to let her escape. But she said nothing. She didn't want to involve them—they'd already lost too much.

The adjacent elevator door opened. Two men burst out of it and Edie's heart caught in her throat. More eco-rads, she was sure of it. One was no more than a teenager, the other a burly man with bright red hair and a complexion to match. What the hell were eco-rads doing at the port? At that moment it felt to Edie like they were here just for her, but that was impossible. There were any number of reasons for them to be here—what station or colony didn't have something going on that the eco-rads objected to? From bombing mineral mines to raiding medfacs that engaged in gene jiggling, wherever human technology advanced beyond what the rads deemed appropriate they would be hiding somewhere, planning a lethal disruption. They must have been monitoring the comm channels. That was the risk Finn had taken when he sent out a message to find a ship. The rads would have had only minutes to launch an attack, but that was all they needed. Poison darts were old-fashioned and clumsy, but easy enough to smuggle past the sec-check.

As the newcomers surveyed the scene, there was no disguising her identity. Her jacket was torn, her clothes scuffed with dirt, her knuckles bleeding. They looked at her and knew what had happened and who she was. Their target.

The elevator door swished shut on Tilda and Amma and Inga, and they were gone.

Frantically, Edie looked around for a way out. The corridor

was enclosed. Several doors led to booths within reach, but they would be either locked or occupied. If there was anyone else around, so far they hadn't emerged to offer help.

The eco-rads could see she was trapped. They moved with purpose but didn't hurry. When they were five meters away, she saw that the red-haired man had something strapped to his fingers. She stared at the tiny pea-shooter that was going to kill her.

Behind her, the plaz door shattered. She spun around, expecting to face the other eco-rad, but it was Finn. He held a metal pipe in his hands—part of the broken railing from the catwalk. He looked toward her as if he didn't see her, staggered a couple of steps, stopped and tried to focus his eyes again. He was fighting poison meant to kill her, and looked like he might fall over at any second. The other eco-rad was nowhere in sight. Finn must have disabled him.

The teenage boy rushed Edie. She had a split second to anticipate his attack and used it wisely, swinging to the side and lashing out with a kick to his groin. He stumbled back with a yelp of pain. The other rad ignored his plight and kept coming.

Edie backed up against Finn. Despite his being in no condition to fight, her veins flooded with a new wave of adrenaline to replace the abject hopelessness of moments earlier. Whatever state Finn was in, she was glad he was here. She'd already be dead if she'd faced these people alone.

The eco-rad leered at Finn, as if Finn was already out of commission—despite the raised metal pipe.

The rad lifted his hand and Edie heard a small *ping* as something was fired from the weapon on his hand.

Finn took a sharp step backward, looking in disbelief at the dart in his arm. Unlike the other rads who'd wielded handheld darts, this man had a simple trigger in his fist that enabled him to attack at range.

The boy had recovered enough to try again. With a frown of anger and determination he rushed at Finn. Barely looking at him, Finn swung the pipe in a wide arc and struck the boy in the stomach. He dropped, curling into a fetal position, groaning.

The pipe clattered to the deck and Finn sagged against the wall of the booths, clutching his arm. He plucked out the dart, pushed off the wall, and lurched toward the eco-rad. Every instinct told Edie to drag him away, to run. But Finn hadn't given up yet. He swung at the eco-rad, punching the man in the jaw with surprising force. With the rad off balance, Finn lunged, this time knocking him to the ground. Finn went down with him.

The *ping* again. The eco-rad shot Finn in the chest at point-blank range, but he couldn't throw off Finn's weight. Finn brought his knee up and pressed it on the man's throat with the full weight of his body. The man's eyes bulged, his arms flailing, but Finn ignored the blows. Edie dived onto the eco-rad's right arm, the one with the dart gun strapped to his knuckles, and wrenched it up over his head to point it away. Finn had taken three hits of the poison, or whatever it was, and he was still alive, still conscious, still fighting for his life—for her life.

"Stand down!"

Edie looked over her shoulder to see a security guard a few meters away, his spur aimed at Finn.

"Don't shoot!" Edie yelled. "This man attacked us. He's armed."

She didn't want to release the rad's arm, knowing his only objective was to kill her with the dart gun. It would take a split second to shoot her, regardless of Finn's pressure on his windpipe or the guard's weapon trained on them all.

The boy got to his feet and started to run, using the closest exit—the broken door of the booth—ignoring the guard's commands to stop. The guard let him go, deciding to deal with the three battered people on the deck instead.

He approached them warily. Edie focused on Finn, hoping he could remain conscious long enough to get the eco-rad safely dealt with. Hoping he wouldn't kill the rad, and hadn't killed the one in the booth. It would be impossible to avoid

the scrutiny of the Crib if they were detained or if charges
were laid.

"Finn, back off," she hissed. He didn't seem to hear her at
first. She risked releasing one hand from the eco-rad, who
was lapsing into unconsciousness, and grabbed Finn's shoulder. He looked up, eyes glazed, brow drawn low as though in
great concentration. "It's okay, Finn. Back off."

She pushed his shoulder and he eased up, leaving the eco-
rad choking though his compressed windpipe. Edie worked
the dart gun free from the rad's fingers and threw it aside.
Only then did she feel safe enough to release the man's arm.
She stood on shaky legs and tried to haul Finn up. The guard
was only a few meters away now and could see they were
unarmed, no threat to him.

Edie heard the thud before she saw what happened. The
eco-rad from inside the booth, the one she'd locked in and
thought Finn had dealt with, had emerged, bloody and limp-
ing, and had knocked down the guard with one wild swing
to the head.

And the guard had a spur. The rad struggled to rip the spur
off the guard's forearm, and in those few seconds Edie knew
she would have to tackle him. Finn was crouched on the
deck in a daze, breathing heavily, as though forcing himself
to stay conscious.

She approached the rad, hands up in what she hoped was
a nonaggressive gesture.

"You don't have to kill me," she said. "I don't work for the
Crib anymore. I just want to help people—like those two
women and the child."

"You're a murderer!" the rad yelled, still struggling with
the spur. It must have some sort of lock to the guard's arm.
"I hear their souls screaming. Trillions of souls screaming
each time you rape another planet. Murderer!"

The rad lifted the guard's forearm, pointing it toward Edie,
and wrapped his hand around the guard's fingers, trying to
locate the trigger.

The elevator doors opened. Edie whirled around and stared in disbelief at a familiar face.

Zeke.

Despite having spent the last hour determined to escape the rovers, Edie felt nothing but relief at seeing the op-teck.

Haller stepped out behind him. So, their escape had been discovered and they'd come to find her. And found her fighting for her life. From the determined looks on their faces, it must have been clear to the rad that Haller and Zeke were here for her.

The rad's arm jerked and the bulkhead behind Edie sizzled. He'd got the spur to fire, missing her by centimeters.

Zeke and Haller ran toward him, and the rad swung around, taking aim at them instead. A plate of decking exploded near Haller's feet.

The rad didn't get a third shot.

Ping. Ping. Ping.

The rad flinched. Three shots, and then two more. His body was peppered with darts. For endless moments he hovered on the edge of balance. Then he collapsed, releasing the spur.

Zeke and Haller stared at the body, then turned in unison to find the source of the shots. Finn had managed to retrieve the dart gun from the other side of the deck, and used it to shoot the rad. Now Finn sagged to the floor again, oblivious to everything around him.

Edie rushed to his side as he clung with one hand to a railing on the bulkhead, trying to stop himself sliding all the way to the deck. Sweat dripped from his face. Still trembling from the ebbing adrenaline in her veins, Edie clutched Finn's arm, willing him to remain conscious.

He needed medical help, and fast.

Haller stormed toward her, red-faced, ready to explode into anger. Thankfully he was sensible enough to realize this wasn't the time.

"Stay away from us. Stay back!" she yelled, her arm going

protectively around Finn's shoulders. They had no weapons.
They couldn't make her go with them.

Haller pulled up in surprise, but hesitated only a moment.
He put up his hands in an unconvincing gesture of appease-
ment. "Get up. We're leaving."

Edie's mind flashed back to another dying man in her
arms, years ago. Lukas, choking in his own blood while
Bethany lay dead nearby. Lukas had lived. She would make
sure Finn lived, too.

"They poisoned him," she said as Haller advanced again.
"He needs help!"

"We'll help him. On the *Hoi*."

She didn't believe that. Haller wanted Finn dead, had
planned to abandon him to die. They couldn't go back with
the rovers now. On Neuchasley, Finn would get medical help.
Even if the authorities discovered who they really were, at
least Finn had a chance. Assuming they weren't separated.

Beyond Haller, Zeke glanced nervously around. Like
her, he must expect Security to appear at any moment. Edie
twisted her hands into the fabric of Finn's jacket, anchoring
herself to him. Let Haller try and drag her away.

"*Come on*, Edie." Haller's voice grated with urgency. He
was right behind her, leaning over her. He extended one hand
and closed it around her fist, but she clung tighter to Finn.

Suddenly Haller's free arm swept around her neck, catching her throat in the bend of his elbow. He squeezed his
arm, compressing her carotids, and pulled her back to arch
her spine. Instinctively she grabbed his arm, but he was too
strong. Stars danced in her vision and she went limp, catching Haller by surprise. She drew together all the energy
she could muster and bucked forward, yanking his arm
straighter, easing the pressure off her arteries.

"If you leave him . . . I won't cooperate. If he dies . . ."

Her voice was little more than a choking gasp. Haller
pressed his knee solidly into the small of her back and she
was pulled backward again. The pressure tightened and she
could neither speak nor think. Within seconds the strength

drained from her body. Her head felt light and her vision narrowed.

Blackness rolled over her.

She was in a tiny dark place, and she sensed bodies huddled around her. A voice barked orders. Haller. What was he talking about? They were on some sort of shuttle or taxi, preparing to rendezvous with the *Hoi Polloi*.

They were leaving the station. Leaving Finn.

She tried to say something, but was hit with a wave of nausea that culminated in blackness again, and silence.

CHAPTER 12

Edie turned her head and looked at Finn, lying unconscious on a gurney beside her. His bare chest rose and fell—unevenly, and too slowly.

She waited for her head to clear, for her thoughts to fall back into order. Then she remembered that she hadn't expected to see Finn here at all. They'd left him on the station, hadn't they? Left him to die.

"Enjoy your adventure, teckie?" Zeke's voice drifted across the room.

Her head turned slowly toward the op-teck. Every muscle in her body felt leaden. Her lungs ached to drag in air that was too warm and humid. They must have given her a mild tranq. Her eyes took in the familiar equipment and bulkheads of the infirmary on the *Hoi*.

Zeke came over and helped her sit up.

"Finn's here," she said, because she still couldn't believe it. Her throat burned. "Is he okay?"

"Uh, not really. I mean, he will be, if—"

Edie pushed away Zeke's supporting arm and slid off the bunk. Her knees buckled and she grabbed the edge for support. Looking around the room, all she saw was a blur of lights glinting off plazalloy surfaces.

"Did you identify the poison?"

"Hey, you need to rest up. I've done all I can." His dismissive tone made her realize he didn't consider this his responsibility. "He's strong. Either he pulls through or—"

"Get out." She turned on Zeke with a glare. "You don't care if he lives or dies, so just go away."

She went to the nearest bench and rummaged around for anything she recognized. She wasn't a medic, but she knew biology, biochemistry, physiology. With a sequencer she could identify the poison, find out how it was affecting Finn's system, and reverse it. If it wasn't already too late.

"Dammit, you drag him all the way back here and then do nothing for him?" Furious, she blinked away tears, keeping her eyes averted so Zeke wouldn't see. "Why even bother? Doesn't anyone have med training? Why did no one help him? How long has it been?"

"Only about twenty minutes, I guess." Zeke sounded wounded by her verbal attack but did not leave. "We did what we could. Stimulant for his heart. And a blood thinner, I think. Haller did it."

Edie went to Finn's side. They'd removed his jacket and tee, and his chest bore angry red marks where the darts had struck. Someone had messily smeared medigel on his other wounds, the cuts caused by the broken plaz window. The underlying bruises from Haller's attack earlier in the day made the fresh wounds look worse than they probably were. Still, despite the hard lines of his obviously powerful body, Finn looked as helpless as a child.

The med tom displayed the brutal facts on a holoviz. Finn's heart rate and breathing were below normal, his body temperature was dropping, and his kidneys and liver threatened to shut down.

"I need a sequencer. Treating the symptoms isn't enough. He's dying."

Zeke pulled open a locker and found the device. She drew a blood sample from Finn's arm, flinching at the feel of his clammy skin, and ran it through the sequencer.

She jacked in to watch it work while Zeke hovered in the background, staying out of her way. From the sequencer's readouts, Edie saw that the poison was altering one key metabolic pathway to cause a buildup of toxins, but fortunately not affecting the nervous system. That would have shut down Finn's lungs altogether. While the sequencer couldn't identify the chemical, the med tom suggested an antidote and Edie set about programming it to synthesize one.

She didn't understand why they'd rescued Finn, and it didn't matter. He had to live. The idea of being stuck on the *Hoi* without him was unbearable. If he died, she'd refuse to cooperate. That much she'd already decided. They'd taken away Lukas from her, but this time she'd fight harder.

"I think this will work." She took a seat near the sequencer to wait for the antidote, clenching her sweaty palms into fists. "Why is it so hot in here?"

"Enviros are screwed up. Got the kid crawling around in the air ducts tracking down the problem. We've had a few systems twitching, toms misbehaving. Strange." He shrugged. No doubt he'd remain unconcerned as long as his rigs weren't affected. He pointed to a pile of toms lying haphazardly in the corner, some of them belly-up, others oozing waste. "Haller wants you to take a look at the cleaner toms before the captain notices. Not that Rackham notices much these days. You may as well get started, while you wait."

Grateful for a distraction, she selected a tom from the top of the pile and set it on the bench next to Zeke. He handed her a driver from his tool belt. As she flipped open the tom's port to release a steady dribble of greasy muck, she tried to make small talk.

"We're back under way?"

"Yup. Left port in a hurry, for obvious reasons. Haller had a taxi waiting and with luck the authorities at Neuchasley can't tie it to the *Hoi*."

"When did you find out we were missing?"

"Haller broke into your quarters when he couldn't raise you on the comm." He grinned, showing a mouthful of white teeth. "Your plan was kinda slapdash."

"We had to improvise. We had no choice, Zeke. Haller threatened to kill him."

"He's safe enough now. If he pulls through. Hell, he fought off three rads. We need him around."

"Five rads."

"Five!" Zeke's brow went up. "Well. I'll vouch for him. As long as you make him behave himself."

She looked up sharply. "Don't talk about him like that." Much as she wanted to remain on good terms with Zeke, she couldn't stand the way he wore his serf-handler hat.

Zeke threw up his hands with an exasperated grunt and hopped down from the bench. Asking him to treat a serf as a human being was just too much for him.

"I'm gonna head back to my rigs. You need anything, let me know."

"I might need a hand with these toms. It looks like they haven't reported to a maintenance booth for twenty-four hours. They're all clogged up."

"I know that. That's why Haller wants *you* to fix them."

She didn't miss the word he emphasized. "So, scooping out gunk is my punishment?"

"Believe me, it could've been worse." Zeke stepped out of the infirmary without elaborating, snapping the hatch behind him.

As Edie pushed her finger against the tom's jack point to check its internals, she shuddered to think what "worse" might mean. Her memory of Haller grabbing her was fuzzy but terrifying—the calm, calculating way he'd clenched her neck until she passed out. So unlike the brutal violence of the serf Ademo, and yet they'd both had no compunction about forcing their will on her. Ademo had been desperate for freedom, and Haller had been desperate for—what? Was it only greed that prompted him to use her, or was he truly devoted to helping the Fringers? He'd claimed as much during their first meeting, but it was hard to believe.

She glanced over her shoulder at Finn, stretched out on the gurney, his features relaxed and vulnerable. Her chest constricted with fear for his life. He had been her source of strength for the past two days, her only true ally on the ship for the simple reason they were both here against their will.

The sequencer beeped. Edie washed the oily filth off her hands. Fingers shaking with fatigue, she extracted a vial from the machine and slotted it into a spike. When she pressed the needle against Finn's neck, he stirred but did not wake.

There was nothing more she could do for now. With a med tom keeping watch, she'd be alerted to any change in his condition. What she really wanted to do was sleep. Her muscles were sore, her body exhausted from the fight and the adrenaline rush. Fixing the cleaner toms seemed an irrelevant chore in comparison to her body's immediate needs.

She slipped into the small shower off the infirmary and stripped off. A shower and a long, restful sleep would take priority over doing penance for Haller's amusement.

A hand clamped down on her naked shoulder and Edie spun around, clasping her towel to her. Haller had snuck up behind her as she emerged from the shower. She had the distinct impression that he'd been lying in wait.

Without a word he slammed her against the wet wall. The effort to keep her balance on the slippery floor while keeping the towel around her naked body meant she couldn't use her hands as a buffer, and her head rebounded off the bulkhead.

Haller had worked himself up into a state of fury, and she was terrified of what he might do to Finn in a moment of irrationality. She couldn't see beyond the doorway into the infirmary. She could only hope Finn was all right.

"Don't you dare hurt him," she spluttered.

Haller backhanded her across the face. As Edie's hands went up instinctively in protection, the towel fell away. Her knees buckled and she slid down to the floor, cradling her burning cheek. She had expected sarcastic reproach from Haller, not violence.

As she fumbled for the towel, Haller's boot stomped on it, just missing her fingers, and he wouldn't let her tug it free. She curled up her legs and wrapped her arms around them, covering herself as best as she could.

"Who the hell do you think he is?" His rage was barely contained. "What gave you the idea he has any importance at all to this mission? He's a dispensable lag. I've got six more just like him in the cellblock, and you nearly got us all arrested because of some idiotic idea that he's worth saving."

"Then why did you save him?" Edie's throat ached from the effort to not cry. She would not break down in front of Haller.

"Because I understand now, teckie." He leaned against the bulkhead, blocking the light as he looked down on her. "I understand he means something to you. As long as I have him, I have a hold on you."

That was certainly true, and it might be the only thing that would save Finn's life. She was a fool for expecting Haller to appreciate that Finn had proven his worth as her body-guard against the eco-rads—the very danger this crew most feared. No, Haller didn't care about that. He only cared that she play her role in the mission.

"Get up."

When she failed to obey, he dragged her up by the arm and she forgot about covering herself. Now she was frightened of what he might do to her. In the taut lines of his face, his outrage simmered just below the surface.

"This could have been so much easier for you. So much nicer for both of us." He pressed his forearm across her breast to pin her against the wall, the heel of his hand digging painfully into her sternum. "We made you disappear from the Crib—a new ident, a job, a future. Don't ever underestimate what we did for you. No more chances, teckie.

If you act up again, things are going to get very unpleasant around here."

Over the hammering of her heart, she somehow managed to speak. "I won't cooperate if you kill him."

Haller gave a harsh laugh. "*Kill* him? Will you cooperate if I flog him? Starve him? There are so many ways I can guarantee your cooperation, now that I know you've developed this little attachment." He sneered as he took a lingering look at her body. His free hand hovered near her exposed breast, and he clenched his fist as if to stop himself touching her. "You have no idea who he is, you stupid girl. Why do you think he was a lifer on a labor gang? You don't get life for stealing candy or starting fistfights." As he made each point he jabbed his arm against Edie's chest, pushing the air out of her lungs. "The only reason he's on your side is because he has to be. Don't think for one moment he can be tamed."

He shoved away from her suddenly, tossing her aside. Hastily she grabbed the towel and covered herself.

"Did you fix those cleaner toms? There's a bunch of them crowding the garbage chute belowdeck, just sitting there like dumb fucks. Get them cleaned out and fixed."

"I can't find anything wrong with them." Edie backed toward the door, toward the infirmary and Finn and safety. "It's the system, something in the system stopped sending them instructions."

"So this is what I get for a legendary Crib cypherteck," Haller sneered. "Can't even fix a tom."

"I told you, it's something—"

"I don't want excuses. If you can't fix the toms you can do their work instead. Get a mop and start cleaning."

"What?"

"There's a maintenance cubby aft, deck three. Start there and work your way up."

"You . . . you want me to scrub the decks?" She couldn't believe her ears.

"That's what I said." He smirked at her expression. "Think

you're too good to do the dirty work around here? Think
again. And get him"—he jabbed his finger toward the infirmary—"out of there and back on his feet by tomorrow."

He stormed off.

"He saved your life, you shit." Edie wanted to scream the
words, but they came out as a whisper, unheard.

She dried off mechanically, her legs still trembling. A
beep from the med tom drew her back into the infirmary.
Finn still slept, oblivious to her little drama with the XO.
She checked the readout, which showed his vitals were improving. The knot of worry in her stomach eased, but her
blood still hummed with adrenaline.

She traced her fingers along the shiny streaks of medigel
on Finn's chest. Once they healed and the bruises faded and
the poison broke down, he'd be good as new. Except for the
older scars on his skin. She'd never asked him about those.

"What happened?" Finn's voice was a labored rasp.

She pulled her fingers away and met his eyes, which were
bright and focused.

"We're back on the *Hoi*. Haller—" Her throat closed up
over the name. She dared not tell Finn that Haller had manhandled her after she refused to leave the station, let alone
assaulted her in the shower room. If Finn retaliated out of
some kind of chivalry, things would only get worse. Somehow she had to keep the peace between the two men, for
Finn's safety.

"I mean just now. Something happened, woke me up. I
felt you—"

"No, I'm fine," she said quickly. Damn the leash. Her mind
still whirred with anger and fear and shock.

"I guess our escape didn't turn out so well."

"No." She tried to find a silver lining. "But if the local
authorities had taken us in, they'd probably have handed us
over to the Crib."

"I'd be no worse off than I was a week ago."

"How can you say that? They'd kill you for helping to
kidnap me."

He frowned, unconvinced. "And what d'you think those rads were trying to do?"

Edie sighed, shook her head. "Maybe it's for the best. Seeing those people . . . I wanted to help them. People like them. And the rovers are doing that. They have resources. The *Drakkar* could never have protected us. They're too small and too poor. Hell, Finn, they needed our help more than we needed theirs." She thought of the ragged little girl, brought to a grown-ups' meeting. They couldn't even afford a babysitter.

Now Finn shook his head, a slow roll of his neck on the pillow. "Since when did helping Fringers become part of our plan? Don't make me start thinking you're going to stick with these rovers after this mission."

"No. I'm thinking beyond that. I have a skill the Fringers need. If there was a way . . ." She trailed off, not sure of what she was trying to say. She hadn't thought of what she would do if they cut the leash. She hadn't truly realized there were people out there so much worse off than she was. She hadn't thought she could make a difference.

"Every time you reveal what you are," Finn said, "you're painting a target on your—"

He cut himself off as he glanced at her face, his eyes narrowing when he saw her swollen cheekbone, as if noticing it for the first time. He reached up to touch the bruise, and the brush of his fingertips brought fresh tears to her eyes. She shivered, not from his touch but from the sense memory of Haller's assault. Despite everything Haller had said, she had no doubt that Finn's concern was genuine. He was no brutish lag who could only be controlled by violence.

She held her breath at the stroke of his fingers along her jawline. For a few seconds, she forgot everything else but his simple touch. That yearning for human connection shocked her, and she made a small involuntary movement, shying away from him. Then regretted it, because his attention was the first good thing she'd felt in a long time.

Whether or not he noticed her reaction, Finn dropped his

hand away without asking about her new bruise. Let him think it was from the fight at Neuchasley.

He was right about her being a target, and her heart sank at the realization. If she worked as a cypherteck, there would always be someone, somewhere, who would use her or kill her for that skill. Even the Fringers might hold her captive and force her cooperation. While the rads' desperation was driven by ideological fervor, theirs was driven by pure survival.

"This is where we're safest," she said firmly. "I don't want to admit it any more than you do. Let's get back to our original plan. If you . . . if we behave, Haller will leave us alone. He needs me and we need the creds."

"These pirates are using you."

"You and me both. Right now, we can't change that."

He shrugged, too tired to argue with her, and winced in pain at the small movement. "I could feel you . . . holding on to me. You could have left me there."

"No."

"You're not what I expected."

"I just want you to live."

Finn turned his head away and stared at the featureless bulkhead. "We were almost free."

"We will be free." She wanted to touch him, reassure him, but she wasn't sure she believed what she was saying. "We need to plan things better. We need the creds from this mission. We need to wait until we're out of Crib space, where no one cares about a couple of runaways."

Finn closed his eyes again. She didn't know if he was listening.

And despite her exhaustion, she had work to do.

CHAPTER 13

Edie ignored the pain in her knees and the ache in her shoulders, and kept scrubbing. An hour ago she'd stopped looking back every few minutes to see how far she'd come along the corridor. It was disheartening to see how slowly that distance increased.

A sensor swept the corridor from one end to the other every ninety seconds. The invisible laser scanned for debris and dirt on the gravplating and relayed information to the cleaner toms—except that the toms weren't working. Edie had started out with a bucket and mop, but this wasn't good enough for the sensor. Haller must have turned on its audio alarm, because every ninety seconds it had beeped to inform her she wasn't doing a good enough job. She'd had to resort to getting onto her knees with a scrubbing brush to remove particularly stubborn areas of dirt. Knowing Haller, he'd probably increased the sensitivity of the sensor, too. This much crap couldn't have built up in only twenty-four hours.

But this wasn't about clean decks. The cleaner toms would get fixed, one way or another, or Zeke could put the serfs to work until the gravplating gleamed. Haller didn't care about clean decks. He wanted to control her.

And that infuriated her. Her options had never been so limited as they'd become in the past few hours, and yet her determination to control her own fate had never been stronger.

She sat up on her heels to stretch her back.

"Penance *over*," she muttered. She'd get back to her regular work, prove herself with her strong suit, make Haller feel like he was getting his money's worth. He could hardly expect her to slave away with a scrubbing brush for days when there was work to be done.

She swished the dirty water down the drain in the nearest maintenance cubby and washed her hands. The hard work had left her plenty of time to think. With her fingers wrinkled from the cleaning fluids and her knees rubbed raw, she was resigned to being back on board under the control of her captors. Haller might repulse her, but he wanted her alive. Cat and Zeke were tolerable crewmates. This was simply the safest place to be.

Despite her overwhelming fatigue, she climbed up to top deck. The common area was the only easily accessible place on the ship she'd found with a viewport to space. She wasn't expecting to find someone else there. Cat beckoned her over and they sat on a low plush bench, side by side, looking out at the turning stars. The navpilot did a double take at the ripe bruise coming up on her cheekbone, but if she guessed it was Haller's work she didn't say anything about it.

After a few minutes, Cat spoke. "You ever looked out at nodespace?"

Edie shook her head.

"Not for the faint-hearted. If Haller's got the watch, he shuts the screen. I think it's beautiful." She indicated the inky black landscape. "This, too. All of it."

Edie was grateful Cat hadn't opened the conversation with admonishments about her escape attempt. "Is this why you like flying?"

Cat nodded. "It's so empty and peaceful. I like that. But you can't beat the action of flying the smaller ships—the skiff, the chasers in the war. You really feel like you're part of it."

"Part of what?"

"Everything. The lights out there, the nothing in between. The universe. Sometimes I feel like it's pulling me in, welcoming me home like a long-lost child. And I'm always running away, another ship, another mission. Out there, that's the only place that will always want me back. Don't you ever feel that way?"

Edie frowned, not sure how to answer. "I haven't really contemplated the universe before. My life has been rather confined. But most of the time I'd rather be somewhere else."

Cat gave her a sidelong glance. "Somewhere like Port Neuchasley?"

"Somewhere Neuchasley could have taken me—us."

"That was a pretty dumb thing you did today." Cat shook her head more in sympathy than reproach. "If you want to survive away from the Crib, you need us."

Edie stared at her hands, running her fingertips over the scraped knuckles, knowing that Cat was right.

"You have to understand, I thought Haller was going to kill Finn. I couldn't let that happen."

"I heard about what happened earlier today—Haller was bluffing. There's no way he'd leave him at the port. Finn's already connected to your escape from Talas. If they found his body and linked him to the *Hoi*, they'd be on to us. Believe me, if Haller wanted to get rid of Finn, he'd find a more discreet way of doing it." Cat put her hand on Edie's knee to take the sting from her words. "It won't happen. Haller won't lose sight of the prize. He needs your cooperation. Just try and stay under his radar, okay?"

"Yeah, I'll try."

"I've been here for years and I don't like Haller and he doesn't like me, but it's just easier for everyone if we get along. He's furious with you right now but it'll pass. Hell, even I'm furious with you. The captain puts on one crew supper per mission—tomorrow night—and he got into a snit over this and postponed it. I was really looking forward to some good food." She smiled to show she was teasing. "I can do without his stupid war stories, but you can't get one without the other."

"Why do you call them stupid?"

"Because I don't think they're real. I was Fleet, too. A lot of what he says doesn't add up. Sometimes I think he lives in a fantasy world. Maybe that's just how he gets through this. We're all just trying to get through."

The hint of sourness in Cat's voice made Edie wonder just how committed Cat was to the *Hoi*'s agenda—why she stayed and whether she had a choice.

She dared to ask the question. "Are you here because you have to be?"

Cat tensed, her breath hitching. When she spoke, her cheerfulness sounded forced. "I'm flying, Edie. I can't complain. They tell me where to go, but I'm the one plotting the route, riding the nodes. I can carve out my own path through the universe. I'm not saying I don't have plans—" She looked down abruptly and when she continued, Edie sensed she'd changed her mind about what she was going to say. "I just do the job."

The job. *Scarabaeus*. Edie hadn't given the mission a serious thought since her initial doubts after the briefing. It seemed like weeks ago. The sense of dread that had started when she found out their destination returned in a sickening rush.

Cat touched Edie's shoulder briefly as she stood up. "You've still got a few things to learn. We're not the enemy. At least, I'm not, Zeke's not." With that, she said good night and left.

Alone with the stars, Edie wondered if she, too, might carve out her own path. Her past had been dictated by the Crib, which chose the course of her future, shaped her mind, her talent, her options. It had whittled away her choices until one path remained. She'd never thought to look for another way until she'd stepped onto Scarabaeus's soil for the first time and realized her path was to destroy.

One of the lights out there was Scarabaeus's sun. She should have asked Cat which one.

No, she didn't want to know.

The e-shield dulls her senses. Some people insist they feel no difference, but she's never worn a shield before and is hyperaware of the way it makes everything feel fuzzy under her fingertips, how it waters down the sounds and smells of this alien world, dulls the taste of the air and reflects a disconcerting silver glare onto her retinas. The last thing she wants is for her experiences to be filtered. Tainted.

So she flicks off the shield. Bethany will kill her if she finds out. Alien worlds are never compatible with human physiology, and some are outright toxic. But she feels safe here, though she doesn't know why.

Later, she finds out. Danger is loud and ugly. Danger is the sound of warning sirens screaming, heavy boots thudding over gravplating, the crack of a spur wielded by a faceless rad. The look on a dying woman's face, the acrid smell of scorched flesh and of too much blood.

This is the lesson she will soon learn by experience. But there's no danger here, in this place of beauty—at least not to herself.

She watches the beetle struggling through the moss as she lies under the alien sun. Her vision blurs with tears, her mind reels with the weight of the knowledge that being here is a mistake. Yet no one cares. Not the commander, not the seeding team. Not even Bethany, who seems concerned only that she watches and learns and behaves herself, that the timetable is adhered to, that the rigs function smoothly, that the planet is worked over, torn down, and remodeled to make it fit for humans. They want this world, and no three-billion-year-old ecology will stand in their way.

Bethany, furious, finds her there, lying on the moss. She

*aches with the shame of her disobedience because she loves
Bethany—how else to explain the choking grief when she
dies? But Bethany is part of all this, part of what she now
sees as the Crib's betrayal.*

*And so, rather than save one beetle from its treacherous
entanglement only for it to be destroyed by the BRATs, she
resolves to save everything. She doesn't know how. She only
knows that when the chance comes, she'll take it.*

She's capable of more than any of them can guess.

The stars glowed and contracted into tight points of light as
Edie's eyes refocused. She'd returned to Scarabaeus in her
dreams, time and again. Sometimes the dreams were ach-
ingly beautiful, and she felt safe and welcome on that alien
world. Other times, the emotions dredged up by the mission
overwhelmed her. The shame of inciting Bethany's anger,
the sense of betrayal over the Crib's intent to destroy such a
world, the terror and grief over Bethany's death.

And underneath it all, her own betrayal. The secret she
held on to like the shell embedded in her skin that everyone
else deemed worthless.

She saw Finn's reflection in the window and swiveled
around. He sat on the edge of a couch a few meters behind
her, head forward, relaxing with his hands dangling between
his knees.

"How long have you been there?" No answer. "You should
be resting."

"Med tom says I'm fine."

"Then we should move back to our quarters so Haller can
forget this ever happened."

"Did you get hurt down there?"

She shook her head, frowning. Her injuries were insignificant compared to what he'd been through.

Tapping his temple, he clarified his question. "Why're
you so churned up? I thought you were glad to be back on
board."

"You know that's not really true."

He looked down at his hands, accepting her rebuke. When he glanced at her again, waiting, Edie knew she should say something. She wanted badly to explain everything, to open her past and her thoughts to him, but where to start? He wanted a release from her emotions, not an explanation of them. And thirteen years spent under the close scrutiny of CCU trainers and case workers and doctors had instilled in her a powerful reluctance to open up to anyone.

She thought about what Haller had said—his implication that Finn must have done something terrible to end up a lifer. Edie didn't want to believe that. Nor did she think Finn would reveal anything if she asked him directly.

"If we . . . after we find someone to cut the leash, what will you do?"

He opened his hands, stated the obvious. "Evade recapture."

"But where will you go?"

"It's probably in my best interest not to tell anyone."

She tried not to be offended that he wouldn't confide in her. "I know you fought in the Reach Conflicts. Which planet were you fighting for?"

His jaw tightened and he stared beyond her, at the starscape, hesitating long enough for her to realize he was weighing his words carefully. "None in particular. From our side it was called the Liberty War, by the way."

"I know." He'd avoided the question, and she let it drop. "The part I don't understand is this: they send POWs home after the war. You're still here. They said you were a lifer."

He gave her a dark look that made her regret bringing it up. "Whatever you think I've done, you don't fear me. You never have."

"Haller wants me to fear you."

"He wants you to control me."

With the voice snag gone, the drub sitting in her quarters, and her promise not to use the jolt, Edie wasn't doing a very good job of that. She was uncomfortable talking—or even thinking—about the reason she wasn't afraid of him.

"Do you have family?"

"Truthfully, I don't think about it."

"I just wondered if you were a decent, upstanding citizen, once upon a time." That was what she really wanted to know—who he was, what he had once been.

Finn gave a low growl and said with real annoyance, "Too many damn questions. And no, I was never that."

His restless aggravation was covering for something more profound, and she was itching to get to the bottom of it. But she kept her tone light.

"You don't like the way I handle you, Finn?"

"You're not *handling* me."

"Well then, I'm doing something wrong."

She was teasing him, and he had enough good humor remaining to let it slide. In turn, he moved the topic away from himself.

"If it's not Haller spinning stories that's getting you riled up, what is it? Is there some danger I should know about?"

He deserved an explanation. Edie sorted through her thoughts before speaking.

"There's no danger that I know of. But I haven't told them everything." Her hand moved unconsciously to her throat, where the neckband of her tee hid the beetle shell. She made a fist to stop the nervous gesture. "They know all they need to know. The rest is . . . my business."

When she stalled again, he raised an eyebrow expectantly.

"Those dead BRATs—that was my doing, Finn. I saved Scarabaeus from terraforming seven years ago."

His eyes narrowed. "How?"

"During our final ground check—they drop the BRAT seeds from the ship, and then go down to check a few at random. The last one was on an island. A beautiful place." She swallowed, caught in a wave of churned-up emotions. "My trainer finished up and we were ready to leave. She told me to jack in, take a look at the BRAT priming. She was pissed off at me—I'd wandered off earlier, doused my e-shield—so she just left me alone with the BRAT. I wasn't supposed to do anything, just look and learn. But an idea came to me. At first I didn't even dare . . ." Edie drew a deep breath to steady her voice and control the bone-deep trembling in her body. "For the first time in my life I had power. Power to control the destiny of an entire world."

Finn stared at her intently, and she guessed her emotions were turbulent enough to be flooding across the leash.

"So I planted a kill-code lock. It's one of the first things they teach you—how to lock down the biocyph, shut it off. I set a time-delay on it, wrapped it all up in a housekeeping tier to hide it. Real simple."

"Why did it affect *all* the BRATs?"

"Because they talk to each other. They have to, to coordinate the terraforming. Just like the keystones these rovers make that send a message to all the other BRATs. The kill-code was transmitted across the planet after we left orbit. A year later, the scout probe reported the BRAT seeds were dead. I couldn't believe I'd succeeded. And no one ever suspected. They'd already moved on to the next project."

"If you saved Scarabaeus, if it's unharmed, why are you terrified of going back?"

Edie sighed. "I saved Scarabaeus because I wanted it left in peace. We should leave it alone."

"It's just a rock and some bugs."

"Right," she muttered, turning back to the starscape. What had given her the ridiculous hope that he'd understand? Why should he care about Scarabaeus? Yet he was right. If only she could put aside her emotional connection to the planet, she'd see Scarabaeus for the soulless rock and biomass it really was. Any other view would be as absurd as that of the eco-rads.

For a long moment Finn said nothing. Then, "You can shut down an entire terraforming operation, but you can't dismantle this thing in my head?" He didn't sound resentful, but his question stung her conscience.

"I'm sorry."

His reflection in the viewing port gave a nod of acceptance as he stared at his hands. His fingers laced and unlaced.

Edie looked at the stars. Cat was right—it was peaceful, and Cat had found her place in that emptiness. It would never be enough for Edie. She craved the freedom, but it left her in a spin. She needed to know where she was headed. Perhaps the fantasy of helping people like Inga and her family was nothing more than a placeholder, a random lifeline because she had to be sure of *something*.

The only thing she was sure of right now was Finn.

He caught and held her gaze in the reflection. A massive physical presence, so strong and sure of himself in many ways, but powerless to take charge of his situation or to control his future. It gave him a vulnerability that made her heart constrict in her chest—a momentary pang of sympathy that she pushed aside without examination.

"I get this feeling from you," she murmured. "You move through the universe like you're on another plane. It never touches you. I know you started out caring about something, and now it's gone. Or they took it away. Nothing matters to you."

His answer came reluctantly. "Truth is, the universe bewilders me. I gave up a long time ago trying to make sense of it."

He looked away self-consciously, and after a while he stood up and waited for her to follow.

CHAPTER 14

Tilt, one of the most popular low-g sports in the Crib, was played in a controlled variable gravity zone. On board the *Hoi*, some time in the past, someone had hooked up leftover gravplating on all six walls of the gym and this served as the Tilt arena. As Edie soon discovered while watching a match in progress, the random system failures affecting other parts of the ship were even more apparent here, and the variable gravity was rather too variable. At unpredictable times the plates would give way and drop all four players from various heights, wherever they happened to be within the three-dimensional field. Seeing the guys trying to maintain their dignity was comical, to say the least.

Cat had bowed out of the match after the first two rounds, to be replaced by Kristos. Haller, who had somehow ended up on the same team as Finn, seemed relieved about the switch, while Zeke still hadn't stopped grumbling about his new partner. Cat was amazing in low-g, launching herself off the walls and accurately judging distances and angles as she maneuvered through the hoops of light projected into the arena. Her skills had unbalanced the teams to such an extent that even Kristos's fumbling moves hadn't made much of an impact on her team's lead.

"Your bodyguard moves well," Cat mused.

Realizing Cat had noticed her watching Finn, Edie flushed. There was a languid grace about him in regular gravity, at odds with his size, and this translated well to low-g where his movements looked natural even if his skill at the game wasn't particularly noteworthy. In fact it looked like he'd never played before, although he clearly had experience with low-g.

Having already completed their morning workouts, she and Cat had left the men to their sport and retreated to the kit room, which overlooked the gym. It had its own gravplating that kept them stable, but still Edie's stomach lurched each time the plates beyond them unexpectedly switched direction.

Edie's gym shoes were off, and Cat was painting the tops of her feet with rosy-brown ink—a striking effect on her pale skin. The fine brush tickled. The normality of the activity was at odds with the way Edie felt. Two full days had passed since her escape attempt. Two days keeping out of Haller's hair, dutifully attending the morning CPT sessions, and spending her shifts with Zeke and Kristos as they prepared the rigs. Always with Finn in the background. Now that he'd fully recovered from the poison, Zeke put him back to work and he did it without complaining. He wasn't free, but at least he was receiving better treatment than a laborgang serf. And Haller seemed satisfied that he'd learned his lesson and would not cause further trouble.

"So tell me," Cat said with a sly look, "is he housebroken?"

"He's clean and basically polite, if that's what you mean." Edie stopped herself from elaborating on Finn's other attributes, like the intriguing confidence she'd glimpsed on Neuchasley, and the way he made her feel safe.

Cat gave her an exasperated look. Enunciating carefully, she said, "What I mean is, are you grinding him?"

"That would be a bad idea."

"Speak for yourself!"

Edie didn't want to put a dampener on the girl talk now

that she and Cat were getting along, but she had to explain. Even if it meant revealing more than she'd intended. "Back on Talas, when I was in the training program, my trainer and her bodyguard were lovers. I don't just mean they shared a bed. They were very close. When she was killed by a rad, he blamed himself."

"Was it his fault?"

Yes. Lukas and Edie had each claimed a share of the guilt. He and Bethany had had a fight that day, a petty personal squabble. He'd left her alone for a while so they could both sulk. The stowaway eco-rad had come looking for her and found Edie first. And so Bethany had walked in, defenseless, when Lukas should never have left her side in the first place.

"Their relationship complicated things. They should've kept it professional."

They gazed at Finn again. He glided past, twisting through a hoop of light just before it winked out. The point registered, and a green holo cube, his team's color, stabilized in the area. Haller and Finn's combined abilities made them the better team in theory and they should have overtaken on the scoreboard a while ago, but they would rather lose the match than work together. Only Kristos's ineptitude and Zeke's frustration was losing the blue team the territory Cat had won earlier.

The gravity shifted again and all four players floated upward in the opposite direction from a new set of linked hoops materializing below them. Zeke began the charge to secure them.

"Well, you can send him my way any time," Cat said with a grin, and then waved away that notion with a flick of her hand. "Listen, if you'd worked around lags for as long as I have, you'd think twice about loosening the reins. Forget those psych evaluations that say he's a sweetie. He'll turn on you if he sees the opportunity."

Haller had tried scaring her the same way, but Cat had no

reason to exaggerate and her words sent a shiver through Edie. She didn't want to believe that could ever be true.

"Zeke said he was a Saeth. Do you know what that is?"

The paintbrush in Cat's hand froze over Edie's big toe. Then she laughed mirthlessly.

"A Saeth, is he? Now I know why Zeke wouldn't tell me much about him before our mission to Talas Prime."

"I don't get it. Finn won't talk about it. Zeke told me to ask you. What's a Saeth?"

"The Saeth were rogue independence fighters. Top of the Crib's most-wanted list. Assassins, basically. They were from the Fringe, but all the Fringe governments denied any knowledge of them."

"So who did they work for?"

"Who knows? Themselves, apparently. Their own private army with their own agenda. Their activities helped prolong the war and disrupted the new independence treaties. You know, I sympathize with the Fringers and I can understand the Crib, but the Saeth turn my gut."

Cat stared at Finn with a new glint in her eye. Edie did her best to add some perspective.

"Hey, the war's over. He's a lifer with a bomb in his head. Is that enough to settle your stomach?"

Cat grinned, lifting Edie's foot to examine her handiwork. "I guess so." She glanced up, chewing her lip. "In case you're wondering—in case anything happens to him—I didn't know about the leash. We used him to grab you, but I was told he'd be freed afterward, and that's what I promised him."

Edie nodded, watching Cat screw the lid on the ink, unsure of what to believe. She was sure, however, that Cat's motivation for explaining herself had more to do with wanting to form a connection with Edie than any real concern about Finn.

"Is this finished?"

"Yes. It's already dry."

Edie admired the artfully painted scrolls and dots all over

the tops of her feet. It had been a long time since she'd done anything to make herself pretty. She looked up to see Cat examining her throat.

"What's this?" Cat reached out to pull the neck of Edie's tee down.

Instinctively, Edie put up her hand to cover the beetle shell.

"What is it? A jewel?" Cat moved Edie's hand and peered closer. "It's beautiful."

"It's just a shell." *Turquoise and black.*

"Where did you get it? Was it expensive?"

"It's not worth anything. Having it implanted cost a small fortune—at least, it was a lot when I was a teenager."

"So it doesn't come out?"

Edie shook her head, hoping Cat wouldn't ask more questions.

"Hey, you wanna have fun with the boys?" Cat grinned at her confusion. "Come on. I couldn't stand it if Haller won."

Cat pulled Edie to her feet and indicated the scoreboard, which showed that Haller and Finn were now ahead by a narrow margin. The arena had more green territory than blue. Kristos flailed around ineffectually while Zeke yelled instructions and cursed the kid's mistakes.

"You can jack in and control the grav," Cat said. "See if you can't tilt it a bit in Zeke's favor."

"I don't even know the rules of the game," Edie pleaded, but Cat had already brought up the control screen and the holo rotated between them.

"I'll tell you what you need to do. Quickly—Finn just took another point."

"Wait—what if I want Finn to win?"

Cat stood back, hands on hips. "Your choice, but would you rather Haller won or Finn lost?"

She had a point.

A kidnapped cypherteck and her unwilling bodyguard were the last couple on a pirate ship that would be invited to the captain's supper. At least that's what Edie thought. Cat, however, insisted that they were both expected to attend the rescheduled event—and that it wasn't optional. What made Edie nervous was that for two days she'd expected a reprimand from the captain about her and Finn's escape attempt, but Rackham had taken little interest.

"He's made himself scarce on this trip," Cat told her. "Not that he's usually the life of the party, but he barely knows it happened. It pissed him off at the time, but it was nothing more than an hour or two's inconvenience. Haller played it down, Zeke even more so, because neither wants to get blamed. *Unauthorized shore leave* is the official verdict."

The upside of the event was that Haller would be on duty, on the bridge. It made the idea of supper more palatable.

"You should put on a dress," Finn said. They were in their quarters cleaning up.

Edie wrinkled her nose. "I'll put on a dress when you comb your hair."

He grinned and ran his hand over the thick dark fuzz on his scalp. It was growing back in, balanced by the evening shadow along his jaw. "Couple more weeks, then."

Her face warmed at the idea of wearing a dress for Finn. She had the strange feeling they'd just made a deal.

By the time Edie and Finn arrived, the captain was already there, along with Cat, Kristos, and Zeke, and two engineers whom they had not yet met. The engies, Yasuo and Corky, were introduced but didn't speak a word to Edie. The younger one, Yasuo, spared Finn a dubious look. Corky, the beefy, tattooed chief engie, seemed more interested in working his way through the captain's expensive wine.

The dining room was the best-dressed room on the ship. It was easy to forget you were aboard a shabby long-range mining vessel when surrounded by genuine wood, richly woven fabric, and handmade knickknacks from all corners of the Reach. And Rackham, it turned out, was not only a collector of exotic furnishings and artwork but also a connoisseur of fine food. Gia was used to serving up bland meals en masse for the crew, but was also capable of extraordinary culinary feats, according to Cat.

Finn seemed to know his place—he went to sit in the galley off the mess, from which Gia was serving. Rackham didn't miss a beat on the war story he was relaying as Edie slipped into a chair and kept one eye on Cat to follow her lead in the proper use of the cutlery as everyone tucked into soup. Edie was amused to see Kristos doing the same thing—watching Cat and trying to sit upright and tilt his plate properly, taking small spoonfuls and using his napkin.

Rackham had some sort of antique weapon on the table, and began describing its features to Kristos, who apparently hadn't seen it before.

"It's a recoil-operated semiautomatic, point-four-five cartridge. Only seven rounds in the magazine plus one in the chamber, but with a slug that size you don't need more than one. Weighs a little over a kilo. My ancestors' standard issue firearm for a century. Timeless design."

Kristos looked like he wanted to touch it, but Rackham didn't offer.

"If you're going to get the job done, you want a weapon with stopping power," Rackham continued. "What does a spur do? Peppers 'em full of tiny holes, and even if you can stop 'em coming, they get patched up in no time. To get what you want, use maximum force. That's the only way to play the game."

This was only the second time Edie had met Rackham, and his detached air chilled her blood. While Haller enjoyed his one-on-one power games, she had the feeling that Rackham could be far more ruthless on a grand scale. Perhaps that was something he'd learned in the war.

"I have a few other law-enforcement items of interest," Rackham told Kristos, nodding toward a cabinet displaying his collection. "Couple of holographic ident cards that predate the Crib. A nineteenth-century sheriff's badge from Old Earth—hardly a scratch on it. Handcuffs almost as old as this gun. If you have a spare moment or two, I'll show you."

Zeke smothered a snort by turning it into a cough. He didn't seem to think Kristos would be getting much free time on this trip.

"Sha'nim," Rackham said suddenly, carefully laying aside his weapon. Edie hastily swallowed a mouthful of delicately spiced stew that Gia had just placed before her. "Lancer was telling me on the bridge this afternoon that you're a native of Talas." It was unlikely Rackham hadn't already known that, even if he hadn't been directly involved in her kidnapping, and the shift in topic was awkward. "That world warrants a couple of sentences in every history holoviz. I remember reading about the Talasi. That case over there—" He drew the attention of his dinner guests with a sweep of his hand. "Gia, open that case, will you, and fetch me what's inside. You'll recognize this, Sha'nim."

He smiled smugly as Gia hurried to comply. She withdrew the contents of the display case with trembling hands and carried the object to Rackham as carefully as she might handle a soufflé. The captain took the egg-shaped item from her—his hand was large enough to palm it comfortably—and held it up for all to see.

Edie stared in astonishment at the talphi cocoon. Secreted and molded by the female of the species to carry her eggs while on the wing, such cocoons had been a commonplace find during her childhood. What was unusual about this one was simply that Rackham had it in his possession.

"Isn't it magnificent?" Rackham turned the cocoon over in his hands. The iridescent surface wavered and bled like oil on water as it caught the light. "It was created by a native creature on Talas—a primitive flying mammal, I believe. I traded three cases of very good brandy for this beauty. Perhaps you can tell us more about it?" he prompted Edie, passing the cocoon to Cat on his left.

Edie opened her mouth to answer his question politely, but felt an irrational surge of annoyance at the idea of Rackham, or anyone in the Crib, trading Talasi property and putting it on display.

"Talphi cocoons fall under the indigenous trade act," she said. "It's illegal to transport them off Talas. The law was enacted two decades ago to prevent exploitation of the Talasi." She decided not to mention that the law was also intended to protect the naïve—the cocoon contained enough neuroxin to kill everyone in the room but her.

Cat scowled at her, but Rackham was unfazed by what could have been interpreted as an accusation.

"And that's why it was so damn expensive. Still, well worth it in my opinion. I paid a high price for all these treasures. This dreadful beast"—he indicated the sprawling artwork in the corner behind him—"was a gift from a Fringe-world captain. I don't think she liked me. And in that chest over there is an antique Lourches songbird. A beautiful museum piece, although that particular one has never been played in my presence. I've no musical talent to speak of, and I can't persuade Lancer here to take it up."

"Because I have mercy on your eardrums, sir," Cat said tolerantly.

Rackham gave Edie an appraising look. He kept his eyes on her while addressing the room, like a king holding court. "What did you think of your brief trip to Talas, Lancer? The original natives were xenophobic, low-teck refugees from another failed colony world who somehow managed to tame that toxic planet and have thrived for centuries."

"Thrived is hardly the word," Cat said. "We never went dirtside, but on Talas Prime the news-caps were full of the troubles down on the planet. There's friction over trade agreements and whether or not to try and detoxify the ecosystem. Terrorism in the city is rife, despite the Crib's occupation. The economy's a mess. The city dwellers have used bio-bombs on the forests and the natives live in secluded camps. That was supposed to be a temporary measure but it's been—what, almost twenty years?"

Edie nodded, rolling a water glass between her palms, desperately uncomfortable under their scrutiny.

"Talas's ecosystem is toxic?" Kristos said. "How do the natives survive?"

The question was addressed to Edie, but she didn't respond. Rackham, however, seemed eager to share his knowledge. Edie should've guessed from his eclectic collection that he was more knowledgeable about colonial anthropology than the average Crib citizen.

"Their ancestors integrated biocyph strands into their genome. It was as illegal then as it is now. The Crib cut them off, but they were isolationists and didn't care. And eventually"—he looked directly at Edie—"your people were forgotten."

Not my people. She disliked being identified as one of them, and bit back the reflexive response. Why should she identify with people who had rejected her?

Rackham and Cat began debating the pros and cons of bio-bombs as a means of pest control, and the engineers excused themselves to prepare for the next jump—Corky quite obviously inebriated. Through the serving hatch, Edie watched Gia wait on Finn with a mixture of flirtatious smiles and motherly concern—quite different from the deference she reserved for the captain and crew. Finn responded with a friendly appreciation that startled her. After what Cat had told her about the Saeth, the normality of his behavior struck Edie as being entirely unassassinlike.

Rackham was distracted by a quiet but insistent beeping on his personal commlink. He squinted at the message, his brows crawling low over deep-set eyes, and then directed the transmission onto the holoviz so everyone could see. It was Haller, looking worried, awaiting instructions.

"Haller tells me a CIP vessel has been tailing us for the past few hours," Rackham announced, as though he were commenting on the weather.

In the uncomfortable silence that followed, Edie felt the

heat of unvoiced accusations. Was the Crib coming after her? Of course she expected Natesa to send someone to find her, but surely the rovers had covered their tracks.

Zeke finally spoke up. "CIP has hundreds of smaller ships patrolling just outside Crib Central. Might be a routine patrol, coincidentally on the same course."

"That's becoming less and less likely," Haller said. "They followed us through the last two jumps."

"Damn, we're only three jumps from Scarabaeus. Have they made contact?" Cat asked.

Haller shook his head. "They may think we'll take off if they voice any suspicions." In contrast to Rackham's calmness, the XO's voice held an edge of alarm. "At this distance we can still outrun them, disappear into the nearest jump node, and claim Article Seven if they complain. They can't delay a commercial vessel without due cause."

"We can't run," Rackham said. "It'll look like we have something to hide and they'll hound us for the next century—you know what they're like."

Now even his eyes slid toward Edie. For the first time, she wondered if Rackham opposed her presence on the ship. Maybe he'd rather Stichting Corp send the *Hoi* on safe survey missions instead of seeding ventures that required a valuable cypherteck to complicate his rover lifestyle. While the *Hoi* was a legally registered vessel that ordinarily should pass a Crib Interstellar Patrol inspection, there was no explaining away the presence on board of a cypherteck who had recently disappeared from her post under suspicious circumstances.

"Let's play it cool for now." Rackham neatly folded his napkin and with a flourish of his finger called Gia for more wine. "We're well out of Central's control, so they're going to need a damn good reason to board us for inspection. We're a few hours from the next jump, at which point we'll diverge from our scheduled flight plan anyway. So they'll lose us in the node unless they get a hell of a lot closer in order to track us."

"I'll let you know if they close in." Haller signed off.

"Nothing to worry about," Rackham said, taking a sip of wine, but the fingers of his other hand drummed on the tabletop. He thumped his glass on the table. "Dammit, this merlot should be served at seventeen degrees. This tastes like twenty-two, at least. Seventeen, Gia! Seventeen degrees is the correct temperature."

Gia rushed to his side in a fluster. "It's the secondary refrigeration unit, sir, that powers the wine cabinet. Been failing all day."

Cat rolled her eyes at Edie over the rim of her glass as the captain expressed at length his disappointment. Edie was only too grateful that his attention had moved on from her heritage to the precise temperature of his wretched wine.

CHAPTER 15

Haller swiveled his console around to face Edie. "I've given you limited access. Figure out what's going on with these systems failures, and then jack out. Don't meddle. Don't try and fix anything."

He'd woken her at three in the morning after a crowd of toms rattling the captain's air vents had driven Rackham to demand an immediate solution to the random failures affecting the ship's systems. Flickering striplights, screwed-up air mixes in the mid-deck quarters, the gravplating fluctuations during the Tilt game—these minor annoyances had kept the engineers on their toes. With a possible CIP confrontation coming up, Rackham wanted the source of the errors located before something more serious went wrong.

Edie's brain was still a little foggy as she slid into a seat, stifling a yawn. She pressed her fingertips against the dataport, trying not to appear too eager. An overwarm wine cabinet and a handful of misbehaving toms on a decrepit pirate ship didn't interest her, but Haller's failure to track down the problem was an opportunity for her to snoop around the *Hoi*'s higher-level systems.

"Remember, I said don't fix anything." Haller watched the holoviz as Edie filed through the systems routines.

"Wouldn't dream of messing with your precious ship," she muttered.

Finn had come along to the briefing room, and Edie was glad. The two men detested each other, and that would never change, but the more opportunity Haller had to see that Finn was behaving himself, the less likely he'd be to carry out his threats against him. Finn was backed up against the bulkhead, arms folded over his chest as he watched her work.

The error log was now several thousand entries long. She ran it through a filter to detect any patterns. Nothing came up—the failures appeared to be truly random. She kept the holo running an uninformative loop that masked her datastream, just to see if Haller could tell the difference. She needed time to think and explore.

Slipping through the virtual door that Haller had opened for her, she accessed the *Hoi Polloi*'s mid-level secure systems. Her splinter sorted through jumbled tiers, reorganizing them into music she could understand. Like much of the technology on the ship, the system had been patched up over the years with amateurish hacks. It remained surprisingly functional, and that meant the high-level systems were depressingly secure. Ideally, she needed to create a worm—a hidden, self-directed algorithm that over time could break through. But she was no infojack, and such sophisticated coding was beyond her expertise. In any case, there was nothing she could do from this console.

As she filed through the tiers, searching for ideas, Haller's on-edge voice broke her concentration.

"Well? What's going on? Did you find anything?"

She flashed up the error report, pulled back from the datastream, and returned her attention to Haller.

"As you can see, there are blips in here. Doesn't even qualify as a virus. They're not replicating or doing any permanent damage."

"And they won't mess with major systems? I don't want any surprises."

"It's not affecting any systems that require security access."

"So how do we fix it?"

"You told me *not* to fix it. Sir."

Haller scowled. "If that's all it is, fix the damn thing, teckie. Where did these blips come from anyway?"

Edie chased the blips as they played over the surface of the tiers, dipping into the melody of the programming at random—one disharmonious note here, another there. Simple mischief, like a flurry of playful sprites tickling the nose of the ship's systems. Distracting, but never quite enough to bring on a sneeze.

Distracting.

A shiver swept down her spine and her hands went cold. From the corner of her eye, she saw Finn shift position as her rush of anxiety sent a spike of awareness to his brain.

"Where did this thing come from?" Haller repeated, oblivious to her reaction. "Something we picked up at port, a bad piece of code—or what?"

"It's a distraction," she said quietly, lost in the code.

It took Haller a second to catch on. She saw the spark of panic in his face before his eyes slitted as his mind started working again.

"You mean a diversion?"

"Yes."

"Shit. Engineering has been chasing these problems around the ship like legless toms for three days . . ." He raked a hand through his hair and looked wildly around the room as though the answers might be found there, while Edie channeled the code visuals to the holo.

Finn came over and leaned on the console, taking in the information. "So, what should we really be looking for?"

"I don't know," Edie said. "It's curious, though—the blips haven't spread from a common source. They've been introduced into the ship's systems over and over again during the last few days."

"Does it matter?" Haller said. "You have my permission to get in there and fix it. Then maybe we can figure out what we're being distracted *from*."

"Something keeps tapping in, feeding new code. There's no point clearing out these blips when new ones are appearing all the time."

"Yes, but from where?"

"Maybe you have a stowaway," Finn said sardonically.

Haller snorted. It was an insult to suggest that a ship the size of the *Hoi Polloi* could carry a stowaway this far out of port without detection. Haller's security wasn't that sloppy. "What about a hackscript?" he suggested.

"No, it's deeper than that." Edie turned the layers over in her head, teased them apart to peek inside, noticed the pits and wrinkles in the clean coding, like high frequency dropouts in a poor quality recording.

Haller shook his head. "A worm, then? Seems like overkill, considering the kind of problems we've been having."

"Maybe they're planning ahead," Finn said.

Edie bit her lip to suppress a grin, because a worm was exactly what she'd been wishing for, although one that disrupted cleaner toms wasn't going to help her and Finn.

Then she found it. "I think they already succeeded."

The holo displayed the bones of the ship, rotating slowly over the console. A series of orange dots ran the length of each corridor, and more glowed to life in the cargo holds, the gallery, the crew quarters, everywhere.

Haller squinted at the display. "What are those?"

"Access ports for the maintenance toms. They jack in to recharge, to receive instructions, to report their status. My guess—someone planted an infected tom, it infected more, and they've been injecting blips every time they jack in."

"But toms can't affect any secure systems," Haller said. "They can't do much of anything except clean up trash and fix leaky faucets."

"If they're programmed right, they can also scurry about unnoticed, squeeze into tight places." Edie called up the tom roster and overlaid the current location of every tom on the ship. "And burn through locks."

At least half of the toms were clustered in one location: belowdeck.

The cellblock.

Haller slapped his commlink and started yelling.

It took several tense minutes for Zeke to get out of bed, get to the cellblock, and report back. Three cells open, three serfs missing.

Haller finished updating the captain over the comm, then turned to Edie. "Can we get an idea of the lags' location—heat sensors, movement trackers?"

"The toms have thrown everything out of whack. We can't trust the sensors until I've cleaned out the blips and shut down the toms' access."

"Get to the engine room and do it." As he studied the holoviz, Haller kept the link open to Rackham. "Sir, tell-tales are reading that the armory is still locked up. But they showed the cellblock was, too. No way to know what's going on from here."

The captain ordered Zeke, Haller and Kristos to the armory. He and Cat would secure the bridge. "If they get a hold of the rifles . . ." Rackham said tersely.

"They'll blow holes through the hull," Finn said, finishing the thought. "They have a lot less to lose than the rest of you." He eyed Haller, who was checking his spur as he headed out. "Hey. We need weapons."

"How do I know you're not involved in this somehow?"

"He's never even met those serfs," Edie pointed out.

Haller hesitated, self-consciously fiddling with the spur on his arm, no doubt considering the pros and cons of letting Finn roam the ship armed versus letting Edie roam the ship without adequate protection.

"Fine." Haller went to a locker near the hatch, thumbed it open, and pulled out a spur. Just one. He tossed it to Finn.

"What about e-shields?"

"Unfortunately, we store them in the landing skiffs, ready

for dirtside missions." He pointed at Edie, his face drawn. "Take the main route to the engine room and get the sensors up to speed. We need to be able to track those lags." As his gaze rested on Finn again, his lips tightened. If he'd planned to throw any order Finn's way, he changed his mind and settled for less. "I'll be taking that spur back and counting the rounds when this is over." He left the room.

Finn slipped on the spur and checked it. "You ready?" Edie nodded numbly. "Okay. Let's go."

"Wait. Finn." She had to ask. "Was this . . . *Did* you have anything to do with this?"

He glanced over his shoulder from the doorway. "No."

"I thought maybe it was another plot to escape or—"

"No."

No elaboration, no explanation. She believed him.

They moved cautiously through the common room on deck one and climbed down to deck two using the aft access ladders. Emergency shafts ran around the inside of the hull, and it was more likely the escaped serfs would use those to get around than the open routes. Edie and Finn didn't want to meet up with the escapees—that was Haller's intention, not theirs.

Deck two was freezing cold and in total darkness. Edie walked into the void, touching the striplight at various points without result. Enviros were screwed up here. Finn went halfway down the next ladder to check below.

"Stay close."

He was alert but calm, and she was surprised at feeling absolutely certain he could protect her. She hadn't felt that way since Lukas. Whatever Cat thought about the Saeth, Edie was glad to have an ex-Saeth on her side right now.

I won't let you out of my sight. Lukas used to say those words to Bethany, and never forgave himself for breaking his promise. Then he said the same thing to Edie, and had kept that promise scrupulously until the Crib forced him to break it and made him disappear.

In the eerie, icy dark, she started expecting serfs to jump out of hatches and access covers. Backing up closer to the ladder, she waited for Finn's all-clear.

Something flickered at the far end of the corridor. She gasped—and then felt stupid as Finn darted up from the ladder well to see what the problem was.

She waved him down. "There's nothing there." It was a striplight on the blink.

"Get back against the bulkhead," he hissed. His head and shoulders were above the level of the deck, his spur aimed into the dark.

A shadow crossed the struggling striplight. Finn sprang into action, jumping onto the deck in a fluid, silent motion. He pushed Edie firmly behind him. She held her breath, flattened against the bulkhead, the length of her arm and thigh pressed against his side, the heat of his body soaking through her. She felt helpless and light, unanchored in the darkness and in danger of floating away. The solidity of his muscular frame pulled her away from the emptiness. His self-assuredness helped to ground her, but he wasn't bullet-proof. And she was unarmed.

"Move into the light," Finn said, not loudly, but with enough force to carry his voice down the corridor.

Another dart of movement as someone shot out of the infirmary. Then a thin voice quivered down the corridor. "Don't shoot!"

Edie almost laughed with relief. "It's Kristos."

"Jezus." Finn lowered his weapon, but when she started forward he crossed an arm over her to hold her back.

"You're supposed to be in the armory," she called out to Kristos.

"No fuckin' way!" Kristos sounded both scared and petulant. Edie's eyes were getting used to the dark now, and she could see him edging his way up the corridor, casting fearful glances to the forward ladder well he'd climbed. "There's three serfs loose, did you know? I didn't hear any orders. I didn't hear."

The kid was lying, but in his current state he wasn't going to be much use in any case.

Finn must have realized the same thing. "Stay on this deck," he said. "Stay away from the skiffs and the emergency shafts. You got that?"

"I got it." Kristos slapped open one of the hatches—his quarters. "I'm not coming out till it's over." He slipped inside and locked the hatch behind him.

"Tough guy," Finn muttered. "Come on."

They went down to deck three, which was in better shape. The striplights were running on standby and enviros maintained a reasonable temperature. Instead of continuing down to the engine room, Finn hesitated in the shadows.

Edie drew an unsteady breath, wondering what he was planning. "We're supposed to—"

Finn held up a finger to silence her. He was watching the armory, forty meters down the corridor. Haller and Zeke emerged, talking in low urgent voices. The two men climbed up to deck two without noticing them.

"Armory first," Finn said. "Stay close."

She followed. Now was not the time to wonder how Haller would react to Finn's insubordination.

Her commlink buzzed and Haller spoke over an open line to all crew. "They got to the armory. Toms must've been burning the locks for a while, so it was open by the time they got there." He sounded breathy from adrenaline and simmering panic. "They took the rifles—all five. They can't be shooting those inside the ship. And there's a couple of spurs missing."

"Did they leave anything for me?" Edie asked dryly.

"You're better off unarmed," Haller said. "If any of these lags has a humane thought left in his head, he'll be less likely to shoot an unarmed girl."

She wasn't convinced, considering the way serf handlers prided themselves on dehumanizing men. And she didn't want to think about what they might do instead of shooting her.

"We're now in the port emergency shaft, both of us,"

Haller continued. "I sent the engineers into the starboard shaft in case the lags double back."

"And where the hell is Kristos?" Zeke called from somewhere in the background.

"Uh, haven't seen him." Edie wondered if Kristos would have his pay docked for blatant disobedience. But right now they had other things to worry about.

"Listen," Haller said, "we've got nothing but spurs. Can't risk provoking a gunfight anywhere near the hull with those rifles. We're sitting tight until you get those sensors back online, teckie. They don't have boundary chips so they might head for the skiffs—even the lifepods if they have outside help coming. I need to know where they're going so we can cut them off. Vent them if we have to."

Shit. Haller was scared, and that scared Edie. She glanced at Finn as they reached the armory hatch. His expression was hard as he toed aside a dead tom before hauling open the hatch. The lock was a smoldering mess. Half a dozen toms lay scattered on the deck around the hatch, all of them belly-up, inactive.

"You reached the engine room yet?" Haller asked.

"Almost," she lied. "I'll let you know when sensors are back, sir."

She signed off and grabbed the spur that Finn handed her off the rack. He strapped a second weapon to his left forearm and hooked on a spare clip.

They jogged back to the ladder well and climbed below-deck. Forward was the cellblock, still housing the three remaining serfs. The bolt on the outer hatch hung at an odd angle, looking like it had been chewed through.

The aft hatch took them into the control booth of the engine room. A plaz window filled the far wall, overlooking the expansive engine pit. Down each side of the pit ran a raised catwalk, accessed from doors on either side of the control booth. Edie gazed out over the pit. She knew enough about engine teck to recognize the fusion reactor—a series of four-meter-tall laser rings lined up like skinny donuts, glittering with ice crystals, with the fuel containment chamber running through the center. Behind the fusion reactor, suspended in a web of girders, was the I/M converter mass—a matte-black ball big enough to entirely fill the *Hoi*'s gym.

A gentle whirring sound came from the magnetic fields that spun the plasma fuel, piped in from external tanks. For all that intimidating machinery, the room was surprisingly quiet.

While Finn guarded the hatch, Edie sat cross-legged on the deck and pressed her fingers to the dataport on the control desk. Many of the maintenance systems were centralized here, and it was her best bet for eliminating the confusing blips so that the sensors could be trusted. Shutting down the toms' access ports was the logical starting point, so that no more blips could be released. Without instructions, the toms would end up wandering aimlessly once their regular schedules were done, but they were harmless enough in that condition. Next, she coded a sniffer and set it loose throughout the system to tag the existing blips. Then she sent a patcher to chase it. The disharmonious blips were nudged back into place, restoring the melody, note-perfect.

"Can you do anything useful in there?" Finn asked.

"I've destroyed the blips, so the sensors should read right. I'm rebooting now to—"

"That's not what I meant."

She threw him a look over her shoulder. He was talking about the future, about an escape plan after the mission. "Okay. I've been thinking about it, about how to get into the more secure areas. If I could get access to navigation . . ."

"Would you know what to do if you had that access?"

Edie shook her head with a grimace. "Enviros, then. If we control their air, we can threaten them. Force them to let us go."

"The thing about threats is, you'd better be prepared to follow through." Finn squatted on the floor beside her. His voice was low, intense. "You'd better have nothing to lose."

She had something to lose—someone. Given the chance, Haller wouldn't hesitate to counter her threat by threatening Finn's life.

"What else can I do? We have nothing over them."

"Can you access external comms?"

"To send a message? Where?"

"What about that CIP patrol ship?"

Edie's heart missed a beat and her face flushed with anger. "No. I'm not going back to the Crib." Back to being a pawn in their game of galactic imperialism.

It disturbed her that, not for the first time, Finn thought he might be better off with the Crib than with rovers. He must have seen the determination in her eyes, heard it in her voice, felt it through the link, because he backed down.

"At least find a way to keep that option available. Jam open your access to comms so we can use it later if we find someone who can help us. Can you do that?"

She nodded, returning to the datastream. Working quickly—she couldn't stall Haller forever, and they were, after all, in real danger from three armed serfs on the loose—she tracked down the external comms and coded a link between it and internal comms. The link would allow her to access an external line even after Haller revoked her security privilege. It wasn't perfect. A leak between security levels wasn't something that would go unnoticed for long, but unless someone was looking for it they'd be unlikely to find it. It might hold until they reached the Fringe.

Just as she finished, the console beeped, its reboot complete. The reboot had cleared any remaining echoes of the damage, and she called up the sensor readings again.

"It's done. Best I can do anyway," she told Finn.

"Good."

He stood and pulled her to her feet so she could check the holoviz. She thumbed her comm. "Haller, sensors are up."

"About bloody time. Where are the serfs?" Haller's panic

was lessened now that he was no longer blind. Without rifles, however, he was still effectively declawed.

Finn examined the holo with her. The sensors picked up the body heat of everyone on the ship and relayed their locations to the holo, along with the commclip ID of those who wore them—herself and Finn in the control booth, Kristos in his quarters, the captain and Cat on the bridge. The three serfs still in captivity showed up as unlabeled splotches in the hold.

"Who's that?" Edie pointed to a glowing shape in a stateroom near Kristos's.

"That would be the cook, in her quarters," Finn said.

She mentally chastised herself for forgetting Gia. "Okay. And these are our four guys in the emergency shafts." Their heat signatures were indistinct, the ID labels fading in and out because the sensors were on the other side of the bulkhead, not in the shafts.

"You ready to give me my options yet?" came Haller's voice.

"Where are they?" Edie whispered, going over the layout again. The serfs were flesh and blood with beating hearts and body heat—they had to show up. "I don't see them," she told Haller, and was rewarded with an impatient growl.

"Any chance they're no longer on board?" Finn said.

She checked the security logs on the skiffs. Both were docked and secured, as were all six lifepods, and she reported this to Haller.

"Maybe they're stone cold dead," Zeke quipped.

"They escaped maybe thirty minutes ago, at most," Edie said. "If something killed them they'd still be warm."

"Yeah, but it'd solve all our problems," he grumbled. He must be feeling particularly peeved about the escape, since the serfs were his responsibility.

"You sure you fixed those blips, teckie?" Haller said. "Maybe a skiff launched and they've left a false log."

"No, the skiffs are there. I'm sure of it." Wiping the errors was a simple patch, and there wasn't a chance she hadn't recognized a deeper problem.

Nevertheless, she heard Haller ordering the engineers to Beta skiff. They could eyeball it from the emergency shaft without exposing themselves in case the serfs were there. She could see from the holo that he and Zeke were going to Alpha skiff. The lifepods were a less likely target for the serfs, as they couldn't get far in them.

Edie checked over the sensor readings again. "Where could they be hiding?"

Finn stared out the plaz window, at the engine. "What's the air temp around the I/M mass?"

"Cold enough to frost up the room, but that shouldn't affect the sensors."

"Yeah, but it sucks up the heat from the fusion reactor, right? It's a heat sink." He squinted across the fusion rings to the girders housing the black ball. "So there has to be a hot zone out there somewhere."

Edie's breath caught as she zoomed in on the sensor readout for the engine room. Finn was right. The sensors showed the rippling colors of heat gradients—below freezing throughout most of the room, colder still where the I/M mass was located, and a river of heat streaming into the I/M mass from the fusion reactor.

She examined the readout for any signs of uneven heat distribution.

"There." Finn pointed at the holo. Tiny flickers wavered in and out of view near the I/M mass. Three men hiding out in the zone that was invisible to sensors and had a tolerable temperature.

"I'll tell Haller." She reached for the comm switch on the control desk, wondering how the hell the XO would resolve this. If the rifles were dangerous near the hull, then surely they would be catastrophic in here.

Finn stayed her hand. "He'll kill them. Is that what you want?"

"Of course not."

Finn looked out again, eyes narrowed. Then he stripped off both spurs and walked to the door at the side of the booth.

"What are you—?"

"Don't call Haller."

He went out onto the catwalk.

CHAPTER 16

Edie was too stunned to call after him. Through the window she watched Finn walk away, his hands open and empty. One of the serfs came out from his hiding place among the girders, rifle pointed at Finn's chest. Edie wiped sweaty palms against her thighs, her throat constricting.

She needed to calm down. It would help Finn far more if she could squash her emotions, leaving him with a clear head.

From what she could see, the serf was middle-aged and wiry. He was dirty enough to make her wonder if he'd crawled through access tubes to reach the engine room. Perhaps the escapees were unaware that the crew's firepower was so inferior to theirs, and had decided to hide until they could make a run for a skiff.

The serf's hands shook, either from fear or desperation. Edie glanced at the comm switch on the control desk, every instinct telling her to call for help, but Finn had told her not to. She had to trust that he knew what he was doing.

"I'm unarmed," Finn said, loud enough for her to hear through the window. He stopped twenty meters from the man, his breath misting in the freezing air. Edie could make out two more serfs hovering in the shadows. "If you're trying to get off the ship, you went the wrong way."

"They sent you to talk to us?" the serf sneered. "A lag? Or are you one of them now?"

"They don't know you're here yet. I came to help."

The man's rifle dropped slightly. If there was anyone on the ship he might listen to, Edie hoped it would be a fellow serf.

Finn took a few more steps, stopped again. Now he was too far away for her to hear his words, but the rifle gradually sagged lower and lower, and the other two came out of hiding to listen. They were much younger. If all three attacked Finn, even without weapons, he'd be in trouble. Then again, he'd handled himself well with the eco-rads . . .

Haller buzzed her comm, startling her.

"The skiffs are docked. I'm adding extra security loops to prevent them being stolen. Engineers are checking the lifepods. Anything to report on your end?"

"No, sir. Still searching." Her answer came reflexively. Whatever happened out there, it would only be made worse if Haller knew about it.

"Let me know as soon as you've got a trace."

He signed off, and she took a deep breath. She couldn't stall him forever. Eventually the engineers would return and see for themselves what was going on.

One of the serfs was talking to the other, gesturing wildly, and Edie hoped he was persuading him to listen to Finn, to surrender. But his young friend shook his head and hefted his rifle over his shoulder. He grabbed a second rifle from the older man and started up the catwalk, pushing past Finn. For a terrifying moment Edie thought he was going to walk all the way back to the control booth. But he reached an access panel, kicked it open, and disappeared inside.

Finn glanced up at Edie, then turned back to the two remaining serfs. More words were exchanged—it appeared as if Finn was trying to persuade them to give up their weapons. They clung to the rifles, shivering in the cold. But whatever else Finn was saying, they were listening.

A minute later, Finn was back with her in the control booth.

"Did they surrender?" she asked.

"No, but they will. They're thinking about it."

"What did you say to them?"

"Told them this wasn't the right time. That they'd get themselves killed. Until we reach the Fringe, they've no chance of survival off the ship."

"What about the other one?"

"Well, that's the stupid one. Claims he knows how to fly—he's going to make a run for it, the idiot. He *will* get himself killed."

"If he's heading for the skiff, we have to warn Haller." She didn't want an ambush on her conscience.

Finn hesitated for only a moment, then nodded. With relief she punched the comm.

"Sir, we've found them. One's crawling through the portside access tube, on his way to the skiff, armed with two rifles." Edie checked the sensor readout. "He's about a hundred meters from you, moving fairly slowly. Two are holed up in the engine room."

"Are they armed?"

"Yes, but it looks like they'll surrender. Finn talked them down."

"You said portside? That's Alpha skiff. I'm still here with Zeke. You need to stop that lag before he reaches us."

"How?"

"I don't care!" Haller's voice rose again. "We can't defend ourselves here, not against rifles. Turn off enviros in the tube, overheat it—"

"I don't have that sort of fine control," Edie said, searching for options. "Wait, I have an idea. Stand by."

She jacked into the infirmary on deck two, holding up her hand to silence Finn when he opened his mouth to question her. They watched the holo as five red dots raced out of the infirmary, tumbled down two ladder wells, and skittered over to the portside access tube, meters from the skiff's airlock.

"Those are toms?" Finn asked after a moment.

"More precisely, med toms. Armed with tranqs."

He gave her a crooked grin that she decided to interpret as respect for her brilliant plan. She told Haller what she'd done, and they waited a couple more minutes until the red dots converged on the heat signature from the serf. Within a few seconds he stopped moving.

"I think he's down," Edie reported.

"Damn right!" came Zeke's exuberant voice. "He just rolled out of an access hatch at my feet. Nice to know some of these toms are still on our side."

It was over. She could finally relax. The two men in the engine room huddled on the catwalk awaiting their fate, rifles discarded. They made for a pitiable sight.

A warning klaxon went off.

Both serfs shot to their feet, looking up, and Edie followed their gaze. White speckles drifted down on the men's faces.

The bulkhead over the serfs' heads exploded, and a torrent of white foam gushed into the engine room, covering them from head to toe and blanketing the fusion rings.

Edie stood rooted to the spot by the absurd display on the other side of the window. "What the hell is that? Is there a fire?"

Finn leaned over to punch the comm. "Haller! What the hell are you doing?" There was no answer.

She caught the note of panic in Finn's voice. "What's going on?"

"He's venting the engine room."

In disbelief she stared at the white froth rapidly filling up the vast space around the engine. "But why all the foam?"

"You vent when the engine overheats. The foam sucks up the heat and gets ejected. Haller must've tripped the foam to force the room to vent."

Fear for the serfs pushed Edie into action again. She

pressed her fingers into the dataport of the control desk and accessed the engine room emergency protocols. They told her the vents would open in twenty seconds. The override screamed its demand for authorization, which she didn't have. Haller had already revoked her security privileges.

"We have to get them out." She was at the door and onto the catwalk before Finn could stop her. "Get out of there!" she yelled into the whirling whiteness, hoping she could be heard over the klaxon. "Back to the control booth!"

Powerful arms reached around her and pulled her backward. Instinctively she struggled against Finn, still screaming a warning to the serfs now lost in the thick foam.

An indistinct shape staggered along the platform, meters away. The older man plunged through the foam, choking, blindly grasping for the railings.

"Go back!" Finn bellowed in Edie's ear. He pushed her against the door and moved toward the serf.

She couldn't breathe. Blinking stinging suds from her eyes, she looked toward the far bulkhead where rows of slats were tilting open, drawing chaotic streams of foam through them.

Beyond that, empty space.

Finn had the man by the shoulders and half dragged, half supported him to the door, clutching the railing with his other hand. Edie grabbed the doorframe to keep her balance, trying to drag the dwindling supply of air into her lungs. The pressure inside her ears built painfully.

She helped push the serf inside the control booth. By the time the door snapped shut, her limbs were so leaden she could barely stand. Still, she pulled herself up on the control desk, choking the foam out of her lungs, and watched through the window as the foam shot out into space.

Seconds later, the engine room was clear. The klaxon cut out abruptly and the vents closed.

There was no sign of the other serf, or of the rifles or anything else that hadn't been bolted down.

Edie sucked in air, still spluttering. Her clothes felt sticky and wet. She wanted to shout her outrage but had no voice. Finn sat beside the man he'd rescued, who had collapsed on the deck and lay coughing and retching—but alive.

She hit the comm switch. "Haller." Her voice came out as a croak. "I told you they surrendered."

There was a brief pause before he answered. "You told me they were still armed. Are they both spaced?"

The image of a nameless young man tumbling through the void speared her mind. "We saved one."

"I thought you said they were armed!" He was accusing, angry. "Forget it. I'll send Zeke to fetch him. Get back to your quarters."

A minor serf rebellion, a dead man, two no doubt facing severe discipline. But it was over for Haller, simple as that.

"Did we lose the other three rifles?" Haller asked.

"Yes."

Haller swore and cut the link.

CHAPTER 17

"Damn labor-gang activists, that's who it was." Zeke dropped a dead tom at Edie's feet, his usually soft brown eyes fired with anger. "Probably a dockworker. They smuggled one bloody tom on board with our supplies, and ended up killing a serf instead of freeing any."

Edie didn't point out that it was Haller who had killed the man. His death, and the fate of the other two escapees, weighed heavily on her mind.

"Did the serfs know about it beforehand?"

"I don't think so. Looks like the idea was just to cause mayhem and give them a chance to mutiny. Idiotic plan. Those activists are as shortsighted as the eco-rads. Ranting on about forced labor, completely disowning any responsibility for setting free hardened crims."

She'd never seen him in such a foul mood. The tension on the ship had been rising all day, with the Crib Interstellar Patrol vessel following them through the last jump and still tailing them at a distance. Haller was short-tempered, Zeke yelled at Kristos for the slightest mistake, and even Cat had stopped smiling.

"Did you want me to take a look at the tom?" she said, in the hope of appeasing Zeke.

"Waste of time. We know it was this one. The kid spent all afternoon tracking it down."

She didn't envy the young teck that job. Kristos now sat in the corner of the hold wiping and rebooting every tom on the ship. The toms clustered around him like eager children waiting their turn. A simple master program would achieve the same result, but making Kristos do it manually was his punishment for hiding out in his quarters while the serfs were loose. This, along with Zeke's scolding, had left him subdued.

Finn, meanwhile, had barely spoken a word to her since the death of the man in the engine room, and she worried that the events of the previous night had given him second thoughts about their plan to finish the mission. For now, though, he was being cooperative, helping a couple of serfs move all the illegal equipment into the skiff so it could be temporarily jettisoned if CIP boarded.

Edie followed Zeke through the hold to the cellblock, where he'd gathered the tools needed to fix the broken bolt.

"What happened to the other men who tried to escape?" She wasn't sure she wanted to know, but she hadn't seen them all day.

Zeke waved his hand dismissively. "Aw, don't worry about that. We dealt with them."

"What does that mean?" She glanced at the closed hatch leading to the lockdown cell—the railings Finn had been chained to a couple of days earlier had looked suspiciously like a flogging post.

"I'm the handler. I handled it. They'll be back on duty tomorrow." Zeke's tight voice, so different from his usual joviality, warned her to drop the subject.

She did so, and consoled herself with the fact that, if nothing else, at least the serf revolt had given her the chance to meddle with the *Hoi*'s comm systems. Not that she could think of a single soul on the outside to contact at this point.

"What about this CIP vessel? Are they after me?"

"Who knows? They finally made contact this afternoon,

demanding our manifest. Claiming we underpaid the tariff at the last jump gate."

"Can't you just pay up and get them off your back?"

"No, because they know that we know it's a bullshit excuse. If we cave in, they'll know we're covering for something else."

At the far end of the corridor, a flustered Haller jumped down the ladder and marched toward them.

"Are you reading my memos? Did you program those nanofinds?"

"Uh . . . nanofinds, sir?" She had no idea what memo he was talking about.

He glared at her, his color rising, and seemed to be waging an internal battle as to whether he should smack her. She was grateful that Zeke was right there and Finn was nearby.

"Read my fucking memos, Edie! If we can't avoid being boarded, you and that serf need to get to the skiff. We'll give you a shove into the jump node and you can hide out until it's over. We need nanofinds to wipe the *Hoi* clean. Get it done. Then report to the bridge. We might have a problem with the BRATs."

He stormed away.

Edie turned a questioning look on Zeke. "What's he talking about? He wants to dump us inside a jump node? In that tiny skiff?"

"If it comes to that." Zeke shrugged, as if it wasn't a big deal.

It was a very big deal to Edie. If the skiff needed a push from the *Hoi* to enter the node, it must mean there was no gate. And with no gate, the skiff would be stuck wherever it exited until the *Hoi* came back for it.

That sounded like a terrible idea.

"Isn't this illegal?" Finn's dry tone emphasized the irony of his question. Was anything these rovers did legal?

"Completely illegal. The primary use for nanofinds is to scrub a crime scene."

"But you've done it before?"

Edie shrugged. "It's biocyph. I figured out how to make them when I was a kid." They were in the infirmary, where she drew blood samples from them both and dropped them into the DNA sequencer. "Never made them before to wipe out all traces of my own existence."

Their med records had already been wiped. It was a strange feeling to scroll through the ship's logs and find herself erased. Even Haller's memo vanished as soon as she closed it. She scanned the system to find that he'd put a rather clumsy precoded worm into action an hour ago, presumably when the danger of being boarded had become too great to ignore.

Finn watched her working but fell silent again. He was hardly the most talkative person she knew, but today he'd seemed preoccupied with his thoughts.

"Are you thinking about that serf?" she said.

"I'm thinking about CIP."

"The ship out there?"

"Ever thought about turning yourself in?"

Her hand froze over the sequencer. "You can't be serious. Go back to the Crib? I've told you why I can't do that. Natesa, Project Ardra—"

"What about me?"

He was right. She had to consider what was best for him, too. But that was never going to be the Crib.

"After what Haller did—murdering that serf," he went on, "I believe you now. I believe he'll find a reason to kill me."

"Cat thinks otherwise. Listen, what Haller wants is to get through the mission with maximum profit. We're doing this for the creds. Our goal and his are the same. The Crib isn't the answer."

"It might be the only answer to deactivating the leash. Crib tecks are the best."

She couldn't argue that point, and they'd agreed from the start that the leash was their first priority. But the situation had changed. After witnessing the Fringers' misery first-hand, she'd lost any remaining faith in the Crib's integrity. They'd discard Finn even quicker than Haller would.

"What about afterward?" she said. "Even if they do cut the leash, you'll still be their slave and I'll still be Natesa's pawn. The Crib has nothing to offer us."

He inclined his head in a gesture of withdrawal from the discussion, but not exactly agreement with her argument. Edie didn't pursue it, didn't want to hear him come up with more reasons. He was simply wrong if he believed either of them had a chance of freedom in the hands of the Crib. His peculiar mood singed the air.

Using a standard wet-teck generator, she imprinted their DNA codes onto a matrix. A few minutes later she held between her fingers a vial of genetically engineered nanofinds to be distributed through the aircon. They would multiply rapidly, spread through the ship, and selectively target only the DNA for which they were primed—hers and Finn's. They would break down all traces of hair and dead skin cells they came across and then quietly self-destruct into unremarkable dust, to be mopped up by cleaner toms.

Edie was prohibited from the bridge, which made Haller's summons all the more unnerving. Her crew key failed to snap the hatch and she was about to hit Haller's callsign when he opened the hatch from the inside.

"That report you wrote," he said without preamble, leading her to a console at the rear of the bridge. Finn hung back and the bridge crew ignored him. "Because the BRATs were dead, you said, the Crib scout ship knocked out the satellite that the original mission left behind." He flicked on a holoviz, which displayed various projection lines on an image of Scarabaeus. Behind her, she was aware of Captain Rackham in conversation with Cat at the con, and one of the engies.

"That would be standard procedure. If the BRATs didn't germinate, they would've disabled the satellite to prevent its transmissions drawing the attention of rovers."

"But you don't know for sure?"

"No," she admitted. Her report contained a large amount of speculation that she'd presented as fact, based on her accumulated knowledge of standard CCU seeding procedures.

Haller's holoviz was starting to make sense now. An animated sim showed the satellite's projected tracking path and ground coverage arcs.

"Our advance probe is picking up transmissions that exactly overlay this pattern. That means the satellite is still functional."

"I guess so." What did he expect her to do about it? It wasn't her fault CCU had left a beacon behind. "Surely you have to deal with this problem all the time—isn't that what you rovers do? Hit and run. Disguise your ident transmissions within the system, do your dirty work and then disappear before CCU can respond to the satellites that detected your presence?"

"It's not detection I'm worried about. Yes, we can disguise our approach." He gave her a look that said he wasn't about to tell her how. "The satellite is receiving information from the BRATs."

"Okay, that's normal. There would be latent broadcasts from the surface regardless of whether the BRATs germinated."

"I'm not talking about weather reports and positional scans and security beacons." Haller's voice was tight, controlled, masking something very much like panic. "The satellite is picking up activity *within* the BRATs. Our probe sent back a preliminary reflection and it looks like nothing I've ever seen."

He flashed up the data packets. The content was Crib-encoded so he'd been unable to access it, but the packets contained far more information than could be accounted for by the housekeeping blips of dead BRATs.

Stunned, Edie could only murmur, "What's going on out there?"

"CIP is on the line," Cat said sharply from her console,

and Edie turned to catch the wary glance the navpilot threw in her direction.

"Off the bridge," Rackham snapped at Edie over his shoulder, sparing Finn a brief glare as well.

By the time they reached the hatch, everyone's attention was on the main holoviz. In a spur-of-the-moment decision, Edie ducked behind a console, pulling Finn with her. She needed to know whether CIP was after her, and she wasn't going to rely on Haller's secondhand report to find out.

"Put them on," Rackham said.

A young, square-jawed CIP official appeared on the holoviz.

"*Hoi Polloi*, this is CIP Inspection and Quarantine on the *Laoch*. One hour ago you were ordered to power down and prepare to be boarded."

"One hour ago," Rackham replied coolly, "you sent an illegal order to inspect our manifest. You've since provided no acceptable reason to delay us and no justification to inspect our holds, despite numerous requests from my crew. Your spurious excuses are unconvincing. This continued harassment is unwarranted, and I intend to take it up with your superiors once we return to the Central zone in a few weeks."

The young man didn't falter, reciting his orders like an automaton. "You are required to comply with all CIP requests for inspection."

"Cut the bull, young man. Those regulations apply within Crib Central space, which we left two days ago."

"You registered an incorrect mass at jump dock thirty-three AVID, within the Central zone. Therefore—"

"Therefore, you should have stopped us then. You missed your chance. Not that it matters, because we both know that there was nothing wrong with our mass or with the tariff we paid to traverse that node."

The CIP official set his jaw in frustration, and Rackham turned to Cat with a cutoff signal.

"Captain!"

They all spun back to the screen at the sound of a new

voice, and Edie suppressed a gasp. A familiar face now filled the screen.

"Captain Rackham," the woman said in the snide voice Edie knew so well.

"Who the hell are you?" Rackham barked.

"Liv Natesa. Crib Colonial Unit, Special Branch."

Edie crouched lower behind the console. There was no more pretending that this was a routine CIP inspection, although rovers must run into such trouble all the time. Natesa was on board the *Laoch*. It could only mean she suspected Edie was on the *Hoi*.

"Captain, I have the authority of Crib Central Intelligence behind me. You need to listen to me."

That got Rackham's attention. The bridge went quiet.

"Say your piece, Ms Natesa."

Edie had to give him credit for sounding entirely calm, something she'd never felt in Natesa's presence. She knew the woman too well. Natesa had a way of crushing all arguments, all obstacles that impeded her mission. She always won. Rackham just didn't know it yet.

"I have information that you may be harboring a criminal," Natesa said, "by the name of Edie Sha'nim."

A *criminal*? What was she talking about? Was she planning to accuse Edie of desertion? Or worse . . . of Ademo's murder? Edie saw her future with the Crib more clearly than ever. If Natesa threatened her with criminal charges, her choices would be Project Ardra or life in a prison camp.

And Finn's choices? None at all. He'd participated in her kidnapping, or desertion, or whatever Natesa planned to call it. As a serf, his status was below Natesa's threshold of humanity and his future was a swift execution. Even if Edie could plead his case, he was at the mercy of the leash. Natesa would never allow him to stay at her side. He would be discarded. There was no hope for him.

That realization set Edie's heart pounding. Going back to the Crib meant death for Finn.

Finn's breath ruffled the hair on the crown of her head as

he crouched behind her. He pressed against her, warm and solid, and closed his hand around her upper arm. With his lips against her ear he breathed, *Shhh*. She fought to calm herself.

"You will submit to an inspection so we can clear you of this allegation," Natesa continued. "Otherwise I'll be forced to impound your vessel immediately and arrest your crew to face serious charges."

"This is outrageous," Rackham blustered. "What's with the charade? How dare you trail us like a Priscian vulture with accusations about our manifest and tariffs, and now this nonsense about harboring a criminal. What are you going to think up next—our taillight is out?"

As Rackham's voice rose, Edie hoped he wouldn't lose his cool. The captain struck her as a man who always chose his words too carefully to say something stupid.

"I wouldn't dream of concerning myself with your taillight, Captain. From your ident I note you're a loyal Crib citizen like me. A decorated vet, no less. You've done your duty for the Crib. Now let me do mine."

Rackham started another protest, but Natesa simply spoke over him without even raising her voice.

"The *Laoch* is increasing speed to rendezvous with you in twelve minutes. Please hold course and we'll spare you the trouble of decelerating. I strongly recommend that you comply."

Natesa cut the connection. Edie sagged against Finn, intently aware of his protective touch. But there was no real safety in his arms. He couldn't protect her from Natesa's plans, and she certainly couldn't protect him.

She peeked out at the bridge, where Haller paced the deck. "We can still outrun them, can't we?" Haller said.

Cat gave an uncertain shrug as she checked her console. "We could make a dash for the jump node, but if they open fire—"

"We're not going to run." The bridge crew stared at Rackham. "We're a prospecting vessel for Stichting Corp, no more, no less. They may not have an entirely legal reason to search us, but if we don't comply we'll never hear the end of it. How far are we from the jump?"

"Six minutes at current speed," Cat reported.

Rackham spun on Haller. "Send the cypherteck to the skiff and we'll push her through the jump. We've got to get her and those rigs off the *Hoi*. Lancer, you mapped a course for the skiff?"

"Yes sir, did it yesterday."

"Are we close enough to give them a shove into the node?"

"With our bulk shielding the skiff from CIP sensors, we've got about four minutes to launch the skiff before they come within range to detect it."

"Four minutes. Go!" Rackham yelled.

Haller ran right past Edie and Finn, and ducked through the hatch. His boots clattered on the ramp as he descended to the deck below. Rackham continued barking orders at Cat and the engie Corky, giving Edie and Finn the opportunity to sneak out.

Haller's voice boomed over the shipwide comm. "Edie, where the hell are you? Get to Beta skiff immediately."

Edie hit his callsign on her comm. "We're on our way." The idea of being jettisoned into a jump node horrified her, but it was preferable to ending up in Natesa's hands, where Finn's life was worthless.

They ran the length of deck one, climbed down two decks, and doubled-back to find the floor hatch that led directly to the skiff's airlock. It was a shorter route than going via deck four's hatches. Finn jumped down, landing lightly, and caught her around the waist as she followed him and slid to the deck. They could hear Haller up the corridor yelling at Zeke, who in turn yelled at the serfs.

Haller's face flooded with relief when he saw that Edie had arrived. "Get in there. In a few minutes this place is going to be crawling with CIP drones, and you need to be *gone.* Skiff's on auto. Cat's patched through the flight specs, so you sit tight until we come back for you. Don't touch anything."

Edie and Finn stepped through the hatch as two serfs bolted out on Zeke's command. They'd been dragging in the last of the illegal equipment.

"Secure the inner hatch, then get up to the cockpit and strap in," Haller instructed as the outer hatch cycled shut in front of his nose, with him on the other side.

Edie turned to survey the hold—it was stuffed full of equipment, every piece of junk that could possibly incriminate the *Hoi*, as well as Zeke's treasures that he probably didn't have the proper paperwork for. The sharp edge of Zeke's booster scraped her shin.

"You guys ready to go?" It was Cat on the comm.

Edie went over to the comm panel and answered, her voice unsteady. "Yes, we're set."

The events of the last few minutes were slowly sinking in. They were about to be launched into a jump node with no means of getting themselves back out. And Natesa was out there, bearing down on her, determined to bring her home. And calling her a criminal.

Perhaps Natesa was making it all up as a ruse to get aboard the *Hoi*. But Edie had known the woman since she was ten years old. Natesa had the power to carry through those charges—frame Edie for desertion and accessory to murder, or at the very least blackmail her with the threat of prosecution.

Returning to the Crib was completely out of the question, and seeing Natesa's face again, hearing her voice, only heightened Edie's resolve. She could never go back. *Never.*

CHAPTER 18

Edie's knees gave way and she sat down on the booster casing. Her heartbeat was starting to return to normal after the frantic rush belowdeck, but her mind still whirred. She looked up to see Finn standing in front of the inner hatch, facing her.

"We have ninety seconds before the *Laoch*'s close enough to detect your launch," came Cat's voice. "You better get that airlock sealed."

Edie was about to tell Cat it was sealed when she noticed the gap between the two halves of the hatch. Her eyes followed the line of the gap down to the deck, behind Finn's boots. He had wedged a piece of pipe there, to chock open the door.

She rose to her feet in disbelief. "Finn . . . what are you doing?"

"Rescuing you."

She stared at him. So he was taking control now. He was going to ruin everything.

"Listen to me, Finn. We can't go back."

He stood there, resolute, arms crossed, blocking the hatch. There was no point even trying to get past him to free the doors herself.

"They'll kill you."

"Or make me a hero for saving you."

Edie sighed shakily. "Trust me on this one thing, Finn. They'll kill you. Natesa will see to it, just to spite me. They'll separate us and let you die."

Her words had no impact. When he spoke again, his tone was eerily bemused.

"Go ahead and jolt me. You can end it that easily."

What was he up to?

Haller started screaming Edie's name over the comm. The telltales flashed—he wanted visual engaged so he could see what was going on. He must be back on the bridge already. Edie ignored him and stared at Finn.

"Oh, that's right," Finn drawled. "You swore never to jolt me again."

And then she knew his game. He didn't care if the Crib captured them or not. It was irrelevant. He wanted to see what she would do, whether she would break her promise.

Whether he could trust her.

"What's going on down there?"

Edie slammed her palm down on the comm panel and Haller's enraged face came into focus on the holoviz.

"The hatch is jammed, sir." She felt strangely calm. "Safety override is preventing the skiff detaching."

"You better fix the problem, young lady. You've got thirty seconds before that patrol ship comes into range. If they detect the launch, you are history."

We all are history, she mentally corrected him. She glanced up at Finn, who had not moved. "Finn's working on it."

It was a full ten seconds later that Finn's expression finally changed as he realized she wasn't going to trigger the jolt. With a crooked smile, he turned to shoulder the hatch a fraction wider, kicked the pipe out of the way, and let the doors snap shut.

Haller's readouts informed him that the skiff was secure and a wave of relief crossed his face.

"Detaching."

He wasted no more words and cut the connection. A slight and momentary shift in the grav field was the only indication they had broken free.

Finn was already heading up the ramp to the cockpit. Too exhausted to follow him, Edie slumped on a crate and squeezed her hands into fists as the pain of his mistrust welled up inside her. After all they'd been through, he still needed to test her, to make sure of her, to take her to the brink of despair and force her to put her freedom in his hands.

Seconds later, Finn's voice on the comm spurred her into action again.

"You better grab on to something. We're entering the node."

Edie jumped up and looked for a handhold. "How long?"

She didn't have to wait for an answer. The skiff lurched and shuddered, and half a dozen untethered items, including Edie, lifted off the deck and sailed meters through the air in various directions before tumbling down as the grav field stabilized again. Edie crashed into the bulkhead halfway up the wall, hitting her left shoulder hard. She slid down to the deck and landed in a heap, winded. There was a moment's panic as she tried to drag in a breath, and then a sharp pain shot down her arm as her expanding lungs pressed against her injured shoulder joint.

"You okay?" Finn, over the comm.

Edie moaned in response, gathered herself up and stumbled over the booster, now lying on its side. Zeke would be furious if that was damaged. In their hurry, the serfs hadn't had time to secure everything to the deck. Part of her hoped that something really important had been smashed beyond repair.

Finn took two steps down the cockpit ramp to look into the hold and check she was on her feet. The fact that she was staggering about didn't seem to worry him, as long as she was alive and mobile. He beckoned her up and returned to the cockpit.

Edie kicked a couple of crates in frustration as she crossed the deck. She went up the ramp and into cockpit, wincing as she rubbed her shoulder. The viewscreen was closed, so there was nothing to see but the blinking colors of the holoviz readouts. Finn turned in the pilot's chair.

"Anything broken?"

She scowled and slumped into the seat beside him, wondering if he was referring to her bones or the equipment in the hold. "What happened?"

"Ship this size, with no nav guidance locked on—the systems don't cope too well with the node horizon."

"What do you mean, no nav guidance?"

"The skiff isn't supposed to jump at all. Doesn't have the mass. The *Hoi* gave us a push and lent us a few seconds of nav guidance to stop us crashing into the horizon." Finn checked the controls as he spoke, frowning at some of the displays and scrutinizing others more intently. She couldn't tell if he was confused by the readouts or concentrating on analyzing the cryptic information.

"You know how to fly this thing?"

"Nope. You?"

She shook her head.

"Wouldn't that be ironic," he mused. "They give us a ship, emergency rations, and a hold packed with gigacreds worth of equipment . . . If we knew how to steer this boat, we'd be home-free."

"But you said the skiff isn't capable of jumping by itself."

"Not when there's no jump gate. But we could exit the node at a mapped point, somewhere near a system or a commercial route, get ourselves picked up, trade the junk down below for passage. Hell, that stuff would pay the galaxy's top teckie ten times over to cut this leash."

"Nice fantasy." Edie tried to get comfortable in the seat, but every move was rewarded by a sharp pain knifing through her shoulder. "Anyway, we're on autopilot so there's nothing we can do, even if we did know how to navigate."

"You could disable that in a flash." He grinned at her. "I

hear you're good with that sort of thing. Not that it matters if we don't have a pilot."

"Exactly." She didn't appreciate his good humor, his attempt to put the incident down below behind them. "Would you really have let the Crib catch us?"

"Would you really have jolted me?"

"No! You're the one who backed down. I didn't jolt you."

"And I didn't get us caught."

"Then what exactly was that stunt all about?"

He turned serious. "I wanted to see if you would."

"I promised that I wouldn't."

He shrugged that off. "Just words."

"I just put my entire future in your hands by keeping that promise. Do you believe me now?" She'd meant to sound accusatory, even indignant, but the effect was spoiled when her voice came out choked with emotion.

"Yes."

His simple answer flooded her with relief, but it wasn't enough to wash away her disappointment at the way he'd chosen to test her. He watched her rubbing her swelling shoulder joint. He must be deliberately concealing how her pain was transmitting through the leash, but his face registered a faint look of concern. Far too understated for the agony she was suffering, in her opinion.

Finally, he said, "You injured something?"

"Don't know. Hurts like hell."

"Must be a medkit around here somewhere." He spoke offhandedly, turning back to the console. "Try the lockers down there."

Edie dragged herself out of the seat and used her good arm to pull open the hatches that covered well-lockers under the deck, one by one, angrily slamming them back down again. She blinked away tears, furious with herself for getting hurt, furious with Finn for not caring.

Each locker was three meters deep with a ladder down one wall, and contained crates of rations, various tools, and EVA suits dangling off their racks like deflated life-sized dolls.

She found a large medkit and hauled it up onto the deck. The case opened out to reveal the usual first aid equipment, mostly geared toward stopping bleeding, restarting hearts, and opening airways—not useful right now. There was a portable imager that would give her an internal view of her shoulder, but she couldn't even find the on switch. She found the manual and started to scroll through it before coming to the conclusion that she'd rather suffer the pain than take a crash course in diagnostic anatomy.

Finn crouched on the floor in front of her, having finished whatever it was he was doing at the flight console.

"Take off your jacket." He was already firing up the imager without so much as glancing at the manual. And his voice was softer now, no hint of derision.

She attempted to comply, but couldn't move her injured shoulder far enough to get either arm out of its sleeve. Finn helped pull the jacket off and she bit down on a cry, making him wince in sympathy. He examined her shoulder briefly through her tee by probing with his fingers, efficient and surprisingly gentle, backing off when she gasped in pain.

"Do you know what you're doing?"

"Raise your arm. Rotate it."

She could do neither very successfully and her shoulder was on fire. Finn scowled and shook his head as if to clear his mind of the signals of discomfort her brain was sending him.

"I have to admit," she said, "it makes me feel better to know you're suffering along with me."

"Not for much longer."

Finn smiled, amused. So, her attempt to play the tough guy wasn't very convincing. Watching the curve of his lips, she found the pain suddenly worthwhile.

He produced a spike from the kit and gave her a shot in the neck. Edie relaxed against the bulkhead as the drug coursed through her system, washing away the pain. Something her doctor at Crai Institute once told her drifted through her mind . . . something about certain drugs not mixing well with her neuroxin-dependent biochemistry. She decided he was very, very wrong about that.

"Let's take a look."

Finn pressed the imager against her shoulder blade for a minute or so, allowing the scan to run its cycle. The holoviz projected an interesting view of her joint and muscles and blood vessels, but it meant little to Edie. She was feeling so peaceful and relaxed that a diagnosis of imminent death wouldn't have fazed her. Finn watched the holo, too, but unlike his puzzling over the flight controls, he showed neither confusion nor interest in this readout. He simply took in the information.

"You do know what you're doing," she murmured as consciousness began to fray.

After a long pause, in which his eyes remained fixed on the readouts, he responded. "Trained as a field medic."

"Oh. The way you handle Zeke's rigs, I thought maybe you were a meckie."

He gave a shrug but didn't answer. Why did he have to be so damned elusive about everything? He ran the scan through the autodiagnostic program and then rummaged around in the first aid kit.

"Medic, meckie . . . you're a smart man, Finn. How'd a guy like you end up a serf in the Catacombs? Did you do something bad after they caught you?"

"You tore your supraspinatus."

"My what?"

"It's a muscle in your shoulder."

"Sounds serious."

"It's not. It's a very small tear."

He produced a prepackaged spike and injected it into the site of the injury. Dulled by the first spike, the pain was nevertheless severe enough to push the air out of her lungs in a groaned curse. Then the pain quickly fizzled out.

"What was that?"

"Synthetic matrix to speed up the repair of the muscle

fibers. By tomorrow you'll have most of your range of movement back." He cracked open a packet of straps. "You need
to take that top off."

She grinned. Couldn't help herself. "I bet you say that to
all the girls."

His head ducked as he concentrated on unrolling the supplies, but she caught his smile. She let him unzip her tee and
ease it off her left shoulder. Instinctively, she drew the other
half of the garment across her chest for modesty, though she
didn't really care what he saw. Didn't care about anything
anymore, although she wished he would meet her eyes. He
was examining the shell between her collarbones while his
hands unraveled the straps. The turquoise shimmer reflected
in his dark eyes.

He really was looking rather longer than he should.

"That's not very professional," she whispered, and his eyes
flicked to hers with a gleam of something she'd never seen
before. Something inappropriate. Playful desire? So hard
to tell with this man, and whatever it was, it was quickly
doused.

He began strapping her shoulder, and her brow furrowed
as she considered the mystery of who he really was.

"Will you tell me why you're still a serf? Why didn't they
send you home after the war? Were you an assassin?"

He barked a laugh. "A what?"

"Cat said the Saeth were assassins who messed things up
for everyone."

"Cat's parroting the Crib line."

"Tell me the truth, then."

"Some other time."

He pulled firmly on the strap and tied it off. He was so
close, she could reach out and touch the scar on his throat.
Didn't realize she'd done so until it was too late.

"What about this? Tell me why they snagged you."

"Tell me why the first thing you did was take it off."

"To win you over."

"There's more to it than that."

"No, there's no more." She frowned, thinking he was right, there must be something more, and while she struggled to control her thoughts she watched her fingers move up his neck, over the sharp angle of his jaw. Felt the roughness of his cheek and the smoothness of his lips. "I like the sound . . ." She couldn't tell if she was speaking out loud. Her tongue felt thick and lazy, and the words didn't come out right. "I like the sound of your voice."

He captured her hand in his. "I think we'll ease up on the painkillers next time, okay?"

She nodded, which made her feel even woozier, and closed her eyes. She was almost gone. Finn got to his feet, pulling her up against the unyielding pillar of his body, and even though she desperately wanted to sleep, she could have stood there forever, supported against him, clinging to the hard ridge of his biceps, soaking up his heat. She heard the soft whirr of a servo as he opened out the two seats at the rear of the cockpit to form a bunk.

Next thing she knew, she was horizontal, and it must have been some time later because she was cozy under a blanket yet didn't remember how it got there, and Finn was back at the console, turned away from her. He had opened the shutters over the large viewscreen. Cascading torrents of glowing strings twisted and curled out of the void to envelop their small ship.

Nodespace. It was beautiful. Serene in its monotony, and terrifying.

There was no sense they were hurtling forward, and maybe in nodespace there was no such thing. More like tumbling out of control within an endless mesh of gnarled fingers of light. It reminded her of Captain Rackham's grotesque artwork—reaching out to grab her, stroke her, catch and release her only to let her tumble down again.

She closed her eyes to the view, closed all her senses, and let the comforting arms of sleep drag her back under.

CHAPTER 19

Sirens. Lukas pitches forward through the hatch, clutching his chest. A faceless man kicks him aside.

She takes a faltering step toward Lukas, but the man points his spur at her head.

Eco-rads. On the ship. But rads have principles, don't they? They only kill the cypherteck, the heart of the mission. They're not supposed to kill Lukas.

"Don't be an idiot," Lukas says through a mouthful of blood. "She's not the one you want. Look at her! She's too young. She's just an op-teck."

The rad stiffens, his spur blinking impatiently on his arm. So it's true—they don't kill indiscriminately.

Bethany rushes in, crying out for Lukas, and the rad spins around, recognizes his target, and fires. Bethany collapses silently to the floor as Lukas screams. He tries to drag himself up. Bethany lies in a crumpled heap.

The sirens wail.

Lukas grabs the rad's ankle, brings him down. But Lukas is already losing consciousness. It's not much of a struggle.

She watches and does nothing. Bethany is dead. Lukas is down. There's nothing to do.

The rad races out, his only objective now to get off the

ship, but there are milits on board. He won't evade capture.

She kneels at Lukas's side, too shocked to speak or cry. She can't look at Bethany again. Her stomach churns at the smell of burnt flesh. Shouts and footfalls echo down the corridors, and the intermittent crack of gunfire.

The ship's medic arrives, and others. Someone pulls her away, draws her outside the room, asks if she's hurt.

Everything hurts.

She passes the eco-rad on her way off the ship. Demasked, lying crumpled against the bulkhead where they brought him down. A teenager, not much older than herself. His eyes follow her and she stops. Does he even care he was caught? The cypherteck is dead—mission accomplished.

A milit jerks his head to tell her to move on, but she takes a step closer.

"You failed," she says, looking down on his young, hard face. "I'm no op-teck. I'm a cypherteck, her trainee. You should have killed me, too."

His eyes flare with anger, then turn cold. "Look at what you've done," he whispers. "You've destroyed a world."

Later, they tell her that he died from his wounds. She hopes it's true.

And Lukas, his shoulders stooped under the weight of his guilt, his uniform still stained with Bethany's blood, vows to never let it happen again.

Edie splashed her face with water and allowed herself for just a moment to remember Lukas and Bethany. She'd known little of their relationship while it was happening. They were too discreet, and she was very young—naïve and oblivious to many things. But afterward, during the two years Lukas was Edie's bodyguard, she could see how he changed. No friendly banter, no personal discussions, no careless laughter and no squabbles. With Edie he was professional and dedicated at all times.

Yet somehow he became her friend and mentor along the way.

Staring in the mirror, Edie's face warmed at the vague memory of her recent behavior with Finn, and she chastised herself. Lukas was the one person she trusted and respected most in her life. She needed to take heed of what she'd learned from him. Pursuing any kind of attachment with Finn was simply too dangerous.

Having staggered down the ramp to the primitive facilities to wash up, Edie now struggled one-handed into her clothes, her skin still damp and soapy. She returned to the cockpit and stuck her wrist back into the sling Finn had fashioned. Her shoulder was purple with bruising but the sharp pain was gone, replaced by a dull nauseous ache.

The sight out the viewscreen didn't help. She averted her eyes and sat beside Finn. He pored over starcharts, and the look of puzzlement was back. Clearly he didn't know what to make of them.

"Any idea where we're headed?" She'd been asleep for several hours. The spike had worn off and the water had woken her up, but she was still groggy.

Finn looked up. "Flight plan says we're a few minutes off our exit point. I can't find our position. No idea what's on the other side."

"You mean Cat's sending us through an unmapped exit?"

"Looks that way."

"That's crazy. We could be heading into anything."

"Odds are in our favor that it's a deserted chunk of backwater space."

Edie knew the odds, more or less. There were millions of nodes throughout the Reach—known space—nine tenths of them unmapped. Of the mapped ones, most exit points had been found to lead nowhere special. Some of them brought a ship closer to another node that *did* go somewhere, and so they became important. The most valuable nodes were those with exits within star systems, and, occasionally, near planets—like the one near Talas that prompted its recolonization and the construction of the space station fifty years ago.

It was sheer foolhardiness to enter or exit unmapped nodes. That was the job of mapping crews, who earned hefty hazard bonuses for their troubles. It was insanity to exit a node in a skiff that lacked the mass to traverse nodes of its own volition. She and Finn were about to end up on the other side of a jump node without the means to reenter it and find their way back. They were entirely dependent on the *Hoi* coming after them, and if CIP impounded the *Hoi* they'd be stranded.

Despite the lingering dread in the pit of her stomach, Edie reassured herself that—either way—at least they were safe from Natesa and the Crib.

"Is there any way we can control our exit point?"

"No. Autopilot." Finn sounded unconcerned. "And why would we want to? The *Hoi* can't find us if we deviate from the flight plan."

"So you've given up the idea of taking the skiff and running?"

Finn leaned back in his seat. "Just a fantasy, like you said."

Edie fidgeted with her bandage, chewing her lip. She hated not having any control over their destination. "What if we exit in the middle of a skirmish or an exploding supernova?"

"One in a billion chance."

"There could still be danger. You hear about mapping crews disappearing all the time."

"Mostly because their ships get ripped apart on the node horizon, because they're stupid enough to take risks with their shielding. Those guys are already crazy or they wouldn't be in that line of work. Listen." He leaned toward her. "Sometimes you have to let things play out. There's nothing we can do just now."

She nodded and turned back to the viewscreen. Tried to make sense of the swirling strings of nodespace outside, as she might decipher a datastream, but no patterns emerged. After a while, she became mesmerized by the display.

"What's that on your feet?" he said out of nowhere. He was staring at the patterns on her bare feet, propped on the edge of the console.

"Cat did it."

"She branded you."

"No, she painted me."

Her warning tone stopped him commenting further. She wasn't in the mood to be baited when they were going to be trapped together in close quarters for a couple of days. She much preferred the man who had pulled her into his arms after tending her injury a few hours ago. The man who'd seemed on the verge of opening up. Now that she was in full control of her faculties again, perhaps he would.

"You said you'd tell me the truth about the Saeth." When he didn't respond, she tried again. "At least tell me about the chip in your head. I know the Crib set up the boundary trigger and the bomb, but they didn't put the chip there in the first place."

"What makes you say that?" His look betrayed nothing.

"I know Crib teck when I hear it. I don't recognize your chip. Who put it there?"

Finn drew a deep breath and let it out slowly, and she got the feeling he was stalling while he decided whether to answer.

"All the Saeth had them. It's a comm chip, or was, before the Crib wiped it. We learned to transmit basic signals and instructions to each other. Nothing fancy, but they helped us get the job done in silence."

"What job?"

Finn shifted awkwardly in his seat.

"Come on, Finn. Don't you want to set the record straight?"

"Telling you about it won't change a thing."

"It will for me." She smiled, and to her relief he returned it—but it only made him look sad.

Then he settled back and told her.

"The Fringe worlds spend half their time fighting each other over old grievances. They always have. The push for independence, the Liberty War, gave them a common goal but it didn't always stop the petty disputes. Some of them, the ones that could afford it, put aside their differences long enough to assemble an allied special-ops force—the Saeth. They funded us and we vowed to fight for all Fringers, not just our homeworlds."

"So you weren't assassins?"

"We spent most of our time blowing up Crib munitions factories. Recovering impounded ships and weapons. Escorting refugees. We did anything the rebel factions were too disorganized to do themselves."

"How did you get caught?"

"I was captured four years ago, right after the ceasefire."

"*After* the ceasefire? That makes no sense."

"The Fringe worlds denied responsibility for us because they didn't want to risk the terms of their fledgling treaties. They got their independence, such as it is, but they sold us out, handed us to the Crib on a platter. The Crib spun it so well that even the Fringers came to believe we were never on their side. We were on our way home and . . ." His voice cracked, and when he went on it was with reluctance. "Milits tracked us down. I held them off so my men could get away. Thought I'd be smart enough to escape later. It took longer than I expected."

"*Your* men?"

"I was a sergeant."

"Sergeant Finn." She tried the name on him.

His lips quirked. "That's not my real name."

"Then what is?"

"It's not important now."

"Why did you join the Saeth in the first place, instead of fighting for your homeworld like the other rebels?"

He hesitated, smiling grimly at some memory. "Well, there was a woman."

Edie grinned, but only to mask the unexpected pang of jealousy that lodged in her chest.

A woman. In Finn's past.

Of course there was a woman.

"Because of her, I took up a cause. And learned my lesson eventually—to take care of my own survival first."

"That's why you're so reluctant to help the Fringers now."

"Let's just say I lost comrades fighting for the Fringe worlds. They didn't do it for the glory, but they wouldn't have expected to be disowned and abandoned when it was over. My men . . . there were four of us left. Two with families. We had to find our own way home, through Crib lines and our alleged allies. A few days after my arrest, I heard my men were gunned down, trying to run from a patrol." Finn drew a deep breath and exhaled unsteadily. "A Fringer patrol."

As he stared off into the distance, lost in the memories, Edie waited for him to say that he blamed himself. He didn't say it, didn't need to. He didn't need pity from her.

"Why did the Crib let you live?" she asked.

He looked at her as if he'd suddenly remembered someone was listening. "At first no one knew what to do with me. After that . . ." He shrugged. "Suppose I got lost in the system."

Edie could see now how his incarceration had affected him. He'd commanded men, accepted responsibility for them, fought for entire worlds, and asked for nothing in return. To have it all stripped away and be rendered helpless, and now the leash . . . There wasn't much worse that could be done to any man, but especially a man like him.

She felt the urge to put things right for him, to make it fair. But what could possibly make up for what the Crib and his own people had done to him? The task was too big for her. And beyond their joint survival and cutting the leash, it wasn't her problem. She pushed those thoughts aside.

Remembering the marks she'd seen on his back, she asked, "Why did they whip you?"

He grimaced. "Took me a while to figure out I should behave myself if I wanted to survive in one piece." Absentmindedly, he touched the faint scar on his neck. "I've been out here a long time. Seen a lot, heard a lot. I heard the Talasi have a nonvocal language, that they speak in sign. Is that why you took off the snag?"

Pieces of their earlier conversation came back to her. He'd asked her this before, and she'd been unable to coordinate an answer. A week ago she hadn't thought about why she wanted his voice snag removed—she only knew she hated it. His suggestion made sense.

"I guess so."

"So the Crib taught you to speak?"

"I learned to speak Linguish from the camp guards."

"You get into trouble for that?"

"Yes. No. Not me. I wasn't worth disciplining. Their superstitious nonsense didn't allow for the existence of a half-breed, so no one took much notice of me. But there were some children : . ." Edie sighed—she hadn't intended to open up to him, but it was a fair exchange after what he had given her. "Four of us were caught talking to the guards. The elders were always warning us against it, against any outside influence. But we were curious. Fascinated by their stories." Her voice faltered as she thought back to that dreadful day. "When the elders found out, they made an example of the others. Me, they just ignored. Most of them were glad to be rid of me when the Crib took me away."

"What happened to those other kids?"

She swallowed as an old hate boiled to the surface. "The elders cut out their tongues."

She didn't meet Finn's eyes but sensed him freeze in the seat beside her. So he could still be shocked, even after all he'd seen and heard.

"The Talasi were mistreated for thirty years by the new colonists on Talas," Edie explained. "After they were put into camps, the Crib's policy was to not interfere with their culture, so they did nothing about it. But culture isn't sacred just because it's ancient. Some things . . ."

"Some things are just wrong."

She nodded, wondering how he'd managed to get the story

out of her. She'd never spoken of it before. Tracing the delicate painted lines on her feet, she felt him studying her.

"Who was that woman?" he asked.

"Natesa? She's my boss. My patron. She rescued me from poverty and neglect. She came from a deprived world, too, and assumed that gave us a connection—that we shared the same dreams. I'm a disappointment to her." Edie had never voiced that idea before, but as she said the words she realized they were true.

"You don't sound like that bothers you."

Edie's shoulders heaved in a deep sigh. "Even at the age of ten, I knew she wasn't choosing me out of benevolence. From that moment, she dictated everything in my life. There were times when she terrified me, because I couldn't see a way out from her influence. I used to run away, every so often, just for the taste of freedom. She never understood that." Edie couldn't look at him as she spoke. Compared to his grievances, hers sounded petty. Even that childish wish for her mother's return, a yearning that had tarnished her relationship with Natesa from the start, seemed irrelevant.

"You feel like she used you."

"She did."

"You're not a pawn, you know. She needed you—you could've taken advantage of that."

Now Edie looked up in surprise. "Are you saying I *should* have? Didn't you just say you behaved yourself in order to survive?"

"No one *needs* a serf. One man's as good as the next. Making trouble only makes it worse when you don't have the upper hand. When I do—if I see the smallest chance of success—I'll fight." His attention was drawn to something on the console, and he sat upright in his seat. "Looks like we're about to exit nodespace."

He pulled the seat harness over his shoulders and Edie did the same, securing herself tightly this time. For a few seconds the view outside the skiff didn't look any different, but as she was about to remark on it her seat lurched violently as the grav field stuttered. Her stomach flipped. She heard the equipment in the hold being thrown around again—they should have clamped down the loose stuff, but neither of them cared enough to think of that. Edie gripped the seat arms and closed her eyes, thankful for the harness because this ride was rougher than their entry into the node, hours earlier.

The skiff shuddered again, evened out, and she braved a look. She'd never been so happy to see the still, speckled expanse of starfield. A couple of telltales blinked red on the console. One of them turned amber, then green, even as she watched—whatever was wrong must have self-corrected. The other one remained red and Finn pushed buttons to get a readout on the holoviz.

"External vids and sensors are down," he reported. "And here's why we won't be running anywhere." He pulled up the fuel gauge, something neither of them had thought to check before. It had been bled dry.

Edie jacked into the comm. "They've disabled communications, other than a short-range link to the *Hoi*. No calling for help."

"How short-range?"

"I'm not picking up any comm buoys in the area, so the *Hoi* would have to be right here in the system with us. What now? We just sit and wait?"

Finn unfastened his harness. "I found a couple of memos coded for you. They were flashed over right before we hit the node."

Edie made a face and pressed her fingertips onto the dataport. Haller's memos were never much fun.

"It's the probe telemetry from Scarabaeus. He wants me to analyze it."

In her fear over being chased down by Natesa, she'd put Scarabaeus out of her mind, preferring to believe Haller was mistaken about the satellites picking up BRAT activity.

"What do you think it means?"

"I don't know. It's probably nothing. Those BRAT seeds are *dead*. I killed them."

"If something's going on down there, we need to know. Might be dangerous."

She scoffed. "Scarabaeus is ferns and lichen and beetles."

But she pulled up the data anyway. She *did* want to know what was going on, although not for the same reason as Finn. She'd spent the last seven years thinking she'd preserved Scarabaeus. The idea that she'd find the planet terraformed beyond recognition was too unbearable to contemplate, but she had to know. If the Crib found out, they'd colonize it. That was exactly what she'd tried to prevent.

The coding was Crib standard and she unlocked the data, choosing a three-sided display to sort it on the holoviz. At first glance, nothing made much sense. The BRATs were certainly active, and that made her stomach sink, but she couldn't find the usual terraforming protocols.

"This doesn't tell me much. There's some activity, but that doesn't mean the biocyph machinery is engaged. Even if the BRATs are rambling—running calculations and transmitting data that the satellite picked up—my kill-code lock should make it impossible for the biocyph to respond or to change the ecosystem."

"What if you're wrong and the ecosystem *is* changing?"

He was still thinking about possible dangers, but her concern was something else entirely.

"Then I'll have to fix it."

CHAPTER 20

Six hours later, Edie had learned frustratingly little more. She needed more information, was hungry for it—but that would have to wait until they reached Scarabaeus. The most likely scenario was that the BRATs were simply talking among themselves, perhaps the result of a remnant chunk of programming that the kill-code had not affected. If it was more than that . . . Edie tried not to imagine that scenario, but it haunted her. More than half a decade of terraforming would have severely impacted the planet. Was there any chance she could heal the wound that humankind had inflicted? The BRATs would have a record of Scarabaeus's original ecosystem, and once they made planetfall perhaps she could switch the target back. Not every species, not every plant and animal and metabolic pathway—it would leave a scar—but she felt compelled to try.

Edie pushed back in her seat and switched off the holoviz. She'd spent so many hours engrossed in her work that she'd lost track of time. It was early evening. Finn had spent the day tinkering in the cargo hold. He must be feeling caged in, with nothing to do and little space to move. Descending the ramp, she found him pulling packing material into a clearing he'd made on the deck, next to the drilling rig. The rig itself was in pieces.

"What are you doing with that?"

"Rethreading the mounts. I noticed they were off when I was cleaning it the other day."

"But they don't use it."

"Just bugs me to know it's not been done right." He grinned and indicated the makeshift mat he'd made. "You up for some training?"

"Are you still worried we'll find trouble on Scarabaeus?"

"You told me it'll be all beetles and bunnies, right? No, I'm planning for the future. After this mission we need to think about cutting ourselves loose. Out there on the Fringe, I'd feel better if you knew how to defend yourself."

"What about my shoulder?"

"I'll get you another spike. Take off your boots and find us some e-shields." He went into the cockpit where the medkit was.

Edie complied, grateful for the excuse to distract herself from Scarabaeus. She hadn't thought too much about what would happen after the mission, only that they'd need to be alert for any chance to escape. Then, find an infojack to cut the leash. And then what? She'd be alone on the Fringe with no contacts, probably no creds left, and a skill she'd have to hide if she didn't want to end up being used or killed.

Finn returned, spike in hand, and administered the shot. "Quarter dose this time. Let me know if you get dizzy."

Dizzy. A safe euphemism for what the painkillers had done to her earlier. She blushed as she remembered the things she'd said, the way she'd clung to him. The look in his eyes.

They clipped e-shields to their belts to soften the blows and went through some blocks and strikes. With one limb out of action, Edie's body readjusted and her overall balance improved. Finn favored his left side where his ribs were still sore.

They wore themselves out. They ate and slept and worked

out through most of the following day as well, concentrating on legwork to avoid stressing her shoulder. There was no word from the *Hoi*.

The physical activity felt good. Finn's style was less tutored than she was familiar with. He showed her simple core principles to make her defenses more generic, adaptable, and efficient at dealing reflexively with unexpected attacks from unpredictable opponents.

"Who taught you?" he asked her late into their second day on the skiff.

"My first bodyguard, Lukas. He was a tournament expert in Halen Crai."

"That explains it. You fight like a man."

"Thank you."

He threw her a curious scowl. So, it hadn't been a compliment.

"You play a little too close to the rules," he explained. "That won't help when you're fighting for your life."

She opened her mouth to defend Lukas, but he relented before she got the words out.

"Listen, it's not so bad. Your legs are strong, your feet are quick. But you need to fight like a girl because you'll never have brute force on your side. And you're thinking too hard instead of letting your body react."

As they drilled the blocks and falls, she was aware of her body becoming used to his touch, fuzzy as it was through the e-shields. She had to secretly admit she was enjoying herself, despite the monotony of the passing hours and the uncertainty ahead. They were in limbo, suspended in time and space, out of reach. Powerless to control anything beyond these bulkheads, but they could shape the universe within their tiny ship. So she let herself watch, admire, feel. It would be over soon enough, but she could enjoy it for as long as it lasted.

She surprised him by hooking her leg around his, shouldering him in the chest with her good arm, and successfully sweeping him to the deck for the first time ever, and he

laughed. Edie pulled back at that unexpected reaction. Looking down at him, at his relaxed handsome face, his vitality,
she saw in a flash of recognition that he was not the serf whose
voice she'd unlocked, not the bodyguard she was forced to
work with, not a fellow prisoner with the common goal of
escape—he was a man, and she was attracted to him.

And even though she knew that was dangerous, she ignored the danger.

One second later, he returned the favor and she was flat
on her back.

"What happened there?" Finn demanded. He'd brought
her down by twisting his legs around hers, breaking her fall
at the last moment to protect her shoulder. He had her pinned
to the deck with his legs, her right wrist imprisoned over her
head so she couldn't jab at his throat like he'd taught her.

"Uh, I wasn't paying attention." Too busy admiring the
way his white tee clung to his chest, and similar nonsense.

"Okay." He eased off and she waited for him to jump up
again, like he usually did, but he seemed to have no intention of doing that. "Your first move was a good one, though.
Took down a man twice your body weight. Impressive."

"I'm learning to fight like a girl, huh, Sergeant?"

"That you are. It's all in the leverage and timing." Their
shields arced and hissed where they clashed. He reached
down and cut them both. "But you screwed up in the follow-
through. You should've shot me, cut me, stomped on me
while you had the chance. Or run away. Now you're on the
ground and you've given up ninety-nine percent of your options."

She gave an experimental wiggle, but he was immovable.
"So what happens next?"

His dominating position should've scared her, but she
was sure he'd get up if she told him to. Fairly sure. And she
wanted him to stay right where he was.

"What happens next," he said thoughtfully, "depends on
my intentions. I reach for my shiv or for my zipper."

"Either way, I'm fucked."

His eyes narrowed with amusement but he didn't move. She was hyperaware of his easy strength as he lay over her.

"So I'm supposed to give up?" she said.

"It should never have come to this. Your only option now is to exploit a weakness."

"Finn, I don't think you have a weakness."

He ignored that, his gaze lowering to the V of her tee where the zipper had been pulled open a notch by the fall. He ran his fingers over the beetle shell at the base of her throat, trailed two fingers down her sternum to ease the neckline open further. Further than she'd anticipated. When his hand reached her stomach, she stopped breathing and his eyes briefly met hers.

"Checking to see if you got any more of these on you." His voice was soft, like honey poured over his usual gravel-edged growl.

She managed to drag in a lungful of air. "No. Just the one."

He stroked the shell again, making the surrounding skin vibrate. "Is this a tribal thing?"

"It doesn't mean anything."

"Sure it does."

Damn him. Was the leash turning him into a mind reader?

"The Talasi do mark their bodies," she conceded, "but not like this. And they never marked mine."

Well, there was the occasional black eye or fat lip . . . She closed her eyes and kept talking—talking made it easier to block out his scrutiny. But that made her more aware of the weight of his body against hers, and of his smell that had become so familiar.

"What it means is . . . Scarabaeus. I found a beetle strug-gling through the moss and I didn't save it. Didn't see the point. But it must've hitched a ride in my clothing. I found it, weeks later, in my pocket. Dead, dried up . . ."

Her breath caught as he settled more closely against her. His palm curved around her ribs, skin to skin, impossibly warm, and the fabric of her open tee slipped aside, exposing her breast to the cool air. Breathing became difficult again, but she kept going.

"There was this woman I befriended. She had a shop in the outer loop of Halen Crai. I used to run away from the institute and visit her. She did tattoos, jewel inlays, that sort of thing. I had her implant the beetle shell into my skin. I didn't tell anyone what it was. I don't know why I did it."

"To mark yourself with a piece of that planet."

His mouth drifted across her throat as he spoke, and she shivered. She wanted him to kiss her. Even as the thought formed in her mind, she turned her face away so his lips wouldn't find hers.

We can't do this.

He must have sensed her change in mood because he raised his head. Every place he'd touched her skin, she could still feel the trail of heat.

"Edie."

His solid presence rushed back in, calm and compelling. She opened her eyes, looked into the gold-flecked shadows of his. His brow furrowed in that crease that warned her of the emotions intruding on his mind. For once, he didn't complain, but she could tell he was suffering. She drew a deep breath, trying to stay in control for his sake.

"You've never said my name before," she murmured.

"I haven't?"

"You seemed to think I was called 'Hey'."

He smiled, not at her but at some private thought. Her gaze was drawn to his full lower lip that bore the scar of Haller's fist from last week. She couldn't take her eyes off it. But in her mind's eye she saw Bethany, crumpled and stained with blood, and Lukas cradling her, crying her name. Lukas broken and empty. Bethany dead.

"This is a bad idea," she whispered. "We can't—"

"Hush."

He watched his own hand as it explored her body, circled her bare breast, thumb brushing the nipple, and she gasped.

How could one hand radiate so much heat? He traced the curve of her ribs with meticulous intent, stroked her belly. His fingertips turned downward to slip beneath the low-slung waistband of her canvas pants. The intimacy of his touch pulled every visceral thread of emotion into a tight knot of need. Her body betrayed her, arching involuntarily against his.

A low groan escaped his throat and she knew it was the leash. Her arousal threatening to thwart his efforts. He seemed determined to ignore it. He shifted his weight again, fitted his hips against hers.

He had to stop. Stop now, or never stop.

She squirmed beneath him and he pulled back slightly.

"Finn, this won't . . . we can't. I'm sorry." She swallowed past the lump in her throat. "It's dangerous."

His eyes darted back to hers, clouded with confusion. From what little she knew of him, she understood why. Danger for him was the battle zone, the serf handler's arbitrary cruelty, the unknown perils of an alien world. Not *this*, the comfort and warmth of connection with another human being.

But he rolled off without a word and moved away. Edie stood and zipped up her tee, wanting to explain. He picked up a piece from the drill he'd dismantled and became pre-occupied with reattaching it to the mount. When he didn't look her way again, she went up into the cockpit and sank into a seat, shaking.

They could never be close in that way. She trusted him to take care of her, to keep them both alive. She didn't trust either of them with the complications that would arise from a deeper relationship. And unlike Lukas and Bethany, he didn't have the luxury of living if she died.

She watched the starfield, its almost imperceptible rotation across the screen with the lazy spin of the skiff. It threw a tint of fear over her mind, this endless velvety view. She closed her eyes and heard silence. Then, after a while, the sound of the skiff's enviro systems. She had to concentrate to hold the sound—not because it was too quiet, but because

her ears had acclimatized to its constant hum so that her
brain ignored the stimulus. The dull drone permeated her
body and after a while she could distinguish slight variations in the pitch and tone, until it sounded like the skiff
was whispering. Sometimes she caught a syllable, a half-
formed word, but as her mind struggled to make sense of it,
it drifted out of reach like a dissolving dream. The effort to
understand made her uncomfortable, and the sound became
annoying. She tried to push it away, make it inaudible as it
had been before. Was this what the leash was like for Finn,
this constant irritation skirting the edges of the mind but
never coming into focus?

From down below came the sound of metal grinding on
metal as Finn put back together the pieces of his meaning-
less project.

She felt safe having him around, but too near and it scared
her. No more swapping life stories, she resolved. No more
wanting to reach the place behind those enigmatic eyes. No
more feeling so damn good at being exposed to him, body
and mind, and at the intimacy of his wandering hands.

Thoughts of food and sleep were interrupted by an incoming
signal. Edie stretched out her back, stiff from sitting slumped
in the seat for more than an hour, and hit the comm.

"*Hoi Polloi* to *Charme*."

"Cat?"

"We just left nodespace. I see you on the scope. You guys
doing okay?"

"Who's *Charme*?"

"Hey, you named a planet. I named a skiff. We'll be on
you in about eight minutes. Sit tight."

"That's what we've been doing for two days."

That, and other things.

CHAPTER 21

The moment they docked, the *Hoi* jumped back into nodespace. Edie wanted nothing more than a few hours' sleep on a proper bunk, not only because she was exhausted but because it would postpone having to deal with what had happened between her and Finn. While Zeke ordered Finn back into the skiff to help him assess the damage to the rigs, Edie made her way to her quarters. Halfway down the corridor on deck three, Haller met her coming from the opposite direction.

"Come with me to the briefing room."

"What? Sir, I . . ." She looked longingly at the hatch to her quarters.

Haller waved away any protests. He looked angry and anxious, a combination that gave him a wild-eyed appearance. She remembered the way he tended to fracture when things weren't going his way, and decided to cooperate.

"We just got the telemetry from a direct survey of the planet. You need to take a look. And turn your comm back on. You're on duty."

It was already an hour into the nightshift, but Edie avoided making a sarcastic comment about the duty roster. From Haller's attitude, he must think the telemetry meant bad news. She hurried along behind him, eager—despite her exhaustion—to examine new information about Scarabaeus.

"What happened back there on the skiff," he asked as they climbed up the decks, "right before we launched you?"

"The inner hatch was jammed."

He stopped and eyed her with suspicion. "Jammed. How?"

"A glitch with the servo. I don't know, sir. Finn gave it a kick and it was okay."

"What a hero." From his sneer, she got the feeling he didn't entirely buy her explanation. "Tell me, what's your history with that Natesa woman? All in all we had a rather . . . unpleasant encounter."

As they continued through the common area and into the briefing room, Edie took a moment to enjoy the idea of Haller and Natesa having to put up with each other.

"She's on a holy mission and I'm her lucky charm."

Haller scowled. "You've brought us precious little luck." He flicked on the holoviz and it projected Scarabaeus, a serene globe suspended in midair, slowly rotating. "That planet down there is seething with life."

"You knew from my reports that there's life there. Too much life for CCU to have been messing with it in the first place."

"That's not what I mean." Haller tapped the holo, and the image zoomed in on one of the continents. "These survey scans are showing regions of high concentrations of life, and the distribution exactly matches the distribution of the BRATs."

Edie stepped closer and studied the holoviz. Surrounding each tiny red dot that represented a BRAT was a green splotch. An inkblot of life.

"Maybe the local wildlife has moved in around the BRAT seed husks, established habitats," she suggested.

"No, no, no!" He jabbed his finger at the ghostly image of the planet to punctuate his words. "I'm talking about regions of intensely concentrated life spreading out from each BRAT for a radius of several kilometers. What the hell is going on down there?" His words tumbled out as he worked himself up into a state of panic.

Edie dropped into the nearest seat and puzzled over the display. The BRAT seeds did not germinate—she'd made sure of it. That's what CCU's unmanned probe had reported, and that's how she'd interpreted the data from the advance probe.

Could the germination have been delayed for a year? She'd never heard of that happening. And even if it had, this pattern of localized concentrations of life was entirely atypical. In fact, this looked like something she'd only read about, and if she was right, it was very bad news.

"I need to study this. I can't give you an answer right now."

From the look on Haller's face, that wasn't going to be enough. He needed something to latch on to, a convincing explanation, a plan of action. Behind him, she saw Finn leaning in the hatchway. She hadn't seen him arrive and Haller hadn't noticed him.

"Have you heard of a megabiosis?" she asked Haller. "It's theoretical. In sims it happens when the target ideal is lost."

"A mega what?"

She called up a basic seeding routine via a softlink to illustrate her point. "The BRATs release cyphviruses to sample the biosphere. Then the biocyph models the biosphere and figures out how to transform it into the target ideal—a Terran world. It writes new programming, creates heritable cyphviruses that infiltrate the genome of every living thing in order to remodel the ecosystem. One biochemical pathway at a time, planetwide."

The sim followed her lead and bloomed with new life.

"You're not telling me anything I don't know." Haller was one notch short of yelling. He pushed his red face closer to hers, and Finn tensed at the aggressive stance. "The bioreadings on this place are bizarre. I can't make head or tail of them. It's one big mutated mess down there."

"Scarabaeus had advanced lifeforms—if the BRAT seeds did germinate, the results were always going to be unpredictable." Edie's thoughts raced, her throat tightening as she contemplated the implications. "The biocyph is meant to adapt. My best guess is that it couldn't cope."

She'd studied dozens of seeding operations, knew more than most people about how biocyph worked. But this pattern of distribution was more than unique—it should be impossible. She wanted it to be impossible.

"I've only seen this in sims. Theoretically, you get systemic feedback loops. Pockets of hotbed activity. A megabiosis. The cyphviruses are changing the genomes they encounter but with no clear direction. Each of these pockets"—she highlighted a few green areas on the holo—"is like an independent organism, caught in a feedback loop that keeps it localized but constantly evolving under the instructions of biocyph that's lost its target ideal."

"So what does this mean for the mission?" Haller sounded somewhat placated now that she'd given him an explanation, however little he understood it.

"Let me take a closer look at the data. I'll write you a nice report if that's what you want, but in the end all that matters is the BRATs have germinated. They've been brewing for perhaps as long as six years, put down taproots. We can't extract them."

"Nonsense. We can't leave empty-handed. We have to salvage something."

"There's nothing we can do."

Nothing she could do. It was the worst possible outcome she could have imagined. Scarabaeus was surely beyond healing.

"There has to be a way to cut the taproot—"

"You can't just—"

"—drill a parallel shaft, or bomb the damn thing out of the ground." Haller paced the deck, looking up and away again without comment when he noticed Finn. "These BRATs were supposed to be *dead*."

"We'd be wasting our time," Edie choked out through the grip of despair squeezing her chest. She caught and held

Finn's gaze, knowing he sensed the weight of her feelings if not their exact nature. They weren't supposed to be here. They didn't belong on this ship with these people, or on this mission, or on Scarabaeus. They belonged in the *Charme*, in that timeless bubble where nothing mattered but the two of them.

Haller's pacing came to a halt. "We are not leaving here without getting something from that planet."

In an attempt to satisfy him, to make him go away, she said, "I'll think of something. Maybe Zeke has some ideas." In truth, Zeke was the last person who'd persevere in the face of this kind of setback.

Haller leaned over her, grabbing the arms of her chair. Finn stiffened.

"It's time to prove your worth, teckie, and justify the risk we undertook to bring you on board, not to mention the expense. Figure out a way to get those BRATs out of the ground. Final briefing is at four tomorrow morning."

He pushed past Finn and stormed out.

Edie sagged in the chair, her energy drained, eyes stinging with tears. Finn came into the room and leaned against the far end of the console. Between them floated the glowing sphere of the planet that awaited them on the other side of nodespace.

"You still think you can fix it?" When she shook her head, he leaned toward her and the patterns of light created by the holoviz played across his skin. "I don't understand. It's a rock with some wildlife. Nothing sentient. Nothing to ponder what's happened, nothing to feel regret or grief. Why does it mean so much to you?"

He was right, of course. As a sixteen-year-old, her impulsive decision to save Scarabaeus had come from an emotional reaction to that unthinking, unfeeling wildlife. But over the years, it had come to mean so much more—her greatest act of defiance.

"It was the only time I truly beat them. Or thought I had."

"Did we come all this way for nothing? No paycheck?"

The leash, the creds to unhook it—that was what they were really here for. Scarabaeus was not the priority, no matter how she felt about it.

A shudder swept the ship, combined with a sudden change in engine noise, indicating their reentry into realspace.

"Ladies and gentlemen, welcome to system VAL-One-Four," Cat said over the shipwide comm. "We reach orbit in nine hours."

Nine hours to figure out how to turn the BRATs on Scarabaeus into their freedom ticket. Edie flicked off the holoviz. The image dissolved and she stared at the empty space it had occupied.

"I'll find a way."

Finn nodded with a look of trust that she hoped she could live up to.

"You get some rest," she told him. "No point in both of us being exhausted."

He hesitated, as if he might protest, but then nodded and straightened, rubbing his hand across his forehead. He looked as tired as she felt—but she had work to do.

More than ever, the mission now depended on Edie. If she was going to get paid, she had to come up with a solution.

Zeke thought the whole thing was a joke. No bonus pay for this mission, but what did he care? There would be other missions, and there was no way anyone could blame *him* for this failure. So he wasn't too happy when, at the briefing early the following morning, Edie put forward a plan of action that placed a large share of responsibility for success squarely on his shoulders. She knew exactly what the objections would be, and the op-teck didn't disappoint her.

"You're gonna get *inside* the BRATs and rip out their guts?" The stark whites of Zeke's eyes flared as he crudely paraphrased her idea. "There's fuckin' milit-grade security holding those BRATs together. Every time we've tried before, we've wrecked the damn things. You may be able to jack in and talk to the biocyph, but no way are you gonna get physically inside one after it's germinated. And even if you can, the biocyph will be useless. We've taken stuff that's twelve, maybe eighteen months old before, but after it's been brewing for *six years*? It's hardwired into that planet's ecosystem now, no good anywhere else. It's worth shit to us."

He turned his incredulous look on Haller, but the XO wasn't interested in Zeke's opinion. He was waiting for Edie to salvage his mission. Kristos and Finn stood nearby, taking everything in. Having worked through the night, Edie was in no mood to pretty things up for any of them. She explained as concisely as she could.

"It's not as valuable as embryonic biocyph, that's true. I still think I can hijack it and merge it with some of the seeding machinery you've got lying around here, and put together something useable for your Fringe-world customers. Not keystones. Maybe some sort of gene jiggler."

"Can't we just reboot it?" Kristos asked. He had little comprehension of what was going on, but had picked up on the nervousness of everyone else.

"We'd need the biocyph templates in order to reboot." Edie glared at Zeke. "And unless Zeke's been doing some real creative trading lately, I know you don't have those."

Haller ignored the implied accusation about Zeke's extra-curricular activities and moved on. "What about the inbuilt security?"

"Zeke's right," she said. "We can't force the BRATs open, not without destroying them. My plan is to jack in and try and persuade them to open up."

"Uh-huh. Just like that?" Zeke said.

"Those BRATs are primed to respond to cyphertecks, although not usually after germination. There has to be a way in."

"And you've done this before?" Haller looked dubious, but interested—he was willing to be convinced that it would work.

"More or less." Closer to less, but she tried to sound confident.

As Zeke opened his mouth to protest again, Haller waved him into silence. "What about the alarm system? If the *Laoch* is still out there, two jumps away, we don't want any alarms triggered."

Edie drew forward a holoviz display of a standard terra-forming BRAT six years after germination—a honeycomb of biocyph matrix housed inside a six-meter-tall plazalloy case, half buried in the ground and anchored by a taproot five times its own height. A network of organomeck rootlets reached out from the taproot, spreading hundreds of kilo-meters in every direction, growing ever finer toward the periphery—some breaking the surface to form shrublike growths on the landscape, some intercepting and intertwin-ing with the rootlets of neighboring BRATs.

"We need to set up a shield around the immediate area, about fifteen meters in diameter." She demonstrated this on the simulation by a fuzzy purple sphere to represent the boundaries of the shield. "We use trackers to monitor the flow of information between the BRATs, and to prevent the BRAT talking to the satellite and raising any alarms."

"My rigs can't do that." Zeke was unwilling to agree to a job that sounded impossible.

"Yes, they can. Won't be easy because the biocyph in your rigs has been hijacked, stalled, de-merged, reprogrammed, and tripped so many times it's virtually senile." Zeke looked taken aback, but he was listening. "Once I've jacked in, there'll be Crib security locks to bypass. Then, if I can find my way down to the original initiating sequences, I should be able to persuade it to open up."

"And once we get inside," Haller said, "how do we take out the circuitry?"

Zeke snorted. "Wire cutters."

"Very careful use of wire cutters," Edie corrected him. "We'll need containers to store it—about half a cubic meter per BRAT."

"That's what the lags are for. Easiest assignment they've ever had," Haller said. "How long will this take? We can make up some of the lost time, but we'll only have five days dirtside if we're to make our rendezvous on the Fringe."

"The first one will take the longest. Maybe eight hours."

Haller looked horrified. She was fairly sure it would take no more than one—either she could do it or she couldn't, and she'd know after one hour—but she intended to use the rest of that time for something else entirely. Once jacked in, she planned to find out exactly what had happened on Scarabaeus, and if possible do something about it. She couldn't reverse the process but perhaps she could halt it. Perhaps there was something of Scarabaeus's original beauty left to preserve. She only needed to adjust the programming of one BRAT. Within minutes it would communicate with all the others and spread the new code. The rovers planned to remove only a small percentage of the BRATs, not enough to severely impact her plan.

"After the first one," Edie continued, "we've got an average one hour's flight between each site, plus two or three hours working on each BRAT."

Haller had his own ideas. "That's not enough. We'll be working with about seven hours of daylight, six of dark. Gravity is point-nine-four, weather is temperate. Ideal conditions for fast work. We'll split into two teams—you'll rotate between them. You'll crack open a BRAT for team one to work on, and then Cat will ferry you to the next site, where team two will have already prepped the area."

"Uh, are you allowing any downtime in that schedule?" Zeke said. "I can't work five days straight."

"We'll play it by ear." That was the best Haller would offer.

Edie had a headache just thinking of the workload ahead, but she had an even greater concern. The BRATs were hundreds of kilometers apart, well beyond the range of the leash. Outside the bulkheads of the *Hoi*, there was a real chance she and Finn could get separated by a lethal distance.

Zeke turned to Edie. "You said there was advanced life on the planet. Anything we need to worry about?"

"The ecosystem was analogous to a late-Paleozoic period of evolution." She was met with blank looks. "Nothing a standard e-shield can't handle."

They seemed satisfied with that.

"Obviously, Finn will stick with me."

"Obviously," Haller echoed with a smirk. "So, any idea how we're going to fool our buyers on the Fringe that they're getting what they paid for?"

Edie returned his smirk. "That's your job, sir, not mine."

CHAPTER 22

Once they reached orbit, Haller allowed Edie a one-hour break before showtime while the rest of the crew continued working. Her mind was on overdrive. Unable to nap, she'd spent the time going over the specs for the toms they were taking with them. When her eyes refused to focus anymore, she grabbed a change of clothes and headed across the corridor for a shower. Maybe that would wake her up.

Just as she flicked on the water, a dark shadow approached the stall—Cat, stripping as she moved, leaving her clothes where they fell. Due to her untidy habits, Edie had found her belongings in the bathroom before. Bangles and scarves and pretty scraps of underwear.

"Hey." Cat stepped into the jets, gesturing for Edie to make room. "Sorry. This is my last chance at hot water for days. I've got syscheck on the skiff in five minutes. You gonna be ready to leave at oh-six-hundred?"

"I guess so."

Cat pulled a handful of decorated pins out of her black hair and untwisted the locks. Edie hadn't realized Cat's hair was so long and thick—she always wore it knotted up, speared with pins at strategic locations. As she soaped up, she looked at Edie for so long that Edie started to wonder if she was planning to make a pass at her.

"Did you happen to read those memos on the skiff?" she said at last.

"The data from the advance probe? Not much use—we learned more from the later surveys."

"I mean the other memo."

Edie frowned as she recalled that there had been two memos. She'd been so engrossed in the first, she'd never got around to reading the second.

"What about it?"

Cat shrugged. "It really doesn't matter now."

"Then why mention it?"

"Because I wanted you to know . . . I tried to help you."

"What are you talking about?"

"I sent you a new flight plan for the autopilot."

Edie wiped soap from her eyes and stared at Cat. "You wanted us to escape?"

"It would've taken you to a shipping lane. Given you a chance. I told you before, Edie, I didn't know about the leash until it was too late. What they did to Finn wasn't fair."

"What *they* did? That infojack did it. The one you were fucking, remember?"

Her anger seemed to upset Cat. The navpilot held up a hand to calm her. "He was hired by Stichting Corp. He didn't tell me about the leash because it had nothing to do with me. The point is, I had a change of heart."

"Well, the skiff had no fuel so it was never going anywhere, flight plan or not."

"I didn't know that."

Something about the look on her face made Edie think she was telling the truth about that, at least. The rest didn't quite add up.

"On the day you kidnapped me, you rejoiced at the death of that other serf. I find it hard to believe you care what happens to Finn."

"You're right. I didn't care about either of them at the time. Just wanted to get the job done." Cat flipped off the shower without asking if Edie was ready. "Anyway, none of this matters now. You didn't find the flight plan. The skiff had no fuel. It's like it never happened."

But if it had happened, Cat had tried to redeem herself. Her loyalties were flexible—she'd said as much herself. Would she help them again, when the time came?

"Listen, Cat." Edie grabbed Cat's arm as she exited the shower. "Thank you for trying."

Cat smiled but she didn't look happy. She wrapped herself in a towel, picked up a few of her dropped pins, and left for her quarters.

Edie dressed in fresh oxor-cloth pants and a gray V-neck, and pulled on her jacket. In her quarters she found Finn sitting on the deck, spine pressed to the bulkhead, eyes closed. She stared at the crease of worry between his brows, knowing the turmoil in her head was responsible for it.

She unclipped her diagnostic rod and called up the scan she'd done days ago, when he first complained of the strange sensations in his head. She'd done nothing about it, but perhaps she should try. He didn't need the distraction of being linked to her emotional state any more than he needed the distraction of a sexual relationship with her.

It must be because they'd used a biocyph strand in his splinter. It made the link unbreakable, which was the most important thing as far as her captors were concerned, but it was also able to crudely interpret the transmissions from her brain. From her mind to his, translated through two wet-teck interfaces, the result was the distorted signal that he described as white noise.

What she needed was a way to reduce the signal.

"Finn." She spoke just loud enough for him to hear, not loud enough to wake him if he was dozing. "I thought you were working on the trackers with Zeke."

He didn't move. "Came to fetch you. It's time to go."

"I have an idea."

He opened his eyes and looked at the holoviz hovering over the diagnostic rod.

"About the leash?"

"Yes." She sat beside him. "Were you meditating?"

"I was trying to clear my mind. Of you. I guess that's meditation." He stretched his neck and ran his hand over his head, lingering at the back of his skull in a gesture of irritation that was becoming all too familiar. "What's your brilliant idea?" His smooth voice seductively encouraged her to give him what he wanted—help, hope, relief.

"The problem is that our respective wet-teck is transmitting and receiving too much information. We need to find a way to attenuate the signal."

"If the signal drops, won't that . . . you know, blow up my head?"

"Not if the attenuator is at your end, between your splinter and your brain. My signal will still come through loud and clear, but your mind will be oblivious."

He liked the sound of that. "Do it."

"After the mission, I promise. I have to take my time with this, get it right."

"Okay."

She fiddled with the diagnostic rod, the silence between them buzzing with unresolved tension.

"I'm sorry about what happened in the skiff. That I had to make you stop." He said nothing, so she forged on, unable to look at him. "If we could've stayed there forever . . ." She bit her lip, annoyed at herself for such a ridiculous fantasy. "I would've let you . . . do whatever you wanted." Damn, that was something she'd barely admitted to herself yet. Her body pulsed with the memory of his warm hands. "But we're back to reality, and it's impossible. My trainer died because she and Lukas couldn't prevent their personal relationship from affecting their jobs."

"It was just sex." His voice was soft, his tone just careless enough to make her wonder if the nonchalance was faked. "One time only, if that's all you wanted."

Was that all *he'd* wanted? Their eyes met, and in his she saw a blaze of emotion that belied his offhand manner. Then it was gone. Pragmatically she reminded herself that the leash transmitted her arousal to his head in unpleasant ways, which meant what they had done was probably as far as they'd ever get.

"Forget it," he said, getting to his feet and grabbing his jacket from the bunk. He held out his hand and she took it. His steady strength flowed down the length of his arm and into her body as he pulled her up. "Concentrate on the job. Let's get through this."

With a few minutes to go before the departure at six, Edie climbed up to deck one, to the viewing port, and looked out at the world—a ball suspended below the ship, streaked with aqua and white. Small enough to hold in her palm, as beautiful as Rackham's stolen talphi cocoon. From space it looked as serene and fragile as she remembered it. Her throat constricted when she thought about what they might find down there.

She made her way belowdeck to the skiff where Finn and the rest of the landing team had assembled. In the cockpit, Cat was running her final checks. Zeke ushered the serfs into their seats toward the back of the hold. Among them, Edie recognized the man Finn had saved in the engine room. He didn't look her way.

Along the bulkhead, inside the hatch, stood a line of compact backpacks and calibrated e-shield pods—one set for each team member. Edie clipped an e-shield to her tool belt, where it sat snugly against her hip. There was a rack of spurs and two rifles—the latter for Haller and Zeke. They'd lost the rest when Haller vented the engine room.

Haller went through the final plan. His mood seemed elevated after his recent decline into panic and frustration. He was at his best when he had a job to do, and despite the difficulties ahead, at least they had a plan.

"We've got six BRATs targeted for today, all within a three-thousand-kilometer diameter. Our base will be this island"—he pointed on the holoviz—"where Cat will stand by with the skiff."

Their landing site was on the main southern continent of
Scarabaeus. Edie had suggested the site because the region
was temperate, as opposed to the more extreme climates of
the northern landmasses, and the cooler, drier climate had
resulted in slightly less dense vegetation growth around
the BRATs—the only noticeable difference. Still, it was
an important one. That physical barrier would be their big-
gest hassle in terms of time and effort. Rather than hacking
through kilometers of dense jungle in order to reach each
BRAT, they would climb down from the canopy and winch
up the biocyph.

They squeezed into the cockpit—Haller up front next to
Cat, Kristos and Finn behind them, and Edie in the back, in
the foldout seat built into the bulkhead. Zeke stayed below
with the serfs. Edie would've appreciated his irreverence and
humor up on deck. Cat and Haller were all business, while
Kristos's jittery nerves made Edie feel worse. She glanced
guiltily at Finn's profile, wondering how he was coping with
the nausea in her stomach, but there were no clues written
on his face.

The skiff plummeted toward the planet, the gravplating
equalizing out the gees so that, if not for the riotous view
out the viewscreen, she'd have thought they were motionless. Edie concentrated her gaze on a light just above eye
level on the opposite bulkhead, in order to avoid the tempta-
tion to look sideways out the screen. When she did chance a
look, they were coasting through the clouds.

If her attempt to sabotage the terraforming mission seven
years ago had worked, Scarabaeus would be as untouched
now as the day she first visited it, except for those thousand
inert metal bullets lodged in its skin. If the Crib had succeeded, Scarabaeus would be on its way to becoming a new
and perfect world for humankind to colonize.

Instead, it was neither. As the skiff glided high above a
dark, still ocean toward its destination, all Edie knew for
certain was that no Eden awaited them.

CHAPTER 23

In the drizzling rain, she sees neat rows of fence posts interrupting the desolate plain. From this distance, she recognizes the woven roof of the council meeting hall, the long
nursery building, the hog pens tucked away in the corner of
the compound.

And the guard tower, the shuttle pad, the fence itself—
stark reminders of the Crib's control over the Talasi.

In six years she has run away from the institute many
times, but she's not left the city before. Last night she paid
for a landcruiser ride across the continent by jacking into
Halen Crai gov's criminal records and wiping out the driver's insurance violations.

She doesn't understand why she's here—never has she
entertained the idea of returning to that life. She wants
nothing to do with those people. But tonight she will leave
Talas for the first time. Its ecosystem is in her blood and
she'll have to return, but for a while she'll be . . . somewhere
else at last. Free. She needs to take one more look at the
camp, at the place where she came from.

Just one look under a gray morning sky. Then she turns
away. Talas made her blood. The Crib made her skills. But

it has not made her identity. That creation is left to her, and the future.

As she turns away, the driver scratches at his hair—bone dry in the rain. He's wearing an e-shield—terrified, as are all colonists, about contamination from neuroxin. "That's it? Leaving already?"

"I have to get back to Halen Crai."

"What's the hurry? We only just got here."

"I'm taking a space flight. I'm going to turn a rock into a new world."

"A new world, huh?" He doesn't believe her. To him, she's just some street kid whose knack for dry-teck will keep him out of jail. "Sounds nice."

"It will be nice. I'll make it beautiful."

"Sure you will, hon. Send me a postcard."

As they speed back to the mountains, back to Halen Crai and the stone walls of the institute, the sense of impending freedom lifts her spirits. She imagines the perfect world she will help create, and the people who will call it home, and she envies them.

From the stratosphere, the megabiosis was a gleaming, scalloped brooch on the rugged landscape. Edie couldn't take her eyes off it—as bizarre and unnatural as the sculpture of a tortured artist, yet entirely organic.

The skiff banked to make a slow pass over the area, and the megabiosis tilted out of view. Edie turned her attention to the external vid feeds. A thick web of matted vines covered the knot of jungle—three or four different species, judging from the variation in shape and coloration. Here and there a spindly feeler escaped the tangle to extend skyward, but the vegetation mostly turned in on itself, exposing only the unbroken curves of the vine stalks. The appearance of thicker, grayish branches indicated a sturdier arboreal species beneath.

A thousand of these megabioses peppered the surface of Scarabaeus, each ten or more kilometers in diameter. The rest of the landscape looked bleak by comparison, far more desolate than she remembered. Retroviruses sent out by the BRATs had formed the pockets of jungle by reworking the ecosystem, but they must also be affecting the areas beyond, killing off native species. There was very little groundcover. Edie choked back a sob. Her perfect world was ruined, countless species wiped out or changed beyond recognition. Finn turned in his seat, gave her a look that made her wonder what her heartbreak felt like to him.

She drew a deep breath, telling herself to hold it together. There was a still a chance she could do *something* down there to make things right.

Haller sent team one into the cargo hold. Edie, nearest the hatch, was first down the ramp, with Finn following closely, as if he was eager to get to the surface. Zeke handed him a spur and took one for himself. The sight of the men strapping on weapons reminded Edie of previous missions. She'd had the protection of Crib milits, but that hadn't prevented the raids. In fact, the Crib's state-of-the-art firepower only encouraged their attackers—fanatical eco-rads, greedy rovers, and desperate Fringers—to band together and arm themselves comparably, exacerbating every confrontation. Edie could only hope that no one knew about this small team of rovers salvaging biocyph from a ruined world.

The skiff shuddered in the air currents, hovering at low altitude. Zeke slapped the control pad to open the internal hatch.

"Shields on," he ordered, using a button on his belt to activate the serfs' shields as well as his own. They could not be trusted even with their own survival. "We'll move out in two groups. The serfs and me, then the three of you." He nodded toward Edie and Finn, and then Kristos, who fidgeted in the shadows. "Cheer up, kid," he bellowed. "My little buddy here goes first."

He tossed a tom into the airlock, closed the internal hatch, and opened the external hatch.

Edie had modified the tom to take some basic readings,

and it was linked remotely to a holoviz. For now, though, they all watched the skiff's external vid as the tom dropped into the canopy of the megabiosis. It scrabbled for a grip and took a few cautious steps.

"Can that vegetation take our weight?" Haller asked over the comm. He had the same vid feed as they did.

Edie called up the data collected by the probes and overlaid that visual with the tom's readings. An indistinct dome wavered in midair between her and Zeke, the holo becoming gradually clearer as readings from the tom streamed in.

"Ultrasound shows dense cover almost all the way down— seventy meters," Edie reported.

"Gonna be tough, hacking through that." Zeke gave the serfs a quick look. That would be their job. "The vines seem to have good structural integrity down to the last few meters. Then it's open at ground level."

At the center of the holo, the dark, impenetrable shape of the BRAT waited in a clearing.

Edie had programmed the tom to climb straight down, but it was having trouble finding a large enough gap in the vines. It skittered in a circle, testing the vines at each spot, returned to its starting point, wandered off in another direction, and didn't come back.

Zeke banged the vid feed, as if that would help. "What the . . . ?"

"I think the transmissions from the BRAT confused it." Edie watched the holo as the tom's transmissions became increasingly nonsensical, and then dropped out altogether.

"Well, we've got a general image of the environment down there. I've scanned for weapon sigs and signs of human life. All clear," Haller said. *Human* could only mean eco-rads.

Zeke cycled the airlock and corralled the three serfs inside. They obeyed mutely, dull-eyed, doped up on tranqs. Ready to work. They carried cutting tools—simple water torches—and packs of equipment needed to set up the shield, cut out the biocyph, and haul it back up to the skiff. The *Hoi* hadn't come prepared for this job, and the torches were the only tools on board that were suitable for hacking through the jungle while being safe to place in the hands of serfs. E-shields could effectively absorb or deflect the impact of a torch's high-velocity water stream, in case any of them got trigger-happy.

Edie watched the serfs disappear through the outer hatch, following their progress on the vid feed. Zeke winched each man onto the matted canopy, and then himself. Finn repeated Zeke's actions with the airlock, venting the dangerous air of Scarabaeus so as not to contaminate the skiff. The inner hatch opened and he stepped inside, along with Edie and Kristos.

Finn opened the outer hatch to face a blustery morning. Edie's e-shield muted the feel of the wind on her skin, but not its sheer force.

"I'll go first," he said, raising his voice over the wind and engines instead of using the link. "Just grab the winch and I'll catch you." He didn't offer Kristos any guidance. His job was protecting Edie. "You ready for this?"

She nodded. "It's our payday," she said, too quiet for him to hear, but he read her lips and gave her a quick grin.

Finn disappeared over the lip of the hatch. Her stomach flipped as she peered over the edge, but he landed safely on his feet, smooth and steady as a cat. The winch rebounded and she put her foot through the loop, wrapping her hands around the rope. Like Finn, she wasn't going to trust Kristos with the controls. She worked the panel herself and descended slowly the four meters or so to the canopy. A gust of wind caught her, swinging her underneath the skiff and back again, and then she felt strong hands on her, guiding her down.

Finn helped her off the winch, and she leaned against his sturdy body. He pulled her down into a crouch like Zeke and the others, because the wind and the uneven surface made everyone unstable on their feet. The vines looping up from the dense vegetation formed convenient handles, and Edie grabbed on to them. Zeke yelled instructions up to Kristos as he made his way down. The young teck dropped the last two meters, landing on his back, limbs flailing.

Zeke clambered over to help him up. "Damn kid couldn't find down in a gravity well."

"Everyone safe?" came Cat's voice over the open line, and Zeke yelled back in the affirmative. "Back in a few hours to collect you guys, and whatever you dig out of there. Stay in touch."

The skiff ascended in a steep climb, turned, and flew away.

Through the e-shield, the vines felt slimy between Edie's fingers. Her injured shoulder protested as she clung on, finding footholds to work her way closer to Zeke, always aware of Finn nearby keeping a close eye on her.

It took twenty minutes for the serfs to cut a hole into the vines. The water torches sheared through the clot of vegetation and the serfs used brute force to push it aside. Zeke went after them, followed by Finn and then Edie. Above Edie, Kristos was the last one in. He moved too fast, lost his footing, and kicked her in the head.

"Watch it!" she said, and he stuttered an apology.

She rubbed her skull, looking down to make sure she didn't do the same thing to Finn. She could see the top of his head, his broad shoulders, and his arms reaching out to grab the vines. It was slow going. The serfs had to make the tunnel wide enough to accommodate their equipment, which took time but made it comfortably wide for the rest of the team.

"This is fuckin' crazy!" Zeke yelled from somewhere down below, but he sounded like he was enjoying himself.

"Stay closer," Finn called up. He sounded annoyed that the gap between him and Edie was increasing. Her shoulder ached fiercely now, refusing to take the weight of her body, so she had to look carefully for every foothold.

"I won't let you out of my sight," she muttered, wishing more than ever that her first bodyguard were here. Lukas would have offered encouragement, made her feel okay about being here. Even when it wasn't okay.

"What did you say?" Finn was suddenly right behind her. He had either climbed up, or stopped to let her climb down. Their descent was so slow, with long periods of immobility, that she hadn't noticed. Now his lips were at her ear, his body against hers.

"Lukas used to say that. *I won't let you out of my sight.*"

Finn said nothing, but when he moved again he adjusted his pace so it matched hers, and the gap between him and Zeke widened instead.

It took ninety minutes to climb halfway down. Sunlight still penetrated but it was darker. Unidentified sounds came from all directions—soft chirps, rustling, buzzing. The vines were looser and softer here, and Edie had plenty of time to examine them during the stop–start descent. While she despaired over the loss of the native species on Scarabaeus, she couldn't help but be fascinated by the new alien life before her eyes. The thickest vine species, white and almost translucent, had a purple, thready parasitic fungus growing along its branches, and the green leafy tendrils of another species twined up from below, using the main vine structure as scaffolding to climb upward to the light. Occasionally she caught a glimpse of a blue-winged thriplike insect darting through the gaps in the vines.

"What's that?" Kristos yelped. She looked up to see him flapping his hand around his head, swatting at a tiny thrip. It was attracted by the aura of the e-shield. It flitted toward the shield and disintegrated with an audible *zap*.

"What setting is your shield on?" Edie called out.

"Um . . . maximum."

"We're not in combat!" Zeke yelled from several meters beneath them, having heard the exchange. "Crank it down or you're gonna set this place on fire."

That was an exaggeration, but maximum shield strength was overkill. And while their other equipment was of dubious origin and quality, Zeke hadn't skimped on the shields.

They were first-rate. They kept the temperature and air mix stable within the barrier, filtered out organics, and deflected or absorbed minor physical impact.

"What if, you know, the BRAT knows we're here," Kristos said, quietly this time so no one else could hear.

"It's not going to notice a few hacked vines," Edie threw back.

"But there's all those airborne viruses, or whatever, that sample our DNA and change it—"

"They can't get through the shields, even on minimum. Just don't turn it off or you'll be mutating within the minute."

She couldn't resist teasing him, but it was true. On her previous visit, Edie had turned off her e-shield for a few minutes, trusting that the alienness would not harm her. But now the environment was drenched in cyphviruses released by the BRATs. They sampled everything in the ecosystem, transmitting the data to the biocyph in the BRAT, which analyzed it and wrote custom-designed retrovirus code. This was transmitted back to the cyphviruses, triggering them to recode their embryonic DNA-analogs and integrate the new DNA into the host organism's genome. Thus the organism was transformed, at the genetic level, to become more like the target ideal that the biocyph was working toward.

The target ideal was supposed to be a Terran-like ecosystem. It was not supposed to look anything like this.

It seemed like a long time later that Zeke called out, "We're setting up the shield now."

He and the serfs must have reached ground level. The sphere of protection from the shield would isolate the BRAT, enabling the team to work without it communicating to the other BRATs or to the satellite that it was being interfered with. Edie stopped her descent to perch on a sturdy vine, and pulled a diagnostic rod from her belt. It registered the shield coming online, its edge ten meters below her and about the same distance to her left. The holo displayed a sphere overlaid with a grid—a diagrammatic representation of the shield's structure.

"I'm getting a broken grid," she reported, using the comm to avoid shouting.

"Looks fine to me." Zeke sounded out of breath, like he'd been exerting himself down there.

She reinitialized the rod and examined the holo again, switching through different views. "Interference or something. Are you sure about the integrity?"

Finn climbed up to wedge himself behind her so he could take a look for himself. Their e-shields melded and she felt the warmth and pressure of his body along her spine. She shook her head for his benefit. It didn't look like a break in the shield—not quite. But something was wrong.

"Zeke, can you power it down and reboot?" she said.

Above them, Kristos made an impatient sound to get them moving again. Finn swung to one side to let him pass, but when Edie started to follow he held her back.

"Let's wait here till we sort this out." His hand gripped her belt, holding her there.

"It's just a sensor glitch, Finn."

"You on your way down?" Zeke bellowed.

"On our way." Edie glared over her shoulder at Finn. "Let's move."

"First you clear this glitch."

She tapped her comm again. "Zeke, power down will you? I need to check something."

"What would I want to do that for?"

"Just do it."

She heard his muttered curses, but he complied. The holo flickered out and it took several minutes to reappear as Zeke rebooted, bringing the shield online again. This time the anomaly was obvious.

"There's another shield down there," she reported.

"There's five other shields, teckie. Five men. Supposed to be seven, so get your ass in gear. Jezus, it's a frickin' swamp down here." The comm crackled as Zeke moved about. "Come on in," he sang to himself, "the jungle's fine."

Edie magnified the distorted area on the grid. The

interference came from the overlap with another shield. Not
an e-shield, but a weak sphere similar to the one they were
using on the BRAT. Much smaller.

She tensed against Finn's chest. "I think someone got here
first."

The jungle exploded beneath them.

One deafening crack that sent shock waves reverberat-
ing in all directions. Edie slipped downward, instinctively
grabbing on to the vines to slow her descent, oblivious to
the screaming pain in her shoulder and the sharper pain in
her eardrums as they threatened to burst. She was deaf and
blind and numb, senses caving in swiftly. She didn't fight it.

CHAPTER 24

Consciousness returned in increments, one sense at a time. Pressure against her neck, almost cutting off her windpipe but not quite. The e-shield protected her. She jerked her head clear and was aware of pressure in other places where her limbs were tangled in the vines. Her brain felt hazy and soft, like it was sparking in slow-motion. Time stood still. She heard . . . silence, then the falling of heavy vegetation and the distant scrambling of unseen creatures. She must have blacked out for only a few seconds.

And other noises—none of them human. Clicks and whistles and moaning. The e-shield permitted a faint tinge of harmless ozone to reach her nostrils.

These thoughts got her brain working again. Zeke. He'd been on the ground. They all had, except—where was Finn? He'd been right here with her, and now he was gone.

She opened her eyes and blinked away the flashes in her vision. There was no longer a tunnel below her. Even as she watched, the vines moved, slithered all around her like a nest of serpents, entwining and matting together again until she was cocooned within their grasp. She stared in disbelief. Everything about the vines told her they were plants, but this behavior was more like that of an animal.

"Well, I'm alive, so I know you're not dead."

Finn. Somewhere down below, but close. The blast must have knocked him a few meters lower.

She managed to drag in a deep breath. Her first breath. Now she knew she was alive.

It took Finn ten minutes to hack through to reach her, using brute force and a blade from his tool belt to rip the vines aside. She didn't think Zeke had assigned him a shiv—he must have lifted it before they left the skiff.

She worked her limbs loose, and the feeling gradually returned to her hands and fingertips.

"Why am I shaking?" She wasn't cold or afraid. She felt nothing.

"Shock." Finn pulled himself up in front of her in the small hollow they'd made amid the vines. "Listen, we're gonna have to go down to the ground. No way we can climb back up."

With great effort, she tilted her head and saw that he was right. The vines had closed in overhead, healing the wound the alien intruders had made. It would take forever to cut through that, and Finn's shiv wasn't going to be enough. And her shoulder would never handle the climb, even if the path was cleared.

He checked the spur on his arm. She watched his deft fingers, then his face. Her mind finally caught up to what her eyes were seeing, and then she tracked back over the moments before the explosion.

"Edie, you have to calm down." Finn wrapped his hands around her skull. Her misfiring brain was affecting him. She focused on his dark, calm eyes, feeling the pressure of his fingers against her skin. "Only a few more meters. The vines thin out directly below us. You can drop straight through. Follow me."

She nodded and he released her.

"What happened?" she managed, her voice a whisper.

"Pulsed EM discharge combined with explosives and a shitload of shrapnel. A flash bomb."

"Hidden in that low-strength shield?"

He nodded. "So low we missed it on the sweep from seventy meters up, but it was enough to mask the signature from the bomb. Probably dropped from the air. They can drill through rock, so this place would've been no problem."

"That shield . . . it had the same frequency as our shield for the BRAT. That's why it was barely detectable. They knew which BRAT we were heading for, they knew the shield frequency."

"Those details were only finalized in the last twelve hours."

She didn't like where that line of reasoning was going. "Did someone on the *Hoi* betray our location to eco-rads?"

"Or launch a guided flash bomb to the surface when we entered the system. Someone who's not too fussy about who died."

"Died? Are they all . . . ?"

"Well, they were right on top of it."

Edie closed her eyes against his indifference.

"That shield they set up around the BRAT saved us," he said. "The blast was more or less contained within the perimeter. They were inside, we were outside. Hand me that."

He took the diagnostic rod from her and widened the scan range. As he checked for other shields in the vicinity, she was struck by his calm professionalism. A soldier in a battle zone, immune—at least for now—to the death surrounding him.

"I'm not finding any more." He handed the rod back. "This thing is bleeding out."

"What?" The power cell was less than half full—that couldn't be right. She'd fully charged it before they left.

"The EMP's caused the charge to leak. We'll lose everything soon—comms, diagnostics, e-shields."

Edie's mind suddenly felt sharp as a blade. "We can't lose the shields. We can't survive without them." She checked hers. The plan had been to recharge at the skiff every twenty hours or so. "I still have fifteen hours. What about you?"

"About the same." He tried the comm. "This is almost

dry, too. I'm getting a weak signal but unless Cat boosts the power at her end—and fast—we can't contact the skiff."

He began climbing down. She followed his footholds, and after a few meters the vines thinned out. She dropped beside him onto an uneven bed of roots and broken vines. Briars and a dozen species of reeds and grasses sprung up from the marshy earth. Large stumpy growths protruded from the ground, forming anchors for the stalks of the vines. A spiny plant clutched the edge of one stump, its creamy, enameled petals glistening silvery pale in the dim light. Interspersed with the vegetation were boulders, some twice Edie's height, that had been part of the original landscape. And strewn over everything was a pale gossamer thread woven by some unknown creature.

After the strange behavior she'd observed in the vines, she looked at everything twice, half expecting these plants to start moving. But for now, the vista remained serene.

Too serene—in shock, perhaps.

The only movement came from above, where the vines still churned through meters of canopy. She and Finn would never get out that way.

Finn set up a couple of lamps. The thicket surrounded them, but a natural clearing had formed over this shallow swamp where the vines had grown up and over, twisting together to form a living cave. The air was dank and still.

Edie's knees almost gave way as she pushed through the thicket. The ground was marshy in places, rocky in others. Every step was a struggle.

"We'll have to get out of here at ground level." He gave the jungle a grim look. "Let's grab what we can from the others and get started."

The others. The bodies.

They found the first hidden in a bed of fallen vines and splattered with mud. One of the serfs. Finn worked the man's tool belt loose and took what he wanted, then turned the body over carelessly to raid the backpack. Nearby was another serf, his face turned toward Edie, expressionless, almost peaceful. She dropped to her knees and touched his head. She hadn't given the serfs a second thought, and she knew no one else would, but this man came from somewhere, had a past, maybe had hopes and dreams if the tranqs hadn't knocked it all out of him.

His e-shield generator was damaged beyond repair and the battery pack was leaking. She clipped it onto her belt and pried the water torch out of his clenched fist.

She caught a glimpse of the BRAT through the undergrowth, a towering gray giant, its featureless casing mostly free of growth, since there was nothing for moss or vines to cling to. In the opposite direction, a body had been thrown into the undergrowth by the force of the blast. Only the torso was visible, but she recognized it as Zeke.

His body twitched.

"Zeke's alive!" she yelled at Finn, who was trudging through mud to reach the body of the third serf. Kristos was nowhere to be seen.

Zeke's shield hissed and flickered, its integrity breached. They had to get him out of there, and fast, before the cyphviruses found him and changed him. Even as Edie processed that thought, she knew it was too late. Within minutes his body would be invaded, his genome transmitted to the BRAT. The BRAT would redesign his DNA according to its unknown target parameters and send out the retroviral code to make changes. Even if they got him off the planet quickly, his body would be infected by those viruses and he'd die without the very finest Crib medical attention. Probably even with it.

She was too far away to extend her shield around him. And if he was infected, it was too late anyway. He had to be quarantined.

She made her way toward him, climbing over rocks and dragging aside foliage. Finn finished raiding the body of the last serf and followed her.

"Don't touch him!" he called out, having noticed the spluttering e-shield.

Edie adjusted her shield's frequency slightly so it could not merge with Zeke's once she got close enough. Zeke's limbs were twisted at strange angles, his skin slashed by shrapnel and stones thrown up by the bomb. When she saw the blood soaking through his jacket in patches, she drew a sobbing breath. His e-shield desperately tried to remain online, sparking and cycling. It threw a flickering ghostly aura around his body but his left arm was exposed where the connection had malfunctioned. His head lolled to one side and he wore a huge grin.

Come on in, the jungle's fine.

Edie forced herself step closer, then recoiled in shock. Zeke's fingers were gone. No, not gone . . . the creeper vines on the ground had latched onto his arm and entered his fingertips with wriggling tentacles. The veins under his skin pulsed with life. Not his life, but the life of the plants. They had merged with him, drawing his flesh into themselves.

Finn came up behind her. "It's happening to one of the others, too."

Zeke's body twitched again and he opened his eyes. Bloodshot eyes, huge with surprise.

"You're not leaving me here, are you?"

"No, Zeke," Edie said. "I won't leave you."

He turned his head to look at his hand. The flesh squirmed with slivers of alien vines that had entered his body.

"Doesn't hurt." His breath rasped.

"Zeke, it's okay. We'll get you out of here."

Edie swallowed hard and tried not to look at his arm, his smashed-up chest, his haunted eyes. Whatever it was that had invaded his flesh moved up his forearm and into the muscles of his shoulder, even as she watched. It ate away his hand until the end of the limb was grafted into the surrounding lattice of vines.

"Where's the kid? Where's Kristos?"

She couldn't answer him. Zeke's shield failed for a full second, then flickered back on. Off again. On.

"Turn off the shield, teckie," he whispered. "No point wasting it."

"Cat will be here any minute with the skiff," she lied.

"Cat . . ."

The breath hissed out of him and he stared at Edie. Unblinking. His arm quivered briefly with new life.

Finn moved to grab the rifle but Edie stopped him.

"Let me." She couldn't bear to see him treat Zeke's body like he had the others, like a dead animal. She collected the shield pack and rifle and unstrapped Zeke's spur, trying to hold her tears in check. "He was a good man."

"If you say so."

Finn had known the serf handler, the drub, the discipline. She remembered Zeke's shiny laughing face and his good-natured irreverence, their shared resentment of the Crib, and how she had liked him from the start—even if she could never quite trust him.

As she stood up and turned away from Zeke, her comm-link buzzed and stuttered. It was Cat, trying to get a message through. Edie went to answer it, an automatic reaction, but Finn stayed her hand before it reached her belt.

"If she's responsible for this, or Haller, do we really want to be talking to them now?"

Edie faced him squarely. "She's our only way out of here."

"Zeke, Zeke, do you copy?" Cat's voice came through clearly now.

Finn put his finger to his lips and Edie hesitated. He hit his own commlink.

"This is Finn."

"What the hell happened down there? I picked up a massive EM pulse in the vicinity. Did you guys get hit?"

"Yeah, flash bomb, masked by a low-level shield. We have multiple casualties. The serfs are dead, and the op-teck kid, and Edie."

He looked Edie in the eye—a warning. She stayed quiet.

Cat was silent for several seconds. "What about Zeke?"

"He's alive. Badly wounded."

"Let me talk to him."

"He's unconscious."

Another pause. Then Haller came on the line. The message track indicated he wasn't on the skiff. Cat must have already dropped him and his team of two serfs at the next megabiosis, but he'd been listening in.

"You said Edie's dead?"

"That's right." Finn's voice was flat.

"Fuck."

"She was on the ground setting up the BRAT shielding with the serfs."

"But your lag ass was clear?"

"I was securing the perimeter with Zeke, doing my job, *sir.*" His lip snarled on the word. "Everyone inside the perimeter took the hit."

"Please forgive my lapse in logic," Haller said, "but isn't your brain supposed to fry when the cypherteck dies?"

Finn didn't miss a beat. "You underestimated her. She found a way to disable the leash days ago."

Haller muttered another oath while Finn drew their attention to more immediate problems.

"The EMP did some damage to our equipment. We're losing power on our shields, and the commclips will be dead in twenty minutes or less."

"How long do you have on the shields?" Cat asked.

"Hard to say. I should be able to cobble together enough power to last the two of us until we get out."

"You've got a six-kilometer trek through the jungle hauling Zeke . . . six hours, at least," Cat estimated.

"Cat, return for my team first," Haller said. "We're only a few meters into the canopy—we'll climb up and you can winch us out. Then we'll decide on the best approach for retrieving Zeke."

There was a pause as Cat considered the order. Clearly, she'd rather come for Zeke first, but there was more chance of success with Haller and two more men helping in that operation.

"Fine, sir. I'll check in with Captain Rackham. Stand by, Finn."

"I'll be here." Finn flicked off the comm with a humorless grin. He climbed back over to the area where he'd set up the lamps, and gathered the salvaged equipment together.

"Why pretend I'm dead?" Edie called after him, struggling to keep up. "If they thought I was alive, they'd race back here to save me."

"No, they'd tell you to fix that shielding on the BRAT and complete the mission, what's left of it. If the cypherteck is dead, the mission is over. Home time. Much as I want that paycheck, I won't die for it."

"They wouldn't make me do that, not now that it's clear the rads were here. It's too dangerous."

Finn gave her an exasperated look. "There were no rads, Edie. Rads kill the cypherteck. That flash bomb was designed to wipe out an entire team."

Her breath caught as the truth of his words sank in. "Then it *was* someone on the crew. Cat, Haller, Rackham, the two engies . . . who?" As rovers these people had been through a lot together. She didn't want to believe they'd betray each other.

"Don't forget the cook," Finn added. He couldn't be serious—Gia didn't have the resources for something like this. "Or the kid. I guess Cat and Haller are off the hook, assuming they really do stick around to rescue us."

"That's why you told them Zeke was alive—so they'd come back for him."

Finn gave a harsh laugh. "You think they'd come back just for me?"

CHAPTER 25

By the time Cat called back a few minutes later, after consulting with Rackham, Finn's comm was dead. He answered using Edie's, only to find that Cat had more bad news.

"Just tried to take off—but I'm not going anywhere for a while. My flight stabilizers are shot."

"How the hell did that happen?" Haller barked.

Edie and Finn exchanged a look and Edie mouthed the word *sabotage*?

"I have no idea, sir." Cat's despondency sounded genuine, but it might be an act. "Controls felt a bit weird when I landed on the island after dropping off your team, and then they burned out when I fired up the engines again just now."

"Call Corky," Haller said. "Tell him to come down in the other skiff to help with repairs."

"Already did that. This is going to take a while," Cat said. "Finn, head due north from the BRAT. If we get there before you make it out, Haller and the serfs can start cutting in from the other direction."

"Understood." The comm crackled. Finn checked the power and shook his head in dismay.

"We won't leave . . . won't . . . without Zeke." Cat's transmission broke up and faded out altogether.

"You think she's telling the truth?" Finn gave the comm-clip a little shake, as though it had trapped Cat's last few words.

Edie remembered Cat's claim that she'd tried to help them escape by sending a flight plan to the skiff. "Yes, I think so."

They didn't speak aloud the fear that the traitor on the *Hoi* would try again. For now, there was nothing they could do but get out of the jungle.

Edie packed up the salvaged shield batteries and anything else that looked useful—there wasn't much left. She strapped on Zeke's spur, hoping she'd remember the firearms lessons Lukas had given her, if it came to that.

Finn shrugged on his backpack. "You set?"

Edie was aware of the creature a split second before he was, saw the pale shape scuttling through the overhead branches. Finn sensed it, looking up just as it flung itself onto his chest trailing a milky white thread.

Edie automatically raised her arm and the spur slid into position. Her thumb hovered over the trigger. But the creature was already falling off Finn, zapped by the shield. Its lightning-fast movement had given her a false impression of its size. It was no bigger than Finn's boot, beside which it now dangled motionless, its multiple legs curled up underneath its flattened carapace, suspended from a thread anchored overhead. It looked like an overgrown slater.

"What were you gonna do, shoot me in the chest?" Finn yelled.

Edie lowered the spur, surprised by his anger, and realized how stupid her reaction had been. The shields protected them from any creepy crawlies this place could throw at them, but set on low they couldn't deflect projectiles from a spur. She might have killed him.

"Sorry," she said sheepishly.

He scowled, grabbing one of the lamps as he moved past her. "Probably one of those friendly bunnies you told me about."

"I never said anything about bunnies. That was your idea."

They'd taken a few paces across the clearing when a very human groan stopped them in their tracks. Edie whipped out her diagnostic rod and scanned for e-shields in the vicinity.

"To our right."

It was Kristos. From the readout, his shield appeared to be intact. They found him tangled up in debris some way back from the rest.

Edie cut through the vines with her shiv and pulled him clear. "You okay? Were you knocked out?"

"I think so." Kristos staggered to his feet. He looked over his limbs and seemed satisfied he wasn't injured.

Edie saw his e-shield crackle on a stray leaf. "You didn't turn your shield down."

Kristos blushed defiantly, and Finn laughed at him. "You got lucky, kid. But check your power meter." While Kristos's face turned from shame to horror, Finn explained. "The blast damaged the batteries. Turn your shield down now or you'll never last long enough to get lucky again." He turned away, ready to move on.

"We should still check for concussion," Edie told Finn. He carried the medkit in his pack.

Finn relented. He shone his penlight in Kristos's eyes. "You remember what just happened?" he asked gruffly.

"There was a bomb or something . . ."

"You feel dizzy?"

"No, I'm okay. Where's everyone else?"

"Cat's having engine trouble. She'll fetch Haller's team and then come for us," Edie explained. "The others are dead."

The young op-teck's ruddy face went white and his eyes teared up. She pitied him—his only two runs with the *Hoi Polloi* had both ended in tragedy.

Finn returned the light to his belt. "Got a headache? Weakness in your arms or legs?"

Kristos shook his head numbly.

"If you throw up or fall down, let me know." He turned to Edie. "He's not concussed. Come on, let's get out of here."

Edie shook her head at the good doctor's perfunctory examination, but he was right—they had limited juice in their shields and they had to move. She helped Kristos get his pack sorted out and followed Finn into the clearing. From there they set off due north.

At point position, Finn had to work the hardest to clear a path. They avoided the low-hanging vines because it was impossible to hack through them—ever since the explosion, they took to quickly closing over wherever they were damaged. The rest of the vegetation was less dense, but much of it was too thick to cut even with a water torch, and they had to climb over it. Then the water torch ran dry and they used shivs. The ground was uneven, thick with prickly undergrowth and punctuated with slippery boulders. Edie's mind automatically categorized each new lifeform it registered— mosses, ferns, arthropods, worms. Only a few meters into the thick of the jungle, and despite the low light levels, she'd already counted dozens of species. Each one was unlike anything she'd seen before, but was recognizable within broad categories. And each one, she knew, was unlike what it had been seven years ago. Every living thing on Scarabaeus had been transformed at the genetic level as the BRATs controlling the ecosystem beat to their own strange drum.

Finn looked back frequently, checking their progress. Perhaps he thought Kristos's survival meant they shouldn't rule him out as the traitor. Edie was more concerned with Kristos's emotional health. Kristos ploughed on in subdued silence.

The jungle was a cocoon of indistinct shadowy shapes lit by broken rays. They'd been on Scarabaeus for five hours, and it was mid-afternoon. Finn climbed a large, craggy boulder almost as tall as he was, and leaned down to help Kristos and Edie up. On top of the boulder, Kristos put his hands on his knees, catching his breath.

"How much farther?"

"Kid, this is going to take all day," Finn said. "If you're not up to it, don't bother tagging along."

Kristos looked up with a flash of anger. He wasn't used to being spoken to like that by a serf.

Edie put her hand on Kristos's arm before he said something stupid. "We'll make it out of here. A few hours, okay?"

The other side of the boulder was a sharp drop. Finn jumped off, losing his footing momentarily in the soft mesh of plant material on the ground. He staggered a couple of paces, as if the ground had shifted underneath him, before regaining his balance.

Kristos was already following him.

"Wait!"

Edie reacted instinctively to Finn's shout, dropping to her knees and grabbing for Kristos's jacket as he went over the edge, but she missed. She peered over the boulder. Kristos had landed in the spongy patch of dark undergrowth. It was littered with what looked like crushed and broken exoskeletons.

"My boots are stuck!" he called out.

"Grab my hand." She reached down as far as she could. Preoccupied with pulling his feet out of the sticky bed, Kristos didn't look up.

The ground shifted again, forcing Finn to back up against the ferny vegetation of the jungle. Kristos lost his balance and landed on his backside.

A long thick pad snapped across Kristos's body, then two more. They curled in on him like fingers closing into a fist. Edie realized they had unfurled from the edges of the marshy area where Kristos was stuck. The fingers twisted from the base like a corkscrew, tightening into a massive, fleshy tuber that swallowed up Kristos's body with more speed than any plant should have been capable of.

Finn reacted instantly. Leaping forward, he grabbed the edge of one pad and pulled until it separated from the adjacent one, and plunged his arm inside.

"Stay there," he yelled at Edie as she moved to climb down. As Finn grappled with the tuber that enclosed Kristos, she noticed a row of pale markings along the edges of the fingers. Photosensitive pits. The tuber, despite looking more plant than animal, had eyespots similar to those of primitive invertebrates. From their crude structure she guessed they could differentiate light from dark and probably even the direction of light rays.

Finn grabbed his shiv with his free hand, but it had little effect on the fibrous plant. A strangled cry came from within the tuber as the fingers tightened further, and the entire structure slowly twisted and tightened.

Edie couldn't just sit there and watch. She slid down the side of the boulder, keeping clear of the corkscrew fist, and joined Finn around the other side. She helped him pull on the fleshy pad to widen the gap he'd made. Finn braced himself against the ground to avoid being pulled inside as the plant inexorably drilled itself into the earth.

"Got him." Finn's jaw clenched with the effort.

He had a good grip on Kristos's arm, and yanked hard. Edie caught a handful of Kristos's collar and did the same. The edges of the tuber's fingers peeled back to reveal a layer of inward-directed spines on the inside that worked against them, holding Kristos firm, although his shield protected him from being impaled. It sizzled against the spines as it resisted them.

The tuber had wound itself halfway into the ground, forcing Finn and Edie to their knees as they pulled without making much progress. There was a terrible crunch as bones broke.

"Kristos! Turn up your shield."

His head bobbed against his chest. Edie thought he'd passed out, but then he raised his chin, eyes wide with terror. She yelled at him again, urging him into action. One hand came up and gripped the edge of the tuber, as if he might try to pull himself out, but his weak effort made no difference. His other arm was still trapped.

Edie reached down the side of Kristos's hip, now below

ground level, and searched blindly for the shield generator on his belt, feeling the tug of the tuber as it sucked at her arm.

"Stay clear," Finn shouted, doing his best to keep a hold on Kristos's arm.

"We need to crank up his shield."

Another crunch as Kristos's lower body was crushed. He was no longer moving at all.

"Get back!"

She ignored Finn, frantically grabbing at Kristos's belt, her arm sinking up to the elbow. The force of the twisting motion was incredible, and she wasn't sure her shield could protect her bones for very long. A sudden jerk pitched her forward and her arm slipped deep inside the tuber. She struggled to keep her head free. Pain shot through her arm as it was slowly forced to bend the wrong way at the elbow joint. She could barely gasp a moan of agony.

Finn released Kristos, who disappeared into the clutches of the tuber. His strong hands closed around her shoulder and he tried to lever her arm free.

"You have to grab Kristos," she gasped. "It's crushing him. Grab him!"

As Finn pulled hard on her arm, Edie cried out—in frustration more than anything. She should have known Finn wouldn't waste time with someone else when she was in danger. His priority was her life, because her life was his life.

And her life was in danger now. The tuber was not giving her up. She didn't know how deep it would drill into the ground, but if it didn't let go she'd be buried alive.

The strength of Finn's body pulling against the plant suddenly deserted her. He stepped back and hauled his rifle into position.

"Don't move."

He fired twice into what remained of the tuber above ground, angling his aim to avoid hitting Edie.

The rounds exploded with waterlogged pops, and sap spurted from the tuber. Edie felt an immediate relaxing on the twist of the fingers, and her arm came free. Before Finn had time to object, she plunged both arms back inside, desperate to take advantage of the damage that had been done to the corkscrew. It must rely on water pressure to maintain turgidity, because as the sap leaked out its grip grew weaker and weaker.

She felt Kristos's limp body and grabbed handfuls of his clothing. The lack of resistance as she touched him told her his shield had burned out under the pressure. The tuber fingers wilted and she was able to pull him halfway out.

"Finn, help me."

Finn stared into the jungle, his rifle slung, and Edie followed his gaze. There was a ripple within the ferns. The tangled mass of vegetation coiled itself up, as though waiting to strike.

Then it pounced. Not an animal, surely, though it moved like one. The tip leapt out like a whiptail, striking a blow to Finn's shoulder, hard enough to make him stagger. His shield sizzled and absorbed most of the impact, but the reedy stalk, as thick as his arm, held fast around his neck. Its inertia dragged him to his knees. The shield kept the pressure off his windpipe, and he was able to twist and fire into the thing with his spur.

Edie fired into the undergrowth an instant later. The whiptail retracted quickly, thumping along the ground like a wounded snake.

A squeal came from the undergrowth. All around them the jungle rustled. Edie cranked up her shield a notch, seeing Finn do the same. He made a quick turn, full-circle, warily taking in their surrounds. They were cocooned on all sides, and above, by the close jungle, with no room to run and nowhere to hide.

The tuber that imprisoned Kristos sank to the ground like a deflated balloon.

"We have to get him out," she said.

Finn nodded and took a step toward her.

Something hit the side of Edie's head and she yelped. The

sensation was muted by the shield, but it still felt like she'd been punched. More whiptail attacks on Finn came in quick succession, from all directions, leaving him whirling in confusion. They bounced off his shield and he held his fire. Edie leapt to help, pulling up when one more fell short, the tip landing a meter from her boots. It writhed on the ground, possibly injured by Finn's first shot.

"Stay close," Finn said as she went to his side. "Stay low. And stay *calm*."

She nodded, crouched, spur at the ready, peering into the living jungle. For a tense minute, nothing happened.

"What the hell is this stuff?" Finn said.

"I don't know." She just wanted to get to back to Kristos.

"Come on, you must've seen a lot of weird shit in your time."

"Not like this."

She'd never seen anything like it. A half-meter-wide flattened reed anchored the creature or plant, or whatever it was, within the vegetation mass. At the other end its tapered tip folded and twisted in on itself like origami. More than anything the tip resembled a locust, as long as Edie's leg. She caught glimpses of moist, speckled pink flesh within the squirming folds.

Her heart pounded, and that wasn't good for Finn. She took deep breaths and concentrated on looking out for the next attack. Were these things harmless or not? They couldn't penetrate the shields, but prolonged physical battering would drain the batteries as the shields wasted energy dispersing the impact. With shields down, they'd be exposed to the cyphviruses that permeated the planet.

Which was already Kristos's fate, if he was still alive.

Behind her, Finn continued turning a slow circle. What terrified Edie more than the whiptails was the way the jungle moved around them, shifting and heaving like a leviathan waking from slumber. To get out of this place they were going to have to go through that.

Two more whiptails lashed out, one catching Finn's leg

and almost tripping him up. He fired in the general direction of its anchor, but the vegetation was too thick and tangled to accurately judge where they were coming from.

Edie grabbed a stick and prodded the half-dead fleshy thing near her feet. It reacted instantly, coiling around the stick, holding it fast. Then it let go. It had either died or decided the piece of debris wasn't worth its time.

And then the jungle seemed to inhale, and she held her breath with it. She heard only silence, but felt the pulse of the jungle beating. Faster.

Finn sensed it, too. He shifted uneasily. "What the hell . . . ?"

A quick, violent quake shuddered across the landscape. It wasn't the ground that moved but the things around them, vibrating as one beast. Again the whiptails shot out, but this time a dozen or more at once, in a coordinated circle from every direction. Finn pushed Edie to the ground and covered her with his body as the heavy tips battered him. One caught his wrist and he snaked it free. She felt him fumble for his rifle, and as soon as the whiptails withdrew he rolled onto his back and opened fire in a wide arc into the undergrowth.

The foliage exploded, disintegrating amid hissing steam. Edie covered her head as fronds and branches tumbled to the ground. Higher up, the vines scrabbled for a hold, thrashing about as their scaffolding was cut out from beneath them. Those that broke and fell landed on Finn and Edie, bouncing off their shields in a patter of sizzles and pops.

The air smoldered. Unseen creatures shrieked and scurried.

Finn shouldered the rifle and surveyed his handiwork.

Edie gasped in the scorched air, cranking up the filters on her shield. "Must've been the flash bomb. We were fine until that went off. Some sort of defensive mechanism kicked in."

Thick vines squirmed around them, unraveling, creeping in from every direction, reaching with seeking, trembling tendrils. The area was fast becoming a choking, tangled web and soon it would be impossible to move through it at all.

An alarm sounded on Finn's shield. He checked the monitor on his belt and threw Edie a worried look.

"Must've been damaged. Thirty minutes left. How much on those battery packs you salvaged?"

"A few hours, all up, but its leaking just like you said. Mine too—it's reading five hours left." They weren't going to make it. "We have to get back to the clearing. To the BRAT. Maybe I can recharge our shields from its power source."

Finn slapped a fresh clip into the rifle and nodded curtly. "This way."

He grasped her hand and pulled her along at a half-crouch, back toward the boulder, ducking a new wave of whiptails that flayed their shields. They approached the collapsed tuber that encased Kristos. Cocooned in a tight mass of vines, all that remained was a desiccated husk, its surface gray and cracked.

"I need to check . . ."

He was dead, she already knew it, but she needed confirmation. Something stuck out between the twisted fingers of the tuber: Kristos's hand, clutching at nothing. If he'd kept his shield higher, if the jungle hadn't attacked them, if they'd managed to pull him out . . . But he was dead, and if she and Finn didn't get to safety before the jungle overwhelmed them or their shields ran out of power, they'd end up the same way.

They climbed up the sheer face of the boulder, easier now than it would have been ten minutes ago because the jungle had descended and there were low-hanging branches to haul themselves up with. On the other side, confronted by shifting tentacles of foliage that latched onto their limbs and whipped across their faces, they made a dash for the clearing, retracing their steps even as the path was obliterated. It was only fifty meters or so, but they fought the jungle every step of the way.

When they finally broke free of the dense vegetation

and emerged into the swamp clearing, things weren't much better. Shadows shifted and wavered in the half-light and the same whiptail reeds snapped and withdrew, over and again, wherever they moved. Above them, the tunnel they'd made through the canopy had closed over as though it had never been there, and the jungle pressed down. The living cave was collapsing.

They fired when they had to, when the whiptails grabbed them or blocked their path, but it seemed that each shot only amped up the jungle's violent reaction. As the writhing vegetation edged closer, they were forced toward the center of the clearing, into the shallow swamp. Every nerve-racking step through the mud could lead them into another trap like the predatory tuber that had taken Kristos, or some other unknown danger.

"Need a damn flamethrower," Finn muttered, checking his ammo. "Can you get us inside that thing?"

The BRAT lay ominously silent a few meters away.

CHAPTER 26

There's always a way in.

Bethany's presence flooded the datastream that flowed through Edie's mind. So many years since she'd jacked into Bethany's coding. The familiar sonnets brought a wave of pleasure. The way Bethany riveted her tiers together with glyphs, using the actual glyph as a bridging subroutine instead of a simple marker. The way she wedged extra commands into empty layers to create a more compact and efficient program—more efficient for the biocyph, a nightmare for the cypherteck trying to tease the strands apart, but Edie was used to it. Edie had adapted the technique, improved it, used it herself for years.

Bethany's frank, confident, innovative personality was written into the code.

Finn stood guard beside Edie, gritting his teeth, wary of every movement of the jungle around them. From the way he rubbed the back of his neck, he was equally aware of her heightened mental state that messed with his head. They had made it across the swamp to the BRAT, dodging flailing whiptails and vines, so she could jack in. They'd emptied their spurs in the process and discarded them.

Behind them lay Zeke. Edie avoided looking at him.

The first priority was to get inside the BRAT casing, which would provide physical protection against the attacks. Then they could figure out how to recharge the shields and brace themselves for the long trek out of the megabiosis.

To get in, Edie needed to convince the BRAT to open up. She'd used the Crib's emergency codes to get past its security barricade, leaving it open to surface-level reprogramming. Now she had to decide the best way to proceed without annoying it to the point that it threw her out of the link.

She'd drained half of her remaining shield power into Finn's damaged shield, but his was draining fast as he kept the jungle at bay with the occasional rifle blast. He asked after her progress only once, and she answered him with a scowl. He kept quiet after that.

Crouched low, Edie leaned against the BRAT, fingers pressed into its single dataport.

Bethany's coding had never been the harmonies that Edie could create. No one else could do that. Bethany's sonnets were fragments of music, without melody but always melodious, like sultry wind chimes dangling in a light breeze. Endless variations on a theme. Edie could lose herself in there, in the familiar cadences, in the memories. She filed through the datastream looking for the layers she needed to work with.

The softlink physically connected her to the biocyph within the BRAT, but it was a tenuous link. It relied on the BRAT giving up its data to her, usually something it was more than willing to do—biocyph relied on external stimuli to function, and was primed to respond to cyphertecks. But this biocyph didn't want to let her in. It had built security blockades throughout the tiers, making them difficult to demerge, as though seven years of playing the same tune had imprinted an irreversible habit upon it.

But it wasn't the same tune, Edie saw that now. A BRAT seed's instructions were to transform an alien ecology into a Terran-like environment. To use the genomes available within the existing web of life, to make simultaneous changes from the microbe level up, in every metabolic pathway in every living thing through every level of the food chain, to create ocean, soil, atmosphere, and biosphere where humans could thrive. But after a year of dormancy brought on by Edie's kill-code that had spread from another BRAT on a faraway island, from the moment the BRATs on Scarabaeus had managed to reactivate, their instructions had changed.

The BRATs had proceeded along a new path. Checking the log, Edie found no record of external disturbances over those seven years. No one had tampered with the biocyph. There was no aftertaste here of any other cypherteck.

It was Edie's signature—warped almost beyond recognition, but it was hers.

Her heart pounded as she processed the implications, not wanting to reach the inevitable conclusion.

They'd turned off the temperature regulators on the shields to conserve power, and it was getting cold in the depths of the jungle. Finn had been circling the BRAT to get a better view of their surroundings. He came back around the edge to report.

"Something's happening."

She followed his gaze out into the jungle. The vines were turning opaque, and instead of their constant shifting movements, they seemed to be freezing. Finn reached out and touched the tip of a petrified vine. No longer flexible, it was now rigid and brittle. It broke off in his hand, sizzling against his e-shield. The broken end dribbled a milky sap.

The jungle was eerily silent all of a sudden.

"What did you do?" He nodded toward the panel where her fingers were pressed into the dataport, as if she was somehow responsible, but she'd not yet made any programming changes to the BRAT.

"Nothing. Maybe it's a normal process as the sun goes down."

Finn looked dubious. He fired into the canopy, not quite directly overhead. The explosive bullet sent a torrent of vine shards raining into the swamp and the area surround-

ing it. Distant shrieks ripped through the air, and some not
so distant.

He fired again, with the same result. Now a blanket of
razor-sharp pieces of crystalline vines covered the dead men
and the remains of their equipment. Looking up into the
cone-shaped tunnel that had been formed, Edie saw patches
of gray, late-afternoon sky.

"Maybe Cat will see that when she flies over," Finn said.
"She can winch us out."

It sounded like a good idea . . . until Edie realized the sky
was disappearing. The tunnel was caving in. She grabbed a
lamp and shone it upward. Ribbons of sap spurted from the
broken vines. The thick fluid congealed almost instantly to
melt the edges of the tunnel back together, once again forming an impenetrable mass. Considering the mobility of the
vines in their flexible state, it made sense that the fluid inside
had a controllable flow.

Finn raised the rifle to fire again, but Edie pulled his arm
down.

"Save the bullets, Finn. There are hundreds of tons of biomass up there. Clearly it doesn't want to have a hole carved
through it."

He turned a curious look on her. "You talk about it like it
has intent."

"It does what it needs to, like any organism. Its survival
must depend on the structural integrity of the megabiosis."

A keening sound drew her attention back to the melted
patch of vines. Shapes crawled through the mangled mesh.
Then small creatures dropped out of the canopy—hundreds
of them, scattering in all directions. Some dived into the
vines and struggled to free themselves, screeching in distress, the broken edges tearing their flesh. It seemed unlikely
this was natural behavior. The rifle shots must have disori-
entated them.

A group of the creatures plummeted straight toward the
BRAT in a chaotic cloud. Finn was thrown off balance as
they hit him, his shield sparking limply. Edie realized with

alarm that its power was almost dead. He hunkered down, shielding her. She felt the *thud, thud, thud* against his body as the creatures flung themselves at him in a frenzy, trying to get a grip. His shield no longer absorbed the impact of their blows. The creatures fell to the ground and scurried away on tiny legs. They were the same slaterlike creature that had jumped on Finn earlier. She saw now that the carapace lifted up and opened out, like a hard-shelled beetle, to reveal softer wings inside. And everywhere they went, they trailed a silken thread.

The slaters found Zeke's body. Edie watched in horror as they swarmed over him, cracking the vines that cocooned him, ripping the clothes on his body, and then the flesh, into thin shreds with their tiny busy jaws. The air roared with the sound of clicking wings, shattering vines and the slaters' screaming.

She leapt back into the biocyph connection. They needed a fast solution. Finn's shield was about to fail, hers wouldn't hold out much longer, and the slaters had an appetite for human flesh. She shut out the noise and fear, steadied by the grip of Finn's hand on her arm where their shields merged. She grabbed the flickering echo of her signature, buried deep within the tangle of new coding that the BRAT had written. The biocyph knew her, but that didn't mean it wanted to obey her. She captured the signature with a glyph and then laid a passive trail back through the tiers, networking multiple trails from each glyph, then more networks from each of those, so that they fanned outward in a crescendo of increasing complexity. She mentally apologized to Bethany for the brutish assault she was about to launch on the delicate workings of a biocyph seed.

She gathered together the thousands of end glyphs and shot multiple copies of a deceptively inoffensive algorithm down every spoke of the fan simultaneously. They raced toward the central glyph, the core access point, following the trail of her signature, their paths converging again and again so that the algorithm snowballed, gathering momentum, until it forced apart the tiers like a wedge. It hit the core like a cymbal crash and burst open to reveal its simple command.

Open!

To her right, a seam in the BRAT quivered and cracked. She banged on the casing to attract Finn's attention. They moved around the edge of the BRAT in a crouch. Edie looked back to see the slaters carrying away the remains of Zeke's body, coordinating their efforts to drag pieces of his flesh into the jungle. The tatters of tissue that got left behind were quickly swooped upon. She looked away, feeling sick.

The slaters clambered all over the BRAT, some of them finding the crack and skittering around it, feelers probing, legs sliding on the slick surface as they tried to hold on. In a couple of seconds the gap would be wide enough for them to slip inside. Finn reached over Edie to knock them away. They curled up and rolled off as his weakening shield zapped them, and for a split second Edie recognized the spark in his shield's aura that signaled the shield had almost failed.

She extended her own shield to envelop Finn and most of the door as well. She expanded it gradually. Too fast and it would simply enclose the slaters along with them. As the periphery of the shield widened, it hit the slaters and they bounced away. The split in the seam was now half a meter wide, and protected by the bubble of her shield. Finn's hands around her waist lifted her up, and she climbed into darkness. He threw their packs in after her, then jumped inside.

Edie took one last look at the chaos outside before jamming the door shut. The seal hissed and locked.

Finn turned on a lamp. They were on a narrow ledge running all the way around the central core of the BRAT—a three-meter well where the biocyph and seed machinery were housed within a network of scaffolding. The casing arched over their heads. This upper part of the BRAT contained the main interface jacks and the parts of the machinery that were meant to be accessible, although not normally after the BRAT seed had been planted and had germinated. On terraformed, colonized worlds, BRATs were left in the ground indefinitely where they continued their sampling and tinkering, fine-tuning the ecosystem for the human inhabitants, suppressing disease-causing bacterial outbreaks and algal blooms and other conditions adverse to humans and their agriculture and technologies.

Edie cranked down her shield so that it enveloped only herself and Finn. It was going to fail within minutes. Pulling the spare batteries out of her pack—the ones she'd charged with the remaining power in the rest of their team's shields— she swapped the cell over, and handed one to Finn.

The thumping and scrabbling on the outside of the BRAT returned as the slaters resumed their attack.

"So much for your bunnies," she said grimly, making her way around the ledge.

"Did the flash bomb damage anything?"

"Biocyph's pretty much immune to EM interference, and the seed casing would protect it in any case." She pointed out the power cell. "Do you have any idea how this works?"

"I thought BRATs were your thing."

"I know what's down there." She nodded into the biocyph well below the ledge. "I don't know how it's powered."

Finn came over to take a look. He flipped open the cell and examined the traces on the circuit module.

"This won't work. Even if we can jury-rig an interface, it'll blow out the shields."

"Are you sure?"

"Yes."

"We have to try. What other option do we have?"

He shrugged and she handed him one of the drained e-shields. She watched him open it up and tease out a wire, which he stripped with careful efficiency using his shiv.

"This is all because of me," she said.

He met her eyes, looking shocked by the despair that choked her voice.

"Finn, I did this. My kill-code. The lock that I put on the biocyph—it's a loop of code, an irreconcilable paradigm. Makes the programming go around in circles. The biocyph gets confused and eventually it just gives up. But here, it didn't shut down. After a year, the BRATs found a way around it. They broke the lock and they've been fighting the kill-code ever since. Fighting to survive. Fighting *me*."

"You think that explains the aggression?"

"Yes. Instead of creating a world for humans, its new target ideal became the creation of an environment to protect itself. The flash bomb was its first big test, made it aware of us as a danger. Then the shooting . . ." Edie slid down the cold, smooth interior of the BRAT into a tight hunch, hugging her knees. Those things that had torn apart Zeke's body, and waited outside to tear apart her and Finn—they were *her* unintended creations. "On any other world this could never have happened, I'm sure of it. This place had different raw materials to work with. Advanced lifeforms, not just algae and bacteria."

"Helluva breeding ground for anyone interested in bio-weapons," Finn mused.

He found the power trace on the circuit module and touched the stripped wire of the e-shield to it. The shield popped and crackled. Sparks erupted out of the connection—a short-lived mini-volcano.

He turned the dead shield over in his hands. "Burned out."

"We can put all our remaining power into two working shields," Edie suggested. "I think we can get about five hours each."

"The shields won't hold charge. Your fifteen hours lasted only two. Mine lasted even less."

"Is there nothing else you can try?"

"This one is beyond repair. The other was already damaged. These systems are just not compatible." He leaned back against the casing and rubbed his neck. "What about you?"

"What do you mean?"

"What can you try?" He shone the lamp into the well of biocyph.

"There's nothing that can help us down there."

"That's all that can help us."

"No—"

He grabbed her shoulder—the injured one. "What's the matter with you? You're giving up?" His harshness sent a shiver through her. "This machinery can create entire worlds."

"There's nothing I can do!" She pleaded with him to understand. "I wish I'd never come here. I should never have interfered."

"Oh, spare me that crap." Finn pushed her away. "You did what you did. That's the past. Maybe you can convince yourself you deserve to die here, but don't make me the victim of your guilty conscience." His eyes held more emotion than she'd ever thought him capable of. Fury, even hate, but above all a passion for life.

They faced off for breathless moments.

And then, with the same passion brought firmly under control, he said, "Don't you let me die."

CHAPTER 27

Edie climbed down into the heart of the BRAT, leaving Finn on the ledge in the dark. She knew the inside of a biocyph seed intimately, could have found her way around without the lamp, but Finn clipped it to her belt anyway.

Here in its underground belly, the BRAT composed its retroviral music. Using the data collected by the airborne cyphviruses, it analyzed the existing ecosystem, creating endless simulations until it hit upon a combination of changes that needed to be made in order to bring each organism closer to the target ideal. It wrote the code for a tailor-made retrovirus, which it transmitted to the target cyphvirus. The cyphvirus was activated, the host cells infected, the genome transformed. Adenine, cytosine, guanine, thymine—the simplest of musical scales. Four notes that combined three-by-three to create the arpeggios of life: amino acids to be endlessly shuffled and assembled into proteins that controlled the physiology of all lifeforms.

Perhaps only a slight modification would be made, unnoticeable to the organism. Perhaps a major change. And every change in an organism required multiple simultaneous changes throughout the ecosystem to support it. The biocyph coordinated this global transformation using a plan that allowed for change over a timescale of decades, until it birthed a world that was safe and nurturing for humans and their kind.

Edie jacked into the biocyph, still with little idea of what she was planning to do. The datastream was a dense, complex cacophony that would take hours to untangle. She searched for something to latch on to. The original specs were still there, along with an accumulation of data gathered over the years by cyphviruses from all the BRATs that had infiltrated every level of the ecosystem, from the mountaintops to the deserts to the depths of the ocean.

And the distorted, mutated instructions were clear now. The biocyph was sending out instructions that changed by the day, feeding back on itself as it sought only to protect the megabiosis from the enemy—the kill-code lock she'd implanted.

She toyed with the idea of dismantling the kill-code, reactivating the initial parameters of Scarabaeus, and reversing the process. It might take a millennium of guided evolution, but the planet could come to resemble the world she remembered from her first visit. The desire to fix the damage she'd caused overrode even her survival instinct.

Hours of work to be done—time she didn't have. She would've done it, let her e-shield dwindle and die while she worked on restoring Scarabaeus . . .

If not for Finn.

Was everything he'd done for her only to protect his own life? She'd seen enough to believe that wasn't true. He'd tried as hard as she had to save Kristos. He'd risked his life for the serf in the engine room, too. She'd glimpsed beyond that implacable exterior over the past two weeks. She'd witnessed his anger and frustration, his humor. She'd experienced his tenderness. None of that should surprise her—he was human, regardless of what the Crib or the *Hoi*'s crew thought of their lag laborer.

He deserved to live. When it came to a choice between Scarabaeus and a man, Edie had to choose the man. She wanted Finn to live. If she could've given him more, restored

all that he'd lost, she would've done that, too. For now, all
she could give him was life. And that meant keeping herself
alive.

The e-shields were useless. Even without the power bleed
caused by the EMP, the physical attacks from the creatures
would quickly drain them. They needed to survive without
shields, and they needed the aggressive wildlife to ignore
them. *We made you disappear.* Haller's words. If she could
disappear from the entire Crib, surely she could hide for
a few hours from a terraforming seed and its hostile lifeforms.

Perhaps there was a way. She tried to get her head around
it. Cyphviruses sampled everything they touched, treating
the environment like a single complex organism. The biocyph calculated how to integrate all the components har-
moniously, regardless of whether individual components
could survive the transformation intact. The e-shields had
so far protected her and Finn from that sort of transformation, but their presence, like the flash bomb and the weapons
fire, jammed the blades of this massive ecological blender.
Jump-started by the bomb, the ecosystem had perceived the
physical intrusion and triggered a defensive reaction.

What if they could pass through the blades unscathed?

Edie teased apart a tier within the biocyph's algorithm-
processing center and wrote a new tune. Nothing too ob-
trusive. Nothing the main program pathways would notice
for a while. She drew threads from nearby subroutines—
whispers and pulses of melody. She diverted them, pegged
out a new route and marked the way with glyphs. She lost
herself in the rhythm as she created her new tier, bleeding
the edges into the surrounding tiers so that it became fully
integrated.

She made it sing.

And Scarabaeus whispered back to her. At first she barely
listened, too caught up in her plan as she modified the
BRAT's instructions so they could escape the jungle. But
there was something here, something not buried in code or

hidden between programming tiers. As she lingered in the datastream, the whisper intensified until she could no longer ignore it. Her wet-teck soaked up the music of Scarabaeus and recognized a pattern.

She grasped at the pattern, pulled it apart, studied its details, but it disintegrated. She gathered it together again and realized there was nothing to see unless she viewed the coherent whole. It was not something to be examined note-by-note or even by melody, but to be absorbed as a symphony.

Through manipulating the ecosystem's genetic code in order to defeat the kill-code lock, the biocyph had learned more than just how to survive. Scarabaeus had its own song now.

A new song that would change everything.

"Finn." She gently shook his shoulder. She'd been working for an hour, at least, and he was dozing, the rifle lying across his thighs. "Finn. I've finished."

"What . . . ?" He rubbed a hand across his face. The lamplight picked out the gold flecks in his eyes.

Edie crouched beside him. "It's safe. As safe as it's ever going to be."

"How much longer on the shields?"

"Forget the shields. I switched them off."

That riveted his attention. "You *what*?"

"I needed to let the cyphviruses in."

Into their bodies, hers and his. She knew the idea would make his skin crawl. That was the standard reaction. But not Edie's—she'd been born with it.

"You mean . . ." His lip curled. "There's nanoteck running around inside me?"

"I had to give the BRAT a picture of who we are—our biopatterns. The cyphviruses will transmit our biopatterns to the BRAT, but it will recognize us now. I've instructed it to ignore us instead of trying to change us. Even the local bacteria will leave us alone."

Finn narrowed his eyes as she explained. She could tell he

wanted to believe her, wanted to be convinced. He wanted to live.

"Jezus." He tilted his head back against the casing, peering into the gloom as if he could see the nano-sized particles Edie had exposed him to. "Couldn't you just take a blood sample?"

"Blood contains your DNA—the template that made you. But it's not *you*. Terraforming biocyph needs the complete picture, all the metabolic pathways. It'll take a few hours to take effect, so we can't leave yet."

"What about the creatures that attacked us?"

"The jungle should ignore us now. Every aspect of this ecosystem is controlled by biocyph, and I've programmed it to treat us as inert components. We have to stop shooting at it, though."

His hands closed around the rifle. He wasn't going to give it up that easily.

"There's something else. Something amazing, Finn." She could've kept what she'd discovered to herself, especially since she had no idea yet what to do with the information, but they were in this together. "The biocyph creating these megabioses—in learning to overcome my kill-code lock, it's evolved. I can *feel* it in the datastream . . . It's so adaptable, I could develop it for use in any ecosystem. It could be used to crack the locks on the BRATs on other worlds."

Finn sucked in a breath. "If you're thinking of taking *any* of this mutated mess offworld and spreading it around—"

"It's only mutated because the BRATs lost their target ideal. I'm talking about an algorithm, a cryptoglyph that can be programmed into BRATs on other worlds. It will teach the BRATs how to permanently override their inbuilt annual shutdown. No more renewal keys. No more slapdash keystones."

"You realize what that would mean?" Finn shook his head, as though it was too much to contemplate. "What are you going to do about it?"

"I don't know. Maybe I should just—" She stopped herself, because the idea of keeping it secret was unthinkable. "It could free the Fringe worlds forever."

"The Crib won't stand for it." Finn was still shaking his head. "This is not your fight."

With a twinge of disappointment, she realized he was talking himself out of it. She wouldn't let him do that. Once he'd been the kind of man who'd have jumped at the challenge. It was her job to make him remember that.

"We can make it our fight. I *made* this hell, Finn, and it's produced a revolutionary technology—"

"Revolutionary? You don't want a revolution, believe me. You're talking about starting a war."

She understood then. Finn had already been there—fought for a cause and lost everything.

"Something good will come from this mess that I made. I have to take this to the Fringers."

"No matter the consequences?"

"It's their chance for freedom. They can refuse, but I have to offer it. I have to try."

Finn didn't meet her eyes. Was he ashamed of himself for not wanting to get involved?

"I promised you we'd cut the leash," she told him, "and we will. But whether you agree with my plan or not, I'm taking it with me."

"How?"

"One of Zeke's stock biocyph modules would be ideal right now, to imprint the algorithm on. I'll have to store it in the wet-teck in my splinter." She turned to jump back into the well of the BRAT.

"Wait." Finn touched her shoulder, frowning with uncharacteristic uncertainty as he searched her face. "Use mine."

"Why? You said this was all a bad idea."

"Yes, I did. But this thing makes me valuable."

"You think I'll leave you behind? Is that it?"

"That's not what I mean. I trust you, Edie, even if I don't agree with you on this. But I have no value to the rest of the crew. If we get out of this place and off this rock, this gives them a reason to keep me alive. Put it in my head, just temporarily, and make sure only you can download it. At least then I have something to bargain with."

"Okay," Edie said automatically. She was still absorbing the impact of his admission that he trusted her. It meant more to her than it should—after all, he was talking about his survival, not his feelings.

He followed her into the bowels of the BRAT, sat patiently while she jacked into his splinter. She'd have preferred to create a new tier in which to store the data, to confine and protect it, but she'd already tried and failed to modify the biocyph in Finn's splinter. Most of it was unused anyway, an empty matrix to store the cryptoglyph.

She jacked into the BRAT's core and recovered the dismembered symphony. She had isolated and extracted the algorithm from the biocyph to leave only raw code, like sheet music without an orchestra. There were just enough linkages intact that she'd be able to recreate a functional module later, by recombining the algorithm with fresh stock biocyph that could be coded for use on another world, another ecosystem.

The BRAT knew her now, and Scarabaeus gave up its secret willingly.

If Cat's repairs had gone well, she'd have picked up Haller's team by now and ferried them to Finn and Edie's location. They had no way of knowing, and could only hope someone was waiting for them outside the megabiosis. As for the *Hoi Polloi*—if someone up there was responsible for trying to kill them all, would the ship even be in orbit anymore?

There was little point worrying about it yet. It would take a couple more hours for the BRAT to make the necessary changes and transmit its new programming out into the jungle. Until then, the only thing on Edie's mind was rest.

Finn settled against the BRAT casing, and there wasn't

much room to do anything but curl up beside him. The cold from the metal soaked through her jacket, making her shiver.

He watched her with a flicker of concern. "You doing okay?"

She hadn't slept in thirty hours and was tired beyond belief, physically and mentally. He must sense that. "I'll be fine."

She edged away from the cold, leaned against his shoulder, already drifting, not protesting when he shifted to move his arm around her so that her cheek rested on his chest. The intimacy of the position was at odds with the painful knowledge that he would walk away from her, and her future, as soon as he was able.

He tangled his fingers into her hair, at the nape of her neck, holding her there in a gesture that felt more possessive than tender. She didn't have the energy to think about it, and his heartbeat was a lullaby.

CHAPTER 28

Everything looks the same as the mission briefing begins. Everything is the same—but Lukas isn't there. He retired, they tell her, but she knows it's a lie. He would never leave without saying goodbye and explaining why. More than that, he would never leave at all.

It will be her sixth mission, departing in a few days. The fifth without Bethany, the first without Lukas.

For the first time in two years, she runs. They'll find her soon, but for a few hours she's anonymous and free as she follows the endlessly twisting caverns of Halen Crai. In the outer loop she enters a shop and a crowd of toms descends on her. Toys, really. Ridiculous species of all shapes and colors, flashing lights and chattering, waving their appendages as they wheel aimlessly around the floor. One runs over her foot and she nudges it aside. Confused, it spins around a few times, speeds off, and bangs into a wall. Others bump into her ankles, staggering around like blind drunks. She's never seen such disorder and cheery nonsense, and she likes it.

The vendor emerges from a back room to apologize. "Fringer junk. Non-standard teck. They can't tune to the local navbeacons."

She sympathizes. She's never felt at home here, either. "I could take a look at them, maybe reset their protocols . . ."

The vendor eyes her appraisingly. "You a teckie? What will it cost me?"

She pulls something from her pocket. Everything that belongs to her, Natesa takes away—but she's managed to hide this for two years. It's all she has left.

The vendor steps forward and touches it with her finger. Each of the woman's fingernails is pierced through with a gemstone, and the nails grow around the gems in distorted ridges. It's beautiful and grotesque at the same time.

"That's what I want." So they can never take it away.

"So what is this? An insect or something?"

"Can you graft it onto my skin, like you've done to your fingernails?"

"Suppose that would work. Is it worth anything?"

"Only to me." A reminder of Scarabaeus, the world she saved, and now of Lukas, who she couldn't save.

With a nod of approval, the vendor says, "When you find something you care about, you got to hold on to it."

As the seal hissed open, darkness greeted them. Finn shone the lamp into the jungle, etching the twisted milky vines with a bluish light and casting distorted shadows on the surrounding vegetation. Scattered pieces of equipment were the only indication humans had ever intruded. There was no sign of the slaters, no sign of the bodies of the three serfs who'd died here, or of Zeke.

But she'd saved Finn.

With the shield off, Edie could smell the jungle properly for the first time and she breathed deeply. Clean, moist, earthy, but sharper than seemed natural. The nanoteck in their bodies would take care of any reactive substances they inhaled—or so she hoped. And if not, there was nothing more she could do about it. They'd know soon enough.

Finn leaned against the outside of the BRAT, checking his rifle. "Smells like standard-issue soap."

He slung the weapon over his shoulder and handed Edie her pack. His endearing nervousness about the nanoteck had evaporated. The jungle was a danger he could shoot at, notwithstanding her warnings—shooting might set off the jungle's defensive reaction again. In any case, he only had a few rounds left in the rifle.

Together they looked out at the jungle, lit by the puddle of light from the lamp. The vine growth matted into a dense network low over their heads. Beneath that lay the tangle of wide supporting stalks of arboreal species, surrounded by pale open-faced flowers with crooked petals stitched together like patchwork.

Everything was drained of color, washed out and semi-translucent. Unlike the original ecosystem, photosynthesis could no longer be the main process that sustained these organisms. Yesterday Edie had seen only one green species of plant winding its tendrils up through the vines toward the light. Maybe the organisms fed like funguses—absorbing nutrients directly from the soil and air, and perhaps from each other.

Edie checked her compass and set off, due north as planned.

"Wait!"

"I know, I know, stay close," she muttered, glancing over her shoulder at Finn.

He was a few paces away, shining the lamp over her head. She looked up to see a slater, suspended by a silken thread. Its legs were curled under its carapace, and the jaws on its underside twitched. She couldn't detect any eyes, but it was aware of her. Its legs started to unfurl.

Finn spoke between gritted teeth. "I thought you said—"

It pounced, its multiple legs scrabbling for purchase among the flaps and ribbing on the shoulder of her jacket. She dropped to her knees, into the soft mud. Its grip was surprisingly powerful, its weight heavier than expected for a flat creature not much bigger than the palm of her hand. Then it was on her neck, its jaws gnawing against her flesh. She forced herself to endure it.

"No!" she yelled as Finn advanced, and he pulled up short.

Its bites were superficial—she knew that from having seen what they did to Zeke. It had taken dozens of these creatures to rip off his flesh in thin layers, gradually working down to the bone. She could handle a few bites—but damn, it hurt.

Around her, the jungle rustled with movement. Finn's boots crunched on the moist litter as he turned around warily, rifle at the ready.

"They're everywhere," he said.

"It's okay."

The slater scurried down Edie's chest, over her hip, and across a meter of ground before launching a pale glossy thread into the vines above and clambering away. In the tangle of vines above her, dozens more slaters—some dangling from threads, some clasping the vines—were just visible in the dim light. They remained motionless for several seconds. Then they moved, but not to attack. They swung across the vines on their pendulums of silk, scuttled over the jungle floor. Some opened up their wings and flew across the clearing. Going about their business.

Finn hunkered down beside her, dumping his pack and rifle on the ground. Having realized the slaters were ignoring them, he turned his attention to the graze on the side of Edie's neck.

"It needed to have a taste," she said.

"I can see that. Jeez . . ." He had the medkit open and started wiping the wound.

Edie watched the jungle. "It worked. Its cyphviruses recognized my biopattern from the baseline I programmed into the BRAT, and the BRAT told it to leave me alone."

"And they'll all leave you alone now?"

"The jungle is like one organism. Everything talks to everything else."

"What about me?"

"The slaters weren't interested in you." There must be a reason why. Then she saw the back of his hand, where the skin was lightly peppered with tiny marks. "The jungle already knows you. Look."

"Something bit me?"

"An insect bite, looks like. Whatever passes for insects in this place."

He smeared medigel on her wound and it set into a thin, transparent layer, the anesthetic numbing the stinging. Then he snapped shut the medkit and packed it away.

"Let's get out of here. And no more surprises, okay?"

Without e-shields it was cold in the depths of the megabiosis. They moved as fast as possible to keep warm, weaving around trunks and boulders and cushiony growths of pallid fungus, cutting through hanging foliage and bracken on the ground, and avoiding the sharp crystalline vines. The pale, moist vegetation glittered in the ghostly predawn light so that the jungle no longer seemed dank or dangerous.

Life rippled around them. Edie swung the lamp to examine as much as she could. Wormlike invertebrates burrowed into fleshy flower petals and tiny multilegged creatures crawled in neat lines along their feathered veins. Some species were physically attached to the stalks and vines by tendrils and nodules, blurring the boundaries between plant and animal.

After three long, tiring hours, there was enough weak light filtering through the canopy to conclude that dawn had broken. Within minutes, the vines lost their crystalline rigidity and became translucent again. Nine hours after the bomb blast, they seemed to retain some memory of that violence, because they moved restlessly, knitting and unknitting in a sluggish dance.

Finn estimated they were more than halfway to the perimeter when they stopped briefly to eat and rest. With the end in sight, Edie couldn't hold her main fear inside any longer.

"What if the *Hoi*'s gone? The skiff can't make that jump."

"We can use the satellite to send a distress call through the node."

"But the nearest ship is probably that patrol vessel with Natesa on board."

Finn raised his shoulders in a small shrug as he chewed on a pro-bar. "Let's hope not. First hurdle is Haller. If he's seen even a fraction of what we've seen, I'm betting his mind's still set on taking biocyph from that BRAT and using it to create something he can sell." Something unique and dangerous and valuable—a tempting combination. "He'll send you back in there, with or without me."

She knew what he meant. Haller would kill Finn if he had to. "So what's the plan?"

"Let's veer off course a little, in case he's digging through to meet us. We'll exit a few hundred meters from where they expect us and make our own way back to the skiff. I'd rather deal with Cat than with him."

As he took another bite, a flash of purple and red crossed his knuckles. Edie stared at her own hand, where color streaked across the skin. She looked up and drew in her breath.

All around them, the once colorless jungle lit up with glimmering rainbows. The translucent vines, glistening with moisture, refracted the sunlight, acting like an endless network of shifting glass prisms. Shafts of light vibrated through the mist creating ethereal curtains of jeweled lace. Everywhere the jungle wildlife shimmered with dappled flecks of every hue.

Her catastrophic failure had transformed into an exquisite wonderland.

"Look at what I made, Finn."

He watched her, a smile playing on his lips. "It's just physics."

More than that: she'd have one good memory to take away from this place.

As they continued on, the effect faded whenever the sun moved behind clouds, only to burst into a radiant kaleidoscope again minutes later. For a full hour they walked through the dazzling new world, and then the sun moved higher and the angle of light changed, and the jungle was again reduced to ghostly shades of gray.

After another hour, the vegetation thinned out noticeably and they picked up the pace. Occasionally they caught glimpses through the undergrowth of open land and mountains. From the initial flyover, Edie knew the terrain out there was pretty rough, but it couldn't possibly be harder to move through than the jungle itself.

A glint caught her eye, several meters ahead. This wasn't another trick of the light—it was a flash of metal. She pointed it out wordlessly for Finn, two paces behind her, and he signaled for her to get down. It could only mean one thing—they'd met up with Haller and his team. But that shouldn't have happened. They'd deliberately gone off course.

They crouched and waited, listening. The sounds of the jungle permeated the air—the chirps and calls of concealed creatures, the scuttling of tiny legs, the rustle of slithering vines overhead. But nothing human, other than their own breathing.

Finn hesitated, and she knew he was uneasy about leaving her unprotected, but they had to know if Haller was nearby. As Finn moved off, Edie quickly lost track of where he was. For a big man, he moved with amazing stealth. Then came the click of the rifle engaging. She tensed. But there was no shot. Moments later he was back at her side.

"One of the serfs. Must've decided to take his chances in the jungle instead of with Haller."

"He's dead?"

"Stripped to the bone, like Zeke." His tone was unemotional, but from the abrupt way he stuffed his things back into his pack, Edie could tell he'd been affected by what he'd seen.

He started moving again. Edie jumped up to follow.

"Maybe the slaters dragged him there."

"I don't think so. All his stuff is still with him—belt, pack, shiv. That's where he went down. It was—"

He stopped, turned to her, changed his mind, and kept walking.

"Finn?"

"From what's left of him, I think it was the guy from the engine room."

"The one you saved?"

"Yeah."

He moved faster, perhaps still not entirely convinced they were safe from the slaters.

Within half an hour, the layers of vines overhead became a loosely woven web, a matted roof that curved downward, so low Edie could reach up and touch it. They were meters from the perimeter, where the vegetation was both less varied and less vigorous. This was the growing edge, the boundary between the new world and the old. They pulled aside the drape of vines and stumbled into the open.

"There she is."

Finn pointed to a plateau several kilometers away, the only flat land in sight. In the bright noon sunlight, the skiff glowed. Just one skiff. Cat had said that an engie was coming down in the other one, but there was no sign of it.

They followed the perimeter of the megabiosis for a hundred meters, checking for further signs of Haller's team, and then Finn turned sharply away and headed out across the uneven scrub.

Edie looked back at the megabiosis, a tangled infestation spilling out from the central BRAT, latching on to and mutating the existing native wildlife, and sprouting up from the earth from the BRAT's network of rootlets.

Look at what you've done.

The words of Bethany's killer. She didn't want to think of what she'd done. Her childish folly had recreated a world and it had tried to kill her. Let it fester now, or fail. Scarabaeus had given her its song, and she was determined to use it.

She heard a sound behind them, from within the jungle. The strangled scream of something dying or half dead. Something human.

"Finn—wait!" She ran around the perimeter and found a place where the vines had been hacked away to make a large hole. It had partially closed over, but this must be where Haller and the two serfs on his team had entered. Cautiously, Edie climbed inside.

Haller had almost made it back out. He was only twenty meters from the entrance. His body hung from the overhanging vines, grotesquely distorted, bones sticking out through ripped flesh. This wasn't the work of slaters. Every part of his exposed skin was pierced by tendrils that snaked into his body. His chest cavity, partially open, pulsed with blood and muscle, the organs almost unidentifiable because they were covered in a mosaic of glassy growths. And body parts were missing. From the hips down there wasn't much left at all—the stumps of his legs blended into the undergrowth. Where his nose should be was a spongy nest harboring tiny crawling worms, and areas of his skull were cracked open.

Yet he was alive. The jungle was digesting him but it was also feeding him. Haller's eyes followed Edie, bright with fear.

Finn drew a sharp breath as he pulled up behind her. Nearby, buried under debris and vines, lay the body of the second serf on Haller's team. His flesh was shredded, his tunic riddled with the unmistakable signs of spur bullets.

"That guy got the better deal," Finn said.

Edie glanced from the dead serf to Haller's mangled body and could only guess at what had happened. Something had spooked them, perhaps, or an argument had started for some reason. With Haller, it seemed, such incidents seemed to escalate quickly. If his shield generator had been damaged in the fight, the serfs' shields, connected to his, would have failed as well. Haller had shot one of them, and the other had run off and fallen victim to the slaters.

Haller gurgled blood and spittle as he dragged air into his lungs, his face twitching.

"Did you see . . ." he rasped.

Edie moved closer, sickened by the sight but drawn out of sympathy.

"Did you see all the colors?" He must be talking about the light show earlier. He had been here much longer than that, though. His eyes refocused on Finn.

"Wouldn't say n-no to a bullet in the brain. Can the Saeth sh-shoot straight?"

Finn turned on his heel and walked out.

CHAPTER 29

"Finn!" Edie ran after him, tripping on the debris littering the ground. "You have to finish it for him. Please!"

He didn't slow down. "Not worth wasting a bullet."

She grabbed his arm but he shook it loose, almost knocking her down. There was no point trying to wrestle the rifle from him. They were out in the open again, in the rocky foothills of a distant mountain range, and the skiff beckoned. She stopped and looked back at the jungle, her instincts telling her to stay near Finn, but she couldn't leave Haller like that.

And not so long ago she'd been thinking kindly of Finn for trying to save Kristos. He'd do that, but he wouldn't end this man's fear and agony.

"Finn, get back here!" She remained resolutely at the jungle's edge while he ignored her, striding on ahead. "You walk twenty minutes in that direction and you'll be out of range. You'll be dead!"

He continued up the rocky incline. She tried a different tack.

"I'll jolt you," she yelled after him, tears squeezing from her eyes. "I'll zap your fucking brains!"

He stopped, turned slowly, and came back. Stepping up close, he glared down at her.

"What did you say?"

"Give me the rifle or I'll do it."

He cocked his head as if calculating the likelihood she was serious.

"I'm serious," she said, for good measure.

He gave her a slow, cold smile, turned and started retracing his steps up the slope. He didn't look back.

Damn. She was furious, but it wasn't enough to break her promise to him.

She ran in the other direction, into the jungle, to confront Haller again. Finn wasn't stupid enough to go out of range. He would wait for her.

Suspended above her, Haller wept watery blood that made pink trails down his face. A white worm crawled over his skin, sucking up the tears, leaving puckered red marks in its wake.

"You can do it, there's a g-g-good girl." His eyeballs rolled around in their sockets, as if he was having trouble controlling them.

"No spur," she said.

"Ohhhh . . ." He sounded disappointed.

Haller's weapons were nowhere in sight. The rifle must be buried under the nest of vines that had formed around him, and as for his spur—if he'd been wearing it when this happened, she couldn't tell now. Most of his right arm was gone, blending seamlessly into the vines in a medusa-like tangle. His left arm bubbled beneath the skin, oozing a yellowish fluid, and tiny stalks sprouted along a deep split down the length of his forearm.

She had a blade, but she couldn't physically reach his chest or head, the two places it seemed likely a stab wound would kill him. She couldn't believe she was even considering doing such a thing.

How to kill him mercifully with her bare hands? She could no longer tell where he ended and the jungle began.

The vines rippled over and within his body, pulsing with life. With a shudder Edie realized the jungle was not going to kill him, not for a while. It was integrating him into the ecosystem. The men who died had been torn apart by the slaters for food. Kristos had died quickly, in the end. Zeke had avoided that fate for as long as his shield lasted, and then he too was devoured. But Haller had been taken alive, his body invaded by cyphviruses, and the biocyph was using his living cells as the machinery to create something new, as though he were a welcome part of the ecosystem.

"Do something." His voice was thready and raw, his eyes stark with terror. "I can feel it inside me, thinking my thoughts. Nooo . . . I'm th-thinking its thoughts . . . We . . . I don't like it."

"I can help you." She hardly dared acknowledge to herself that she'd thought of a way. "But I need you to help me."

No way to tell if he was still listening. One of his eyeballs caved in, pulled through from the inside, and the remaining eye lolled about.

"Someone on the *Hoi* planted that flash bomb," she said, and a ragged eyelid blinked over his eye. "Someone wanted Zeke's team dead. Who did it? The captain? One of the engies?"

From what was left of his throat, Haller made a sound that might have been a snort of derision. "What're you doing here, teckie? Lag said you were . . . d-d-dead."

Ignoring the non sequitur, she tried again, worrying that he would become delirious before she could get anything helpful out of him. "Listen to me, Haller. I can give you a quick death—that's what you want, isn't it? Tell me who betrayed us. Was it rads? Did someone give away our position? Was it you?"

"I would never hurt you. It was . . . I didn't think it could be. Didn't think. But t-two ambushes, what're the odds? It's the baby . . ." Haller rambled on, making no sense. His voice was a hoarse whisper, and she moved closer to hear. ". . . a b-b-baby grandson. He wants out."

"The captain? Haller, are you talking about Rackham?"

"Rackham . . . he's no war hero, let me t-tell you that. Listen to the trees . . ." He drew a breath and cried out, but the sound was nothing more than a silent, coarse rush of breath. "Can you hear them? Why did you never do what you were told? J-jump when I tell you, teckie. Do what you have to. Make it all go away. Th-that's an order."

Edie's shiv swam before her eyes. She pushed up her sleeve and cut into her forearm, inside the elbow. Using the tip of the blade, she dug the implant out of her flesh. There was no pain—at least, the pain didn't register.

She focused on the shard of plaz from her arm, a centimeter-long sliver, slippery with blood. It contained several months' worth of the drug that kept her alive. Even small doses were lethal to non-native Talasi—a few seconds in contact with Haller's bloodstream would be enough. She just needed to deliver it.

Edie grabbed the vines, finding footholds, climbing closer to the shreds of Haller's body. His single eye watched her. Open wounds all over his torso leaked blood, some infested with worms.

"Are you . . . are you going to do it?" Haller slurred the words through distorted lips.

"Yes." Her voice cracked on the word.

"All over now. All over . . ."

She could only get close enough to reach his arm. She pressed the implant against the torn flesh, taking care to keep a hold of one end between her fingertips. His muscle tissue twitched as the tiny device, sensing no neuroxin in Haller's blood, pumped the drug into what remained of his body.

Haller convulsed and the vegetation attached to him shook. The neuroxin was acting faster than she'd expected. Before she could jump away, the jungle began thrashing like a crazed beast with something distasteful caught in its jaws. Worried she would lose her grip on the implant, Edie withdrew and closed her fist around it. She slid down the vines, landing on her back, and rolled free of Haller's nest. Above her, the vines snarled and writhed, ripping apart his flesh.

The jungle thrummed with rage. Edie struggled to her feet, jamming the implant into the pocket of her jacket, and ran clear of the megabiosis. She scrambled up the incline, following the path she'd seen Finn take.

She looked back only once. The jungle seethed around the gaping hole where Haller had been entombed and then collapsed in on itself, crumpling and compressing, sealing the wound.

Edie climbed for only a few minutes before she came upon Finn, hunkered down against a rock. He faced away from the slope, not watching for her approach, though he must've heard her. He took a swig from a water tube. He didn't ask what had delayed her, didn't comment on the patch of blood soaking through the sleeve of her jacket, if he even saw it.

Wiping his mouth with the back of his hand, he looked up at her, squinting against the high sun, and said flatly, "Don't ever threaten me again."

Her mind still reeling from what she'd just seen and done, she gathered together every gram of willpower to fight back the anger and more tears. He'd refused to help a dying man with one merciful bullet.

"I don't understand why you wouldn't help."

"Yes, you do."

The brutal honesty of his reply disarmed her. Yes, she understood. His experiences meant he didn't think like she did. She just hadn't thought that would make him immune to human suffering.

That was an unfair assessment. He'd tried to help Kristos and the serfs in the engine room. He'd already explained himself: he wasn't going to fight for someone who considered him worthless.

"Then you must understand why I threatened you," she said.

"I understand you were angry. I don't understand why

you'd make a threat you had no intention of carrying out." He got to his feet and rubbed the back of his neck. "You had no intention of jolting me, right?"

"Right," she conceded grudgingly. "Please don't tell me this was another test to see if I'd keep my promise."

"No. This time I trusted you. I didn't help because Haller deserved what he got."

No one deserved that. But she wasn't in the mood to argue the point. Right now, what mattered was getting off this rock.

"He thinks Rackham betrayed us. If that's true, the *Hoi* probably left orbit hours ago."

Finn didn't look surprised. This was, after all, a confirmation of what they'd already suspected.

"Let's get back to the skiff." He started up the slope. "It can accelerate faster than the ship. We might stand a chance of catching up before he reaches the jump node."

And then what? They still had to convince Rackham to let them board, which would be a tough task since he apparently wanted them dead.

"Maybe we can count on the engies." Edie didn't even remember their names.

CHAPTER 30

"They've gone! The *Hoi*'s not in orbit."

Dwarfed by the landing foot of the skiff, Cat yelled across the scrub. She must have seen them approaching and left the airlock. Finn jogged the last fifty meters across the plateau, a natural ledge cut into the foothills. Too tired to run, Edie trudged after him. To her right lay a desolate view over the valley, and the megabiosis they had escaped stood out clearly—a tight button on the landscape hiding its deadly secrets within.

She heard Cat's exclamation as the navpilot saw their shields were off, and Finn jerked his thumb in Edie's direction, as if that explained everything. Cat stared at Edie accusingly.

"You're supposed to be . . . Where's Haller and Zeke?"

"Dead."

"No . . . Zeke . . . ?" Cat looked out over the megabiosis as if she might catch a last glimpse of him. The aura from her e-shield glinted.

"I'm sorry, Cat. The flash bomb killed Zeke and the rest of the team. It triggered a defensive reaction in the jungle, and it looks like that spooked the serfs on Haller's team. I don't know exactly what happened, but Haller lost his shield and the cyphviruses got to him. He didn't get very far inside."

Cat shook her head. "I dropped him off about an hour after nightfall. Lost contact a couple of hours later, but he'd told me not to leave the skiff under any circumstances. In any case, I still had repairs to do."

"There was nothing you could have done, once his shield failed. Even if you'd retrieved him."

Finn climbed the ladder to the exterior hatch. "Is the skiff ready to fly?"

Cat looked taken aback by his take-charge attitude, and Edie anticipated an argument. But Cat seemed to think better of it. She surrendered her position at the top of the chain of command and spoke to him as an equal.

"Yes, it's prepped. But the *Hoi*'s gone. Last I heard from them was ten hours ago. Corky was supposed to come down on the other skiff but he never did. I thought at first there might be a rad ship in the system, or that patrol vessel, and that they were maintaining comm silence."

"No," Edie said. "Rackham is responsible for the bomb."

Cat's jaw dropped. "Are you sure?"

"That's what Haller thought. And it makes sense. It had to be someone who knew the shield frequency of the BRAT, and knew our landing site."

"I suspected . . ." Cat looked devastated, like she couldn't quite get her head around it all despite the plain evidence. "The skiff was sabotaged, I'm pretty sure of it. Somebody . . . Rackham didn't want us to leave this planet."

"Then let's surprise him," Finn said. "Can we trust those engies?"

"Yes, absolutely. They wouldn't have abandoned us without a fight."

"Then let's hope they succeeded in stalling him for a few hours."

Finn snapped the hatch and Cat cried out in horror. "Hey! You can't come on board stuffed full of retroviruses from the planet. Isn't that contagious?" She turned to Edie. "You said there was no cure."

Edie moved past her, climbed the ladder, and joined Finn at the airlock. "It's okay. I reprogrammed the BRAT when our shields failed so it wouldn't make retroviruses to infect us. And since you haven't been exposed to the cyphviruses at all, the planet doesn't even know you're here."

Below them, Cat wavered, one foot on the step.

"You can't leave us here, right?" Edie said. "You have to trust me. I fixed everything."

Not quite everything. She couldn't fix Scarabaeus.

Their only option was to chase after Rackham and trick, bribe, or beg their way on board the *Hoi Polloi*. Edie strapped herself into the seat next to Cat, who was running through a quick syscheck.

"Haller seemed to think Rackham had a gripe against the client," Edie said. "Do you know anything about that?"

"I never heard him speak a word against Stichting Corp. I mean, no more than the usual crap we all bitch about." Cat still looked stunned. "What about the last mission? Oh god, did he have Jasna killed? I don't believe it." She sounded like she believed it all too well—she was just having trouble digesting it.

She slapped the holoviz controls and the skiff powered up, its steadfast vibrations sending a surge of relief through Edie.

"And Zeke . . ." Cat's voice cracked.

"I'm sorry." Edie briefly touched her hand. "I know you could have left the planet hours ago. I know you stayed here for Zeke, not for me."

Cat was staring at something on Edie's jacket. "What is that?"

Edie followed her gaze. Her breath caught as she saw the faint glow emanating from her pocket. Sensing her distress, Finn jumped up. Edie took the neuroxin implant out and wiped off the blood and dirt. The reservoir that comprised one half of the device was glowing electric-blue.

"My implant. I used it to kill Haller." Edie stared at it, her heart thudding.

"You killed Haller?" Cat said. "Poisoned him?"

"I did him a favor, believe me."

Finn grasped her wrist to steady it and stared at the implant. "Why is it glowing?"

"It glows when it's empty."

She felt the shock wave of his reaction, mirroring her own.

"Why the hell did you do that?"

Edie glared at him. *Because you wouldn't!* "I didn't know this would happen. I thought it would just pump in enough to kill him."

She should have thought before she acted, but her desire to help Haller had been instinctive. His flesh and blood had merged with the ecosystem—she hadn't just dosed him, she'd dosed the entire megabiosis. The implant's pump had drained itself dry trying to keep up.

"I should've just shot him," Finn said.

"Yes, you should have."

His expression hardened at her blunt reply, but he said nothing. She knew he regretted his action, or at least understood hers, and wasn't going to defend himself.

He pushed up her sleeve to examine the small wound inside her elbow. "How long can you survive without neuroxin?"

"I don't know. It breaks down fast. When it's gone, my body will start breaking down neurotransmitters instead."

"We have to get you to a medfac," Cat said.

"No." Edie tipped back her head against the seat as her world closed in. "Neuroxin can't be synthesized. I have to go home."

Home to Talas. Home to Natesa's clutches.

Her eyes met Finn's and she saw him in chains again, or worse.

"Let's deal with our problems one at a time." Cat pulled back on the control stick. "Let's catch that evil bugger."

The skiff lifted off smoothly from the scrub, raising whorls of dust in front of the screen. Edie closed her eyes, not even wanting a last look at Scarabaeus.

She opened them minutes later to the safe emptiness of space.

As soon as they set a course toward the jump node, the *Hoi Polloi* appeared on their scopes. Finn leaned over the co-pilot's chair as they all examined the holoviz.

"At least he's still in-system," Cat said, "but he must have left orbit hours ago. He's only twenty minutes from jumping."

Edie pointed at the comm switch. "Can you contact the engineers? Assuming they're on our side."

"Of course they're on our side. And no, not without Rackham knowing about it. All external comms go through the bridge."

"Then you have to persuade Rackham. Beg him to take pity on you. Tell him you picked up something valuable from Scarabaeus to add to his collection." Edie exchanged a glance with Finn. They *had* picked up something valuable, but trading it to a rover would be a last resort. And a cryptoglyph was not pretty enough to add to Rackham's museum. It wasn't enough to tempt him.

Cat's hand lingered over the comm. Her hesitation made no sense. Why would she want to be stranded out here?

Finn ran out of patience. He leaned over to hammer the switch. "Call the damn captain."

"Wait." Cat blocked his fist before it made contact. "There's another ship coming. I don't mean CIP. I made . . . arrangements." She looked from one to the other, gauging their mood. "I made a deal with the infojack, Achaiah."

"What kind of deal?" Edie kept her voice level but her blood ran cold.

"He's giving me a new ident, passage to the Fringe—freedom."

"What does he get in return?" Finn said.

Edie's knew the answer. "Me." She glared at Cat, recalling the liaison between the navpilot and the infojack at the medfac. "He's going to double-cross Stichting Corp, sell me again, get paid twice."

In Cat's guilty silence, Edie's mind raced. She glanced at Finn, knowing he was thinking the same thing as she was. Achaiah had created the leash and he might be the only one who could deactivate it. Could they make a deal with him in exchange for the cryptoglyph from Scarabaeus? The idea of handing over something so precious to an infojack curdled Edie's blood. He might simply sell it to the Crib, and the Crib would destroy it, thus preventing it from ever reaching the people it was supposed to help.

But she'd promised Finn they'd cut the leash, no matter what. Perhaps Achaiah would accept something else in payment. With Cat's help, perhaps they could persuade him to do the right thing.

Then again, why count on Cat's help? She'd planned this from the start. Her change of heart three days ago suddenly seemed less impressive.

The silent conversation passing between Edie and Finn had gone over Cat's head. Perhaps she thought they were about to turn on her, because she panicked. She jumped up to explain herself.

"You think you're the only unwilling crew members on the *Hoi*?"

Finn stepped between her and Edie, grabbing Cat's arm to jerk her away. Cat shook him loose but her temper flared.

"We're all prisoners of the client. We're all forced to serve—one way or another." Cat jutted her chin, defying them to question her explanation. "Even imbeciles like Kristos, who thought he chose this life of adventure and crime. Even Haller, who convinced himself he was happy being bribed to serve a noble cause. We knew we could never leave. This is my ticket out."

"At our expense," Finn said.

Cat ignored him. "He'll save your life, Edie! He won't let you die—he'll get your meds, somehow. What difference does it make anyway? Rovers are rovers—your situation won't change."

Edie found her callousness hard to swallow. "What about Finn? What if the next rover crew decides they don't need an unwilling serf hanging around?"

With visible effort, Cat calmed down and dropped back into the pilot's seat. Despite the ache of betrayal by a woman she'd finally convinced herself was on their side, Edie felt sorry for her. There was something good in Cat, something that had made her try and do the right thing a few days earlier. Something that could be reached.

Edie tried to reach it. "With your help maybe this can work out. We need Achaiah to cut the leash. At least that protects Finn's life. So change the deal. We can pay him with what we have—the skiff, the equipment down below."

"You really don't have any idea how much you're worth, do you. We have nothing to give him to match the price he'd get for a Crib-trained cypherteck. In any case, infojacks deal in information and skills, not things." Cat looked at them, pleading for understanding. "I never wished any harm on either of you. I mean that."

"Act like you mean it."

Cat closed her eyes for a moment, her expression troubled as she came to a decision. "Okay, I'll do what I can. We just need to sit tight for a few days—"

Edie's hopes faded. "A few *days*?"

"We're three days early for the rendezvous."

"Three days plus however long it takes to procure neuroxin from Talas . . . It could take weeks. I don't have that long." Perhaps it was only Edie's imagination, but the muscles in her limbs already felt weak—the first sign of neuroshock.

"I have contacts," Cat said. "We'll get your drug somehow. We just need a good thief."

That didn't convince Finn. "There must be some medication that can help. What exactly is happening to you?"

"Neuroshock," Edie said. "It's a catastrophic failure of several key biochemical pathways. An amino acid cocktail might help for a while, but I need neuroxin. There's none on the *Hoi*." As she said the words, she remembered . . . there *was* neuroxin on the *Hoi*. "Rackham's talphi cocoon—it's full of neuroxin. If I can figure out how to extract it, it should keep me alive a few days."

Finn turned to Cat. "Talk to Rackham and get us back on the *Hoi*."

"I thought you wanted to cut that leash?" Cat said.

"Finn's right," Edie said. "I—we could be dead in three days. We're back where we started—we need that cocoon on the *Hoi*."

"You sure that's what you want to do?"

"It's our only option."

"Okay." Cat gave a lopsided grin. "Zeke always boasted he had contacts at every port. I know some people, too. I'll find someone near Talas and persuade them to buy or steal what you need."

"How was Achaiah going to board the *Hoi*?" Finn asked Cat. "By sweet-talking his way through the airlock?"

"He gave me a worm that I planted in the system. When the time came I was going to activate it, and it would give him access to the ship's main systems—weapons, engines, nav control. He could effectively shut down the ship for a few hours. Then he was going to board and . . . well, with my help, grab Edie."

"Can the worm be triggered remotely?" Finn asked.

"Edie could do it." Cat looked expectantly at her.

"Uh, I don't see how."

"That link you set up between internal and external comms when Haller briefly gave you security access—"

"You found that?"

"Sure, but I couldn't figure out how to disable it. It would never have worked, by the way. You simply can't send a message out that doesn't go via the bridge. But we can use it now in the other direction."

Edie saw where she was going. "If you can get Rackham to answer a hail, I can sneak in via the link and access the internal systems. You just need to keep him on the line long enough."

"If the topic of conversation is himself, it's not that hard to keep him talking." Cat turned to the console and sent out a hail. "The worm is hidden in the navcharts. It's programmed to migrate randomly, so you'll have to hunt it down."

"How were you supposed to find it?"

"It's timed to make an appearance in three days for easy access, and then disintegrate after a few hours." She grimaced. "Things aren't really working out the way they were supposed to."

"No shit," Finn growled, hovering over them.

"When you find it, the activation code is Cameo." As the *Hoi* answered the hail, Cat hit the comm switch. "*Charme* to *Hoi Polloi*. Captain Rackham, please respond."

"*Hoi Polloi* here. Cat Lancer. How delightful to hear your voice again," came the sardonic reply.

Edie pressed her fingers to the access port and piggy-backed along the comm line, quickly finding the link she'd made to the internal systems. The higher levels were impossible to breach remotely, but that was what the worm was for—if she could locate it. She shot a seeker, primed to track anomalous code, down the line. It would find a worm faster than if she trawled through the navcharts on her own, even if it turned up a few false positives in its eagerness.

"Sir, please don't leave without me." Cat sounded suitably distressed. "They're all dead and no one knows I'm here. Wait for me."

"I'm afraid I'm not inclined to wait, Lancer. I'm so sorry."

Cat closed her eyes as if fighting for control. Her façade shattered. "Dammit, I know you planted that bomb and sabotaged the skiff. You're responsible for all of this. For Haller and Kristos and Zeke. Have you killed Corky and Yasuo, too? And Jasna . . . you got Jasna killed."

"Jasna was assassinated by eco-rads. You know that."

Edie shut out the voices and concentrated on the seeker. It replicated and widened its search pattern, squeezing between the tiers. She sifted through the datastream, examining every discordant chunk of code the seeker threw her way, discarding the obvious errors and mutations that every system acquired after decades of use.

"Why did you do it?" Cat said, her voice choking.

"You wouldn't understand. You're too young. But my reputation, my family . . . they're all I have. They mean everything to me."

Cat screwed up her fist in frustration, but again she calmed herself down. It was one thing to keep him talking, another to piss him off so much he cut the link. "Captain, please don't abandon me here."

"We made a good team, didn't we, all these years?" he mused. "But I have other considerations. Now, I suggest you get back to that planet, young lady, before you maroon yourself."

It sounded like Rackham was about to sign off. Edie snapped her attention back to the comm and jammed it open at Rackham's end. It would buy her a few more seconds until he physically pulled the plug.

"What the . . . what's going on?" came the captain's puzzled voice. "What are you up to, Lancer?"

"At least jettison an escape pod," Cat said. "Leave me with supplies. Give me a chance out here."

"What the hell are you doing? How did you . . . dammit . . ."

From the captain's increasingly frustrated cries, Edie could imagine him jabbing buttons on his console, trying to figure out why the link wouldn't close. He was no teckie.

While he raged, Edie listened to the music of the *Hoi*.

Deep inside the complex rhythms of the navcharts, exotic

notes wafted through the datastream. She understood the meaning behind the melody, but every note, every phrase of code held a foreign trace. The worm, elegant in its sophisticated simplicity, was the work of a master crafter. Suspended commands hovered over the security mesh, awaiting orders.

"I hear you," she whispered. "I hear you."

CHAPTER 31

Cameo.

Cat's homeworld, the hellhole where the Crib had found her. They had that much in common, Edie and Cat. They had the Crib to thank for saving them, and to curse for what they'd become.

Edie sent the password and woke up the worm.

The worm uncoiled along the datastream, a disturbing bass note beneath the melody. In tune but offbeat. It attacked the highest security level, choking the internal access points and effectively cutting off the crew from the main systems. Edie changed the security codes to lock them out. Meanwhile, she had full access now for as long as the comm line remained open.

Edie gave Cat a nod to indicate she was in, and the skiff's console lit up with the *Hoi*'s nav controls. With the *Hoi* only minutes from jumping, Cat punched in a new course so it veered away from the node.

"I want you to know, Rackham, you won't get away with this," Cat said. "You'll pay for what you did."

Rackham's line crackled. "Not in this life."

Edie watched the navpilot's painted fingers flying over the console as she set the *Hoi*'s engines to a hard deceleration, followed by a full turn and a new course back toward the skiff. Now Rackham couldn't fail to notice—

"What's going on? Lancer! Is that cypherteck with you?"

"Go to hell, sir."

The comm dropped out at his end. He must have finally yanked the right line. But it was too late for him. The *Hoi* was locked on a new course and Rackham was powerless to stop it.

Edie pulled her hand from the port. Her fingertips were white from pressing too hard. Finn gave her a rare smile. Hope burned in her chest for them both—an unfamiliar sensation.

Then he got back to business. "How long until we reach the *Hoi*?"

Cat checked their position. "I've set her engines to a crawl. Too much acceleration and she'll be a bitch to haul around again. At full tilt, the *Charme* will meet up in about four hours and be less than an hour from the jump by the time we board."

"What kind of weapons does Rackham have at his disposal?"

"The *Hoi* has a couple of cannon but he's locked out. He has his personal spur. If he killed the engies"—Cat's face twitched in anguish—"he has two more, plus whatever ammo's in the armory. What about us? I've got a full clip." She indicated her spur, hooked over a panel on the bulkhead.

Finn twisted his lips. "One round in the rifle. That's it."

Edie gasped. "Only one?"

Cat wasn't worried. "Forget the rifle. It has limited use inside the ship anyway. You'll hole the hull."

He glared at her. "Only if I miss."

"What about the worm?" Edie asked to deflect their attention off each other. "How long will it last?"

"A few hours," Cat said. "There should still be something left of it by the time we dock." She looked to Finn. "So what's the plan?"

Finn took a seat at the back of the cockpit. "Get to the bridge. Eliminate the crew. In whichever order works best."

"I told you, Yasuo and Corky will support us," Cat said. "And I want Rackham alive. I want him to pay."

"Death is a pretty good payment."

"He deserves worse."

Finn shrugged, perhaps in agreement, but didn't offer another option. Edie watched the two of them squabble, felt the tension of their uneasy truce. Cat was giving up a lot to help them—if things worked out she'd have control of the *Hoi*, but it was the new ident that had truly tempted her. Without it, Stichting Corp could still track her down.

Would Cat join her on her mission to the Fringe? Finn would only stay as long as the leash forced him to, but perhaps Cat could be persuaded to take up a cause. For the right price.

"I just want to find out why he did it." Cat's voice was drained of anger. "I want to watch his face while I smash his precious antiquities to pieces. I want to see him hurting." She drew a sobbing breath. "I want him to pay for killing Jasna and Zeke. Finn, I want you to leave him alive. Give me the chance to—"

Finn interrupted with quiet force. "Lady, you don't have the right to *want* a damn thing from me."

Cat fell silent, her nostrils flaring as she breathed hard.

Leaning against the bulkhead, Finn closed his eyes, but Edie knew he had not let down his guard. She avoided Cat's imploring look. Mediation wasn't her job, and in any case perhaps Cat needed a reminder of the part she'd played in putting them into this position. Her sense of guilt was working in Edie's favor at the moment.

Edie settled into the copilot's seat and watched the scope. The *Hoi* drifted on the far side of the node, still decelerating as it started to turn. Nausea rippled in her stomach. Neuroshock. She gripped the arms of the seat until it passed, wondering if Finn sensed it. She didn't want him worrying about whether or not she'd be able to make it through this. She had to make it through.

A soft jolt woke her.

"We're here." Cat turned to Edie in the seat beside her. "You okay?"

Edie nodded and pulled herself up, fighting wooziness.

"We should start with the engine room," Cat said. "With the worm, we can access most systems from there."

Finn nodded, leading the way down the ramp. At the hatch, they found a couple of charged e-shields in a storage locker, and Cat still had hers. Not that they would offer much protection in a gunfight.

Cold silence and semi-darkness greeted them on the sleeping *Hoi*. Four hours earlier, Edie had set the worm loose on the nav controls, but enviros shouldn't have been affected. Something else had happened here.

Finn moved his arm across Edie to nudge her into place behind him, his body blocking hers from danger. In the glow of the emergency lighting, the equipment hold's haphazard stacks of containers and racks looked like a twisted cityscape bathed in moonlight. Edie saw upturned crates, panels hanging loose, cables swinging from the ceiling. Zeke wasn't the tidiest person but clearly this was more than that. This was the scene of a struggle.

Cat hit her commlink a few times. "It's working, but no one's answering."

Rackham would know the skiff had docked, of course, and could determine their location by tracking their heat signatures. What mattered was getting to the engine room quickly before he could stop them. They stepped cautiously onto the deck and headed aft. As the only one properly armed, Cat took the lead.

Edie's heart beat a rapid tattoo. One look at Finn's self-assured stance as he quickly surveyed their surroundings helped soothe her adrenaline rush. In take-charge mode he was in his element, and she felt a flush of pride as she saw again the man he could be. The man he *had* been before the years of chains and drubs. Confident, competent, determined . . . irresistibly attractive. She pushed away that last thought. With her nerves jangling from lack of neuroxin, her heightened senses must be getting her confused.

Something clattered in the distance, and they froze as a group. Finn tilted his head, listening.

"Just a tom." Edie whispered. The little machines would continue their routine tasks regardless of the human drama around them.

A volley of shots rang out. Edie dropped to the deck as crates fell around them, Finn sheltering her from above. While Edie's ears still rang from the noise, Finn pointed aft to indicate to Cat where the shots had come from. His perceptiveness amazed Edie—she had no idea of the direction.

They regrouped behind a barricade of crates. Footsteps moved through the hold, followed by another round of fire. Cat darted out and returned fire—not very effectively. Overhead, a coolant pipe ruptured and hissed in protest. Finn took Edie's hand and led her in a crouch to the next stack of crates under the covering fire.

Cat joined them.

"You never told me you were such a lousy shot," Finn muttered.

Before Cat could retort, a voice called out.

"Why'd you do it, Cat?"

Cat looked horrified. "It's Corky. I thought . . . dammit. Rackham's got to him somehow."

"Captain told us what you did. Now you're back to finish us all off, eh?" Corky's words were slurred, and he sounded scared, like he was in over his head.

"Drunk bastard," Cat muttered. Then she yelled back, "Don't be a dick, Corky. Rackham did it. He's responsible for what happened down there."

"Give me the spur," Finn hissed.

"Fuck, no!"

Finn glared at Cat like he might just take it anyway. Edie had no doubt that he could.

"You are not going to kill him," Cat hissed. "It's not his fault—he doesn't know the truth."

Finn didn't waste time arguing. "Stay here," he told Edie. Then he slid away, out of sight.

"You betrayed us to the eco-rads again," Corky called into the hold. "You killed everyone!"

Cat crawled along a line of crates, keeping low. Edie stayed where she was and peeked through a crack between two stacks to see Corky standing near one of the seed husks, closer than she'd realized. His tattooed face should have looked fearsome, but he was unsteady, swaying from foot to foot.

"Rackham planted a bomb," Cat said from a few meters away. "We all know he has an arsenal of that crap."

Corky swung around and fired in the direction of Cat's voice.

"Hold up, Corky! Listen to me. He killed Zeke. You know I'd never do that."

"He said it was you!" But his voice wavered with uncertainty.

"I didn't kill anyone. Let's put down our weapons and talk for a minute."

"Where are you?"

Edie watched Cat step out into a clear space on the deck, spur retracted. She had guts, for sure. Corky lowered his spur and took a few sloppy steps toward her, and they faced each other uneasily.

"Now, listen." Cat held one hand palm-up in an appeasing gesture. "Rackham's being blackmailed. I don't know the details, but we both know he's not the hero he claims to be. He abandoned us on that planet, but three of us made it back."

"Three of you?" Corky looked around the dark hold. "Who? Where are the others?"

Edie knew exactly where Finn was—stepping out of the

shadows behind Corky, rifle raised. Cat did a good job of not reacting to the sight.

"They're not coming out while your finger's on the trigger," Cat said.

"And I'm not throwing down my weapon until I know what's—"

Finn struck Corky cleanly in the back of the head with the butt of the rifle, and the engie slid to the ground. Finn disarmed him in a second.

"Hey, I could've handled him," Cat said.

Finn said nothing, but rustled through junk on the deck and pulled out some wiring. He started binding Corky's limp body.

"I said, I could've handled him!" Cat's voice rose. "I've known him for years. He's a friend."

"Friends don't shoot friends. He's a loose cannon."

Cat came suspiciously close to pouting. "With Haller gone, I'm second-in-command of this ship."

"And I'm first-in-command of this mutiny." He stared Cat down with such intensity that Edie saw the navpilot's face melt in submission.

Face down on the deck, Corky groaned and started moving. Blood tricked from his skull, soaking the collar of his jacket.

"Where's Yasuo?" Cat demanded. "Is he still alive?"

"Damn kid's too tough to kill," Corky mumbled. "Captain ordered us to leave and he locked himself in the engine room for hours. Then we had to chase him all over the decks . . ."

"Where is he?" Cat insisted.

Corky wouldn't or couldn't respond. He seemed to pass out.

"Get us back on course for the node before we lose that worm," Finn told Cat.

Cat turned on her heel and stomped down the main corridor leading aft to the engine room.

"Will he be okay?" Edie asked.

"He's fine." Finn finished tying Corky to the gravplating and checked the man's spur. He shook his head. "I guess Cat could've handled it after all. He's out of ammo. Let's check the armory."

On deck three, they found the armory hatch welded shut. The captain had prepared for their arrival.

Finn glowered. "We need cutting torches."

They returned belowdeck to the engine-room control booth, where Cat looked harried.

"We're headed for the jump node," she reported, "but the worm's dying—I only have partial control and I'll lose that in a few minutes. Internal sensors show Yasuo's in the cell-block. Rackham's on the bridge with Gia, and it's locked down tight."

"Can Rackham override our course?" Edie asked.

"Once the worm's gone, yes. But I imagine he wants to leave this system as much as we do."

"Can he handle the jump?"

"He's a fair pilot, but I'd rather be on the bridge myself when we cross the horizon."

"Well, he's welded the armory hatch and the lock," Finn said. "It'll take me half an hour to cut through."

"Half an hour? We'll be in nodespace by then."

"I'd rather be armed before we tackle the bridge."

"Then with your permission, I'd like to free Yasuo," she said sarcastically. "He can help us." Edie understood her anger wasn't really directed at Finn. She'd been betrayed by her captain and now the chief engie. Zeke was dead and her plans for a new future with a new ident were dead with him.

"Do that." Finn moved aside to let her pass. "Can you take out the internal sensors?" he asked Edie. "It'd be nice if Rackham couldn't track us through the decks."

"But then we can't track him, either."

"I don't think he's leaving the bridge any time soon."

Edie found the relevant tier and with the last vestiges of the worm, accessed it and scrambled the internal sensors.

Cat called on the commlink. "Found Yasuo. He didn't fall for one word of Rackham's story and he put up a good fight. Got himself shot a couple of times in the backside. I'm taking him to the infirmary."

"Okay. Then get back to the engine room. We'll be on deck three." Finn started heading out. "Let's track down some cutting torches in Zeke's cave of wonders."

Edie pulled free of the connection, hesitating at the last moment. "Wait!" She drew in her breath as a new presence filtered through the datastream. The jangling chime of an infojack. Riding the worm. "There's someone here. In the datastream."

"Who?"

"I don't know. Someone's patched in remotely."

"*Someone?* If they're jacked in, they must be in-system."

Finn switched to the external scan and put it on the holoviz, homing in on the jump node. A vessel had just come through, decelerating hard on the other side as it prepared to swing around.

"It's that CIP vessel," Finn said. "The *Laoch*."

CHAPTER 32

Edie felt a cold sweat gathering on her skin. "Natesa . . ."

"Find out what the infojack's doing."

Edie followed the infojack for a few minutes as he burrowed into the tiers of the *Hoi*'s system, tramping awkwardly through the melody like an amateur musician trying to keep up with a symphony orchestra.

"He's just poking around right now. He can't actually *do* anything unless he finds the worm."

Finn pulled up the ship's specs just as Cat walked in. She stared at the holo.

"What the hell?"

"It's CIP and they have an infojack in the *Hoi*'s datastream," Edie said.

"Achaiah's on that ship?"

Edie shrugged. "I don't know who."

"He's not due for days. Maybe they caught him skulking on the other side of the jump node."

"Maybe it's not him. He doesn't seem very skilled." It didn't matter who the infojack was. What mattered was that Natesa had tracked her down at last.

Finn was more concerned with examining the specs. "The *Laoch* is Wolf-class. Impressive weapons range. At least four milits on board. Fast acceleration but slow to maneuver. It'll take them twenty minutes or so to decelerate and come about. We should still make the jump before they come in firing range."

Cat wasn't happy. "I don't trust Rackham to handle the node horizon at full tilt. Even if we make it through in one piece, we can't regulate our exit. He could take us anywhere."

"Let's worry about that when we no longer have sixteen plasma cannons aimed at us. Edie, can you stop the infojack from turning the worm against us?"

Edie had continued to monitor the infojack. "This is really strange. He had his chance to use the worm, but now it's too weak to be of any use. He's not interfering." She frowned. She had no desire to fight an infojack on a dryteck battlefield, but it surprised her that he wasn't even trying. In case he knew some tricks she didn't, she jammed a tangle of code into the peripheral tiers of the *Hoi*'s systems, giving her own signal immunity. The worm's haunting, dying notes jangled as it hit the barrier. It plucked at the edges of the tangle, while the infojack did nothing to unravel the mess.

"It must be Achaiah," Cat said. "Under duress he might have told them a few things about the *Hoi* and its mission, but he'd never willingly aid the Crib."

Finn gave a derisive grunt. "Being *under duress* tends to weaken a man's will."

"I made things hard for him," Edie said, "but I don't think he's a danger. I think he's stalling them. How's Yasuo?"

"Knocked out on pain meds," Cat said. "He'll live."

"Is Rackham in communication with that ship?" Finn asked.

Edie tapped into the comm system. "There's some traffic, yes. I can't access it, though."

"That's bad," Cat said.

"He'd turn us in? Even himself?"

Cat twisted her lips. "Rackham would make a deal with the devil to save his own hide."

They watched the nav readout showing the *Hoi* icon heading for the jump node. With the worm dead, they were at Rackham's mercy now.

Then, with an unremarkable *bleep*, the icon changed course.

"Oh . . . no, no, no . . ." Cat muttered, her finger tracing the *Hoi*'s route on an adjacent holoviz. "We're turning to meet the *Laoch*." She dropped into a seat, pushing hair off her forehead, and ran through the nav systems. "They're still coming about. On this vector we'll meet up with them in . . . twenty-four minutes."

"No time to break into the armory, then," Edie said.

Cat looked at Finn's rifle. "Will that shoot out the bridge hatch?"

"One bullet? Not a chance," he said. "That's one hatch you can't force."

"Explosives? Zeke has some locked up somewhere. Or we could see if Rackham had more."

Finn shook his head. "The amount it would take to dislodge the hatch would blow a hole through the hull."

Cat looked helpless. "What the hell do we do?"

Finn thought it over for a full ten seconds. "We have to plan for the *Laoch* docking. Cat, if you can handle Rackham, I'll deal with the milits. You need to lure him off the bridge and kill him."

"I'd be happy to kill him." This latest betrayal had changed her mind, it seemed. "But how do I lure him out?"

Edie knew Rackham's weakness only too well. "I know how."

"Rackham, you've got thirty seconds to open up, or one of your pretty things is going to get intimate with a crowbar."

Cat sounded like she meant it. Edie knew the navpilot would rather take the crowbar to Rackham himself, but until he showed his face that wasn't going to happen.

Edie stood in the dining room, crowbar clenched in her

fists, considering her first target. Outside but in Edie's line of
sight, Cat hid herself to the side of the bridge ramp, waiting
in ambush, spur extended. At the far end of the deck, where
Edie could neither see nor hear him, Finn worked on the
main airlock hatch, welding its seams to slow down a board-
ing party if she and Cat didn't get onto the bridge in time to
stop the *Laoch* docking.

Cat hit her commlink again. "Rackham, I know you can
hear me. You're almost out of time. I'm deciding what to
smash first. That damned songbird you kept asking me to
play? How about that framed splotch of paint on the wall
that you call a masterpiece? You know I always hated that
ugly thing."

When she got no response, she gave Edie a quick nod.
Edie turned a slow circle in the dining room, making her
selection. It had to be something that would make a lot of
noise, so Rackham would hear it across Cat's open link.
She flipped open the crystal chest containing the songbird,
raised the crowbar and brought it down hard on the elegant
instrument.

The songbird broke open with an ear-jangling crash, revealing a nest of strings and pegs and cogs. Edie raised the
crowbar for another strike and staggered, almost losing her
balance. That single hit had drained her energy more than
she'd anticipated. Her legs trembled under her own weight
and she had to fight to stay upright. At least long enough
to bring down the crowbar again, with all her remaining
strength. She fell to her knees as the crowbar hit with a satisfying crunch.

"Hear that, Rackham?" Cat taunted. "One priceless arti-
fact down, ninety-nine to go."

Edie dragged herself to her feet and decided to try something smaller. Neuroshock had not only drained her, it also
made her muscles shiver and she was losing fine motor control. Still, she couldn't face using that crowbar again for a
while. She went to the wine cabinet and jabbed the crowbar
handle against the glass doors to break them.

"I'm going for the wine now," Cat informed Rackham. The idea was to make him believe she was in the dining room doing the dirty work, so he'd not be expecting her attack if and when he did come out. "This is going to hurt me as much as it hurts you," she added. "You know I always enjoyed a good drop of red."

Edie reached carefully past the shards of glass and pulled out a bottle of wine. Her first attempt to break it on the dining table failed. The bottle bounced in her hand. She tried again, this time against the edge of the table, and the bottle shattered. She reached for another and broke it the same way, then another.

Above the sound of exploding bottles, she almost missed hearing Rackham's voice on Cat's commlink. She stopped to listen.

"You're making a helluva nuisance of yourself, Lancer." He sounded outraged. "Do you know how much those things are worth? This is who you really are, then—nothing but a vandal."

Cat was unmoved. "A vandal and a nuisance, that's me. Come on out, *sir*. It's the only way to stop me."

Edie continued smashing bottles, barely aware of what she was going. Her arms ached and her vision spun. Perhaps it would've been a better idea to have Cat do this . . . but Edie was the last person capable of taking out Rackham. Cat might not be the galaxy's greatest shot, but she had the required bloodlust.

Rackham screamed over the link but he wasn't coming out. Edie leaned against the table leg to rest. She needed to sleep. She needed neuroxin. Her breath felt shallow in her chest, and her hands shook. She hoped Finn could hold off the milits long enough, because Rackham was being more stubborn than they'd anticipated. A terrifying sense of guilt overwhelmed her. If the Crib caught them, her life was safe. Cat's life of crime, culminating in kidnapping a Crib cypherteck, would send her to prison for the rest of her days. But Finn—even if they couldn't find an excuse to summarily execute him, they'd haul him away and let the leash do their dirty work.

She had to keep going. She went to one of the display cases and yanked on the doors until it started to tip, then slid out of the way. It crashed to the deck, its delicate contents destroyed.

"There goes your Bascian vase and that pornographic little statue from the Best Times brothel," Cat said. "You should thank me—one less thing to have to explain to your wife."

Rackham's furious response was incoherent.

"Edie, are you okay?"

It took her a moment to realize that Finn was on her commlink.

"More or less," she said. "I'll manage."

"Just remember to stay out of the way if he comes out."

If? He *had* to come out. It was the only way to escape.

"Where's the *Laoch*?" Edie asked, not wanting to hear the answer.

"It's right on us. Maybe three minutes until it docks. The welding will hold them a few minutes longer."

"Then what?"

Finn didn't reply. Did he even have a plan beyond that?

The engine sounds were different, she realized. Rackham was maneuvering the ship to dock.

Edie looked around, her head spinning, searching for something else she could easily break. Her gaze fell on another display case, and she was drawn to it by something familiar inside. It took a moment for her brain to catch up with her eyes.

The talphi cocoon. She had to preserve that. She opened the case and took out the cocoon, cupping it in her hands. Her lifesaver. She just needed a way to extract the neuroxin. She crushed the cocoon flat so it fitted in her jacket pocket.

"Edie!" Cat hissed from outside the room. "Keep going. I think he's—"

The bridge hatch snapped open. Edie moved quickly to

the bulkhead just inside the door and peeked out. Caught off guard, Cat took a second too long to respond and Rackham took two steps down the ramp. Then she swung into action, opening fire from her position below him, protected by the ramp railings. Rackham kept coming, and Edie saw why. He was wearing body armor and a helmet similar to those worn by milits on the battlefield, although the design was unfamiliar to her. It was in poor condition, cracked and stained, but it did the job.

Cat realized the futility of her spur and was forced to move. Rackham's first shots missed, and she had time to reach through the railings and punch his knee. He tumbled over and rolled a few meters down the ramp.

Cat opened fire again. There had to be a vulnerable spot somewhere in that armor. But Rackham had already rolled off the other side of the ramp, putting a barricade between them.

"Edie, stay back!" Finn yelled over the commlink.

Edie froze, her heart thudding. She watched Cat work her way slowly along the side of the ramp, crouching low. Then the navpilot sprang up, firing as she vaulted the railing and dived over the other side. Edie could hear the scuffle and Cat's screams as she vented her rage on the man who'd murdered Zeke.

But moments later it was Rackham who extricated himself, staggering backward with his spur raised. His helmet had fallen off, but other than that he appeared unharmed.

"It's been fun, Lancer," he said, aiming to shoot.

Without thinking, Edie ran out of the dining room. "Rackham, don't!"

Rackham swung his aim on Edie.

Edie gulped, pulled up sharply, and kept talking. "Listen to me. Is this what you really want? Milits on your ship? We have to leave *now*!"

From the corner of her eye she saw movement in the aft corridor. Finn had crept forward, keeping himself hidden from Rackham's view. Like Edie, he must hope that Rackham wouldn't shoot her—would he? He needed her alive so he could take credit for returning her to the Crib.

"What I *want* is an end to all this," Rackham said, coming around the ramp to face Edie. "Was that you, smashing my precious things? My only regret is that I must restrain myself from punishing you for it."

Behind Rackham, Cat was pulling herself over the railings. She made a dash up the ramp for the bridge hatch. Rackham swung around and fired, and Cat stumbled over the lip of the hatch. And didn't get up. She'd been shot, Edie was sure of it.

Before she had time to process that, the ship shuddered and a loud clank reverberated through the hull. The *Laoch* had docked. They were too late.

Rackham marched up the ramp, his expression smug, and turned at the top, spur raised, guarding the entrance.

"I know that lag is hiding back there," he said. "Why don't you come out and face me?"

Edie had to divert his attention before he went after Finn. Maybe, just maybe, Finn could hold off the milits at the airlock. In any case, she was not going to let Rackham kill every last one of his crew.

"Why did you do it?" she asked.

"Why did I work for Stichting? Because they made me a war hero." Rackham projected his voice as though addressing an audience. "After fifteen miserable years in Fleet, flying goddamn supply ships, Stichting Corp found me and hooked me up with a war record my family could be proud of. And they gave me the creds to buy all those pretty things." He sounded wistful. "I should never have trusted them. Told me I could retire after ten years, but they kept extending my contract. One more mission, one more . . . and I had no choice but to obey, because they held my life in their hands."

Now a clanging sound came from the main hatch. The milits were forcing their way in. On the bridge, Edie saw Cat stir.

"Why did you have to kill your crew?" Edie asked, in the vain hope that by keeping him talking she could somehow distract him long enough to allow Cat to recover and take him down.

"Because the eco-rads found out what was going on. Can you imagine it?" He carelessly waved the spur around. "I was being blackmailed by both of them. The client forced me to run missions, the eco-rads forced me to sabotage them."

"You set up missions to fail?" He was as callous as Edie had feared. And the idiocy of his plan made her wonder if his deeper motive hadn't been simply to get revenge on Stichting Corp in the only way he could. Wasting other people's lives to achieve it. Her throat tightened as she remembered Zeke's death-grin, Kristos's terrifying struggle for life, the serfs' bodies stripped to the bone, and her incompetent but popular predecessor, Jasna. Even Haller, much as she despised him, would haunt her dreams.

"There was no way out for me—until a few minutes ago, when your boss showed up offering a deal that solved all my problems. She has a lot of pull, that woman." He pondered that for a moment. "With one word she can ensure my war record remains untarnished, no matter what the rads or anyone else tries to do. All she wants is you, teckie. I hand you over and my sins are forgiven."

"Do you really think she'll keep her word? You're headed for the smallest, dirtiest prison cell in the Reach, Rackham. I promise you that."

"Forgive me if I trust the word of a high-ranked Crib 'crat over a pathetic half-caste child with no idea of her place in the world." Rackham glared at her with the sudden anger of a desperate man. "I have a new baby grandson. It's time for my family to have me back. I'm a *hero*!" He looked over his shoulder. "Gia!"

The serf appeared in the bridge doorway.

"Find out if any of the wine was spared in the rampage. A celebration is in order."

Gia looked as astonished as Edie felt—that Rackham could be thinking about refreshments at a moment like this. The old woman shuffled down the ramp, hurried past Edie without catching her eye, and went into the dining room.

"I do hope they'll let me keep my collection," he mused, crossing his arms awkwardly over the spur on his forearm. "What's left of it. Oh, the wine isn't so important, but most of those things are irreplaceable. Tell me, what is that lag doing back there?" Rackham took one step down the ramp, craning his neck for a better view. "He doesn't have a hope, you know. Gia!"

Edie saw Rackham's face turn white as he stared over her shoulder. Edie spun around in time to see Gia raise the captain's antique gun and fire.

CHAPTER 33

Instinctively, Edie dropped. Gia walked forward, firing re-
lentlessly, stopping only when Rackham's body toppled over
the ramp railing and hit the deck. As Edie crouched there,
she found herself face-to-face with the captain. His face
was frozen in a look of shock. Blood frothed from his open
mouth.

"You keep trusting the wrong people," Edie whispered.

Rackham's throat bobbed as he tried to speak, but instead
of words, his final breath hissed out. Edie's heart stuttered as
she remembered Bethany. As a wave of dizziness hit her, she
closed her eyes and gripped the cold metal deck.

Gia dropped the gun as if it burned her hand, her face as
pale and shocked as her former master's. She looked toward
the main hatch, confusion etched on her lined face.

"Are they coming to save me?" she whispered.

Edie didn't know what to say. Gia meant nothing to the
Crib, to Natesa, to the rovers—even to Edie, if she was
honest. No one was coming to save Gia. No one cared that
she existed. Edie hadn't even realized Gia wanted to be
saved.

Finn was standing right there. He took Gia's hand and

turned her to face him, tenderly, like she was a beloved grandmother.

"*I'm* here to save you."

Her watery eyes met his. For a moment she looked confused, staring up into his steady dark gaze. Then her expression lifted, as though she saw him at last for who he truly was. Her liberator.

She looked at Rackham's body. "He's done so many terrible things."

"Yes, he has." Finn looked at her earnestly, and she returned his gaze with adoration. "But some of us survived, and we'll take care of you. Now, stay on the bridge with Cat. You'll be safe there."

Gia nodded, drinking in his every word, then turned to walk up the ramp. Finn helped Edie to her feet and they went onto the bridge. Cat was sitting up, her right shin soaked in blood. Other bullets had grazed her neck and ear, leaving bloody gashes. Gia pulled a first aid kit out of a panel at the back of the bridge, her eye on Cat's wounded leg.

"I'm okay. I'm okay," Cat muttered. "The *bastard*!" Edie helped her stand. "It'll take me a few minutes to power up so we can break free."

"How long do we have?" Edie asked Finn.

The answer was a muffled explosion from the main airlock.

"They're in." Finn turned to Edie. "Lock yourselves on the bridge. Cat, keep the link open."

He left the bridge, ignoring Edie's cry of alarm. She followed, stopping at the top of the ramp to watch him jump down the ladder well to deck two. From the other end of the deck came the sound of wrenching metal as the milts forced their way past the ruined airlock.

"Come on!" Cat yelled with renewed energy. She clapped her hand on the hatch control pad. "Edie!"

Edie's legs carried her in the opposite direction. Somehow enough strength returned to get her down the ramp and to the ladder. She heard Cat's expletive and the sound of the bridge hatch snapping shut. Cat was safe from capture for a while anyway. But Edie couldn't leave Finn.

She tumbled down the ladder. On deck two, Finn had already run to the far end of the corridor and was tying off the aft ladder well hatch, the one directly below where the milits were now entering the ship.

"Close that hatch!" he yelled.

Seconds later, he was at her side, climbing the ladder a few rungs so he could reach up and tie off that hatch, too.

"What the fuck are you doing here?" His voice was controlled but shaking with anger. "I told you to stay on the bridge."

There was no time for explanations and excuses. "Just tell me how to help," she said.

Finn jumped down and looked at her, his eyes wild with adrenaline. He must have known there was no point in recriminations. It was too late for Edie to go back. Above them, they heard the milits barking orders. Someone tugged on the hatch directly overhead, trying to open it.

Without a word, Finn took Edie's hand and led the way down the corridor. The intimate gesture felt out of place, but it calmed Edie.

He stopped at a hatch and readied his rifle.

Edie hadn't been paying attention to exactly where they were. "Whose—?"

Finn fired at the hatch lock and it splintered. The hatch shifted a few centimeters, then jammed. Finn wedged the rifle in the small gap for leverage, then shouldered open the hatch. He pulled Edie inside.

Rackham's quarters.

"Let's see what else the captain was hiding," Finn said.

He moved efficiently through the large suite, checking every locker and cabinet. The room was filled with more of the captain's treasures, but it was immediately clear some of these were not for the eyes of the rest of the crew. Unlabeled crates, mostly, not exotic items meant for display. Edie tore them open with her fingers, checking for anything they could use. What did a flash bomb look like, anyway?

Cat's voice came over the comm. "Finn, what's going on?"

"Sit tight," Finn responded. Edie watched him pull something out of a closet—a heavy tubular device the size of a barstool but half as tall. "Don't break away until I've disabled the *Laoch*."

"You're going to disable a Wolf-class cruiser?" Cat did not believe him.

"Just keep this link open and do what I say." He looked at Edie, and she noticed the change in him. He wasn't angry now. "Edie, they're going to get you. There's nothing you can do about that. They'll have their own heat sensors—they already know where we are. Just don't let them take you off the ship. I need fifteen minutes. You have to stall them."

"What are you going to do? Is that a flash bomb?"

He didn't answer, but tipped out the random contents of a duffle bag on Rackham's bed and shoved the bomb inside the bag. Then he headed out the door with the bag over his shoulder, along with the empty rifle.

One of the overhead hatches was already partially wedged open. Edie could see light from top deck streaming through, hear the sounds of the milits, see a pair of busy hands packing explosives into the hinges. She and Finn climbed downward, not taking the time to tie off the hatches, past the infirmary where Yasuo lay unconscious on a bunk. They went belowdeck—the best place to hide, but Finn had already pointed out that hiding was useless. In any case, these were the same milits who'd boarded the ship a few days ago when Edie and Finn were on the *Charme*. They already knew the *Hoi* inside out.

They walked past Corky, still bound to the deck.

"Untie me! Dammit, I need to know what's going on!" he yelled.

They ignored him. Finn headed for the *Charme*. With no idea of his plan, Edie was suddenly worried he was going to try and fly it. No, that would quickly put him out of range of the leash. He stepped inside the skiff and took two fresh e-shields out of the cabinet. He clipped them both to his belt. Only when he opened the EVA closet and pulled out a breather did Edie realize what he intended to do.

"You're going outside?"

"Don't have time to suit up. The shields will last a few minutes in a vacuum." He shrugged the small breather reservoir onto his back. "The EM pulse will disable the ship. Cat will break us free, and I'll come back and deal with the milits."

"What? No!" Her voice was little more than a gasp as terror closed her throat.

He didn't waste time with her protestations. "This way—"

He led her to the cellblock and swung open the heavy hatch. When she resisted, he pulled her along behind him to the far end and pushed her firmly into a cell.

"This is just to make it harder for them." He turned to face her, letting the duffle bag slide to the deck, and put his hands on her upper arms, steadying her. "Remember, don't let them take you off the ship."

Don't leave me behind. That's what he meant.

"Finn, you can't defeat them. We have to surrender." She hated the words coming out of her mouth, but all she could think about was getting him out of this alive.

Finn drew his finger along her cheek. "From the beginning, you fought for me. Now I'll fight for you." His tone was gentle, reassuring, and he gave a grim smile. Did he even believe his own words? "Trust me. I've done this before."

Unarmed and alone against four milits? Edie knew it wasn't true. She knew he didn't believe he could do it, either. But he had to try.

She nodded, tried to return his smile as tears burned down her cheeks. She could pretend to believe him, if that was what he wanted.

When he pressed his forehead to hers, pulling her against his body in a desperate embrace, she knew for certain that he didn't expect to survive. And that he was wasting precious time saying goodbye. A sob ripped from her throat.

For a moment longer she clung to him, then stepped back. He closed the cell grille, holding her gaze, and locked it. Then he picked up the duffle bag and moved away. She watched him smash the rifle butt into the console near the hatch, frying the circuitry of the cell locks so the milits would have to cut her free. The lights winked out and she was alone.

Two weeks ago, Edie had faced Finn here, when he had been the one locked up. As she sat waiting, breathing through feverish shivers as neuroshock took hold, she heard voices and movement on the other side of the cellblock door. The milits were here, less than a minute after Finn had locked her in.

The hinged door opened. Bobbing flashlights indicated the approach of the milits. Within seconds, she was locking eyes with a steady, professional gaze that harbored no malice. Only clear intent—to capture her.

"Ma'am, are you okay?"

Capture her . . . or rescue her? His tone wasn't adversarial. As a second milit began cutting through the lock, it occurred to Edie that Natesa really had no idea of the situation on the *Hoi*. And now here she was, locked in a serf's cell, apparently awaiting rescue. Would it help or hinder her now to maintain the pretence that she was entirely the victim and wanted to come home?

Don't let them take you off the ship. That was the most important thing. Finn and Cat had their jobs to do. Edie's role was comparatively simple.

"I'm sick," Edie said. It should be clear to the milits that that was the truth. "I need to get to the infirmary. Deck two."

The first milit ignored the request. "Sir, we've found her," he reported over the commlink built into his helmet. He wore light armor and his e-shield wavered in the dim light of the cellblock.

"Is that deck secure?" came the reply.

"Not yet. We found one guy tied to the deck and he claims there's someone else on deck four, but we're not reading it. They may be blocking our sensors. There's another unconscious in the infirmary on deck three. We've got a lot of ground to cover down here."

"The rest of your team can complete the sweep. Bring her to deck one."

Once freed from the cell, Edie stumbled out and the milit escorted her to top deck. On the way, she counted two more milits roaming the mid decks. On top deck, a milit was cutting through the bridge hatch and another stood at the airlock. Six milits plus the rest of this guy's team below-deck—perhaps two more—for a total of eight. Twice the number Finn had been expecting.

Yet another, this one with commander's stripes, emerged from the briefing room to the left of the bridge ramp. He held a palmet that he must have picked up in there, frowning as he flicked through it while talking over his commlink.

"No, ma'am, I can't do that. The airlock is not secure until we've seized the bridge. I'm not going to lose a prisoner to a decoupling accident." He looked up and cut the link. "Edie Sha'nim?"

Edie nodded.

"Who's the dead guy?" He jerked his thumb toward the body on the deck.

"Captain Rackham. One of his crew killed him."

"And where is this crew? We've only found two others. Are they all on the bridge?"

"I don't know," she lied. "Rackham killed most of them."

The commander nodded thoughtfully. "Search her, then put her over there," he told her escort.

The milit patted her down, taking her commlink and tool belt. Then he extracted the flattened talphi cocoon from her pocket. He looked at it quizzically but asked her no questions as he confiscated it. Edie groaned inwardly, unsure of what to do. If she told them what it was and why she needed it, they might whisk her off to the *Laoch*'s infirmary.

No sooner had the milit settled her on a couch beside the viewport than Edie heard Natesa's voice echoing down the aft corridor.

"I told you, she's not a prisoner! Where is she? Let me through!"

Natesa stormed onto the deck, a flustered young milit in her wake. The commander stiffened, his frown deepening.

"Ms Natesa, this area is not secure. I'll have to ask you to wait on the *Laoch*."

Nothing was going to stop Natesa once she had made up her mind. "Nonsense. I'll wait here with Edie."

Edie stood up to face Natesa, a wash of bitter emotions clouding her mind. Natesa looked impeccable, as she always did, but there was a tightness to her expression that Edie didn't recognize. Was it worry over Edie's fate? Anger? Or suspicion, perhaps. A few days earlier she'd called Edie a criminal—perhaps only as a ploy to get on board the *Hoi*, but Natesa could turn that accusation into fact if she needed to.

Natesa stopped a few meters from Edie, uncertainty crossing her face. That hesitation was new, too. Then she glanced with distaste at the milits roaming the deck.

"Commander Whelan, where can we go that's a little more private?" she demanded.

The commander had given up protesting. He jabbed a finger at the dining room. "In there. Watch out for broken glass."

"Thank you. And bring a medic over. She looks dreadful."

Edie followed Natesa into the dining room and sank into a chair. A milit stood guard at the doorway. Natesa sat at the head of the table and laid her hand over Edie's. Edie forced herself not to pull away.

"Edie, you look like you could use a shower and a nice hot meal. Are you ill?"

Edie nodded, rubbing the itchy wound on her arm, feeling filthy and unkempt in Natesa's perfectly coiffed presence.

"What happened?"

Natesa probably had neuroxin on the *Laoch*—no doubt she'd come prepared—but the price of Natesa's help could well be Finn's life. Edie's thoughts scattered in all directions and she tried to order them. She had to find a way out of this. The despair that weighed on her started to lift as she came to a decision. She would have to tell the truth, accept Natesa's help, and plead for Finn's life.

"The planet," she said, because she had to start somewhere, "it's the same planet we seeded seven years ago."

"Yes, I know. We sent a probe when we entered the system, though it's hardly my priority at the moment. Something is going on down there."

"You have no idea. The rovers took me down there. We found . . . the ecosystem has mutated . . ." Her reluctance to get to the relevant details made her deviate from the point. "It's mutated into something . . . incredible. It broke free."

Their guard stepped back, unconsciously bringing his gun to bear on Edie. "Broke free? Were you exposed? Are you infected?" he said, his voice rising.

Edie stared at him, surprised. She hadn't said that, exactly. But maybe she could use his misunderstanding. Almost without realizing it, she nodded.

Natesa glared and tried to explain it away. "Of course not. She'd be dead already. On a planet like that, exposure to its retroviruses would be fatal within the hour."

The milit turned on Natesa, his eyes widening. "Ma'am, she doesn't look too healthy to me." He backed out of the doorway. "Commander Whelan! Sir! Possible code seventeen!"

Whelan appeared in the doorway looking irate.

"Is there a biohazard on this ship?" he barked. "You didn't mention that possibility."

"Your e-shield protects you," Natesa said. "Just like it protected Edie."

Edie jumped on the opportunity. "Our shields failed. The

captain did it. He sabotaged the mission, tried to kill us all. That's why his crew turned against him."

The commander looked hard at Edie. She let the weakness overtake her for a moment, dropping her head in exhaustion.

Whelan obviously didn't like what he saw. "We can't take her to the *Laoch* until she's been thoroughly checked out. She needs to be quarantined."

"Just send the medic," Natesa snapped.

The milits withdrew, talking in low urgent voices, and Natesa turned a plastic smile on Edie.

"I've been so worried. This has been a nightmare for the Talas team, for the program. I'm so relieved to have you back."

Edie felt the seconds ticking by. Finn had told her to create a delay, and she would do her best.

"How did you find me?"

"We eventually ID'ed the ship that kidnapped you. We tracked it to a node just one jump away and arrested the occupant."

"The infojack?"

"Yes."

Edie's heart skipped a beat. Achaiah was on the *Laoch* after all, and as far as she knew he was the only person who knew how to cut the leash. Despite Finn's decision to fight, surrender was again a tempting option . . .

The image of Rackham's dying face came back to her. People who made deals with Natesa didn't seem to be doing very well these days.

"We caught up with the *Hoi* four days ago, a few jumps from here," Natesa said. "We boarded, found nothing."

"They put me on a skiff and sent it through a jump node," Edie said, stalling for time.

"Incredible. They've been so careless with your life. It's very distressing. You can rest assured they'll pay for—"

The entire deck suddenly plunged into darkness and Edie's

stomach lurched as the gravplating switched off. Hundreds of glass shards and scraps of wood and metal bobbed off the floor, weightless. The spilled wine levitated in treacly globules.

As Edie listened, the engine sounds dwindled away. Moments later, the enviros alarm went off, warning that air and heat were off-line.

The *Hoi* was dead.

CHAPTER 34

Light came from outside the room as a cursing milit lit a chemical flare.

Natesa pulled herself awkwardly to the hatch, ungraceful in zero-g. "What's going on?" She had to yell over the alarms.

In the common area, the milits buzzed around, calling on their commlinks with an ever-increasing sense of urgency in their voices. Edie strained her ears for any indication that the milits had caught Finn, her greatest fear. But it soon became clear that they were getting no response from each other or from their ship.

Commander Whelan came toward the dining room in weightless leaps. "Total systems failure on both ships. Get back in there."

He turned away to snap orders at his men, telling them to find everyone on the lower decks and regroup on top deck. Then he returned to the dining room. He pinned Edie with a glare.

"What's going on?"

Edie waited a few seconds for Natesa to jump in and defend her. Edie, after all, had done nothing. As Natesa regained her seat, Edie saw the glimmer of suspicion in the woman's eyes and knew that wasn't going to happen.

"I don't know," Edie said simply.

"You said there were retroviruses loose on this ship?"

"Yes. Highly active nanoteck from the planet." The lie came easily. Anything that might save Finn was worth trying.

Whelan turned his accusatory glare on Natesa. "We just got hit by an EM pulse. The *Laoch* is off-line. All comms are down, our e-shields are bleeding out, and we've got a major biohazard. I'm ordering my men to return to the *Laoch* and get into hard suits." His voice rose in anger. "You should have told me this would be an issue."

Natesa's eyes glittered in the dark, never leaving Edie. "It's a trick. A ploy to get you off the ship so they can escape."

"This ship isn't going anywhere. It's as dead as the *Laoch*."

"Nevertheless, I don't believe there's any danger."

"Ma'am, nothing that you *believe* is going to rewrite my procedural manual. Stay here if you like, but I'll take no responsibility for you. We're leaving to suit up."

"How long will that take?"

"Five minutes, no more. Are you armed?"

Natesa pulled a tiny stunner out of her belt and laid it on the table, her hand over it. Whelan turned and stormed out. The hubbub outside faded as the milits followed. Natesa sat stiff with anger, her face as white and hard as one of Rackham's sculptures. Edie could think of nothing else to do, so she waited in silence, anticipating a scolding. She felt as tense as Natesa looked, but not because of Natesa or the stunner. She was hoping that Finn had left himself enough time to get back inside before the flash bomb destroyed his e-shield.

Her hair waved gently around her face, the tendrils tickling her neck. Natesa's remained firmly bound up on her head in defiance of the lack of gravity. Natesa narrowed her eyes.

"I'm asking myself if you're really the unwilling victim

here. Are you wanting to be rescued, or were you part of this all along?"

Edie kept her expression inscrutable. "I didn't kidnap myself, if that's what you mean."

"So you'll quite happily walk out of here with me and return to your life on Talas?"

Edie hesitated a fraction too long, rendering any lie unbelievable. "Not happily, no."

The alarms cut out and the *Hoi*'s engines screamed to life. Cat's ploy had worked. Shutting down the ship just before the flash bomb detonated had protected its electronics. The ship rocked, bouncing debris off the bulkheads. Edie instinctively covered her head.

"Hang on tight," Cat said over the shipwide comm.

Edie pulled herself to the deck, where the table provided some cover from the flotsam, and wrapped her fingers around the gravplating. Natesa wasn't so quick to react. The ship jolted violently and a great wrenching sound ripped through the deck as it tore free of the *Laoch*'s gangway.

Moments later, the gravplating and lights came on simultaneously. All around her, the broken pieces of Rackham's collection crashed down. Edie stood on shaky legs and saw Natesa lying on the deck, her legs tangled up in her chair, her eyes wide with bewilderment. The stunner lay half a meter away on the deck.

Edie made a grab for it, but Natesa was too fast. The stunner was back in her hand before Edie had taken two steps. Natesa untangled her legs and hit her commlink a few times, without result. She held the stunner loosely, as if she couldn't quite bring herself to point it at Edie.

"Make it stop," she snarled.

Edie had more important things to worry about. Ignoring the weapon pointed in her direction, she hit the nearest comm panel on the wall.

"Cat, where is he?"

"I don't know. We still have no internal sensors. He gave me a thirty-second warning to cut the power, and I did."

"How did he get out? How was he going to get back in?"

"He didn't tell me. There are several access points, none of them easy. Fuel lines, garbage chutes . . . I don't know. I was listening in on your story about the retroviruses. Good thinking. Did all the milits leave?"

The change in subject didn't help ease Edie's mind. A cold sickness settled in her stomach. If Finn was dead, what was the point of all this? She may as well just go home with Natesa.

Berating herself for her despondency, she replied, "Yes, as far as I know. Natesa is still on board."

"Shit."

"How long before we jump?"

"We're at maximum acceleration, coming up fast on the node. Thirteen minutes."

"What about the *Laoch*?"

"It'll take them a few minutes to recover. I'm not certain we'll be out of firing range before they power those weapons. This could be close."

And if they did make it through the node, Edie didn't want a Crib 'crat on the ship, adding kidnapping to her list of crimes.

Natesa had scrambled to her feet, still trying to contact the *Laoch*. Now she was getting a faint signal. Edie had to get rid of her. But first, she had one more chance to help Finn. From their first day aboard the *Hoi*, the leash had been their priority and it still was. If they could cut it, and if her future must then be with the Crib, perhaps she could negotiate for Finn's freedom. Perhaps seeding Project Ardra worlds for Natesa wasn't too high a price to pay.

It all came down to the infojack. If he couldn't help them, then probably no one could. In that case, she'd take her chances on the *Hoi* and trust Cat could come through with contacts who could help get her neuroxin.

"I need to speak with Achaiah," Edie said.

"Who?"

"The infojack you picked up." Before Natesa could protest, she added, "This has nothing to do with you, the Crib, Talas, or anything else. It's personal."

"Return with me to the *Laoch* and you may talk to him. Edie, don't you dare turn your back on me, on your team, on your duty."

"Rampaging across the Reach, turning planets into mash is not my duty."

"If the project goes ahead without you, our failures will be on your conscience. We need your skills to avoid that sort of disaster. Disasters like the one down there." She waved the stunner to encompass the system they were in. "It looks like VAL-One-Four has become our most magnificent failure yet. Bethany's failure. Poor woman—her final legacy is that mess. I always thought she never really had what it took to shine in this line of work. You, on the other hand, you can save us all."

Edie refused to be wounded by Natesa's insults against Bethany. "Flattery won't persuade me."

"And duty means equally little to you." Natesa drew a deep breath, looked away for a moment, then looked back. "If you won't come back for me, come back for Lukas."

Edie blanched at the mention of his name. "Where is he?"

"We'll let you visit him."

"Where is he?" she demanded, more forcefully.

"I'm sorry to have to tell you—I wanted to keep it from you—but he was a traitor. He plotted against you."

Edie held back a bubble of hysterical laughter in her throat. That Natesa thought she could convince Edie of that lie was an indication of how little the woman really knew her favorite charge.

"It's true, Edie. Oh, he repented eventually, and they tell me he sometimes asks after you . . . from his prison cell on Anwynn."

"I don't doubt you locked him up, even killed him. But he's no traitor." He'd outlived his usefulness to the Crib, and it had discarded him. One day Edie would find out why. For now, Natesa's offer only revolted her.

As Edie's body adjusted to the ebb and flow of neuro-shock, her mind cleared and she felt a little stronger.

"Let me talk to the infojack."

"He's a prisoner on the *Laoch*. It's impossible—"

"Arrange it, Natesa. I need his help with something. If he can't help, then we'll let you go." She leaned on the *we* just a little, to remind Natesa that she had allies on this ship. The stunner wasn't an insurmountable obstacle.

"Is that a threat?" Natesa said.

"Think of it as a deal."

Natesa drew an angry breath, thought better of it, and hit her commlink. As she made the arrangements to get a link set up with the prisoner, Edie sank into a chair while another wave of nausea hit. It wasn't just the neuroshock. She was sick with worry for Finn. He was dead outside the ship with a failed shield or alive inside. She'd find out soon enough.

Natesa set her palmet on the table and Achaiah's face materialized. His blue eyes penetrated the ethereal light of the holoviz and he looked more than ever like the angel Edie had first mistaken him for. Or a devil in disguise.

From his torn clothing and bruised face, it looked like they'd resorted to quick and nasty interrogation methods. He hadn't given in, though. He could have taken control of the *Hoi* with the worm and he hadn't. Leashing one human being to another with a bomb might not violate his ethical code, and neither did trading in cyphertecks, but he wasn't quite as open to selling out his customers to the Crib.

He grinned at Edie, the careless grin of a man with nothing left to lose. In a disconcerting flash, Edie saw why Cat had fallen in with him. His appearance of easy charm reminded her of Zeke, but behind those eyes lay the capacity for unfettered wickedness.

"Sha'nim. Good to see you—conscious, for once."

"Can you cut the leash?"

"That lag is still alive?" His stilted accent was unlike anything she'd heard before.

She wanted to scream at him, *He's not just a lag, and you know it.* "Answer me."

"It's a biocyph lock," he said. "A new line for me, but I like to think I did well."

"Tell me who can break it."

Seconds ticked by as the good humor drained from Achaiah's face, seconds in which the *Laoch* would be powering up to give chase. Finally, he shrugged.

"I was paid to make a link *you* couldn't deactivate. Certainly no one else can."

These were not the words Edie wanted to hear. She gripped the edge of the table. "Not even you? It can never be broken?"

"Sorry." His apology sounded genuine, belying the ice in his eyes. "Is Lancer there with you—?"

"Edie!" Cat's urgent voice on the shipwide. "The *Laoch* is up and running. I could use some help on the bridge. Is it safe to open up?"

Edie cut the palmet link and hit her commlink. "Give me one minute."

Turning back to Natesa, she touched the beetle shell at her throat and thought of Scarabaeus. Her greatest success. Her greatest failure. It was her planet now, its destiny routed through her splinter to an unknown future. She had set it on this devastating path just as Natesa had set her, as a child, on a path. But Scarabaeus would survive without her, albeit changed, and she would survive without Natesa, without the Crib.

"You don't want to be here and I don't want you here," Edie said. "I think you should step into a lifepod and have the *Laoch* pick you up."

Natesa looked ready to admit defeat, but gave it one last try. "What about your neuroxin, Edie? Your implant will be dry in a few months. You'll die if you don't come home."

"I'll figure it out. I don't need you anymore." Edie looked pointedly at the stunner. "Using that won't help either of us."

Natesa thought for a moment and relented, belting the stunner. Edie followed her to the main corridor, which was lined with three narrow hatches on each side—the lifepods. Edie snapped open the nearest one. As the inner and then outer hatches slid open, she stepped back.

Excruciating pain shot up her spine and she crumpled, only registering the sound of the stunner firing after she fell. The deck scraped against her legs as Natesa dragged her toward the lifepod. Edie tried to kick out, but her numbed limbs refused to respond to the orders from her brain. The lip of the pod's hatch dug into her hip and her head banged on the deck.

That knocked some feeling back into her body. Her hand brushed the hatch rim and she put all her efforts into curling her fingers around the edge. She held on tight as Natesa wrestled with her.

"You're coming with me!" Natesa shrieked. "This is more important than you could possibly realize. How dare you turn away from your destiny. *Get in!*"

Edie's vision narrowed and she started to black out. *No!* She wanted to tell Natesa about Finn and the leash and Ademo's blood-filled eyes when his chip exploded . . . No words made it past her throat. Finn was going to die just like that serf—

Natesa gave a cry as something slammed against her. Edie felt a hand close around her arm and pull her out, while Natesa fell into the pod and landed in a heap. As the hatch snapped, the last thing Edie saw of Natesa was her anguished expression framed by locks of hair that had finally sprung free from confinement.

The pod disengaged and fell away.

Edie clutched at Finn's clothing. Her legs were finally regaining some feeling but were too weak to hold her up. She started to slide to the deck and he went with her, crouching in front of her.

"Edie, I've got you." His hand cupped her face as she

leaned into the crook of his arm for support. She wanted to lie there against his rock-solid body forever.

"The milits left," she whispered.

"I see that. Was that you?"

"Yes."

"You're brilliant."

She smiled, basking in his praise. Then she remembered where she was. They weren't free, not yet. "The *Laoch*—"

As the words left her lips, a deafening crack sounded and the *Hoi* tipped sharply, throwing Finn and Edie against the bulkhead.

"Someone get up here and help!" Cat yelled over the comm.

"I can manage," Edie said, and somehow saying the words helped her believe them.

Finn pulled her up and supported her as they hurried through the common area and up the ramp. Cat unlocked the hatch and they joined her on the bridge. Finn led Edie to the nearest seat before stationing himself at a console. On the far side of the bridge, Gia sat at an off-line console, fiddling with pieces of the first aid kit she'd used to patch up Cat.

"They fired a plasma cannon," Cat said from across the bridge, "but they're not up to full power. Must still be dealing with the EM effects. But they still have missiles—those will be shielded against any amount of EM damage."

"Do we have any weapons?" Finn asked.

"Nothing that will do more than scratch that ship. We tend to just run when this sort of thing happens. We have one defense that might work. Get me a schematic of our relative positions and vectors."

Finn punched up a holoviz displaying the positions of the two ships, the *Hoi* overlaid with a red band that indicated the danger zone when the *Laoch* would be within missile range. Edie watched the display, squinting against the bright lights that made her eyeballs ache.

"They'll have orders not to kill me," Edie said. "They won't blow up the ship."

"Maybe not, but they can disable us," Cat said grimly.

The *Laoch* crossed the red band and fired immediately.

"Two guided charges." Cat followed the progress of the missiles. "They're spitting in our eye. Probably aimed to knock out our nav guidance so we can't steer into the node."

"Can you turn off the guidance so the missiles can't lock on?" Edie suggested.

"I could, but then it'll take a few minutes to come back online. That's plan B."

Cat stabbed at her console. From the display, Edie saw that she'd released a beacon transmitting a narrow-band frequency that mimicked the nav guidance transmissions. The missiles went for the decoy, and all three signals winked off the display.

"We're fifty seconds from the node," Finn said.

The *Laoch* launched another volley.

"Do we have more decoys?" Edie asked.

"No. I told you it'd only work once, remember?" Cat sounded calm but her forehead beaded with sweat. She reached over and tapped a switch.

An alarm pierced the tense atmosphere of the bridge.

"What did you do?"

"Turned off the nav guidance."

"You can steer us in manually?" Finn sounded dubious.

"I can try." Cat cut the alarm. "It's better than getting hit. If they take out our guidance, we'll end up stuck on the other side of that node."

The display showed the charges flying past, missing their mark as their target vanished.

"Ten seconds to the node," Finn said. "Eight, seven . . ."

Cat tapped the weapons display. "They've got the cannons back to full power. Here come the big boys."

A barrage of plasma bolts was on the way—Edie knew what that meant. Coherent bulbous masses of atomic particles heated to insane temperatures, carrying vast destruction. With Natesa off the *Laoch* for now and unable to interfere with Commander Whelan's procedures, he was apparently prepared to take undue risks with Edie's life in the attempt to capture her.

Cat clenched her hand inside the control dataglove and concentrated on flying the ship. The main viewscreen showed them drawing closer to the node's blazing ring. With no guidance assisting them, the unsteady pull of the node threatened to send them careening into the edge of the horizon. As the *Hoi* shuddered and slipped, Cat kept them centered.

The ring engulfed the *Hoi* just as a violent jolt rocked the ship. Cat swore and the console lit up.

The viewscreen erupted into the twisting ribbons of nodespace. They were safe.

Edie dragged herself up to look at Finn's console, where he'd pulled up the systems status. "Were we hit?"

"Looks like one bolt hit, aft. Missed the engines by a few meters," Finn said. "Took out our rear end on decks two and three. The bulkheads beyond that are holding. Main corridors are secure."

"Ha! The gym." Cat threw a grin in Edie's direction. "No more CPT."

"And both the bathrooms and the quarters opposite—ours and Gia's," Edie added. There was nothing she would miss, but Gia might have accumulated some possessions. She'd been on the *Hoi* a long time.

Finn got up. "I'll check out the damage. Gia." He held out his hand for the cook, and she went to him. "Come with me. Yasuo needs your help in the infirmary."

"You need to do something with Corky, too," Cat reminded him as they headed out.

Cat moved to the captain's chair and plotted their course. "To shake the *Laoch*, we'll take that unmapped exit where we sent the skiff—about half an hour away. Then we'll jump right back in and head for Barossa Station. I have friends there . . . Zeke's friends, really. I'll send a message. I already did the numbers—they can get to Talas and back in about six days, just in time for our arrival. We should ditch the *Hoi*, though, or Stichting Corp will track us down."

Ditch the *Hoi* and do what? Edie wondered if Cat intended to stick with her. She was too tired to make plans, but perhaps if she put the idea into Cat's mind now, the navpilot would start to think about staying with them for the long haul—despite what this ship, and its missions, had cost her.

"I'm sorry about Zeke," Edie said. "I know he meant a lot to you. I liked him."

Cat nodded sadly. "I was going to come back for him. One day. I don't know if he'd have come with me, but I was going to ask him."

Edie's console flashed unnervingly. "I think that worm has left behind a few shadows. You need to isolate each system and reboot them in turn."

"Will do." Cat swiveled in the captain's chair, slapping the arm rests with satisfaction. "Well, I didn't get to shoot the bastard myself, but I'm sitting in his chair. That's good enough for me. Edie, we made it out."

"Almost. We're almost out."

CHAPTER 35

Edie rested for a few minutes in the captain's dining room, waiting for the dizziness to pass and surveying Rackham's broken treasures. Wondering if anything could be salvaged and whether it would be enough to pay for fuel, repairs, jump tariffs, Cat's mercenary friends and, eventually, a ride to the Fringe.

In her muddy, torn, and bloody clothes she felt like a stain on this exquisite landscape of artifacts. Much as she hated to admit she had anything in common with Rackham, she understood his attachment to these things of beauty.

She climbed down one deck to the infirmary. The talphi cocoon was gone and she didn't know how long she could survive without neuroxin, but she might be able to synthesize some amino acids to alleviate the symptoms for a while.

Gia had made Yasuo comfortable and he was asleep. She was cleaning up the dirty sheets and used med supplies.

"You don't have to do that," Edie said.

"It's my job!"

"Gia, you need to think about what you want to do next."

"How about I make us all some supper? It's past four in the morning, you know."

Twenty-two hours since they'd dropped into orbit around Scarabaeus. It seemed like much longer.

"I meant in the long term. Do you have family? Where do you want to go?"

"Oh, we'll see." She gave a quick smile as she finished what she was doing. Edie wondered if her vagueness meant she had no family, or couldn't remember. Or if she thought of the *Hoi* as her home and had never considered leaving. Perhaps more than anyone else left on this ship, her life was going to change the most.

"I'm afraid a plasma bolt wiped out your quarters. Mine, too."

"Yes, the baffle dropped." Gia pointed down the corridor, where a section of bulkhead had closed off the last few meters of the corridor, beyond which lay the remains of the rooms damaged by the blast. "So, we'll start afresh, won't we?"

"Yes, we will."

"Supper in an hour, then." She left, talking to herself. "I'll make my piquaz stew again. Finn liked that."

"Edie. Wake up."

A hard, wet wall pressed into Edie's spine. She shifted to ease the pressure. A rush of sound filled her ears. Water. It was raining.

Raining inside. Was that even possible?

Something shook her shoulder. Something pushed the hair out of her eyes. She opened them to see an endless stretch of white plaz. Water hit her eyeballs and she blinked and lowered her gaze to look into hazel brown eyes. Reality consolidated around her. She was in the shower next to the infirmary. Cleaning up while waiting for the sequencer to finish. From the engine noise, they were in realspace.

She must have become giddy again and zoned out. She was huddled on a low, built-in ledge-seat in the shower, leaning against the wall as the water beat down.

"Finn. You're all wet."

He was fully clothed and streaked with dirt from Scarabaeus. The water swirling around them was getting muddy.

"I couldn't raise you on the comm. Are you okay?"

"You're making a mess. Take off your clothes."

His eyes crinkled. "Can you get up?"

"In a while. Stay here with me."

He looked at her for an eternity. "Okay."

"But you have to clean up."

He straightened and stripped off, tossing his clothes over the shower stall. He washed quickly while she sat and scrubbed the remaining soap out of her hair. Then she watched him, admiring the view. The soap cleaned the dirt from his skin and it sluiced down the drain, and the water dissolved the remaining strips of medigel on his wounds. It couldn't wash away the scars and bruises.

She began daring herself to step under the jets with him and then reminded herself she'd probably keel over if she tried to stand up. Instead she thought about what an idiot she'd been to reject him in the skiff, and whether her fear about repeating Lukas and Bethany's relationship had all been a sorry excuse.

Then she tried to stop thinking about anything at all, in case his splinter picked up on it.

The comm on her belt buzzed. Finn shut off the water and leaned around the shower screen to answer it. It was Cat.

"Edie! What did you do?"

"What?" She held out her hand and Finn handed the commclip to her, along with a towel. He wrapped another towel around his waist.

"I rebooted the system like you said," Cat said, "and then the navcharts spat out a new file. It's a complete ident package for me—it just popped up from the ashes of the worm."

So that's what Achaiah had been doing during those first few minutes he'd had access to the *Hoi*, riding the worm but not taking over the ship. Being captured by the Crib had demolished his deal with Cat, but he'd still given her what she'd bargained for.

"I guess Achaiah has the germ of a conscience after all."

"I can't believe he did the right thing by me," Cat mused.

Edie glanced up at Finn, leaning against the edge of the shower screen. Cat's good fortune couldn't balance out what the infojack had done to him, but Cat's new ident along with the ones she and Finn had been given when they joined the crew would greatly improve all their chances of surviving.

Edie tucked the towel around herself. "Cat, can you lend me some clothes? We have no bathrooms or laundry facs anymore."

Cat laughed. "I'll send Gia to fetch some."

"Something of Zeke's for Finn, too."

A small hesitation before she responded, "Sure."

Edie closed the link and handed it back to Finn. He sat beside her on the ledge, elbows on his knees, shoulder not quite touching hers. His proximity made her breath catch and her limbs tremble. No, that was neuroshock, surely. To avoid thinking about it, she talked about their survival.

"I'm putting together a spike that might help—acetylcholine, glutamate, glycine, aspartate."

"If you can say all that without stumbling, you can't be doing so badly."

Edie grinned. Nevertheless, his levity couldn't wipe away her fear. "It can never replace the neurotransmitters fast enough, but it might help. If we don't get there in time—"

"We will."

She wanted it to be true based solely on the force of his conviction. But the cryptoglyph was too important to trust to wishful thinking.

"I know you wanted to keep the cryptoglyph, but that was before . . . before I started dying." The words were hard to say, especially when it would be so easy to simply believe his assurances. "In case we don't make it, I'm going to ask Cat to take it to the Fringe. I think she'd do that for me. I want to download it from your splinter."

Finn seemed lost in thought for a moment, and she wondered if he was going to argue about it. She didn't have the strength to stand up to him. But then he nodded.

"I agree. What do you need?"

"Just some stock biocyph. A module from a med sequencer unit will do. And a hardlink."

She started to get up, stumbling against his knee as her legs gave way. Finn eased her back to the seat.

"I'll fetch it."

He brought back the entire unit and set it on the ledge. Edie removed a module from its slot, ran a hardlink to her wet-teck interface, and checked the stock—fresh, amorphous biocyph that was yet to be used for anything.

"Okay, it's ready. Sit there."

He sat cross-legged on the floor in front of her. She was reminded of their first meeting in the freight car on Talas Prime. Then he'd been unable to talk. Now he seemed unwilling, lost in thought. He stared at the beetle shell between her collarbones.

"Ready?"

He nodded, and she touched her fingers to his temple.

The music of Scarabaeus flowed through her wet-teck.

That shouldn't happen. The algorithm was pure code, like raw sheet music lacking an orchestra to play the song. In the fifteen hours or so since she'd put it into Finn's splinter, something had changed.

Her heart raced as she realized the implications.

"The cryptoglyph has imprinted on your splinter."

He looked like he didn't like the sound of that. "What does that mean?"

"I don't know, exactly. The code should just be sitting there on the matrix. On Scarabaeus it evolved to overcome my kill-code lock. I think . . . it's done the same thing to your splinter. Evolved. Merged with the biocyph to create a functional decrypter. I can't extract it anymore."

"Are you saying I'm stuck with this?"

"The splinter can't be removed—we've been through that before. But I can still use it the way I planned. It just means . . . you'd have to be there, on every planet, every time I needed to use it."

He would never agree to that.

He returned to his thoughts while she explored the decrypter. It fascinated her, despite what it meant to Finn—that he was now the most important part of her plan to help the Fringe worlds.

Then she realized what it *really* meant to Finn.

"It can decrypt biocyph locks . . ."

"What?"

"The leash is fused to your splinter with a biocyph lock. And now, the splinter can break biocyph locks."

He drew a breath, hesitated, as if he didn't dare voice his hope. "It can cut the leash?"

"Yes. If I tell it to."

"Wait a minute. Look what happened on Scarabaeus. I don't want anything like that happening in my brain."

Edie dropped her hand away from his head. "That won't happen. It doesn't have the machinery of a BRAT. It just breaks biocyph locks. That's all."

Finn nodded his head slowly, but then his eyes narrowed. "You said my splinter *was* the decrypter?"

"Yes. Lock and key in the same strand of biocyph. When the lock is broken, the biocyph will be destroyed."

"So you'd lose the cryptoglyph."

And she'd lose him.

"You'll be *free!*" Edie insisted. "You won't die if you go out of range. You won't get this interference from my brain waves. No one will be able to jolt you."

Finn looked uneasy. It wasn't the reaction she'd expected.

"It's what we wanted, Finn."

"What about your grand revolution?"

"Our plan was to cut the leash. That's why we cooperated with the rovers, isn't it? Achaiah told me even he didn't know how to cut it. We may never get another chance."

Her words sounded hollow. This was not what *she* wanted, not anymore, and it was hard to admit that to herself. Keeping the leash intact meant she won on two counts—she had a tool to help the Fringers, and she had Finn by her side. She wanted him near, even enslaved. Her own selfish desires appalled her. She felt compelled to act, to overcome them.

She moved her hand to reconnect the softlink. "It'll only take a second—"

He grabbed her wrist. For a few moments she pushed futilely as she tried to touch his temple, a struggle she couldn't win.

"What about those people?" he insisted.

The Fringers. Little Olga and her pitiful family.

"Finn, you deserve freedom."

"So do they."

"You said it wasn't our fight. You were right—I can't start a revolution. I can't do it alone." Her throat tightened as she tried to talk him into making the decision that was best for him, regardless of the cost to her. She swayed forward, pressed her forehead to his, tears flowing freely. "You wanted freedom. I want you to be free."

His thumb grazed her cheekbone where Haller had struck her, days ago, in this very room. Blinking to clear her vision, she looked into the eyes of a man she still barely understood, but did not want to lose.

"Tell me what to do," she whispered.

"You freed me from slavery. You freed my voice. You've made me remember why I strapped on a spur in the first place." He slowly shook his head against hers. "I was never fighting for politics and governments, those bastards who betrayed us. I was fighting for that poor kid on the *Drakkar*. I want my freedom, but not at the expense of hers."

She had no response that could measure up to his sacrifice.

He tilted his face and kissed her. To comfort her, perhaps, but his lips lingered too long for that. Pushing his hand into her tangled wet hair, he stood, holding the kiss, drawing her close. Her body responded with a deep rush of desire.

Finn pulled back with a groan, his fist tightening in her

hair and making her gasp. He released her quickly, turned his face away, but not before she saw the fleeting pain in his eyes. With the leash flaring in his head whenever her emotions were aroused, intimacy would never be possible.

"I'm sorry—" she began.

"Don't be. I made my choice." He recovered quickly, and then that playful look she'd glimpsed once before came to his eyes. "Weren't you going to do something about that?"

She wiped her wet cheeks and smiled, savoring the dissipating rush and the surge of hope that replaced it.

"I will."

First she had to survive the disintegration of her neural metabolism.

Hugging her knees, Edie sat on the couch on deck one and traced the fading ink on the tops of her bare feet. She wanted to scrub it all off and have Cat start again, this time painting the patterns from Scarabaeus. The latticed vines, the glossy slater threads, the dappled mosaics of refracted light . . .

Finn touched her shoulder with such gentle concern it brought a lump to her throat. "Lie down."

Edie obeyed, struggling to keep her eyes open as Finn gave her another spike of the amino acid cocktail that they hoped would slow the progress of her neuroshock symptoms.

Finn turned to the viewport to stare at the stars. They were camping out on deck one. On a nearby couch, Gia fussed with Yasuo's bedding as he slurped down stew and watched toons on the holoviz with the sound turned low. Corky slumped in the corner, contrite, too embarrassed to join the group. Cat was on the bridge enjoying her new favorite seat—the captain's chair—and familiarizing herself with her new identity.

"No sign of the *Laoch*," Cat reported via the shipwide comm. "Listen to this: Caterina Carmel. My new name— like it? Sounds like a movie star."

The *Hoi* jumped into nodespace and the stars evaporated.

Finn's hands tightened on the railing as the view shifted abruptly to become a churning avalanche of glowing colorless ribbons.

After a while, Edie said, "Is the universe still bewildering you?"

In the viewport reflection, she saw Finn smile. "Some things are starting to make sense."

What made sense to Edie was the chance, at last, to choose her future. To throw off the Crib's chains, to undermine its stranglehold using the very thing it had helped her create: the song of Scarabaeus.

What made sense was the knowledge that it wasn't only the leash that compelled Finn to stay with her. He'd chosen her instead of freedom, staking his life on her getting through the next few days.

He rubbed at the back of his neck in that unconscious gesture that was so familiar and unsettling, signifying their bond. It was, perhaps, a ridiculous time to be admiring the flex of his muscles sliding under olive-brown skin, but that's what she did. If she was about to die, there wasn't much else she'd rather be looking at.

She shivered and curled up on her side. Closed her eyes to the universe.

"Finn?"

"Edie."

"Don't let me out of your sight."

FIONA McINTOSH'S

MASTERFUL EPIC FANTASY
THE PERCHERON SAGA

* * * ❧ * * *

ODALISQUE 978-0-06-089911-0

In the exotic land of Percheron, the fifteen-year-old heir to
the throne, Boaz, must assume the mantle of leadership,
guided by his trusted warrior adviser, Lazar. In the midst
of roiling covert intrigue, a headstrong young woman is
brought to Boaz's harem, inflaming unexpectedly strong
feelings in both Boaz and Lazar. And, unbeknownst to all,
the gods themselves are rising in a cyclical battle.

EMISSARY 978-0-06-089912-7

Lazar offered up his life to protect Ana, a prisoner in the
forbidden harem of the great Stone Palace of Percheron,
accepting punishment intended for the bewitching
odalisque. Now, with Lazar's guiding hand absent from
the city, Percheron has become a darker, more treacherous
place, as the young Zar Boaz has to battle the machinations
of his mother Herezah.

GODDESS 978-0-06-089913-4

While enemy ships threaten Percheron's harbor, heroic
Lazar lies afflicted with the drezden illness. And Zaradine
Ana has been taken prisoner by the mysterious Arafanz
and his warriors, and is believed to be with child—carrying
the heir to the throne, the unborn son of Zar Boaz.

FMC1 0709

EPIC FANTASY FROM *NEW YORK TIMES*
BESTSELLING AUTHOR

LOIS MCMASTER BUJOLD
THE SHARING KNIFE

VOLUME ONE: BEGUILEMENT
978-0-06-113907-9

Young Fawn Bluefield has fled her family's farm uncertain about her future and the troubles she carries. Dag is an older soldier-sorcerer weighed down by past sorrows and present responsibilities. And now an uncanny accident has sent this unlikely pair on a journey of danger and delight, prejudice and partnership . . . and maybe even love.

VOLUME TWO: LEGACY
978-0-06-113906-2

While Fawn and Dag's unorthodox marriage has been grudgingly accepted by her people, Dag's Lakewalker kin greet their union with suspicion and prejudice. And when Dag must answer the call to defend a neighboring hinterland from a vicious attack, what awaits him could forever alter the lovers, their families, and their world.

VOLUME THREE: PASSAGE
978-0-06-137535-4

Leaving behind all they have ever known, Fawn and Dag set off to find fresh solutions to the perilous split between their peoples— but their passage will not be ventured alone. On an eventful journey, the ill-assorted crew will be sorely tested and tempered as they encounter a new world of hazards both human and uncanny.

VOLUME FOUR: HORIZON
978-0-06-137537-8

At the end of Fawn and Dag's long journey home they must determine if their untried new ways can stand against their world's deadliest foe.

Visit www.AuthorTracker.com for exclusive
information on your favorite HarperCollins authors.

SK 1109

Available wherever books are sold or please call 1-800-331-3761 to order.